## ALSO BY CHARLES D. HAYES

### FICTION

*The Call of Mortality*

*Portals in a Northern Sky*

*Pansy: Bovine Genius in Wild Alaska*

*Stalking Cindy*

*Moose Hunter Homicide*

### NONFICTION

*September University:*
*Summoning Passion for an Unfinished Life*

*Existential Aspirations:*
*Reflections of a Self-Taught Philosopher*

*In Defense of Liberal Ideas*

*The Rapture of Maturity:*
*A Legacy of Lifelong Learning*

*Training Yourself:*
*The 21ˢᵗ Century Credential*

*Beyond the American Dream:*
*Lifelong Learning and the Search for*
*Meaning in a Postmodern World*

*Proving You're Qualified: Strategies for*
*Competent People without College Degrees*

*Self-University: The Price of Tuition Is the*
*Desire to Learn. Your Degree Is a Better Life*

# A MILE
# NORTH *of*
# GOOD *and* EVIL

BY CHARLES D. HAYES

AUTODIDACTIC PRESS

**Autodidactic Press**
**P. O. Box 872749**
**Wasilla, AK 99687**
**www.autodidactic.com**

ISBN 978-0-9885795-3-8
Printed in USA

First Edition

Book design: BookWiseDesign.com
Source image: Alaska mountains/123RF/ marchello74,
Great Pyrenees/iStock, Wolf/Oregon Department of Fish and Wildlife

Publisher's Cataloging-in-Publication
(Provided by Quality Books, Inc.)

Hayes, Charles D. (Charles Douglas)
   A mile north of good and evil / by Charles D. Hayes.
   pages cm
   LCCN 2015941666
   ISBN 978-0-9885795-3-8 (paperback)
   ISBN 978-0-9885795-4-5 (ebook)

   1. Philosophy—Fiction. 2. Science fiction.
I. Sequel to: Hayes, Charles D. (Charles Douglas). Portals in a northern sky. II. Title.

PS3608.A92M55 2015          813'.6
                QBI15-600110

*Dedicated to the legions of grandparents
whose existence is erased from living memory
as one generation after another passes away.*

*We don't need wars, natural disasters, or threats*
*from the heavens to find meaningful reasons to live.*
*The mortal fate that awaits us all is enough.*

I COULD FEEL THE nurse's gaze, and as soon as our eyes met, I knew it was time. I said, "He's going, isn't he?"

She nodded, finished taking his vital signs, and rearranged his bed. "If you have anything to say, you had better say it now."

For two full minutes, my mouth moved but no words came forth. Then I mumbled something—I'm still not sure what—and it was over.

When my father exhaled his last breath, I'd been on page 276 of Harper Lee's classic *To Kill a Mockingbird*. Boo Radley had just emerged from his cloistered house. While I read about Scout and her brother Jem's violent struggle with an ignorant and vengeful racist, my father lost his battle with time. The background music from the movie version of *To Kill a Mockingbird* began playing in my head, and I began thinking it might be appropriate for a funeral. Mine, perhaps. Not his.

Later that day, my aunt said it best. "The reign of terror is over," she declared. "Buck Sandburg is dead."

And so it was that on a quiet day at the Pioneer Home in Palmer, Alaska, in the spring of 2028, in what would become known as a very ill-omened year, my father died, and with him a big part of the mystery that would claim the lives of two justices of the United States Supreme Court, the Speaker of the House of Representatives, two nationally known conservative radio talk-show hosts, and scores of crimes far too numerous to mention. All in good time, though. There are many other things to consider, and some are far more important for making sense of a world flying apart, coming together, and threatening to end all at the same time.

If you're a person who can find it in your temperament to put gloom and doom aside, and if you've got nothing better to do while the whole world awaits the obliteration of life on the earth and the end of time for our species, then the story makes for some interesting reading. But maybe I'm getting ahead of myself.

If you're not excited by the intrigue of death and the thought of total annihilation, then you should read no further because you are bound to be disappointed. If, however, you are undeterred thus far, let's proceed. It will be a journey of dizzying events, of good and evil, of hope and despair, of love and hatred, and it will stand as an epitaph for a species too ill-informed to long prosper, unless, of course, my judgment is in error.

In any case, I will share with you my early journal entries. If you really want to understand the dark side of existence, time will reveal its nature and the dynamics of good and evil. You will soon realize that, without death, life would have no meaning. Your worldview will be forever altered. I promise.

# STATE OF THE ART

SEVEN YEARS AGO, in 2021, one of the greatest scientific advancements in the history of the planet set the world on an unintended path. Seven years ago was when the Portals System was activated, and its use today is giving clear signs that all life is hell-bound toward the abyss. Named *Adam 21* after Adam Whitehead, the scientist in Wasilla, Alaska, whose earlier work in physics made the project possible, the system defies easy explanation.

Most often Adam 21 is described as an amalgamation of interferometry. Strategic placement of telescopes miles apart enables the creation of an infrared simulation of a cone. By filling the cone with looping transmissions from quantum supercomputers, a mirror is formed that looks back at the earth in time gradients. It is a complete simulation or virtual fabrication of an image reflector that works as if it is real. By placing a time-gradation schematic overlay in the system, it's possible to look back in time at any place at any hour in clear daytime weather.

Adam 21 was implemented under the supervision of Dr. James Tall Tree, scientific advisor to the United States president in those years. To further explain the process, Tall Tree has pointed out that when we look into the night sky, we are looking back in time. If we were now on a distant planet looking at the earth, we would be observing it as it was in the past at a time determined by how long it would take the light to reach our observation point. Adam 21 does precisely the same thing, except the simulation allows you to choose the time and place being viewed.

The image produced is better than if you'd had a camera crew on scene to shoot a movie. It is not possible to view an event in real time, however, as there is a twenty-four-hour waiting period, meaning that one can never get closer than yesterday's observations.

When the system was first activated, researchers could select any time in the last billion years, give a latitude, longitude, and time of day, and view the scene from afar or close up, provided no clouds interfered. Many people couldn't understand why the system's telescopes would be stationed in Alaska, since skies in Alaska are cloudy most of the time. The explanation was that clouds get in the way of transmission only when making an actual observation, not in the creation of the time template.

Once Adam 21 became open to the public, anyone using a personal computer could look back in time at will. Activity became so intense that the billion-year model was halved to preserve bandwidth, giving access to the first half-billion years only to scientists. Bandwidth was an ongoing concern as there never seemed to be quite enough to meet demand.

In many ways, observing the past with Adam 21 is much better than having been there because, if you had actually been on the scene, you would have been able to view the object of your interest only from your own vantage point. Adam 21 makes it possible to examine a scene from any angle, very much like being your own movie producer and having your own film crew with scores of cameras. But this technology enables more dexterity than anything the movie industry might offer, except of course for the special effects department. The biggest drawback is that there is no sound to accompany the visuals, and lip reading over great periods of time is problematic at best.

Before Adam 21 technology, the sheer amount of data being added daily in cyberspace had resulted in a bias for the present in the sense that only the latest information would prove reliable. Anything that had happened more than a half-century prior seemed lost to an ancient chasm, bearing little relevance to the present. Now, Adam 21 has made the past radically important to the present and future, while the most current information is by order of magnitude more important than before.

Being able to watch a Civil War battle, Roman legions in hand-to-hand combat, westward-bound nineteenth-century covered wagons, dinosaurs as they lived, the asteroid that led to their demise, and man's primate ancestors on the Serengeti Plain makes for enthralling entertainment that is both socially and emotionally invigorating and, at times, frightfully destabilizing. The effects have reopened ancient tribal grudges, rekindled ethnic hatred, and fostered myriad conspiracy theories, inciting distrust and smoldering suspicion among people with little education. Simply put, Adam 21 is a revolutionary scientific breakthrough in the course of human history, but it is also revealing itself to be the cause of increasing social unrest on a global scale.

At first, Harry Truman's observation that "the only thing new in the world is the history we don't know" became almost as popular as Coca-Cola commercials, but his words haven't proved nearly as effective as the sales of sugar water. For nonacademic types, Adam 21 has imploded history.

Believing they don't need to know much about the past because a simple search will answer most any query, people are less inclined to recognize the significance of history or of historical events in the context of their time. Infinite amounts of information are available but with little attendant growth in accumulated knowledge. The ability to observe earlier times makes the past seem current, and for some this misperception undermines their sense of autonomy.

Marshall McLuhan's view asserted that "the medium is the message," but when the past is instantaneously available, the present for many can seem like fate, and for others, a trap. Still others argue that egregious accounts of inhumanity are best forgotten and banned from public viewing. Far too many people simply don't understand that without an in-depth knowledge of history, perspective is nothing more than a feeble illusion serving as a shelter for collective ignorance and a platform for arrogance or, worse, ethnocentrism.

Another effect, less often noted but still obvious, is that Adam 21 has added elements of mystery and romance to darkness and more than a little madness. The kind of madness that's emerged has led to an ongoing public discussion of the subject of good and evil. Indeed, Adam 21 has had a dramatic effect on criminal activity.

During daylight hours on clear days, the crime rate hovers near the zero mark, picking up dramatically on cloudy days and then soaring at night, lending to darkness the eerie feel of much earlier times. Psychologists characterize this as something akin to the time when humans were on the menu of wild animals. Because Adam 21 has revealed countless examples of such occurrences during the day, concern has intensified for people's safety at night, resulting in widespread growth among security companies and burglar alarm services.

At the same time, advances in medical technology have helped enormously in forensic science, as extensive backlogs of DNA samples are no longer waiting to be processed. The system for examining and comparing DNA now takes only a few days or hours if deemed urgent, providing expeditious closure to outstanding criminal investigations.

Studies in psychology have declared that you can tell a lot about a family by what they choose for their Adam 21 portals into the past. In fact, the term "family portal" is now so ubiquitous that conventional wisdom says every family must have theirs worked out. The federal government has poured billions of dollars into fiber optics and associated technologies for better bandwidth capacity to keep Adam 21 capability from slowing down the Internet. Recent innovations have made large-screen receptors easily affordable, and the fact that they can be programmed to receive signals from a PC or a tablet makes them very popular.

The term PC, however, no longer applies only to personal computers. The PC is simply considered a personal communication device, and these come in all kinds of sizes and shapes. Some can be worn as clothing or as special eyeglasses, and the contents and display of any device can be instantly transferred to a bigger screen. Digital screens can be connected, making it possible to convert a whole wall in one's home to one big screen. Projection services from museums and galleries throughout the world display live works of original masterpieces in the homes and offices of anyone who can afford to subscribe.

It is commonplace for every home to have wall panels playing continuous video streams of family history, which are constantly being edited, updated, and expanded by social media consultants. The term "back living" is popular in reference to people collecting and stringing together scenes from their childhood. Viewers often acknowledge that their memories of the events are strikingly different from the reality revealed by Adam 21. The nostalgia they feel at these times stands in sharp contrast to the disquieting sense of apprehension that arises when viewing scenes of the current state of the world.

Today numerous hints are circulating about a new technology

soon to be released. It's called Q-Vision and will enable people to view media not on a flat panel but in full three-dimensional mode on stage-like platforms of every size imaginable. There is talk of movie theaters replacing their screens with stages that require no 3-D glasses for viewing. Inventions of this nature continue to be developed. The term "artificial intelligence" has been rendered obsolete because its application is now as obvious as its ubiquity, and the constructive effects are profound.

Unfortunately, the emotional disposition in the country, indeed the mood throughout the world, has tarnished the thrill of these media advances. The general public has grown accustomed to technological breakthroughs. Now, since the media have begun to portend nothing but doom, the anxiety is palpable enough to be sensed as something in the air, something breathable, something foreboding. For those inclined to worry, the feelings of dread have become nearly incapacitating.

# DEMONS IN THE DARK

S ERIAL: FORMED OR arranged in sequence. Cereal: starchy grains or seeds. Surreal: incongruous juxtapositions and imagery. Could these rambling notions provide a clue? Serial killer or cereal killer. Now there was an interesting idea. One kernel or flake out of a whole box of assorted nuts and grains. A surreal killer, perhaps that was more like it, a son-of-a-bitch, weird, off the mark to begin with, living on the very edge of reality. How about just plain killers, or perhaps a team? But why kill over a range of four thousand miles? Why so far apart? Why only in summer and fall? That one should be easy enough to figure out, given a little time. Maybe, maybe not.

Slash, stab, and dismember, multiple cutting instruments, none seemingly used at more than one location, or at least if they were, it hadn't been noticed. But, hey, that might be the whole point. Surely if these homicides were connected, whoever was working the cases would have publicized them. Or would they? Perhaps the incidents were stretched out over so much time and so many miles that no one had put the whole thing together yet.

It was light outside and had been for hours, but the cabin was cave dark. Five o'clock in the morning, and Vince Terrell was wide awake, staring at an imaginary ceiling blotted out by pitch blackness. Since he had moved back to Alaska, he'd been sleeping with black covers on the windows. Summer in Alaska in his youth had been exhilarating, but after returning as an aging adult, he felt as if he was simply not the same person. It was the damned perpetual twilight during June and July that got to him, like now. He took window covers with him everywhere—hotel, motel, it didn't matter. Even when he stayed with friends, he covered the windows in the room where he slept or he didn't sleep at all.

Whatever the circumstances, he awakened frequently. In fact, he seldom slept more than two hours straight without utilizing the darkness to peer into the nature of madness and flirt with demons. Some were his own, and others he petitioned simply to do his job. He had never told anyone he did this, not even Ginger, his wife of nearly six years. But late at night as others slept, he would mingle psychologically with those he deemed criminally insane, as he imagined a domestic dog would romp with wolves if the opportunity to do so safely presented itself.

To begin the process, he would let his mind operate freely, firing randomly without focus, as he was doing now. He learned many things using this method, things only he knew, like how smelling the closet of a victim could give him a special sense of the person, even if it was years after the death. This was one of those investigative techniques you learned from years on the job and one you didn't talk about to anyone for fear of being considered a nutcase.

He had started once to explain to an associate how smelling the clothes of a dead relative could result in a flood of associative memories and how recognizing that smell meant you knew something special about that person, but then he stopped in midsentence. This was not a topic he wanted to share with anyone, especially his colleagues. But to Vince, the whole thing made perfect sense. Vision takes one third of your brain function. If you turn the lights out completely, you can use all of your brain with your eyes wide open, and if your sense of smell does nothing else, it teases your imagination and thus keeps you alert for noticing things others don't.

Sometimes he wondered if his thirty-plus years as a cop had gotten the best of him. After all, his AARP membership card was starting to yellow. He had little to show for all those years of work. True, he had put away some bad people, very bad people indeed, but if he hadn't done it, someone else would have.

Vince's time with the Dallas police department was interrupted a year after the Tet Offensive in Vietnam, when he reenlisted as a Marine. He was assigned to a military police unit and then quickly reassigned to duty as a brig warden, spending eighteen months with North Vietnamese POWs and more than eight years with service members convicted of crimes following the Marines' withdrawal from Vietnam. After ten-plus years, he quit. He would not discuss his time served or even mention his service to other ex-Marines. When he returned to police work after the war, he was a changed man, and now his dreams were frequently haunted by lifeless faces of the North Vietnamese.

No longer a cop, Vince was now a security consultant, a private investigator of sorts. He was semi-retired, but the job he'd recently accepted was rekindling some of his old habits. Lying there in the dark, he returned to imagining the identity of his prey.

One of Alaska's richest men had persuaded Vince to take on an unsolved murder case. Buck Sandburg himself wanted to find out who had killed his granddaughter on the Parks Highway. She was murdered seven years ago, in the fall of the same year that Vince and his niece and Ginger had arrived in Alaska. He'd heard about the incident but had been too busy getting settled to pay much attention. Now the trail was bone cold. It seemed the old man had stewed and festered about it for years before deciding it was the one last thing he had left to do before he died.

The more Vince looked into the matter, the more baffling it became. Every fall but one during the past seven years, homicides had occurred along highways from southwest Missouri to Alaska. But the territory was so big and the incidents so spread out that it was exceptionally hard to detect a pattern unless, of course, you were looking for one. There were twenty-three known victims, twenty-one women and two men. Why the disparity? Common sense suggested it was because these murders were all seemingly associated with hitchhiking, even a mail carrier, whose delivery van had been found broken down six miles from her body. She must have needed a ride.

But maybe he was missing something; perhaps it wasn't that simple. And why, for God's sake, were the crimes so dissimilar? Several of the killings that appeared to have been planned were followed by others that seemed impulse-driven. Could he be dealing with two serial killers whose methods were eerily similar and whose timing was coincidental, or was it just one killer trying to confuse the authorities into thinking there is more than one? What were the odds of that? Hell, what were the odds of Mount Vesuvius blowing its top? Probably not very good, but then it had happened a dozen or so times in the past two thousand years.

He had been toying with the idea of giving the crime scene data to Ellen, his adopted niece. Recently turned seventeen and a virtual wizard with computers, Ellen had schooled herself in classical computer programming from its early stages, when the art was relatively primitive, through its rapid evolution to current practices in mass data management. She credited her insight into the mechanics of data modeling and analysis to her knowledge of that rigid method of coding. Then she had leapfrogged into an esoteric league of analysts, who collaborated in a cloud alliance specializing in pattern recognition and sophisticated puzzle solving. For all the advances in technology, though, it was still the job of someone needing information to have the ability to see the form of a result and to filter out irrelevant data, similar to the way the sieve of Eratosthenes derived prime numbers.

Immensely interested in solving mysteries, Ellen told anyone who asked that someday she was either going to be a homicide detective or a veterinarian, uncertain yet which one she would choose. Studying the evidence would bring her no harm, Vince thought, and it would be something they could do together. Not much of an angle, but one that might be good for their relationship. Of course, he would not show her the most disturbing photos of the crime scenes. In the morning he would review all of the cases while holding on to the notion that there must be a hidden pattern that he hadn't yet detected.

He told no one, not even Ginger, but he was planning to write a book when this case was concluded, even though it was her fascination with literature that had given him the idea. He had often imagined himself writing crime novels over the years, but he had never taken the idea seriously until now. God, if anyone in the country had the credentials to write a book about criminal behavior, he did. So he was sure publishers would take him seriously. There was only one big problem: What if he didn't have the talent? He worried about it constantly and kept putting off actually trying to write a novel because the illusion, at least for now, was more comforting than the truth if he turned out not to have the skill to see it through.

Right now he needed to confirm for Owen Sandburg a connection to his daughter's demise or he was wasting time. Owen's father, Buck, had died only a couple of weeks ago, so the case might be closed anyway. Vince had been reluctant to accept the assignment in the first place, but now he was interested. Oh well, he would know soon enough. But if it really was a serial killer with this much thirst for his craft, then he didn't want to give it up. Time to sleep. Time to play with killers in dreamland.

## STORM CLOUDS

RUBEN SANCHEZ WAS somber, depressed, or just plain down, as he characterized such mood swings. Many times during the past few days he'd half-heartedly acknowledged that life for skeptical philosophers is all the more wretched simply because refuge cannot be found in absurd notions of blissful illusion or the incessant noise of the people he referred to as "significance junkies," whose mindless euphoria was the result of being drunk on the nonsense of happiness talk and maintaining a positive attitude.

Ruben's personal wealth was greater than at any other time in his life, but he'd never felt more alone or existentially anxious for no apparent reason. Deep down, he was tired of trying to get ever closer to reality, to the truth of life, the objective part, if it really existed. On even days he guessed it did; on odd days he felt that the question was unanswerable and that he was disingenuous even to bring it up.

It was still so hard to believe his wife, Esther, was dead—five months now, but at times it seemed like five years. Incomprehensible. In spite of all of his self-regarding intellectual power for speculating about the metaphysics of existence, he was powerless to still his own angst. Nearly seven years had passed since his brother, Ben, was taken by a heart attack. And only a few months before that, Ruben's own heart had nearly exploded.

Ben's death was still fresh on his mind, and now with Esther gone, the future seemed to portend little but darkness, world events daily proving the point, revealing political conflict so viscerally felt and so deeply engrained in ethnocentric hatred that all efforts at remedy seemed hopeless. The winds of war were blowing once more, he thought, but then again, had they ever really stopped? Wasn't there always at least a light breeze of discontent or a gust of animosity and in-your-face hatred? But of course.

Adam 21 technology had given everyone with a computer the ability to look back in time, and the experience had changed the world dramatically. But that much was taken for granted these days. Media pundits were now obsessively focused on the distinct possibility of world war, and Ruben thought that the constant 24/7 harping about the subject would very likely help to bring it about.

Millennia-old grudges received new life almost daily, fueled by images of mass murder. Yet it was not clear in many instances where real guilt should be assigned and, worse, it didn't seem to matter. The only thing that did seem to make a difference was whose side one was on and whose tribe or people one could identify with. Such attitudes stood little chance of changing.

Ruben needed to put these thoughts aside for a while. This morning, deep in the Alaska wilderness near Mount McKinley, he was inhaling the sunrise at the cabin of his friend and financial backer, Robert Thornton, the engaging wanderer he'd met by chance in 2021. After walking away a young multimillionaire from his career on Wall Street, Thornton had changed his persona and pretended to be broke. He'd hitched a ride to Alaska with Ruben, who was driving a used luxury sedan to Ben's car sales lot in Anchorage.

When they arrived, Thornton had noticed a flyer on Ben's wall that pictured a cabin for sale. He surprised everyone by purchasing the cabin and surrounding acreage on the spot, sight unseen except for the photo. In the ensuing years, Thornton had developed an extensive compound on the property, but had preserved Ben's original cabin as a retreat for Ruben whenever he wanted to get away.

At the time of Ruben's heart attack seven years ago, his personal finances were so bad that he and his wife had let their health insurance lapse to keep their bookstore from going under, in spite of the fact that Esther was diabetic. Thornton had paid for Ruben's heart surgery, and since then, the two of them had never spoken of the debt.

Because of Thornton's connections, financial savvy, and belief in its purpose, Ruben's educational project had flourished, and now an office staff of five able employees in Anchorage maintained its web site. The enterprise was like the early days of the Kahn Academy, except the subjects Ruben offered were designed to help students acquire what he characterized as an existential education—a humanities-based curriculum that would help people deal with the anxiety wrought by humans' knowledge of their own mortality and enable them to understand that there is no need to distract themselves by finding scapegoats to blame for the fact.

All this he believed. Indeed, he had dedicated his life to this goal, and yet now his own anxiety seemed to mock his ambition. There were frequent moments when he had doubts about the whole project and felt like a fraud for being egregiously naïve—naïve enough to think that human beings would ever achieve intellectual adulthood en masse.

The objective, as Ruben and his staff described it, was to help people achieve psychological equilibrium through the study of psychology, anthropology, and sociology in order to fully appreciate that the human condition skews one's ability to be objective in a humanitarian sense, unless one takes comprehensive measures to compensate for our faulty predispositions. The underlying theme

...he program was the notion that, both as individuals and as a people, we all need to learn that we aren't really very special, even though our respective cultures lead us to believe just the opposite. Too many of us go about the whole of our lives trying to prove our self-importance through acts of arrogance while listening to constant self-help advice steeped in narcissistic social media and mindless happy talk. Could that be his problem now? Was he taking himself too seriously? Haunted by the question, his supple mind held no answer, and he was tiring of the question.

Alone in the early light, he figured Bob Thornton would be here now to cheer him up, if he weren't in Washington D.C. working on that new nonprofit task force—some kind of global peace effort. Ruben's son and daughter-in-law had divorced recently, and his granddaughter was now living far away and mostly out of touch. At moments like these, he experienced such despair that thoughts of suicide crept about in the periphery of his imagination like playful shadows in a children's fantasy. He had never openly admitted to himself that ending his life was an option, and yet he often flirted with the notion as a way to express his contempt for the meta-physical abyss he'd always suspected belonged at the very core of existence. What would people think if they knew what really went on in the mind of Ruben Sanchez? Would they think him a fraud?

At times he wondered to himself half-aloud if watching a sunrise was for someone in his state of mind an act of hope or self-punish-ment. In his younger days, he had been very much impressed with the philosophy of Ralph Waldo Emerson. Now, with advancing age, he was moving inexorably to Arthur Schopenhauer, whose devotion to misery seemed at times to relish nonexistence, and who had argued that the emotional tax on one's life is too steep, the tax bracket too high for the anguish essential for a person of his station in life. The tax of remorse was to be paid in full, every goal achieved resulting in disappointment, every triumph eventually ending in despair, every aspiration shattered, the very point of it all being utter futility. The long-dead German philosopher nearly made a religion out of art, hated loud noises and women, and lived in constant fear of falling asleep in a trance and being buried alive.

There were times when Ruben felt Schopenhauer had pegged reality far better than contemporary thinkers, himself included, and soon would come a flood of hopeful sentiment, something good happening in the world, something worth celebrating. But then, just as he was feeling hopeful, he would find himself once again on the slippery slope, creeping ever closer to depression and existential angst because the whole country seemed hell-bent on pursuit of narcissistic self-interests, totally unaware of Schopenhauer's notion that such ventures are doomed to despair and oblivious to the radical reality that if real meaning was to be had in the world, it would be found outside the notion of self. According to the German sage of pessimism, the only inborn human error is that "we exist in order to be happy." While a happy life is impossible, "a heroic life isn't," and this was the emotional sustenance that kept Ruben going.

When the radiance of the morning sky began to fade, Ruben went back inside, sat back in one of Thornton's massive recliners, and shut his eyes. An hour or two seemed to pass by in twilight sleep, and he was startled awake by a loud noise from in front of the cabin. The door swung open, and there stood his young friend looking like he'd just stepped out of a Cabela's catalog for outdoor wear.

"Thought I would find you here," Thornton said.

"I didn't expect you back so soon."

"Looks like I'm back to the drawing board. Too many conflicting ideas. I'm not paying the whole tab on this one, so I have to respect the opinions of the others, but I think some of the people involved in this project are idiots."

"What's the hang-up?"

Thornton grabbed a beer from the fridge, popped the bottle cap and sat on the massive oak coffee table close enough for Ruben to smell the hops. "Well, it should be pretty straightforward, but in a way, it may be the most complicated thing I've ever attempted to do, just too goddamned many people involved. And the ultimate goal is elusive because we can't be sure our intended tactics will work. We want to unite a group of wealthy individuals and some corporate conglomerates and government agencies under the banner of creating an aggressive movement for world peace. We're trying to reconcile the world to the idea of making amends for past injustices instead of fueling the hatred that Adam 21 keeps revealing. Most everyone I talk to that I respect thinks we are on the verge of another world war and that the end of civilization is only a matter of time.

"And you don't."

"No, of course not. At least, it's not inevitable, and don't tell me that you believe it is either, because I know you better that that. But the damned media can't seem to speculate about anything but war. The Far East is a powder keg. China, Japan, and Korea have recalled all of their ambassadors and their supporting staff from all of their neighboring countries. India and Pakistan are exchanging both heavy- and small-arms fire, and word from the underground in the Middle East points to the likelihood of an attempt to detonate a nuclear device in or near Israel soon, very soon. If such a prediction is credible, it seems to me they could find a way to stop it.

"The whole world as we know it could be over soon, and we can't even agree on a name for the organization, Ruben. What we need is something simple, something that moves people to aspire to something far beyond the concept of good and evil and ethnocentric nonsense. I don't know why it has to be so goddamned difficult. In the past three weeks, more than 150,000 people have been killed over ancient beliefs. Didn't you tell me once that the Hindu religion is one of peace? We could use some Hindu strategy."

"No, that's not what I said. I said Mahatma Gandhi put a lot of faith in that religion, but it was in fact a fanatical Hindu madman who killed Gandhi in 1949. I used to tell you repeatedly that one of the hardest things to do in this world is to convince people that things are never as simple as they appear, but Adam 21 changed all of that, did it not? Just made the whole premise worse because people blindly ignore the complexity of ancient history. Instead they focus on the ethnocentric sensation they get from bonding closer to their own group because of something bad some other group did to them."

Ruben went to the fridge to get himself a beer, his back to Thornton. "It's a bit early for a beer, but damned if it doesn't seem like a good idea, given what's going on in the world. If you will recall, I used to say that the comedian Bill Cosby was no Cliff Huxtable, that Elvis died on the toilet and John Wayne hated horses, that right-wing wackos often make terrific neighbors and some of the world's greatest bleeding-heart humanitarians are insufferable assholes, that Horatio Alger wasn't a rich man when he died, and that Mahatma Gandhi was himself a jerk to those closest to him. But then, the average man on the street has never been impressed with notions of reality, and the same, I guess, goes for corporate leaders. Except, now that we can see into the past, all of my rhetoric just sounds like pointless bullshit. Of course, things are not as they appear, but 'So fucking what?' is what they say nowadays. Am I right?" He seated himself again in the big chair.

Thornton paused for a moment, pursed his lips and said, "Pretty much. But I'm not prone to lecture like some folks I know, and I can't afford to come across as talking down to some of the world's most powerful people if I want them to cooperate. What we need to ask is that people in every walk of life take the time and effort to look beyond their own take on reality and come together with some kind of sense of community or else we're going to awaken soon in a new dark age, if we awaken at all. So, what kind of an approach would you take, short of a lecture?"

Ruben took a long drink and then stared at the bottle as if he wasn't sure what he was tasting. "The best advice I can offer about getting people to change their minds is to follow some kind of a rhythm of suggestive inference and a questioning agenda of sorts. You can't change most people's minds with arguments. You have to alter their perception. You have to deal with their emotions on an emotional level. The same with reason. I know this sounds a bit flimsy, but you can change more minds with the power of suggestion than by any other means, my friend. Think about it. The world of medicine has always been both fascinated with and ambivalent about the placebo effect. The only thing amazing to me is their inability to comprehend its utility. Give it some serious thought and you will come to the conclusion that it couldn't be any other way.

"How could thousands of generations, in small groups, bound collectively to one another through superstitious belief and spellbound by the special authority of certain members of their group who have the ability to use magical powers at will—how could they escape this experience without perceiving and accepting their illusions as real, with tangible effects both physically and mentally?

"The great mystery would be how humans might have evolved in such an environment *without* developing an ability to kick in a physical response to situations where we feel a psychological need to do so. Our minds are open to suggestion by nature of their duplex construction, which is why most of us are susceptible to hypnosis. We can do simple things that we are consciously aware of and see the effects immediately, but our subconscious is just as competent with our biological processes. Most of the really hard work the brain accomplishes to keep us alive is done beneath consciousness. You need to keep this in mind when you set out to change minds, especially on a grand scale." Thornton stared ahead as if he were listening to his own thoughts instead of Ruben.

"Look," Ruben continued, "if you can successfully plant seeds in the minds of others and nourish them from time to time without being suspected of doing so, then you may be able to get people to cooperate with far more enthusiasm than by appealing to their willingness to accept your argument as more powerful than theirs. Follow me?"

"Maybe." Thornton leaned forward, grabbed his beer, took a drink, and moved to another recliner, lying back as if preparing for a session an analyst's couch. "But I'm never totally sure with you. Sometimes I think you just like playing mind games with me." He sat up again for several minutes with his chin in hand. Finally he said, "I'll tell you this: I need help. Time is critical. This may turn out to be the most important thing any of us have ever done. The same goes for you. If we can't convince a fair number of the world's absolutists that a little bit of tolerance is in order, then everything else may be moot."

"Okay, what's the plan? What's next?" Ruben asked, his effort to show enthusiasm less than convincing.

Thornton had a grim look on his face. "I don't really have one yet, but we have to come up with something quick. I have lots of people preparing summary recommendations of what we should do. Considering that the end of civilization as we know it could be at stake, we ought to feel a strong sense of urgency to get this done. Right? What could be more important than saving the world?"

# WILLOW CREEK

*H*E CRAWLED INTO *bed in total darkness, nudging his naked body against her back. With his right hand he removed her panties, while his left hand slithered under her body and fondled her breasts. He entered her from behind, and she began to move back and forth and side to side for a full twenty seconds before the terror: This was not her husband!*

*There had been something scary about the man in the supermarket. Three times after she left the store she caught glimpses of him. He would have been handsome but not for that look: a Roman nose with nostrils flared as if he were a cat stalking prey. God what an odd character, she thought. Then a couple of hours passed without seeing him again and she put it out of her mind.*

At the spot beside Willow Creek where the Meyers woman's nude body had been found a few days before, Vince sat in his Suburban for twenty minutes without moving. For a split second he wondered if he should just drive off and wait until he talked to Owen Sandburg to see if he should continue the investigation, but it was just not like him to turn a thing loose if he was really interested. Now he wasn't merely curious: the mystery was riveting.

He stared into space as if he had access to another dimension, a warp, or tear in the fabric of time, concentrating so hard that his mind fluttered between total confusion and a sort of slate of emotional braille, something one might feel one's way through by the sensitivity of cerebral touch. This frenzied thinking would help him to refocus in the darkness tonight. Why did he think this homicide had to be connected to Amy Sandburg? That was so long ago. Still, he could feel it, but how and why he hadn't a clue.

He had seen a report on a local newscast that the woman was missing. Then his friend with the Alaska State Troopers, Matt Sills, had called him when her body was found because this was the kind of case Vince was focused on. Unlike the other homicides, this crime scene was still fresh, barely a week old. Samantha Meyers' husband swore that it was not in any realm a possibility that his wife had ever hitchhiked for any reason, whatsoever, and Vince believed him. People who drive BMWs and live in Palmer, Alaska, do not hitchhike, period. And she was a long way from Palmer. That, too, seemed odd.

David Meyers had given the troopers photos of his late wife that seemed to back his statement without explanation. She was a tall, willowy redhead with a beautiful face and the legs of a lingerie model. The photos revealed that she knew how attractive she was, and her husband knew you could tell this about her with only a glance at the picture.

Vince understood that, without a doubt, men watched her all the time, and she reveled in it, but this had been different. Of course, it was absurd to conclude she had been hitchhiking. The thought most likely would have occurred to no one, had not a state trooper written it up that way because of where she was found. Vince was becoming fond of an idea he would not share with anyone because it sounded so sophomoric and unprofessional. He had been investigating homicides for more years than he wanted to count, but something was different here. It was a creepy feeling, so strong at times he felt sure that even when this case was solved and long forgotten the stain on this part of the world might remain. It was less a simple deduction than a gut feeling.

He was beginning to realize, albeit very slowly, that memories of heinous crimes stayed with him over time, often becoming synonymous with the place where they had occurred. What this meant he wasn't entirely sure, but it might mean that he should stop working in the field and start writing before he felt the same way about Alaska that he did about Dallas.

One thing he was sure of was that most of the victims associated with this case had felt extreme fear before they died. How did he know this? He sensed that he could smell it, although he knew he really couldn't, but he stuck with the notion anyway because things that stuck in his mind kept him focused, even when they made no sense.

He was fascinated with the psychology of fear and all of its particulars and manifestations. This revelation occurred to him in the darkness one night after re-watching the classic movie *The Silence of the Lambs* for the umpteenth time. Seeing Anthony Hopkins as Hannibal Lecter immobilized in a stand-up cage, with something like a restraint muzzle mask over his face, a man so dangerous that he could not even be trusted in the same room with another person, even though he was unarmed, was scary as hell, and it led Vince to a new way of thinking about evil.

Perhaps he should tell Sandburg to find someone else. No, that would be no way to end his career as an investigator. This predator had to be stopped. Then it dawned on him that, from what he had intuited so far about this killer, there would be a good chance that he might return to this scene. If so, he would be there to catch him. The state troopers still suspected the husband, whose alibi was that he had been working late that night and came home to find his wife missing and the bed slept in. Vince believed him. The others didn't.

## REFUGE IN RIGHTEOUSNESS

AFTER TWENTY-EIGHT YEARS of service, Staff Sergeant Jonas Blythe left the Marine Corps because of a physical impairment. Twenty-eight years of hard work, hard play, and hard living. He claimed to have drunk enough booze to float a battleship and slept with enough women to send it to sea with a female crew. For most of his final ten years of duty as a hand-to-hand combat instructor at Camp Pendleton, California, he had been routinely introduced to new recruit classes as the toughest son-of-a-bitch west of the Mississippi.

Indeed, his confidence in his skills was the cause of his career misfortune. It wasn't a secret to Jonas that his body language and mannerisms when walking into a bar or encountering any group of strange men, said at both a conscious and subconscious level to all present: *if you are man enough, take your best shot.*

By rights he should have reached Sergeant Major E-9, but his downfall was brawling. He'd been busted in rank three times and would have been booted from the Corps had not the Commanding General of the Third Marine Division declared him the best instructor of his kind in the armed services. Jonas had always assumed he would make up for his misadventures and retire at a higher rank after thirty years, but a training accident had left him partially blind in his right eye and he could no longer pass a military physical. Being discharged as an E-6 was embarrassing.

Having two ex-wives, no children, and no family members he cared to associate with had left him stunned to be out of the service and on his own with no esprit de corps, no unit, no friends, no sense of belonging. He was alone. For the first time in his adult life, he was without a clear-cut mission or an organization to belong to. A modest pension for a man in his mid-forties gave him a little sense of freedom if he watched his debt. But he had no idea, whatsoever, about what to do next. The best thing he could think of was to drink his way across the country and look for a new home and some way to pass the time.

One bright April morning in 2028, he awoke with a severe headache in a jail cell in Lebanon, Missouri. He barely recalled a scuffle in a tavern on the outskirts of town. Vague memories of laying out three or four of the local ruffians like so much cordwood stacked for winter, flittered about in his brain, but his mind wouldn't stay still long enough for him to pin them down to reality. The local lawman, who read Jonas's service record and several newspaper clippings from his backpack about his duty during the Gulf Wars, refused to let the locals press charges without also being so charged with the same offenses. He was holding the ex-Marine just long enough for him to sleep it off, and then he would set him free.

Hung-over with no place particular to go and with nothing more in mind than ridding himself of the vile taste in his mouth and the throbbing pain in his head, Jonas walked into Aunt Betty's coffee shop and homemade pie restaurant, taking a seat next to a heavyset man dressed in black with a white clergy collar. After some friendly conversation, two cups of coffee, and one in hand to go, Jonas accompanied the man to his car. He was Rev. Nathan "Natty"

Baldwin of the Missouri Christian Soldiers Identity Movement, which had a retreat facility twelve miles north of town.

Two days of extended friendship and two weeks among men very much like himself, who seemed to care about his opinions on anything and everything, made the whole world look different to Jonas. Over and over his mind raced through the absurdities of his past life: years of obsessive whore-mongering, drunkenness, brawling for the sake of bragging about his masculinity. All of this nonsense interrupted twice by marriages that never had a chance because they required more of him than he had to give.

Then in a Sunday morning service, when Rev. Natty, amid an organist's rendition of "Amazing Grace," called upon those who would fight for the Lord to stand and come forward, Jonas felt himself moving toward the altar as if his legs were controlled by someone else. Natty decreed him born again, screaming to the heavens, "Go and sin no more!"

For the first time in years, Jonas felt good about himself. Cleansed to the bone and finally at peace, perhaps he was now among his own kind, even more so than in the Marines. His new energizing mission stood out as a clear-cut, black-and-white motive, his very reason for living. Sure, he was an ex-Marine, but now he was a soldier of God. He would smite those who needed it, and the world would be a better place for it.

It made real sense to him: A war for Jesus. This must be why he was on the earth, and yet, there were still times when he had serious doubts about religion and about preachers, in particular. The good reverend was saying that Jonas would be required to submit to a test to make sure his faith met the standards required for membership in the company of God's legions for righteousness. It was a test of character, an enticement to join Satan, a constant invitation to sin among the dregs of civilization, in a camp filled with vile men, scum of the earth, godless mercenaries. Some would kill for the thrill; others would kill for no reason or any reason. Not only would Jonas be expected to refuse temptation, he would also be expected to avoid trouble in a place where trouble festered as a malignant strain of infectious wickedness—a pit of evil devoid of goodness, devoid of grace, devoid of God.

It would be a test of character, all right. What he didn't understand was how, in a world bedeviled and increasingly dominated by evil, he could possibly do anything to make a difference.

## THE PIONEER HOME

WHILE PREPARING TO close her deceased employer's office, Buck Sandburg's secretary had called Vince to say the director of the Pioneer Home in Palmer had an old gentleman living there that he might want to interview if he was going to continue his investigation. Now, unable to get comfortable in the hardwood chair he'd been given, Vince was having second thoughts about accepting the offer. The elderly gentleman across from him fidgeted about as if he were readying himself to jump into a pool of cold water.

"Let's see, officer, where should I begin? I will be ninety-six on Tuesday." And then he was silent for a long moment that made Vince uneasy.

"Or is it Wednesday? Anyway, doesn't matter. The dealings you are interested in occurred a few years back just after I had a stroke that left me without the ability to speak for nearly two and a half years. All I could do was sit, watch, and listen. I'm bettin' that's how the events that brought you here to interview me got started."

He stopped speaking, looked around the room as if suddenly he wasn't sure where he was, and then said, "It all began when Ida Mae Nordstrom's granddaughter came here to the home for a visit. Ida Mae wasn't feeling well so she asked Miss Helen Mabry, who everyone around here just calls Miss Helen, to entertain her granddaughter,

Celia Nordstrom, a tall pretty young lady with orange hair. You know what it's like to be trapped inside your own body, understanding what's going on around but you can't speak?" Pausing again, he seemed to be studying the floor for a moment. Vince made a noise with his chair, and the old man recommenced. "No, I don't expect you do. Till you experience a stroke, hearing about it will never do to understand the feeling or maybe the unfeeling."

Silence for two more long minutes, and when the old man spoke again, he jerked forward causing Vince to jump. "Anyway, it was a couple of months after my spell. Maybe later than that. Hell, I'm not sure when exactly, just that it happened. I was sitting upright in my wheelchair parked like a fireplug in a corner waiting for a dog to piss on my leg, while everybody around here was getting on with their own business as if I was invisible. Talking about me as if I wasn't there, looking not at me but through me. Of course, they still do that, you know. You know how that feels? No, I guess you don't." Now he seemed energized and animated.

"Anyway, I was sitting in the hall just outside Miss Helen's room. Miss Helen was flittering about the room like a butterfly starved for nectar and in search of new blooms after a frost killed most of the flowers, while telling Celia and her friend Amy about her infamous relatives. She went on and on about how her great grandfather Colonel Henderson had ridden with Robert E. Lee in the Civil War and then she went to the opposite wall and to Colonel John Clancy Mabry, who she said served with General Grant and General Sherman and who practically burned Atlanta without Sherman's help. Poor Celia never got a word in edgewise, but then nobody did when Miss Helen was telling about her family heritage.

"But it turns out that the real interesting thing discovered that evening was that little Amy, Celia's young friend, was in trouble. I heard her tell Celia about it on that couch right over there. She was pregnant, don't you know, and that might not have been much to make a fuss about except that she turned out to be Amy Sandburg, and if you've lived in Alaska very long, you know what that means. The Sandburgs are powerful people and have been for as long as I can remember. Do you want me to go on?" A few seconds after he spoke, he leaned forward and appeared to nod off to sleep. Vince got up to look for a nurse, mumbling to himself to calm his growing sense of anxiety.

## FACES OF EVIL

THE TWO SIDE-BY-SIDE computer monitors revealed starkly differing realities of the same general area some distance apart. In the first, an immaculately dressed soldier walked in half-gaited stride beside two little girls wearing pink dresses, holding hands, and skipping to a tune most likely of their own making because there appeared to be no source for music and even less reason for their obvious elation. Their curly ebony locks jostled about in the glimmer of bright sunlight like flowers in a windy meadow, their joyful skipping expressing clear expectations about a cheerful future, the worry-free presence of trusted adults, and the animated naïveté of childhood innocence.

The neatly manicured path took on the spirit of a yellow brick road—with Dorothy and friends on their way to fantasyland, surrounded by fields of ripe grain, colorful flowers, honey bees, butterflies, and nature's air of goodness and virtue. It was, however, early fall 1943 in Poland, and as history would record, Satan himself had assumed control of the country. His name was Adolf Hitler.

The other screen made this clear. It showed the same path, but up ahead a few hundred yards and hidden by the crest of a hill, the scene screamed the death of decency, an overt depiction of madness, of sacrilegious horror, of acts of pornographic immorality carried out with strict military discipline and decor. What the screen revealed was the eye of the abyss: women and children were being put to death with rifle and pistol shots to the back of the head. The contrast for the unsuspecting viewer was beyond comprehension for all but psychopaths, psychotics, and sadists.

The image was to Dr. Wendell Smyth both a surreal and a moral blasphemy; it was the incarnation of evil, a cancer in the bowels of humanity. And yet, he found himself helplessly unable to stop watching it. He had saved the Adam 21 clip in screensaver mode, and it taunted him, even sometimes when he was in another room. He'd memorized every second of the five-minute scene. Being a neurosurgeon by profession, he knew with confidence that it was indelibly etched into the limbic stem of his brain. In this instance, he was grateful that Adam 21 images did not include sound.

Smyth had long ago given up surgery for research, and he now felt frequent surges of exhilaration with the growing realization that someday soon he might be a serious candidate for a Nobel Prize. Oh, his work wasn't really a competitor with the likes of Adam 21, a technology capable of seeing into the past, but for a small-town Jewish lad from upstate New York, he thought it kind of exciting that he might one day be thought of as having brought the power of God to bear on the evildoers of the world.

The real irony and paradox of his accomplishment lay in its style and substance. His godlike miracle was very much of the same form, appearance, and consistency as Jell-O. Of course, it sounded silly as hell on the surface, but it was as big a truth as he had ever encountered and others would soon recognize it as such. He was considering calling a news conference. It was past time. The chemistry worked—he was convinced of its power—and making people believe it worked was easy to do. Too easy perhaps. But this feature would also help to bring a lot of attention to his cause.

In addition to his research, Smyth had a hobby as a web stringer. His web site featured a written narrative interspersed with Adam 21 coordinates so that when you logged on to his URL, you were taken on a tour scrolling through the past with a written or a verbal narrative if you preferred. His site was popular. But then, his subject was genocide, and it came with ample warning: "Do not visit here if you are faint of heart. But if you have the courage and determination to make the world a better place by ridding it of evil, please read on and help support this web site. Help save man from man. The times we are living in demand a sentinel awareness from everyone."

## LIFE WITH ADAM 21 BY OWEN SANDBURG

A T THE TURN of the twenty-first century, psychologist and philosopher John F. Schumaker published *The Age of Insanity*, where he described a Western World increasingly experiencing inward narcissism, alienation, dehumanization, amoral immediacy, mass-produced desire, pathological consumption, modern rage, social fraudulence, environmental dissociation, and overt anti-intellectualism. Then Adam 21 technology took off and things really went downhill.

In the beginning, there was no shortage of predictions about how Adam 21 technology would affect the world. But no one had foretold the big picture with any degree of precision, and most had missed the significant feelings of contempt it would arouse in people all over the planet. Like sticks rubbed together to make fire, resentment created sparks of hatred smoldering and bursting into flame all over the world. Although some pundits had indeed made accurate forecasts about conflict and political turmoil, none that I've found have understood the depths to which ancient acts of genocide could incite present-day calls for vengeance. Apparently, ignorant people are not interested in details, only whose side one is on.

The tools we use to view the world shape the way we perceive the world. Adam 21 has taught us that it is through history that we learn who we are. We have to see who our ancestors were then to know who we are now.

In science fiction movies about time travel when someone changes something in the past, there is often a lot of snap, crackle, and pop short-circuiting-type noise to suggest actual changes affecting the present. In similar fashion, when one looks at events in the past that aren't consistent with what one has always believed to be true, the result can be a severe psychic jolt.

Cultures are analogous to trees. Most of what you see is dead, and only the leaves and the deep interior are living. Likewise, our reasons for doing the things accepted as tradition are largely forgotten. When we let our culture mold us too forcefully, we lose touch with the interior core of what it means to feel truly alive. Just going through the motions is emotionally stultifying.

Adam 21 changed the perception of what perception literally means, and people began to fear they might die having never truly lived. If one's identity is based in large part upon what one has learned to be true about the past, and then that turns out to be false, the result is chaos. Some people experience it thus: If what I've always thought to be true is really false, am I still me?

Scores of prognosticators declared at first that Adam 21 would be a death blow to religion, but the very opposite happened. With the opening of portals to the past there followed a groundswell of fundamentalism in every major religion and too many murky new belief systems to count. Viewing the past without knowing precisely what was being said left interpretation up for grabs. And grab they did—every group with something profoundly inane to claim as the very foundation, the very bedrock of revealed truth, something born of contempt for nonbelievers, something masquerading as concern for humanity, while hiding a festering, infectious and contagious strain of hatred for those deemed outsiders.

A tidal wave of new faiths slammed ashore on every continent as people came together in feverish pursuit of collective delusion. But this phenomenon was now thought to have peaked and appeared to be spiraling down, even though it was still an incredibly powerful societal force—a force to be reckoned with, a point made most often by skeptics whose exasperation seemed at times to border on a penchant for revolution. Few pundits, though, would dare suggest that fundamentalism was not positioned to come back at any given time, even stronger than before. A big part of the global divide was a fracture with Christians on one side and Muslims on the other as each cited Adam 21 examples to disprove the other's religious assumptions.

Simply put, viewing the past unhinged the present, making the quest for some sense of security the uppermost thing on the minds of those who had the least bit of difficulty with ambiguity. Moreover, there was something mystical about watching events in ancient times unfold without sound and without knowing the specific reason for the actions observed. Lip reading gave clues, but too much of what was said was simply lost.

People who feared change were living in a purgatory of accelerating chaos, and they wanted it stopped, the cost be damned, which is why the on-ramp to power appeared to be in interpreting what the past was really trying to show us according to those who presumed they had nailed the truth to the walls of time. The power to convince was, as it has always been, the shortest path to acquiring power, precisely because believers were so willing to trade their fears for assurances of certainty, even if, and especially if, these assurances were metaphysically absurd.

History shows us that if something hard to believe can be accepted by a group, the credulity required for group membership can work as a shield, a barrier, a platform for recruitment, and a lethal weapon against cultural differences, otherness, and uncertainty. By identifying doubt as treasonous behavior, acts of proving one's patriotism would fuel a growing army of zealots, whose zeal was as powerful as their belief was preposterous.

Skeptics, however, suggested that watching ancient history unfold before one's very eyes should offer a demystifying effect. Just as it was hard on the one hand to be sure you understood the precise reason for the actions you were watching, it was just as hard on the other to apply supernatural assumptions about the origins. But of course this didn't stop such efforts. In fact, it brought forth an exponential increase in them, leaving the skeptics distraught, as if they were cheerleaders doomed to always side with the losing team.

Earlier sociologists and literary critics were accustomed to referring to people as rationalists, skeptics, romantics, modernists, and postmodernists, but these categories were giving way to lumping people into historical periods. People were increasingly identified by the century or time periods they were most interested in. Indeed, there were still romantics, but now there were many different subsets of the category. Some focused on relationships in a period, some chose art or literature, and others were mostly interested in other subjects, like architecture, agriculture, warfare, or sexual mores. The same could be said for each and every other assemblage. And, just as the ranks of religious groups had swelled, so had those of the cynics, with the latter beginning to come on strong, selling pessimism as the castor oil of reality.

The most accurate public prediction about career choices prompted by Adam 21 technology forecast the growth of history majors in college, except now there were so many categories of historical scholarship that one could barely keep an accurate tally of their numbers. The great irony is that it wasn't pure scholarship that was sought after; rather, it was some way to make the understanding of history profitable in the business of business, which prompted many cynics to say nothing has changed, that we have learned nothing from history save greed.

Adam 21 rendered all pre–Adam 21 history texts obsolete, making some useful only as guide points for claims that could and likely would be refuted by observation. Nearly all new history majors were expected to master the ability to read lips.

The latest Internet phenomenon was a search grid with an algorithmic menu in which people could locate their interests in the past in a range of value-laden queries like skeptic vs. believer, idealist vs. materialist, emotive vs. rationalist, or liberal vs. conservative approaches, which were followed by nouns, geographical locations, and time periods. All of this information was compiled on one's Personal Page, the entity which had overtaken Facebook years ago. Critics argued that it was nothing short of a head-in-the-sand approach to confirm a worldview one held already, but that didn't detract from the popularity of groupishness. Proponents of group selection said it was an example of nature working as intended, a winnowing out of inferior groups while increasing the size of those with the inclination to come together for common purpose.

A profound change brought about by the technology, and one that a fair number of people had guessed, was that of a revived interest in family lineage. Psychologists declared the beginning of a radical change in the sense of self on the part of the individual, except that it was still too early to tell the full range of the effects. This drama, they said, was underway because of an entirely new kind of awareness of the vast depth of one's connectedness to earlier generations. It meant that past connections to one's ancestors held much more sway over the present than ever before because many of these incidents were simply unforgettable. Moreover, the constant comparison of resemblance among relatives was battering away at the notion of individuality; the more people observed their ancestors, the less unique they felt.

Studying past generations intently was heartening in some aspects and deeply disappointing in others. The change to the psyche of the individual would be profound, they said, but there was little agreement about the likely end result. After all, it was theoretically possible, if you had the time and money, to spend the rest of your life discovering earlier and earlier ancestors with the only restrictions being that you wouldn't live long enough to get to the beginning and, in too many cases, there was uncertainty about who had fathered whom.

Making precise family connections from portals into the past was no easy task, and erroneous conclusions were as easy to make as accurate ones. And yet, many of the physical resemblances between people in the far distant past and their present-day relatives were so striking that incidents of acknowledgment frequently made the national news, complete with photos and interviews about what it felt like to see copies of yourself in centuries past.

All of this activity was often described by pundits as a society flying apart and simultaneously coming together. The whole world seemed perched on the verge of what many said would surely amount to a thermonuclear war, if the shooting were to actually start in earnest.

The most popular prognosticators of the day were making an argument that the newest and most powerful Internet search engine, simply called Hennessey, was so potent that it was on the verge of becoming self-aware, but as many others declared the idea absurd. Nearly everyone, though, admitted that Hennessey had creepy characteristics that made you think you were dealing with a

real person, but that was just because it was so much more sophisticated than any of the previous search engines. It was a massive
bundle of ones and zeroes and nothing more, they said. But then,
who were they anyway to complain and cast doubts and aspersions
on the quest for knowledge? Do we human beings, strung out over
a smidgen of time like sparks in a dark void, amount to much more
than ones and zeroes ourselves? I mean, think about it. Once we are
gone, does an answer to the question even matter?

# LITERARY INSIGHTS

IN THE TERRELLS' living room, a large panel played a four-teen-hour reconstruction of the life of John Henry Peek, the great-grandfather of Vince Terrell. There were scenes of a thin, wiry lad of ten or twelve running in an open field in nineteenth-century Ohio, an idyllic and pristine period of American agriculture in which all of the hard labor put into the land still left little imprint, a time when concrete slabs were absent and the farms were small and quaint. John Henry's boyhood went on for an hour, and viewers could recognize four different family dogs, each a mongrel hound unlike the others.

Flashbacks further into the past showed John Henry's mother and father in their childhood. The scenes were uncomplicated and undemanding, representing an idealized period of youth for both Americans and their European ancestors, although it was crystal clear that life was hard and there was very little to be envious about.

Running in parallel was another life story of the childhood of Vince's great-grandmother Sara Spencer Peek, showing Sara playing on her family's farm and working in a vegetable garden. The film editor had clearly been a professional because the scenes went from John to Sara in such a way as to suggest that the piece contained a trajectory or the implication of a future plot.

Another hour told a very different story, tracing John Henry Peek's Civil War history up close and from afar, from one bivouac to another, from one battle to the next, some won, some lost, and some where the very idea of winning seemed perverse. The scenes were edited for taste, the violence distant enough to make its point but not so graphic as to turn the stomach. The balance of the work consisted mostly of the wagon-train trip of 1865 to California, where along the trail John Henry and Sara met and were married. Then John Henry disappeared. And even though they now had access to details of his disappearance, they chose not to show it. An accompanying narrative explained how fortunate the wagon train had been in light of the Indian raids in Wyoming that had left so many groups with casualties or worse.

One panel in the Terrell home had a subscription to *Adam 21 Late-Breaking Discoveries*, which was a network owned by a media conglomerate. Adam L-B, as the channel was known, featured the latest and most profound discoveries made by Adam 21 researchers, both professional and amateur, from around the world. Each subscription came with a censor level with which to enable or disable objectionable material. The Adam L-B network employed thousands of researchers and film editors working in a frenetic search to beat the other networks to the punch in producing earth-shaking discoveries, which were now pretty much a routine occurrence.

One final screen was a work in progress, a panel in which Vince, Ginger, and Ellen were capturing high points in their current family life as they occurred. Adam 21 took the notion of home movies to a whole new dimension; it was an art form with smoldering levels of emotional nuance. The metaphoric implications were such that people viewed the creations as works of art, and many began seeing their lives in much the same way. The downside was the anguish felt in unfinished portraits, when family members' lives were cut short. What made these experiences so poignant was the rich history portending so much promise but ending so abruptly.

Each day Vince was more and more aware that his whole life was about endings, and he was sure his own could not be that far ahead. At times, it was as if he could feel demise hanging over him like a blanket of fog. The fog might lift but would stay nearby, so he was always aware that it could come back at any moment to cloud the future. That death was a stalker was always present in his mind. He'd made it his life's work to never let the loathsome reality drift so far away that he might be caught by surprise, especially if the adversary happened to be one's own heart.

For seven years, the Terrells had been fans of reading aloud. Their reading sessions had begun on their trip from Texas to Alaska. Ginger's hypnotic voice and the background of the Alaska Highway, contrasted with the nineteenth-century prose of *Moby-Dick,* had resonated so well with their aspirations for the future that now, at least once a week, they partook in family literary adventures of one kind or another. The only thing that usually got in the way was a new discovery on Adam 21. At first it was only Ginger who read aloud. But now they took turns, Vince reading a book aloud from start to finish, then Ginger, and then Ellen. The reader selected the book and the other two had to listen without protest until their turn. Not only did it draw them closer together, but being exposed to each other's subjects of interest was an enlightening way to gain insight about their relationship.

Vince had never considered himself a literary type. He was a cop, not a writer, although he had written so many police reports that he suspected he might really be able to write better than most novices. When he fell under Ginger's spell of unconditional enthusiasm for literature, he began to think seriously about putting his law enforcement experience to the page.

Ginger was always talking about this great work or that, and in addition to their family reading sessions, she was forever leaving material under his nose to read. *Wuthering Heights* affected him to the core. The gothic tale was as far removed from his life as it could be, and yet something about the dark mood of the novel fascinated him. He knew a bit about evil people from having studied the pathologies of criminal behavior for years, but that damned book seemed to have taken him to another level of understanding of the human psyche. He couldn't say why or how exactly, but because of the brooding sentiment and deep-rooted nature of humanity's relish for succumbing to evil, he was awestruck by the possibilities for a breakthrough.

A flash of insight was surely just ahead in the same way that he always seemed to know intuitively when he was about to solve a case. If he could say something, however brief, that could mine his experience with the criminal element, something that rang truer than any modern crime novel, something resembling the gut-level adolescent immorality in *Wuthering Heights*—if he could do that for a place like Dallas, Texas, in these times, then all his years spent in the company of degenerate scum just might make some sense.

There was just one last thing to tie up before he could start in earnest. He had to catch a serial killer, and now he was giving serious consideration to asking Ellen for her assistance. He expected she would be delighted, but he was still having reservations.

His law enforcement experience was vast. He was seldom surprised or brought up short in his expectations about human nature and its perversities. But there was something about his current case that bothered him deeply. Each day he expected it to come to him as a full-blown epiphany, born of subconscious concentration, of deep dreams and a desperate need to understand this sense of evil that flitted about in his mind like a vial of ancient plague virus.

He had lots of evidence but no real clues about this predator. Not only that, but this constant puzzling also made him ill at ease, a tad sick. He was not used to feeling weak and vulnerable—that was something victims likely felt, not men like him. In this case, he would have to prove it.

He couldn't put his finger on a reason, but he felt he was running short of time, and the prospect was worrisome to the nth degree. Time, the very thought of time, what it is, how we experience it, why we are slaves to its peculiarities and finicky nature—Adam 21 had forever changed the very notion of time, which meant it was also changing the nature of what it means to be human. In the dark recesses of his mind, Vince knew this to be the case and it saddened him. Sadder still, was a haunting awareness that his life was nearing an end.

Nothing had ever meant quite so much to him as Ginger and Ellen, and too much of the time, Ellen was in places where he couldn't watch out for her. Now getting her involved in the case could bring her to the attention of a killer, and the very idea was beginning to worry him. What would happen if he were to die before this creep was caught? The thought made him short of breath.

# EVIL ON THE ROAD

WILFRED HOPKINS WAS an average-looking fellow, six foot tall, 190 pounds of well-distributed muscle with light brown hair and pale blue eyes oozing with ego. His image of himself as having Hollywood actor potential fueled his proclivity for arrogance, his taste for expensive clothes, and his fondness for redheaded women. His bags were packed. The special case was ready. He was dressing to leave on his annual sales trek.

Years earlier, he had begun his career selling academic books to schools and libraries, but that had been an unfortunate choice, as selling books had been a dying enterprise long before he got started. One of the old-time book salesmen he met at a convention had said, "Welcome to the harness business." When Wilfred asked what that meant, the older man said, "In-person book selling and harness sales are occupations lost to history, son. You'd better find something else to peddle and fast."

The man was right, of course. That very year, Wilfred lost three of his major lines, without which he could not make a living. He was depressed about it at first because he loved the idea that he was a pusher of literature. He didn't read much of the stuff himself, but it made him seem cultured. The appearance of sophistication was what he relished, not necessarily the knowledge that made it possible. For that he could substitute ego, as he had it to spare, so much so that he would not allow people to call him Willie, ever.

The personal downside of book selling had been that he couldn't take a vacation when he wanted to. Now he didn't have to worry about that because his new job was selling medical supplies and lab equipment. With nearly twenty years of sales experience behind him, he made a pretty decent living. A hell of a lot more money could be made selling drugs and equipment rather than books, the irony of which crossed his mind. What he liked best was his time on the road in the fall. He started north from Missouri in the summer so that on the return trip he would catch and follow the changing foliage in the most beautiful time of the year, taking great pleasure in being alone with his thoughts. Still enamored of being associated with great literature, he carried leather-bound editions of classics with him for show and sometimes listened to audiobooks as he drove through farm country with windows open and semi-pristine air scented with freshly baled hay filling his nostrils.

Today he would wear dark green corduroy pants, a light burgundy silk shirt, and a buckskin corduroy jacket if it got cool after dark—the country squire look he admired. His sales territory included five states and three Canadian provinces. Considering this leg of his annual trip north to be extra special, he had made the geographic schedule a part of his employment agreement. Even though the manufacturers he represented thought it was an inefficient use of his time, his reliability and his sales record prompted them to allow him to schedule his travel as he saw fit. As a rule, he would meet his clients via video sales calls and then visit them in person once a year during the time that in his mind was simply the best season to travel through the spectacular scenery of the North Country.

Seeing autumn colors in the leaves, pumpkins on fences, and jack-o-lanterns in windows added extra satisfaction to his trips, Halloween being his favorite holiday. His birthday was October 30, and he had always felt cheated that he had not been born on October 31. Just saying the words aloud, "all hallows eve," gave him a rush that increased his heart rate. He loved fall. The air spoke of winter to come, implying a sense of finality. Fall hinted of death, and beneath it all his real mission in life was to kill. He had stopped for several years, thinking he might live a normal life, but that was not to be.

Since the beginning of Adam 21, it had become Wilfred's ambition to someday be recognized as the most infamous serial killer ever known, signifying true sophistication and taking the notion of expertise and competence to a whole new level. Convinced that his manner of methodical precision and forensic expertise would render history's most famous killers as rank amateurs, he believed time would reveal him to be the master slayer of all time. It was considered unusual for a serial killer to have long-term goals, and this made him unique and special.

In his own mind he represented evil incarnate. The fact that the general public was both fearful and obsessively fascinated by people like himself—fiends born without conscience—was exhilarating, and it served to feed his peculiar form of sexual deviance. In the company of people considered normal, he could get off on himself solely because of who and what he believed he was. Just being Wilfred Hopkins made him want to kill and to feel good about it.

He often reveled in the fact that the public's need to gawk at the gore in traffic accidents was in large part related to their deep suspicion that they too were capable of feeling good about morbidity, so long as it was happening to someone else, the other, so to speak. Well, he was the *other*, and he knew more about the general public than they knew or would ever know about him. Evilness as pure entertainment seemed to be a gift from the gods.

What the supposedly normal people didn't realize—those simpletons of the general public—was that by scaring themselves on purpose, a thing that only humans do, they were dissipating their own impulses and proclivities for doing evil things themselves. They were using serial killers vicariously as a psychological venting mechanism, and yet they remained unaware of their own complicity. Wilfred loved it that media kept the melodrama of good and evil alive by exaggerating the mythic abilities of serial killers and their inordinate skill at eluding capture.

He wasn't afraid of being caught or being punished. Prison didn't scare him. Such common-man worries were not in his nature. If he feared anything at all, it was not living up to and being celebrated for his grandiose ambition and his constant need for increasing levels of excitement. This is what made him so dangerous. His highest goal was to be remembered as the most compelling reason on the earth to experience nightmares. He would stop at nothing to fulfill his deviant desires and leave his mark on the world. And he would do so without a shred of doubt, guilt, or remorse, as these were human qualities he didn't experience. But, then, he didn't really care because he liked being one of a kind and he would soon prove it beyond any question.

# THE CASE

"THANKS FOR SEEING me, Mr. Sandburg," Vince said, admiring the office's beautiful wall-to-wall bookcases bursting with hardcover books and hundreds of leather-bound volumes.

"You, sir, are my age or older, so I think you should just call me Sam. Everyone else does and they always have, even though my name is Owen. Something my father began, but don't get me started on him."

"Okay, Sam, I'm sure you know why I'm here."

"Yes, I do. I've been told that my late father hired you to find out who murdered his granddaughter, my daughter Amy. Do I have it right?"

"Yes, sir, you do. In case you don't know, I'm a retired police officer, and all I do now is a little consulting work. I was reluctant to take this assignment, but your father was very persuasive. That's not why I agreed, though, Mr. Sandburg. Sorry, I mean Sam. No, he had a genuine sense of desperation about him, and I found it hard to say no. That said, and even though your father gave me a very nice retainer, I will return what I haven't billed if you want to shut the investigation down. It's entirely up to you."

Raymond Owen Sandburg pushed himself back in his chair and studied the man sitting across from him. He looked the part of a straight shooter all right, even if a bit long in the tooth. But Owen purposely acted ambivalent. Amy's death had torn his family apart, and they were just now beginning to work their way back into something that might be thought of as a normal life, if Owen's life could ever be thought normal. He was thinking and watching Vince, who sat perfectly still like a psychiatrist studying a new patient said to be deeply troubled and about to do something desperate.

"Okay, detective, before I tell you what I think, tell me how you see it. Do you want to continue or shut it down, as you say?"

"It's entirely up to you. As I said, I was hesitant to start this in the first place, but I've continued with the investigation even after your father's death. Since I began working on it, I may have made some progress, although it's still too early to tell if it will amount to anything." Vince paused for a moment, and both men continued to study one another.

"I think there is a distinct possibility that your daughter was the victim of a serial killer. Now, I can't prove it at this point by any means, but I do have reason, or maybe I should say I'm relying more on experience-based intuition than reason, to think a serial killer is a real possibility. If you want me to stop, I will turn over everything I have to the Alaska State Troopers. I will share this information with them anyway, even if I continue, so it's entirely up to you, sir."

"Don't you have a preference, detective?"

"All things being equal, I'm definitely interested in going further, but like I said, this is not my call."

"Okay, detective."

"Call me Vince. I'm retired, remember."

"Okay, Vince, then I'm going to ask that you stay on it. If there is a chance in hell that I might keep this bastard from doing the same thing to someone else's daughter, then I don't really see that

I have an option to do otherwise. Just don't in any way involve my wife. I don't even want her to know we are doing this, okay?"

"That's not a problem."

"Okay then, I would like to see your agreement with my father and see if we need to make amendments. I want to be discreetly kept up to date about your progress or the lack of it at least once a week. Okay?"

"Sure, that's not a problem either. I'll send you a copy of the contract, and we'll go from there."

"I'll see you to the door."

Vince nodded as they walked out, thinking what a great loss for a young woman, heir to all this and then losing her life to some low-life piece of shit that never should have been born in the first place. This case, Vince thought, had a feel of evilness to it, and as he stepped off the porch of the Sandburg mansion, he felt himself shudder as if he were catching a cold, or maybe just a killer.

# WRATH AND RIGHTEOUSNESS

REV. BALDWIN SAID God had told him straight up that Jonas was God's man, His avenger, but he would still have to go through the initiation process. Perhaps this really was the man's one true mission in life, but Baldwin still had to get the Seer's approval before moving Jonas into the camp of the righteous and assigning him a mission. This, he had said, would take some time.

Some days Jonas felt as if this religious experience might really be his calling, and on others he felt a little foolish for thinking so. Rev. Baldwin had made it clear that the Seer considered Adam 21 to be blasphemous and sacrilegious and believed it had to be put right with God. "God speaks to you through me, not in my voice but in His," Baldwin said. "Don't you hear it, Jonas?"

Unable to speak, Jonas was spellbound, nodding once in a while, but most of the time sitting very still during these sessions with a hypnotic look in his eyes.

"Jonas, as sure as I'm standing before you, it is God's will that you smite the beast that mocks Him. I saw it in this morning's sunrise; it was a clear vision of you and all of God's glory. It is your fate that you have been wounded in action for your country that you now take up the mantle of Righteousness and that your Silver Star for valor will be replaced by a crucifix blessed by none other than God Himself. You will cleanse the world of the architects of evil.

Someday the name Jonas Blythe will be a synonym for justice. You will be remembered always as the righteous one."

All his ranting about his virtuous role in the world had the opposite of the intended effect on Jonas. He was embarrassed by such overblown language, the words sticking in his mind, memes of doubt, whispering thoughts flooding his mind one moment and disappearing so fast in the next that he was left to wonder if they had actually been real.

Six foot tall, 210 pounds of Marine Corps-tendered muscle, with years of advanced training in all modes of combat, he was certainly the man for the job in the parson's eyes, and there would be many more just like him because the Seer promised as much. Baldwin said they would and should call themselves the Horsemen of the Apocalypse. Sabers in hand, they would rid the earth of the architects of evil and their kin, to serve as a sign of prophesy and as a testament to the wisdom of the Seer.

Training is not what was needed for Jonas. He just needed a mission, something he could believe in, and it needed to be soon. If it was really and truly God's will, he would obtain approval shortly. The reverend was sure of it. Natty claimed that in less than ninety days it would be over, and his destiny would be fulfilled, his reputation celebrated for eternity.

What Natty didn't know, but observation should have revealed, is that his disciple abhorred undeserved praise. Flattery for the sake of currying favor was to Jonas the epitome of disingenuousness, and Marines were taught to detest all manner of pretense, except the promise to kick your ass if you turned out to be a phony.

# OWEN SANDBURG'S JOURNAL: MEDITATIONS

ONE DAY YOU'RE playing children's games, and in the next moment you find yourself in high school, then college. Another flicker of imagination and you're career obsessed and knee-deep in middle age. You're surrounded by people who claim to be your family but who act like strangers when pressed for sincerity about anything that really matters, anything deeper than superficial chitchat. And then, just when you find yourself getting used to the way of things, you find that you have one foot in the grave, your body begins falling apart, and you find it hard to see the beginning of anything without reflecting about the end of it, the end of you, if you are honest. If you can't admit that, you have to find a distraction, and for far too many people someone or some group to hate works nicely.

You try to remember what it was like to be a child, even as a little voice in your head says there is no longer any future in resurrecting lifeless memories. You're an old man, and it's too late to wonder what might have been or still could be. You had your chance and you blew it. Isn't the process of losing one's memory a little at a time a bit like glimpses of death and dying, or is it worse? Is there a fate on the planet worse than being lost in the labyrinth of one's own mind?

You feel an increasingly creepy sense of desperation; you're going to die soon, after all, and among strangers, some of whom will even be sad, but it's of little consolation. You're stunned by the absurdity of trying to make sense of life. After all, just a few moments ago you were playing games, and now look what's happened. Young people roll their eyes when you speak, your belt line is a foot higher than it used to be, you're apt to doze off in the absence of loud noises, and from here on, it's downhill all of the goddamned way to the end.

The world will surely end someday, they say. But does that really matter? You're going to be gone long before that anyway. But then, isn't the whole objective of life in a pointless world to make a point of pointlessness, to make something matter because you can, to spit in the eye defeat, to make an art out of disorder?

Didn't those of us who have always shared a love of ideas, didn't we learn that truth and beauty have to reside deep within in order to know truth and beauty when we see examples? That you either have it within yourself to make such judgments or you don't? Didn't we learn early on that we get precisely what we look for in life and not much else? Are not death and destruction the sum of human self-indulgence? Is there not good before evil? If not for one, the other couldn't exist, so haven't we been doomed from the beginning?

Perhaps I should lay off my medication for a few days and see how I feel about such things. Do you think you could tell the difference if I did?

# SMOKE SIGNALS

VINCE HAD PIECED data together from all of the crime scenes he thought might be connected, including scores of Adam 21 searches both before and after the crimes. He'd spent several thousand dollars of Sandburg's money on a hard-copy mail-out to law enforcement agencies all over the U.S. and Canada. Hard-copy mail was so unusual that it usually got immediate attention. It hadn't taken him long to conclude he'd found a pattern, but still, he couldn't explain it well enough to make his assumptions sound convincing. He just knew that some of these cases had something in common. Of course, he'd felt that way many times before and sometimes it turned out that he was wrong. But if he had learned anything over the years, it was to put faith in his hunches because, if he couldn't make them go away quickly, they usually paid off.

There was something very peculiar with all of those brands of cigarettes left at each crime scene on each body, and sometimes there were more than just one. Some of the reports didn't mention them in the main body of the text, but after reading a few that did, he made it a point to ask and in most cases he was rewarded. Several reports mentioned an empty pack with just one cigarette in it found in the pocket of a victim who didn't even smoke. The brands were odd: Salem, Herbal Gold, Old Gold, Eve, Lucky Strike, and Alpine. Some of the brands, he thought, were no longer being made.

On a hunch, he gave Ellen his data, and boy, was he ever right about doing that. She'd had the information less than a week when she said, "Uncle Vince, all of these crimes are connected. This is the same killer."

"How do you know for sure?" he asked slightly amused, hoping he wasn't sounding condescending.

"Because he's sending you a message," she said.

He could feel the look of surprise imprinted on his face. "What message? What kind of message?"

"It's the same thing and he's repeating it. I'm missing a couple of letters in each message, but this can't be a mistake, Uncle Vince. If you check with the police in Montana, Fort Nelson, and Whitehorse, and if they say that they also found cigarette butts and an empty pack in the victims' pockets, then the killer has sent you a repeated message."

"But what?"

"Uncle Vince, It says HELLO ASSHOLE. You only have to take the first letter in the brand of the cigarettes left at each crime scene to put it together. It was easy to find because he's said it twice. He's gone to great pains to see that the police get the message. The first time he left the cigarettes in random order. But since no one figured it out, he put them in order of his crimes the second time. One more Eve cigarette will complete his message again. He leaves the empty packs because he doesn't want there to be any mistake about the brand."

Vince sat speechless, a look of bemusement and affection in his eyes, and he could tell Ellen could read his thoughts. "Good grief. I think you might make a wonderful detective someday, Ellen, but I hope you can find something much better to do than that."

He and Ginger had adopted Ellen shortly after arriving in Alaska, but she still called them aunt and uncle. Although it may have bothered some people in similar circumstances, the way she said it was endearing enough to convey that she cared as much about them as anyone ever did about their own parents.

For a long time, Vince hadn't found much satisfaction in police work, but now he was getting the feel of it again and it made him forget his health. He had something everyone but his niece had missed. He would send a message to Owen Sandburg right away confirming his suspicions, and he would call his friend Matt Sills at the state trooper headquarters in Palmer. There was a lot to do to make sure this sick bastard was stopped.

In that place where like-minded predators scurried about far beyond the ethics of ordinary people, Vince imagined meeting this fiend in the dark. He would put an end to this freak, write his book, and retire from everything but further pursuit of the happiness he had already discovered. For the time remaining, he would spend his years savoring it. First, though, he meant to see to the happiness of others, to stop this creep. Nothing, but nothing, was more important. HELLO Yourself, ASSHOLE!

# DEEP WOODS

THE COMPOUND COVERED more than five thousand acres. There were three camps. The main encampment began on a heavily timbered hill, where a small church stood supporting an exceptionally tall tower with an enormous bell hanging from it. Radio antennas and satellite dishes were mounted on top, causing it to more closely resemble an attempt to contact extraterrestrials than a place of worship. Thirty yards away was a barracks of sorts, the home of the elders, as they were called: forty-nine men, all white, all over fifty, everyone a zealot, everyone a schemer looking to advance over his peers, all led by a wild-eyed, silver-haired fanatic known as the Seer.

Another three hundred yards down the hill began a vast camp sprawled over flat ground with army-style tents lined up in military precision for a hundred yards in every direction. These tents, pitched over wooden floors with black iron stoves to warm them in winter, housed the true believers, the flock leaders, or God's Praetorians, as they were often called by the elders.

Down the valley another quarter mile lay a hollow that centuries before had been a river bottom and was now the camp of the Infidels, heathens and scum, said the elders, but a necessary part of God's plan. Two hundred or more tents, trailers, and motorhomes, new and old, covered the landscape with no rhyme or reason to their location or layout except for access to water and electricity, which was haphazard at best. No military precision existed here. To one side was an elaborate pit and cage for fighting men and dogs, and to another, a large wooden dance floor had been constructed for Saturday night shindigs and slugfests.

Campsites were first-come, first-served, and the boundaries were how big you made them on proving that you could back it up with force. These men were mercenaries who followed a god that came in so many green-back denominations. They would do anything if the price was right. Some were tattooed nearly head to toe, some wore camouflage, some wore leather. All of them drank heavily, and many used drugs. The Seer had somehow seen to it that the camp was off-limits to local law enforcement. The freedom made the men bold, enough so that several men had already been killed in fights and their remains disposed of in a way that would never come to light. Judging from the behavior of those men, few would be looking for them or even want them to be found.

Jonas had been given a tent and some supplies and had been told to rest up and to pray that he might be worthy of moving to higher ground into the camp of the true believers. If he needed more supplies, he was told to submit a request. It was not enough that he had undergone the baptism of being born again complete with his somewhat sketchy articulation about his willingness to do the Lord's work. He still had to prove himself, whatever that really amounted to. No one ever came out and said what was expected. Getting to the camp of believers required work, evidence of devotion, and as the elder had warned, you have to prove your piety because the world is filled with Sunday-morning Christians, whose commitment doesn't last till the first Tuesday of the same week.

Temptation was purposeful and rampant, with whores, beer, whiskey, and drugs, fist fights, and weekend brawls making the place taboo for the other two groups. Most of the men in the camp were just there to avoid the law, and if a true believer were among them, it would be apparent to everyone from the start. Such a person could do little but watch and pray that one did not become prey.

If there was official business to discuss, members from the lower camp had to be escorted up to headquarters on the hill. There existed only one taboo that could get a person evicted without a second thought and it concerned communication. No Adam 21 technology was allowed at any of the camps except the headquarters. Any deviation from the rules required the approval of the Seer. Even PC use while in camp for anything other than person-to-person communication was forbidden, except for the elders.

Baldwin had whispered to Jonas more than once to keep his distance because there were spies in the place that relayed to the hilltop everything that happened. Though he found himself tempted to drink, he had managed to refuse a beer on two occasions now. At night he would often hear screaming, laughing, crying, even gunshots, but he stayed to himself and away from the organized ruckus.

Jonas assumed the war talk was mostly metaphorical. He spent his mornings and evenings exploring the deep woods. It kept his mind off his needs. Well-beaten trails winding through the woods made the going easy. One early morning he was walking slowly in a mist of light rain. The slate-gray sky gave way to rainbow-like showers of sunlight in places, only to disappear then reappear a few yards ahead. It was like being among a series of timbered cathedrals of ancient oak trees, some that must have been tall when Civil War soldiers rode through these woods. A faint whimper broke the silence. Jonas stopped and stood still. Again silence, but as soon as he started to walk, he heard it again. He was near a landfill, a natural cavern, a half-acre deep in the ground that the men used for dumping their burnt trash.

There, straight ahead near the base of a stack of downed timbers, lay a mass of marbled flesh and clotted blood. Jonas approached very slowly, finding it hard to imagine what he was looking at. Then it became clear. It was a dog, a huge pit bull, with a black and reddish brown hyena-like hide, scarred almost beyond recognition. But not for the blood, it could have been an old saddle, a baseball mitt for a giant, discarded and discolored by weather, or an old leather recliner rotted by time outdoors. The dog was covered head-to-toe in blackened blood that looked the consistency of dark molasses. As Jonas knelt down, he could hear raspy shallow breathing that meant the poor creature was near death.

"Hey, what's the matter big fella?" Jonas said aloud. Taking great care, he picked up the animal and headed back to camp, stunned by how much the beast weighed. He persuaded a man named Samson Cohen, who was camped near him, to give him a ride to town in his pickup for a hundred dollars and to wait for him outside a veterinary office while a doctor examined the dog.

After a few minutes, the young vet in a white coat came out of the examining room with a grim look on his face. "This your dog, sir?" he asked.

"I found him in a landfill," Jonas replied.

"Up north of here about twelve or fifteen miles, I'm guessing."

"How did you know, Doc?"

"Only place around here I know of that has fighting dogs. I'd like to have the place shut down, but there's not much it seems that can be done about it. You belong to that bunch, mister?"

"Don't know if I would say I belong, but I'm camped there for a while."

"Well, I hope whoever did this to this dog gets what he deserves. This animal has been chewed to pieces."

"Will he make it, Doc?"

"I don't know. There's not much more I can do for him. Not much I can do about stitching him up, either. Too much scar tissue. And I don't have any blood for a transfusion. I've given him antibiotics and a tranquilizer that should make him stress-free for a long period, and he needs that more than anything. I'll give you some antibiotics to put in his water. If he lives through tomorrow, he might make it, but I wouldn't bet on it."

On the drive back to the camp, the dog lay in the back of the truck wrapped in a blanket. Samson's name fit him perfectly, a huge specimen of manhood, bald, with a face scarred from acne, and tattoos of vultures on both sides of his neck. As he drove he said, "You've got guts, man."

"What makes you say that?" Jonas asked.

"You know, don'tcha, who that dog belongs to?"

"I found him abandoned in the dump. I reckon he belongs to me."

"That may be, but last time I saw him he belonged to Grover McKinney. People round here call him Red." The pock-faced man looked at Jonas for a sign of concern. When he received nothing but a blank look, he said, "Jesus, man, you in some deep shit. Red McKinney is the meanest son-of-a-bitch in a thousand-mile radius, and in case you ain't looked around, you are in the middle of a bunch of bastards that eats gunpowder for breakfast."

"I don't care how bad he is, there is no call to treat a dog like that."

"That ain't no ordinary dog, neither. How long you been here?"

"A few days. Why?"

"Well, if you'd been here long, you'd have knowd that that pile of muscle and teeth you've got wrapped in the blanket back there is called Satan and for damned good reasons. Didn't get a good look at him until just a few minutes ago. If I'd knowd it was Satan you had in the blanket, I wouldn't have given you a ride to town."

"Satan?"

"Satan, man! The devil dog, himself," said Samson, grinning with a spurt of tobacco juice making a slow and lazy drool down his chin. Samson crouched low behind the steering wheel, moved closer to Jonas, furrowed his face muscles, and squinted as if watching in his mind's eye what he was about to describe. "Man, Red said one time Satan was put in an empty room with, how'd he say it? Oh yeah, he said they didn't know if it was a Burmese python or an anaconda, but it was a humongous goddamned slimy serpent. He said people watched through a window as that snake closed in on its four-legged meal like an exotic dancer gliding through the air, twisting all hypnotic like, this way and that, and then, just as that awful creature froze in midair set to strike, that dog jumped sideways, spun full around, grabbed that snake's head in his mouth and pert near bit it clean through. Ain't no domestic, that dog, no sir. Ain't nobody's pet. He's a killer, just like his owner. Man, if I was you, I'd hightail it out of here and leave that dog behind. We can throw him in a ditch."

"Well, I'm not going anywhere just yet," Jonas said calmly, "and if the dog lives, he can stay with me if he wants to."

The big man behind the wheel gave him a hard look and spat tobacco juice out the window. "Your funeral. If anybody asks, don't mention me taking you to town, okay? Look, I ain't no coward, but I ain't no fool neither." He wiped the tobacco juice off his chin with his sleeve and frowned at the realization that the man carrying the dog was not going to answer his question. He shook his head and mumbled to himself. Pulling over a hundred yards before he reached the gate, Samson said, "I'm gonna let you out here 'cuz I don't want no one seeing me and you with this dog."

"Okay. Thanks for the ride."

"Ain't done you no favor. You in some deep shit, mister, and don't say I ain't told you so."

# ROUGH CUT

EVERYONE WHO KNEW him said Winston Potter was a likeable fellow who would give you the shirt off his back, stick up for you if you were in trouble, or fight a buzz saw if you needed him to, and they said such things frequently. He had been Win to his friends for so long that now he introduced himself to everyone as Win Potter. Of average height and medium build, his complexion bearing evidence of hours in the sun and wind, he was a poster likeness for farm boy USA. He'd just finished the summer wheat harvest in Montana and was headed north with a pocketful of money. Anxious to get home, he was standing by the road, thumb in the air, thinking of home in Talkeetna, Alaska. He had driven south in an old jeep that had blown an engine and wasn't worth fixing. After he got home, he would buy a new vehicle.

For the first time in his young life, leaving was going to be difficult. His mind flashed second thoughts in psychedelic frequency. He'd been working on the Tucker spread in northern Montana. Old man Tucker had taken a liking to him, inviting him home for supper occasionally. His daughter, oh his daughter, Amanda Tucker—had he ever met a more beautiful girl? He couldn't remember a single one. No, he was sure of it, the answer was no. Hell no!

The first time he laid eyes on her was at the Tucker's dinner table. He exchanged glances with her in what seemed like contrived intervals of mesmerizing mysticism. The second time, eating was hard. She stared at him openly and aggressively. On the third occasion, she ran to him outside the house as he was about to drive away in the foreman's pickup. They hadn't even spoken until he had kissed her long and hard. The intensity of the moment sucked his breath away as clearly as if it had been the force of a fist to his gut. They made love in the barn.

The whole experience was a farmer's daughter fairy tale, except it was not a joke; it was as real as anything that had ever happened to him. They talked most of the night. She begged him to stay in Montana. She said he could work for her father. She would guarantee him a job. He said no, but she pleaded and it went on like that for hours. Win wondered how anyone so beautiful could be so lonely, so starved for attention, but then, this godforsaken farm, as great as it seemed to him, must for her be like the outer reaches of the solar system. For most of Amanda's life, her mother had home-schooled her. With a worldview shaped in large part by satellite television, she was forbidden access to Adam 21. She had learned to live vicariously through characters in movies, sitcoms, paperback novels, and daydreams, and she was forbidden to use social media.

Win was infatuated, and yet, he was overwhelmed by her neediness. It was her aggressiveness that scared him most, because he sensed down deep that he was merely a means to an end for her. Had it been another member of the crew who had been coming to dinner, he too would have ended up in the barn. One night together and it was as if he was the prince who had kissed the sleeping princess shielded from life by many years of slumber. But now that she was awakened, what the hell was he to do? Win fancied himself a bit of a ladies man, but Amanda Tucker could have any man on the planet if she really wanted him and that's what bothered him. Out here he would be hers. Anywhere else, he might just be along for the ride.

Following the occasional car with his eyes, he nodded his head. That's what the suddenness and the urgency of her actions seemed to imply—that he was just a convenience, a means maybe to get her off the farm and out into the world. But not for that, he might have stayed, although he didn't know himself well enough to say for sure that this was his reason for leaving. His uncertainty knotted his emotions in a huge tangle of confusion, and he had no idea how to go about untying them.

He'd promised to call and write. Said he'd return soon but couldn't say exactly when. Thank goodness she didn't have a PC or cell phone, or there would be no getting away from her long enough to think this thing through. His resolve for leaving was getting weaker by the moment until an eighteen-wheeler hit the brakes a few yards up the road. Here was the first of his many rides home.

Seven years now he had defied tradition. Most everyone in Alaska who earned a decent paycheck worked on the North Slope oil fields, men and women who lived further south but went to work in the Arctic. Win had it backwards, but it worked for him and he loved the open plains and the great farms. He had been to Prudhoe Bay only once and had vowed never to return.

"Going far?" The crusty looking truck driver broke the silence. "Home to Alaska," Win said. The driver motioned him up to the cab. Win bent down, picked up his backpack, adjusted the sheath on his ankle knife scabbard, and climbed aboard.

# RECOLLECTIONS

O N HIS LAST visit to the home, Vince had wanted to wait and continue his interview after the old man recovered from his spell, but the nurse had said to come back another day.

"How are you feeling, Mr. Taylor?"

"Fine, how are you, young man?"

"I'm not so young, sir."

"Bullshit, wait till you get to my age and see what you think about what's old and what ain't."

"Well, you may be right about that, sir. Do you remember what you told me before about Amy Sandburg?"

"Sure do."

"Could you tell me the rest of the story?" Somewhere just beneath his decrepit exterior, Gregory William Taylor exuded an air of nobility. These people may think he's an old fool, Vince thought to himself, but in there somewhere is a character who must have really been something in his prime.

"What do you want to know?"

"You were telling me about Amy Sandburg. You said she admitted to her friend Celia that she was pregnant."

"Yes, yes, I did say that, didn't I? Well, little Amy was a bit younger than Celia. She needed help ending the pregnancy and said there was simply no way she could tell her father and mother about it. Originally she planned to have the child and was going to attend school away from home. She pretty much had it all figured out and arranged, but then she told Celia that a doctor had said something wasn't right with the baby and it would likely be severely deformed. By then, she was too far along to get a legal abortion without getting her parents involved." Suddenly he leaned back in his chair and closed his eyes.

Vince waited a few minutes and finally said, "Mr. Taylor, you were saying, sir."

The old gentleman opened his eyes as if startled to see he had a visitor. "Oh, where was I?"

"The baby wasn't okay."

"Oh yes, Amy. She went in Miss Helen's room alone. She was gone for quite a while. When she came back she was excited, but all she did was whisper and I couldn't hear what they were saying. A couple of days later, Celia and Amy came back, and this time a young man met them here who seemed to know Miss Helen somehow. That was only a week before Amy's grandfather Buck Sandburg took up residence here himself. He wasn't like an ordinary resident, though. He had a whole wing to himself with two or three attendants that worked for him and not for the nursing home. With his money, I don't even know why he bothered being around people like us, unless it made him feel superior or something. He finally moved out one day and took his staff with him. I'm not sure where he went. Back home where he came from, I guess.

"Anyway, I can only guesstimate that this young man was going to help Amy with the abortion. You see, the trouble was that I think she was farther along than a person should be to consider getting an abortion. But I already mentioned that, didn't I? Oh well, anyway, it's not been such an easy to thing to do, you know, since the Supreme Court muddied up the Roe-Wade decision. Just keep messing with it don't they?" He started to fall asleep again and Vince gently took his arm, saying, "Keep going, sir, you're doing just fine."

"Ah yes, well they talked for a while, and then all three left. A few minutes afterward, the fellow came back by himself. That's the last time I ever saw those girls. Everyone knows, of course, that they found little Amy's body in a creek drainage near the Parks Highway not long after that. But did you know that Celia disappeared a few days later and that to this day she has never been found?"

Vince was surprised. "No, I didn't know. Are you sure? That makes no sense at all, Mr. Taylor. How could the police not connect these two incidents?"

"Beats me. I couldn't talk back then, and this is not the kind of place they come to for clues, you know. They did know she was missing, and I heard people talking about it from time to time, but I'm not sure anyone but Miss Helen knew that Amy and Celia had visited here. You see, Celia's grandmother, who lived here then, got so upset that she up and died shortly after Celia disappeared. The only other person who was aware that both girls even knew each other was Miss Helen, and of course she was as batty as Carlsbad Cavern. Every long once in while they put a picture of Celia on the news and offer a reward, but that's all I know about it." The old man grimaced. "I'm starting to feel sick at my stomach. Could you come back tomorrow?"

The television commercial featuring the missing girl with the orange hair. Yes, Vince had seen it numerous times. Add another victim to the list, a list too long, a list that must not get longer, if there was anything, save moving heaven and earth, that he could do to see to it. He was beginning to wonder if a person could become ill from a growing obsession that could not be satiated in some way. If nothing were done, could this kind of stress kill a person, especially an old detective?

# FIRST MOVE

HOLDING A DOCTORATE in American history, Angela Black had authored a book that, years earlier, achieved wide acclaim among scholars and critics, and drew a favorable review from the U.S. president. She lived for her work, or at least that's how she often heard herself explaining it to others when she was asked about her plans for the future. Whether she intended to marry was a question Angela found particularly disturbing because of her age, and yet it always seemed to be first on the agenda in polite conversation with new acquaintances who still seemed stuck in the last century, surprised that a woman might choose a career over marriage. Indeed, she did derive great satisfaction from "raising world consciousness," as she put it.

When Adam 21 was first brought online, Rev. Sol Worley and Dr. William Dee had become business partners with Angela. Together they established the American Lighthouse for Justice in Law Enforcement, ALJLE. The three of them were very different kinds of people, but they shared a similar worldview about what should be done to make the world a better place. For the past few years, they had been engaged in a nationwide campaign to improve race relations and to shine the light of public scrutiny on police brutality in particular. As a team they were dynamic.

The touch of melancholy that flitted about her could easily

be set aside when she willed it so. Lately, though, Dee seemed to drift away from work into some kind of deep, dark inner refuge. When he did this, nothing she said seemed to bring him back. He answered her questions and even engaged in small talk, but his old self was clearly not present and there seemed to be nothing she could do about it.

At first she was angry, then sad. Finally, she figured he must be lonely and very likely imagining himself close to death. He was, after all, many years her senior, so death could be near. Every once in a while, she thought she saw tears trickling down his face, but she never let on or asked what was the matter; that just wasn't something you would do with a person like Dee. And then, just when she was about to try a subtle new tack at finding out what was bothering Dee, Worley died. Worley had been the partners' emotional center and the source of much of their enthusiasm. Things were not going to be the same without him, and both Angela and Dee knew this without talking about it. Both set about brooding for goodly portions of each day, and the longer it went on, the more each got on the other's nerves.

Early one morning, Angela decided to do something very much unlike herself: she called James Tall Tree under a pretentious excuse she was sure he could see through, and that was the point. In a meeting years earlier, she and Tall Tree had barely been able to keep from locking their eyes each time they looked at one another. It became increasingly embarrassing, and both began looking at the table, the floor, or some inanimate object to avoid eye contact when they spoke. Angela had run into him again a year ago at a conference in Seattle, and the magic still seemed in play. Her friend who worked near Tall Tree claimed to know for certain that he still did not have a serious girlfriend, so she felt she had nothing to lose.

James seemed wildly enthusiastic that she had called, and the two wasted no time agreeing they should have lunch when he came to Denver again. It was as if they had both been given a reprieve or a chance for an exotic adventure. If getting together at this time in their lives was a bad idea, it would likely be apparent sooner rather than later. So why not give it a shot and find out?

With so much trouble going on in the world, so many conflicts, so many threats of war, and so many people dying as a result, not having any intimate relationships seemed to leave you exceptionally exposed and vulnerable to chaos with no one to care if something bad were to happen to you. Angela knew, of course, that there was one word to describe her predicament and the word was *lonely*. Maybe, just maybe, she could fix it, especially if James was lonely too.

# CONSPIRACIES

VINCE WAS TIRED. He wasn't sleeping. The case was hard to piece together, but it was starting to get very interesting. Perhaps intriguing was a better description. Vince had talked to everyone in the Pioneer Home, and most of them had been of little or no help. He interviewed every student still in Alaska who was in Amy's high school class and many of their parents. Old man Taylor was the only one who mentioned that a young man had visited the home and had spoken to Amy on several occasions out of earshot. Now Vince knew who he was.

His name was Paul Rayburn. A man of twenty-six, he was dying of AIDS, an entirely new strain, rumored to have been manufactured in a laboratory as a new tool to be utilized for political assassination. The rumor persisted, and social media was rife with conspiracy theories. This new and egregiously aggressive virus was not at all like the earlier manifestations of the disease—strains that had mostly been rendered harmless years before or were prevented by vaccines. Some HIV strains were even altered to fight certain cancers, but not the newest mutant virus. It was simply too toxic and unpredictable.

Vince expected to find the man in a hospital, but instead, he found Paul in a rundown shack in the woods near Maud Road in Palmer. He had anticipated an obstinate fellow who would likely tell him nothing, and yet Rayburn opened up like a freshwater reservoir whose levy had just burst.

Rayburn's new strain of AIDS had only recently been officially acknowledged by the medical community. It was called the FTA, or Fast-Track AIDS, fast-track because people who were diagnosed with FTA had about twelve weeks to live, sometimes less. All that the drug cocktails seemed to do for the FTA strain was to piss it off. At least, that was the way Rayburn put it. He seemed so relieved to talk that Vince had nearly the whole story in less than an hour.

"Old man Sandburg told me he would pay off my grandmother's house and set her up for the rest of her life if I would cooperate, and with so little time left, I didn't have much to lose."

"What exactly did he want you to do?" Vince asked.

"He didn't tell me all at once. He got me to do a few simple things at first, and then came the hard stuff that actually seemed impossible. Like how in the hell is a person like me supposed to get rid of a couple of Supreme Court justices and the Speaker of the House?"

"You tell me. How?" Vince asked softly, trying to conceal his astonishment.

"I thought at first the old man was crazy, but he was crazy like a fox. He had other people working for him and some of them are pretty smart. I would warn you to watch out for them. The old man was one scheming son-of-a-bitch. He thought he had it all figured out. He said his granddaughter would still be alive but for Justices Harkins and Monroe and a few others. He said black-robed moralists had ruined his life and he would have his revenge if it cost him every cent he had to his name. I'll leave that to your imagination, officer. The old man was loaded from what everyone says."

"I'm a retired detective," Vince said.

"Okay, same difference to me."

Vince nodded approval so as to keep the seemingly good will he had established with the young man. It didn't happen often that Vince would find himself in sympathy with an admitted murderer, but he was having a hard time feeling any ill will toward this sick kid. And that's all he really is, Vince thought, just confused and very sick.

"The old man told me I already had everything I needed to do the deeds running through my veins. Said it was perfect. The sanctimonious bastards would have some time to contemplate their horrid deaths and it would give him great pleasure. After he'd said it, he saw that his words put a dagger clean through me and tried to apologize, or sort of apologize. I suspect a man like him didn't have much practice pretending he was sorry about anything.

"I don't know how the old fart knew about my FTA infection, but he knew damned near everything there was to know about me the first time I met him. He said when he found out that I knew his granddaughter and that I had visited with her several times at the nursing home, he thought that I'd had something to do with her plan to get an abortion. But Amy and I were just good friends. She did want me to give her a long ride somewhere, but I never found out where. He said when he heard I was gay, it put things in a different light. I never figured out what he meant by that." Rayburn leaned far back in his chair as if suddenly nauseous.

"Feeling bad?" Vince asked.

"Yeah, I need to sit still a minute and keep quiet." Vince nodded and wished he had a cigarette, but then he realized that even if he had one, he wouldn't be able to smoke near this dying shell of a human being.

"The old man had a way about him, though, you know. Said I wouldn't have to shoot anybody, just prick them with a couple of drops of blood from a needle that he would furnish and the devil would do the rest. Said he would get word to the recipients about how and why they were dying before they were dead so he could revel in the pleasure it would give him, and he said that just thinking about it gave him a sense of satisfaction that was hard to describe. Weird, huh?

"Said it would be past my time when the authorities figured out, if they ever did, that crimes had actually been committed. No evidence would be left of any notice given to the ones who died. Their accusations that they'd been targeted and had been given a lethal dose of infection could easily seem like hallucinations brought on naturally by the disease. Kind of winced when he said it. I guess it was his way of showing that he was still a human being, even though he had dreamed this stuff up. I had no clue old man Sandburg was near death himself. He didn't have much time to enjoy his revenge."

"So that's what you did. I mean, you got close enough to the judges to prick them with something?"

"Pretty much. It was a lot easier than I thought it would be. All you have to do is carry a walking stick with a needle and innocently bump into people. Hell, they don't even know they've been stuck, and bumping into strangers can happen to anyone anytime, so there was never even any suspicion that anything had been done to the victims. Justice Monroe apologized profusely thinking the whole thing was his fault. Sandburg had someone watch the people I was supposed to tag. Every time the old man mentioned one of the people by name he went into a long rant about how evil they were. Said I was doing a public service."

"So how many were there?"

"I personally tagged five, and I gave blood for others. So I couldn't tell you how many there were altogether."

"How many would you guess?"

"A dozen or so maybe. I don't even know the names of the others involved, but I don't think they will be that hard to find. Sandburg must have figured he was dying as well, so I don't think he was all that concerned about getting caught. He just wanted revenge. He wanted it bad."

"Did you ever try to talk your way out of the scheme?"

"Yeah, I tried every time I saw him. Dr. Mendelsohn said I didn't have much time, and the old man knew that too."

Vince made a mental note. The name Mendelsohn sounded vaguely familiar. Something about venomous right-wing fanaticism.

"I spent a lot of my precious time flying to and from Alaska," Rayburn continued, "and I had to go see Sandburg every time I got back here. But he always went on and on about how evil these people were and saying that if I got a chance to look after my grandmother, I should take it, since she was the only person who ever looked after me. What else could I do?" He looked Vince in the eye when he said this, the question lingering in the bloody sockets where there should have been something resembling eyes.

Vince felt ambivalent about this pathetic creature, and yet, he was spellbound that a character as unsophisticated as this could perpetrate a crime so off the charts in practicality and masterminded by someone who, though filthy rich, was also deemed by most to be a saint of sorts. At least, near the end of his days that's what everyone seemed to say.

When Rayburn finished telling Vince his story, he expected to be locked up immediately, but Vince said that wouldn't be necessary. "How long do you have, son?" Vince asked.

"Doc Mendelsohn got me something he said might give me a few extra days, but it's not for sure. I may have a week, maybe, not much longer. My coming down with the disease has never made sense to me. I mean, it's got an incredibly short incubation period, and I had been celibate for a long time when I got sick. It still doesn't make sense. But there is nothing they can do for me in a hospital, and I would like to stay here. I'm ready."

"Why not stay at your grandmother's where she can care for you?"

"I'd rather she didn't see me like this," he said. "Please don't say anything to her. Would you wait until you hear that I am gone and mail this envelope? It's the clear deed to her house and the passbook for her savings account with a record of my deposits."

"Sure, son, I'll take care of it."

"Thanks for being so candid with me and kind, sir. I don't know what happened that made the old man hire you to find Amy's killer because I always thought he knew what had happened. If he didn't, he sure got a lot of people killed who had nothing to do with it."

"Rest easy, young man. I'll see myself out." Vince walked to the door quietly, stepping lightly so as not to make much noise. He didn't know why, but it just seemed like the thing to do, and he couldn't bear to look the kid in the eye on the way out. He shut the door softly and took a deep breath.

What the hell should he do now? News of Dr. Mendelsohn's involvement was troubling. His name had come up before in local political news. If Vince opened this can of worms in public, it would likely blow up any chance of solving little Amy Sandburg's murder and a serial killer would still be out there having himself a party. He could think of no urgency in blowing the whistle because anyone already infected with the virus would not and could not be saved. Still, Vince was not the type to hold back. What to do? He would have to sleep on it.

Suddenly, he recalled a remark by old man Sandburg that didn't make any sense at the time, but it did now. Sandburg had said he thought he had it all figured out about what had happened to his granddaughter, but if he was wrong, the world needed to be rid of some arrogant people anyway. He'd said, "But where do you start? There are so many."

## ORIGINS OF EVIL

S O BEAUTIFUL WAS the forest on both sides of the road, so green the trees, so magnificent the distant mountain backdrop, that Wilfred drove well below the speed limit, wanting not to miss the essence of what he would characterize as the very reason one needed to kill: that beauty must be made whole by a sacrifice of innocence, some kind of act that offers consolation for the fact that the appreciation of beauty is not long-lasting, never permanent, and thus is but a tease meant to torture those without the gumption to fight back. In his sick mind, beauty was all about perspective. It needed to be accented by death because the two were bound together at the umbilical cord of existence. Beauty demands a sacrifice as a tribute to its emotional adversary, an acknowledgment and tip of the hat to time as the master that uses beauty as a sinister reminder of who is in charge and why.

Wilfred often thought it strange that a person like himself could be so appreciative of beauty and yet so devoid of conscience, but deep down he got the metaphysical connection. He abhorred metaphors and found abstract thought difficult, but beauty and the price to be paid for it was not an intangible in his mind. It was concrete. It represented the dark face of reality, the notion that death awaits all and that death must be acknowledged when contrasted with reasons to live or one would miss the very thrill of being alive.

Wilfred felt special because he understood the association between splendor and demise, because it escaped most of the poor fools he came in contact with.

It wasn't from firsthand knowledge that he'd convinced himself he was without conscience. If you didn't have something, how could you tell? He had learned this much from books. Otherwise, wouldn't feeling a lack of conscience be a sign that fragments of a conscience were still present?

The thought that someday the best psychologists in the country might advance their career by trying to make sense of his psyche amused him, but more importantly it made him feel superior. Of course, he would likely never know of those achievements because he would already be dead. Still, he would die knowing that they would learn who he was. He would make sure of that. He didn't believe in eternal life, but historical infamy in the future would be the next best thing.

The day after his sixteenth birthday, the school's shrink had told his parents that he fit the psychological profile of a psychopath, that he was not only without the guidance of a conscience, but that it might be something even worse. That was when he began to study psychology himself, and now it was rare that anyone could see through his façade. Now, they could only see what he wanted them to see. The idiot who declared him a monster had it wrong. She had said that his bedwetting, his cruelty to animals, and his arsonist tendencies represented the triad of psychological danger and that he should be watched and monitored over the years because he was a textbook example of a true psychopath. Well, he had another triad of traits they would have been alarmed at, but only he knew what they were. The thrilling part was that he couldn't even find them in the textbooks he studied. He was indeed unique.

Sociopaths are thought to be the product of their environment, while psychopaths are created as a result of genetics or an abnormal brain structure. He had both conditions going for him. The important difference between sociopaths and psychopaths is that the former still have the ability empathize with others, while the latter do not. This was not news to Wilfred. He had always known he was devoid of empathy or giving a damn about the feelings or cares of other people. He knew his physiology was different, and the fact that his environment had nurtured his predilection for sinful behavior was nothing short of good luck.

Maybe history would reveal him to be the double-triad killer: The only known living example. What a shame that he was never to be captured alive in a situation where there might be a conviction. The only way they could know about this side of him would be if he were to write it down and leave it behind. Then, when the time was right, the world would know. That's what he'd decided to do. Otherwise, he would not be fully appreciated for who and what he was.

After all, where was that bitch now who said those things about him in high school anyway? Only he knew of her whereabouts, which made him superior by default. The old bag was pushing up daises in a field in plain sight of the school, a field where students now played touch football, going out for a Hail Mary pass, over the very spot where old Mary lay.

He reveled in the notion that someday they would see clearly that he had been one of a kind, a real-life Hannibal Lecter, only smarter by half. Trips like this left him with lots of time to reflect and fantasize. But there were moments, like now, when he seemed to lose control over his thoughts, his memory overtaken by things he wished to forget, things he feared, things his deeds sought to erase, his aversion to bad dreams. When it happened that dreams tormented him, he couldn't help but entertain doubts about his own uniqueness, and this made him anxious and angry. If he didn't quickly change the subject and think about something else, it felt like freefalling into the abyss.

Images of his father's razor strap raising welts on his back made him forget the colorful scenery, but not because of a sense of dread or discomfort. The memories simply spurred his curiosity. His step-mother's shrill voice ranting in the backyard about his yellow-stained sheets was always loud enough to let the neighbors in on his secret. They had a clothes dryer in the laundry room, but she chose to put his sheets in plain sight on a clothesline to humiliate him.

To get even, he set old lady Thompson's house afire, killed both her cats, and spent a month in juvenile hall. He was fifteen at the time. It served her right, though, nosy old heifer, always sitting just behind an open screen window with an ear to the wind solely to listen during his family's squabbles. Stupid authorities never even autopsied the old biddy, thinking she died of natural causes instead of rat poison.

But that was then. Now he was in complete control, except for brief moments of involuntary recollection, which he knew would pass quickly but only after leaving him with an immense burden of anxiety. Stress. It was just self-imposed stress from the need to pay attention to so many details. He vowed he would cut himself some slack because he was by orders of magnitude smarter than the police. Reprieve came quickly when he fancied himself the smart-est serial killer in the history of homicide. He was a breed unto himself. He might very well die with sword in hand, but if so, the whole world would learn of his talent, and it would be at a point in time of his own choosing.

Sloan Bandera was the serial killer he admired the most. Bandera had been discovered only the year before. He'd killed eighteen women before he was exposed and six more after his identity was known. He was a thrill killer, whose torture methods using a wood chipper were so disturbing that most news media refrained from discussing them. Bandera jumped to his death off a ten-story building to keep from being taken alive, a class act.

While he identified mostly with Bandera, Wilfred felt some kinship with other infamous figures from the past. He admired Dennis Rader, the BTK killer in Kansas; David Berkowitz, known as the Son of Sam killer; and also Ted Bundy. With Rader he shared the vicarious thrill of notoriety, the narcissistic impulse to prove his superiority over the authorities. With Berkowitz it was the thrill and rush of excitement of the kill itself, and with Bundy he shared the image of his victims not as people but as objects—objects for his amusement and sexual satisfaction. Though Bandera was a breed apart, Wilfred would soon show the world one breed better.

Some serial killers were known to get continuous elation from iconic trophies taken from their victims or from the scenes of their crime. But for Wilfred the very thought that his celebrity would live on long after his demise was so exhilarating that he frequently had his hair stylist sweep up his hair clippings after a haircut and put them in a plastic bag. The image in his mind of people bidding on locks of his hair after his death resulted in an intoxicating adrenaline rush. He reveled in the feeling so much that he was making plans to have his personal belongings distributed to the online retailers of murderabilia upon his death.

His ambition was that his legacy would make the Green River killer look like a babe in the woods. To do that, he would need to act soon to up the ante to make things interesting and to add dramatically to his body count. After all, how many clues did he have to leave behind before he found a cop smart enough to even suspect he was dealing with a mastermind? What puzzled him most and rattled him in his weaker moments was that he was forever overestimating the intelligence of the authorities, which meant of course that he was still capable of making errors in judgment, and that was troubling. It could lead to a mistake.

For the time being, he would assume the bastards were dumb as dirt, but just as he was about to amend his plans, he saw the Alaska newspaper. Finally, someone had figured it out. This was good but not quite enough. He would send a message, and if that didn't get their butts in gear, he would have to try something else. Now he was tingling with excitement. The adrenaline flow felt good, almost as good as someone else's blood.

## CAMP RULES

JONAS HAD BEEN given a booklet that he was told to read and commit mostly to memory as it was to be returned and not leave the camp. There would be no clemency for breaking camp rules. He was sitting on one of the numerous empty wooden ammunition boxes near his tent, reading the rules over and over, when he heard shouting a few yards away. A crowd had gathered around what appeared to be a fight. Going to look, Jonas found four men on the ground, three of them on top of one very big man on the ground. He reached down, lifted one man off, kicked another, and the third got up and walked away. When the big man got to his feet, the other two assailants left in a hurry.

"Thanks, man, I appreciate it. They was 'bout to get the best of me. I owe you one." The big man spoke as if he were revealing secrets and followed Jonas back to his tent. "Butch Cassum's my name. Some folks around here call me Butch Cassidy."

"Jonas Blythe," Jonas said, extending his hand. "Come in and have a seat."

Cassum sat down, straddling another of the ammo boxes that served as furniture. Seeing that Jonas had been looking at the rule book, he said, "I can summarize that rule book for you real quick-like. You can do any goddamned thing you like in this camp 'cept use the Internet or Adam 21. See that tower?" Butch said, pointing to the hill in the distance. "There's a spammer-jammer up there that will kill any attempt to connect to the outside world 'cept a local call. These people specialize in spamming and jamming. You can use a cell phone frequency here just for a personal call, but people listen to what you say, so it tells you in the book that you are not to mention anything that goes on here to anyone, ever. Got it, bro?"

"Look. First off, I'm not anybody's bro. Name's Jonas. What about up there?" he asked pointing to the outline of uniformly aligned tents on higher ground.

"Different rules altogether for them. Them be the monk-like folks. Set around and pray a lot, from what I hear. Anything goes in this camp but not there. Supposed to be some of them among us in here. Spies they be, looking for men to send to higher ground and those who need to be kicked out altogether. You have to be chosen for moving up and no one knows what the rules are for getting picked. Only been two or three gone up since I've been here, and I've been here longer than most."

"I thought this camp was based on religious principles," Jonas said.

"Yeah, that's what they tell you after you've been through the services, but they put everyone in here with the psychos and sickos to begin with. They get you to say you are saved and then put you in here to see if it really took. Like I told you, not many make it out of this camp, so I don't know how there got to be so many of them in the holy-shit camp to begin with. That's what we call them in the uppity camp, holy shits.

"You have to be some serious scum, though, to be kicked out of this one. I'm just hanging out till things on the outside cool down. I'm never going to higher ground. Wouldn't go if I was asked and only came here to hide out a bit. Only ones I know of that were kicked out just broke stupid rules."

"Wasn't what I was expecting," Jonas said.

"Takes a bit of getting used to. But it's not so bad, Jim."

"Name's not Jim."

"Okay, man, no need to be touchy. You can go to town, but you don't want to be gone too long. And you can bet that up on hill they are watching what a body does out of camp, especially on Adam 21. Don't know how they track it but they sure seem to."

"I thought you said . . ."

Quick to interrupt, Butch continued in a whisper. "Rules don't apply to them on the hilltop. You don't ever want to forget that."

"So who's in charge in this camp?" Jonas asked.

"Nobody official, but there's no doubt about who it is, neither. That'd be Red McKinney. You don't want to get crosswise with him in no kind of way. Hear me?" Jonas looked at him and said nothing. "Remind me to tell you about Red sometime. In the meantime, though, you need to stay the fuck clear of him, if you know what I mean. Look, there he is over beside that trailer."

Six foot three, 280 pounds, with flame-red hair, freckles under his eyes, bulging biceps, and facial features that promised a nasty disposition, Red would stand out in a crowd regardless of any others present. "Don't look so mean to me."

"Damn, Jim, I mean Jonas. Sorry. Talk soft. Don't want him to hear or we be dead meat. Big as I am, I know I couldn't take him, not one-on-one. Done seen him in action too many times. Look, I ain't forgettin' I owe ya one. You ever need to get in touch with me on the outside, just call Sally's Dry Cleaners in town and leave a message for Butch. My aunt will see that I get it. Don't forget, now."

"What about those characters I pulled off of you?"

"Don't worry me none. They be the ones worried now. Cause I'll be watching for 'em. Don't forget 'bout Red, neither. He's a mean 'en."

Partially hidden under a blanket, a scarred pit bull stuck his head out to see who was talking. "Jesus fucking Christ, Jim? I mean Jonas. Jesus." Shaking his head, Butch winced as if he had seen a ghost.

## IN TOUCH WITH EVIL

ELLEN'S EARLY CHILDHOOD seemed ever more distant as good experiences increasingly overrode her memories of the bad times. Her life before coming to live with Uncle Vince and Aunt Ginger had been so painful that she rarely ever let herself entertain those ghostly memories. On the few occasions when she did, she went through a contrived bit of positive self-talk, rehearsing it and repeating it as long as necessary to put things back in perspective.

Feeling genuine confidence in her latent abilities to function in the world, she had learned that she came from good stock, strong women of accomplishment, whose example she would follow in living up to her family heritage. She would make her way in the world, about that she had little doubt, and yet, in moments familiar but unclear in context, she often felt as if the earth beneath her feet was shaky and unreliable.

Sometimes at night she would awaken, imagining that she had no balance and couldn't stand up without holding on to something, a door, a piece of furniture, even the walls. If nothing was in sight, she would go back to sleep, free-falling in timeless space for what seemed like hours without ever coming to rest on the ground. But the next morning she would feel rested, reassured, relaxed, and proud in a spiritual sense, so she didn't worry that her dreams didn't match her feelings. To the contrary, she thought they amounted to a form of mental gymnastics as a way of coping.

There were moments when Ellen suspected that her fondness for animals might have something to do with her mistrust of human beings, but she put such thoughts aside quickly and reprimanded herself for being unworthy of Uncle Vince and Aunt Ginger, whose support and generosity had saved her. Life back in Texas had become a distant blur, old memories of shame and distrust, of her mother's addiction to drugs, and of the countless degenerate male companions who accomplished nothing except add misery and further complications to their lives.

This life in Alaska was life anew, a different planet, another solar system. Aunt Ginger and Uncle Vince were solid, immovable objects in a world filled with spineless frauds, people whose selfish motives were always transparent, even though they pretended to care, and people who would say anything to your face to take advantage of you when your back was turned. This contrast, this new life with real parents, gave Ellen an added sensory aptitude for judging human behavior, and she often said she wanted to be a detective like Uncle Vince. When she thought about it deeply, she sensed that her life experience made her especially suited for it, relating to a world of evil as she did with an eye for realism lost to those whose lives were ensconced in too much shelter from reality.

Ellen had become very fond of the Whiteheads and Robert Thornton, and especially his associate Ruben Sanchez. Earlier, Thornton had had a heavy-equipment operator connect all three cabins with a private trail, but calling it a road was a bit of a stretch. He'd also had his technicians install an intercom phone system to connect the three neighbors' cabins, since cell phones still didn't work that well this close to the mountains. That problem had been solved when Thornton purchased interest in a satellite to accommodate all of their communication systems.

So, every time he stayed at Thornton's cabin, Ruben made it a point to call Ellen using the intercom to see if she was in the area, and whenever possible they got together for long walks. Vince wondered at times if Sanchez's influence on Ellen was really a good thing, but Ginger said anything that stirred that much enthusiasm in a person Ellen's age couldn't be bad.

Ellen had confided in Ruben that she thought her Uncle Vince was planning to write a book. He hadn't told her so directly, but the questions he kept asking made her think he was considering it. She asked Ruben what kind of a book she should read aloud to get him enthused about writing if that indeed what he was planning to do. Ruben had said the answer was a no-brainer, *Martin Eden* by Jack London. "That will do it if anything will," he had said.

Now that she was nearly half-way through the book, she was beginning to think Ruben had been right. Her Uncle Vince had begun giving her looks as she read, as if he suspected her intentions. Vince was aware that Ellen tried to make eye contact with him when she was reading a point she thought important. When she got to the text where London's character Martin Eden rips into book editors, book reviewers, and manuscript readers as failed writers, lacking the fire, talent and originality to write themselves, but taking great pleasure in passing judgment on what they were disparaging because it was genius, he sputtered a cough and looked away.

Wise beyond her years, Ellen knew for certain that before long she would prove her abilities. The school counselors had told Vince and Ginger that Ellen's IQ was near genius level and that her aptitude for technology showed great promise. Ellen knew this, too, because she had read a letter to her guardians from the school that she was not meant to see. Promise was what she would live up to.

She would show everyone what promise was, and she would find a way to demonstrate her gratitude to her new family for having been rescued from evil. The sooner the better.

Ellen could feel her uncle's enthusiasm about her involvement in his case. She loved to surprise him, knowing he was hopeful that she might find something of interest in the material he had given her. The message she derived from those cigarette brands really seemed to astonish him, though all she had done was to create a database of information with algorithms in search of patterns. Vince wouldn't let her see some of the photos of the actual murder victims, but he did let her read all except the most graphic descriptions of what had been done. She was careful not to let Aunt Ginger know the details, or the project would surely come to a halt.

Uncle Vince and his friend Sergeant Sills took her message to the major news media in Alaska, and the syndicates took the story nationwide. The headline read "Alaska Highway Serial Killer Suspicions Confirmed." Sills had a web site put up to ask for public assistance and a special email link to collect leads. What he didn't know was that Ellen had manipulated his email so that each time a message was sent to Sills, she would receive a duplicate. She was going to tell Vince, but then thought better of it. She would wait a while to do that, maybe surprise him again, even better.

Uncle Vince was simply too overprotective of her, she thought. He was always telling her she was too idealistic. At least once a month he gave her the "you never know who you can really trust" lecture, saying repeatedly that it's the respected scout leaders and squeaky-clean clergy that everyone thinks are the salt of the earth who will mug you in the privacy of your own bedroom.

At first she thought these instances of prolonged diatribe were embarrassing, but that feeling soon disappeared. It was clear Uncle Vince cared about her deeply and that he had lived a life among so many unsavory characters that it would be hard for him to accept a peaceful existence without some paranoia, even in a small Alaska town. She would just have to help him adjust.

Messages began to trickle in. Most made no sense. She had not realized that there were so many crackpots in the world. It seemed there were lots of troubled people with little more to do in the world than imagine themselves near the center of a dark mystery. They must be very lonely, she thought.

And then, just before signing off one evening, a message arrived that made her heart race. It said, "You had better get with the program, asshole, or next time there will be no clues at all. It's not much fun trying to match wits with idiots." Her typing speed was off the charts, which made her instantaneous response quicker than her better judgment. She said, "Don't bother asshole. I already know who you are," and hit the send button before she could comprehend the gravity of her actions. Ellen didn't know who he was, but now the killer knew for certain who she was and where she was. She went to bed but did not sleep, feeling too afraid, dreaming with her eyes open, dreaming wide awake of a nightmare to come.

WHAT ?
WHY ?

# STRINGING GENOCIDE

WENDELL SMYTH'S WEB site chronicled genocide only in the twentieth and twenty-first centuries, although he had hundreds of links to sites covering thousands of years. His postings made the point over and over in innumerable ways that these acts were the responsibility of members of the human race who were either still living or were not that far removed from friends and family who still had memories of the events and the culprits involved. After a brief narrative, readers were asked to click on a link for a tour, but not without a warning and not without confirming that you were an adult over the age of eighteen. Upon clicking on the tour icon, a surreal quality took over the screen. Dates flashed faintly with numbers such as 1915: 800,000 to 1,000,000 Armenians are slaughtered by the Turks; 1939–45 6,000,000 Jews exterminated by Nazis.

In one scene filmed from far above, a long line of tunic-clad men in military uniform, stand in formation. In front of each row is a table. Only as the view grows closer do you suddenly see that on the table in front of each man is a severed human head. Stunned, you realize these soldiers are standing tall in celebration of their trophies. They are Turks, and the heads, Armenian.

The dates 1939–1945 are intermingled among scenes of Nazi death camps. Naked women and children by the hundreds stand in lines before trenches; then the scene switches to a formation of men with rifles as smoke bellows up from their breeches. In the very next frame, crumpling bodies fall into the trench like so many discarded rag dolls. In the next, long lines of nude men, women, and children entering what they think are showers, offset with smoke and fire fueled by human flesh. There are frames of people hanging from gallows, impaled on metal hooks squirming in agony. Random clips appear of people being shot in the street in both public and private settings.

Smyth's record of genocide in Rwanda, when, in a three-month siege, the Hutus butchered somewhere between 500,000 to 1,000,000 Tutsis mostly with dull machetes, was so disturbingly graphic, so vile, so unbelievably hard to watch for anyone with a modicum of compassion that a person had to acknowledge three warning screens before access was given.

And then, just when you thought you'd reached beyond your own internal capacity for horror, a small Asian boy of maybe five or six lifts an axe over his head and brings it down with all of his might on the neck of an old woman. She is on her knees with her hands tied behind her. Only this time you are spared seeing the actual blow. What you see instead is the spraying of blood and the repeated swinging of an executioner too small and frail to finish his job. You see that behind him a group of soldiers are laughing hysterically, and you hope to God that the old woman is not the boy's grandmother.

In spite of repeated warnings not to watch unless you were mentally prepared, many people did watch and some complained that the scenes were too graphic and should not be posted. Smyth's response was unapologetic:

"If you can't gaze into the face of evil and defy it with unconditional resolve, then you can't be depended upon to help stop the next Holocaust and are, in fact, helping to guarantee that there will indeed be another one.

"Evil thrives on naïveté, denial, and the avoidance of all things unpleasant. During World War II, thousands of citizens walked by Auschwitz-Birkenau, Belzec, Sobibor, Treblinka, and Dachau daily, turning a blind eye to the purpose of the camps, denying afterwards that they had ever even suspected atrocities were occurring. Ask yourself how this could be possible in a place where 20,000 goddamned concentration camps existed.

"Living in a world purposely partitioned off from displeasure licenses malevolence. If you don't admit the existence of wickedness, you see no need to fight. Instead you turn away, seek pleasurable entertainment, pursue happy thoughts, and live in your own illusionary bubble.

"If you hate violence, hate cruelty, and decry evil, you need to stare into the abyss occasionally to acknowledge their existence, to remind yourself of the threat always present in the shadows. If you choose to look away and avoid the reality of evilness in the world, then your willful avoidance endangers all of us because you won't see it coming, you won't expect it when it surfaces, and you will likely deny it even when confronted.

"If you always shy away from evil, you are accommodating denial. It's akin to the same mindset that led millions of people to walk submissively to their deaths, as if it were incomprehensible that they would be killed. Even though in many cases they could see executions happening up ahead, still they did not resist. Denial acts out behaviorally as overt submissiveness.

"The refusal to face the reality of wickedness is why evil continuously catches us by surprise. Members of my family perished in the Holocaust. Be alert. Be watchful. Remember. Recognize the signs. Stare evil down. Speak up before it's too late."

SOMETIMES I WONDER how much change we can bear as human beings. A few nights ago at a town meeting, I heard a gentleman speak who expressed relief that he would be dead in a few years and that he would not have to endure this nihilistic society much longer. It's an assertion being made by more and more people every day, and I know the feeling. People born in the early part of the twentieth century who lived till its end, grew up with horse and buggies and died with space-shuttle rockets. And although each new scientific breakthrough changed their lives, often dramatically, it happened slowly enough to give them time to come to grips with the changes. But those of us living in the twenty-first century since the advent of Adam 21 have a far different reality to cope with. We are experiencing change at an ever-faster clip, and yet everything we grew up believing about the past is in some significant way not as we thought it was.

The past haunts the present, and at least for now it subtracts from the future instead of adding value. This is not what I expected would happen. I was raised to think that the future would always be an improvement over the past, but that's not true, it seems, not true at all.

Near the end of the twentieth century there existed a developing consensus that the people of the world were becoming more peaceful, more humane and more enlightened, and more forgiving. Now, that reality seems like a fairy tale told by wishful idealists. My generation came into the world believing that people are basically good, and now Adam 21 awards us with daily doses of horror so graphic, so vengeful, and so hateful, that one wonders if there can be any good at all to come from the human race. There are groups of people wanting to censor Adam 21, but many more groups get vehemently belligerent at the very thought of not being absolutely free to examine the past, warts and all. Ralph Waldo Emerson's notion that "no picture of life can have any veracity that does not admit the odious facts" is repeated ad nauseam, but I suspect many people are beginning to doubt it.

It seems to me now that a human can endure an incredible amount of change during a lifetime, provided his or her fundamental identity remains fairly constant. But destabilize us by making us doubtful about who we are as individuals, and especially as a people, and you run the risk of destroying the very ingredient that holds society together.

People naturally tire of change. They always have and they always will. I'm drawn to literature as a means of making sense of the great subtleties we encounter because I was taught early in life that the great artists among us help us to center ourselves into a useful reality. But even if we can navigate our way with ego in check so as not to be overridden by culture and dare to learn to think for ourselves, it's still best not to let on too much about what we have learned, lest we be cast out in exile from our respective communities because we no longer fit.

Now, with each and every day, I'm less sure that the culture I grew up immersed in was ever anything more than an illusion, just one of a multitude of escape strategies used by fools smitten with idealistic notions about life being a gift of some sort. If it's not true that we are indeed a species worth saving, then what's next? How are we to live today? What do I live for if not revenge against those who perpetrated this fraud of humanity's worth? Whom do I punish and will it ever be enough? If no objective good exists in the world, can we find a will to live for sin? If good is nothing but a façade, is evil the only thing that is real? You tell me.

I stopped taking my meds a few days ago. So far, I feel fine, but time will tell, and my guess is that it's not noticeable. Yet.

# HOMEWARD BOUND

WIN POTTER HADN'T said ten words since the truck driver had stopped to pick him up. Aware that a lot of time had passed, he figured he'd best strike up a conversation or he might be afoot again, soon. He wasn't having much luck with rides. Three days on the road and he was not nearly as far from the Tucker place as he should be.

"I noticed you don't use your auto pilot system," he ventured. "Been trucking long?"

"A lot of years, and I'd just as soon do the driving myself," the driver said. "My name is Rudy. What's yours?"

"Winston Potter, but people just call me Win."

"Well, I suspect I was driving one of these rigs long before you were born. Not much difference now, though, except the auto pilot option, the digital engine monitors, the price of fuel, and the new traffic lights and all. About the rigs, though, they do make 'em better today than they used to. I'll say that. What kind of work do you do, son? Bet I can guess it's some kind of farm work by the looks of you."

"You'd be right about that, sir. I'm a wheat harvester. I drive combines and work on them too. At one time or another there isn't much of anything to do with harvesting grain that I haven't done."

"You don't look old enough to have been doing anything for too terribly long," the driver shouted. They were going up a steep incline and the whir of the engine intruded on their conversation. Rudy gripped the steering wheel as if he were navigating a battle ship, clenching his tobacco- and coffee-stained teeth as if these actions alone could help the rig climb the hill through sheer determination.

"Every summer since I was fifteen," said Win.

"With them long hours, I guess you don't hear much news then. Did you know that talk of a world war is about the only thing on the news these days?"

"Yeah, I know about it. I haven't paid a lot of attention to it, but I know about it."

"A young man like you might find himself drafted pretty soon."

"I haven't given that much thought, but you might be right."

It was another thirty minutes before either man spoke again. "Spend much of your time watching Adam 21?"

"A little," Win replied.

"Wish I could say that about my kin. My sister and brother-in-law are obsessed with it. They spend damn near every waking moment messing with stuff not fit to look at. I find it interesting as hell, but you've still got to live your life, you know."

"What time periods are they interested in?"

"Medieval shit, Dracula stuff, although I don't really mean Dracula. You know, the guy they called Vlad the Impaler or something like that. I'm not sure of the time period, a few centuries ago I guess, but he was one mean son-of-a-bitch, ugly too. Dale and Virginia spend hours watching people die of all kinds of torture, people impaled on stakes like a worm on a fish hook squirming in agony for days before dying. Hell, I keep telling them they are going to turn into monsters if they don't stop watching that shit. Beats the devil out of me why people would spend so much time watching other people suffer."

"You got me there. I don't understand it either." They were leaving Alberta now and entering British Columbia.

"Ever kill anybody, son?"

"Just moose, bear, and deer. How about you?"

"Yes, as a matter of fact I have." The silence that followed the admission was becoming uncomfortable when the driver spoke again. "It was years ago and legal, though. The War in Afghanistan, you know. I was in a rifle company. You don't hear much about how it really was over there. There were times when we shot them poor bastards like clay pigeons." He was animated, bobbing his head and rocking back and forth as if a gospel hymn were playing in his head.

"Oh yeah," he added. "There was something else on the news this morning. Did you hear about the killing in Montana?"

Win shook his head and was starting to lose himself in his thoughts when Rudy got his attention. "The local sheriff said she was the prettiest girl he had ever seen. Beautiful red hair, he said, the daughter of a wheat farmer with a big spread not too far from where they found her. Tucker, I think is the name he gave. Told a friend she was going to Alaska to get married. What a shame. The reporter said it looked like she was hitchhiking. Makes you wonder about taking rides from strangers. Don'tcha think?"

## THE MAN CAGE

NEXT TO THE dog-fighting pit stood a cage the size of a boxing ring. Instead of being sunk into the ground, it was elevated and had its own set of bleachers. These were positioned even higher, at a greater incline than that of the pit, so that each and every seat provided a clear ringside view. When Jonas had asked the man who gave him a ride to town about the purpose of the cage, Samson had just grinned, and as his irritation increased, he grinned harder until he broke into a snicker. Finally he said, "I expect you to wind up in there yourself real soon—like when Red finds out you've got his dog, man."

"What are you talking about?"

"Men fight in the cage, either to settle a score or more often to get a routine thrashing from Red when he gets mad. You'll see. Red challenges newcomers all of the time just to make it clear who is in charge around here. If he says get in the cage and you won't do it, a bunch of his cronies will put you in there."

"You ever been in there?"

"No, not me. Don't intend to be, neither."

"What if Red wants you in the cage?"

"Oh, he won't. I made peace with Red a long time ago. He likes me I think. Fighting in the cage is not like the pit for the dogs. In the cage each man wears a leg belt and if the action stops then each man gets a shock, even Red. Hell, I think he even likes it. Like I told you before, Red is one of the meanest sons-of-bitches you will ever run across, mister, and don't say I ain't told you so. He's killed two men in here that I know of, and I'm told there's a lot more I don't know nothin' about. You best get rid of that dog or he be the death of you. Red's gonna be more than just pissed if he finds out. You savvy?"

H E WAS TWO rides past the driver who'd told him about the murder of Amanda Tucker, and he was growing more fearful by the mile. His mind spun out of control, engulfing him in grief-like emotion one minute and in panic the next. He could have made better time if he'd stayed with Rudy, but after the subject of homicide came up, it seemed that the grizzled character didn't want to talk about anything else. Win had mumbled something about stopping to see someone along the way and bid the bloodthirsty truck driver farewell. Surely the authorities would be looking for him by now.

It had taken him a while to figure out how they would go about it. Although, he had told no one about his home town or anything about himself, old man Tucker had his Social Security number. So, it would be simple. Even if they didn't think he was the killer, they would want to talk to him because he must have been one of the last people to see Amanda alive. She had to have told someone she was leaving for Alaska or the authorities wouldn't have known that going there was her intent. So the connection to him was too obvious to overlook.

It was hard to think of that beautiful creature dead. He felt sick but at the same time relieved in a strange sort of way. He would have no decisions to make now as for what to do about Amanda.

WHAT?

The sense of relief made him think less of himself than he wanted to, so he repeated to himself half-aloud the declaration that you can't have it both ways, and he felt none the better for having done so. How could he get across the border into Alaska without being detained and locked up? He didn't have much time to decide what to do, and he wanted to get home before being picked up for questioning.

Win had read about people spending years on death row because of a little circumstantial evidence, and he could only imagine how things must look to the Tucker family. One thing sure, Win Potter was in trouble, big trouble. Even if he were to sneak across the border, the electronic equipment at the checkpoint might read his passport and record his entry. He needed to find something that would shield his passport and block the signal, either that or leave his passport behind, which didn't seem like a viable option. He had to think of something fast. If he had to be arrested, he wanted it to be at home, not at the border. People snuck across the border all of the time, didn't they? But how?

# RED CLOUD AND DISILLUSION

THE FIRST FEW months of Adam 21 technology had passed in a frantic blur of hyper-promotion, celebrations, speeches, dinner parties, panel discussions, and public appearances of every stripe imaginable. But then the stratospheric enthusiasm began to wane as each day became a more prolonged feeling of going through the motions. James Tall Tree grew weary of being James Tall Tree, of being the famous Indian, the Lakota warrior of science, and many other embarrassing media characterizations that haunted his reputation as if, given his heritage, his success was so unusual that it always had to be pointed out.

The plan he'd had in the beginning, which he so far had shared with no one except Native Americans, was to do serious Adam 21 research into the daily lives of the Plains Indian tribes and to show the egregious criminality of whites stealing their land and thus their very heritage. The history of indigenous people in America dovetailed with the iniquity of slavery, and while civil rights leaders were doing a good job of shining a light on the immorality of slavery, a major episode of early American history would not be made clear until slavery and the genocide of Native Americans were put into proper context.

When he was a boy, James listened intently to the elders, whose stories of their ancestors bore no resemblance to the history textbooks he studied in school. There had been runaway slaves who joined his people, and the treatment they had endured echoed of the same genocidal evilness the white man had used to exterminate millions of people in the name of Manifest Destiny. Manifest Destiny was simply a hideous internalization of imagined superiority by a nation of people mad with contempt, drunk with arrogance, morally bankrupt, and consumed by a delusional sense of extreme self-importance. It was white narcissism that tried to force Native American children to expunge their language and customs from memory.

While still in grade school, James had vowed to one day reveal the truth of history, to redeem the dignity lost to his elders. But now, ever so slightly, he could see and feel himself becoming a part of the same power structure that made the oppression of indigenous people possible. He was, in effect, a purveyor of twenty-first century technological destiny.

Frequently now, he was haunted by memories screaming out the horrific injustices he had grown up learning about, crimes every bit as evil in nature as those attributed to the Holocaust. It was all too much for a child to absorb without experiencing a deep sense of trauma. The stories of rape, murder, massacre, torture, the purposeful spreading of small pox and other diseases, mass executions, and theft of land, wives, and children—he remembered them all, and they were still a part of his dreams.

Today, after all of those vows as a boy, he was now one of the most powerful Native Americans his people had seen in a more than a century, and what was he doing to reveal the real truth of history? Nothing of consequence. James had grown up thinking of the Great Plains as a crime scene. And the travesty was that Adam 21 was currently making the account of his people seem even more ambiguous because there was no objective narrative to explain what people were really witnessing.

While still a boy, James concluded that some of the most egregious racist sentiments ever put forth were the legal opinions written to rob Native Americans of their land and sovereignty by simply castigating them as savages—as vicious as wolves, to be precise. American law was riddled with language of racism so vile as to contradict everything Americans were supposed to believe and stand for. These historical documents were in the public record, and yet there was still no outcry, except from those to whom no one listens. The sheer unfairness of this situation and the blatantly unjust standards were baffling and exasperating beyond James' ability to reconcile the corruption and wrongdoing with his dual heritage.

He wanted to take the narrative much farther back to more primitive lifestyles, long before the invasion by Europeans, to put the whole of Native American culture into perspective. Even now, some of his assistants were doing exactly that. By the time he'd actually resigned as national science advisor to the president, he had an overwhelming amount of Adam 21 recordings to sort through. His assistants were first rate, meticulous to a fault. There was nothing much for him to do but watch the segments of video and speculate to himself about what importance, if any, such efforts might bear in the way of practical improvements for Native Americans.

James often reminded himself that many of the Indian reservations throughout the country are worse than the poorest sections of America's major cities. In effect, the reservations, like the nation's ghettos, are home to a stigmatized populace, cultural castaways, people who suffer from the social blemish of belonging to an alienated group—people forced into isolation and then reviled for having learned to talk and act in such a manner that they are easily identifiable as being a part of the outcast assemblage. James viewed the savagery of indifference to human suffering in the vast richness of Western civilization as a mockery of the very idea of morality and something more ethically grotesque than anything ever attributed to the behavior of indigenous people anywhere.

At the same time, he found the darker side of all human beings troubling. Deep examination of history via Adam 21 technology was destroying the romanticism of Native Americans, especially for James. Much of his enthusiasm for showing how the white man had stolen Indian lands was tempered by the reality that, for generations, Native Americans had essentially been stealing land from each other. Of course, they didn't have a Westernized view of ownership of the land, but if traveling through their territory would get a person killed, didn't it amount to the same thing? Wasn't "no trespassing" a declaration of ownership?

Adam 21's vivid examples of the routine brutality of his people was something that took some getting used to, and it shattered every romantic notion of Native American life he had grown up cherishing. He had watched the infamous Red Cloud, whom he had grown up in awe of, do things that were unspeakable, as bad as anything any white man had ever done to the Indians. And he had seen many more examples than most historians had or would ever want to.

James felt himself in the midst of a swirling life phase of existential torment. One day he would think of himself as an Indian, a Lakota blood warrior, only to awaken the next completely alienated from his past, thinking only of science and the future of human civilization. Not only that, but he had something particular in mind, another angle for Adam 21 technology. He had shared his ideas with no one, but he thought it might very well be possible to invert the cone-like simulations and project them in such a way as to study other planets in our solar system and view their past history in the same way reflectors now looked into the earth's past.

It would then be possible to determine if the planet Mars had ever had an earth-like environment.

A part of him wanted to jump head-first into the project with the same fervor that had produced Adam 21, and yet another part of him wanted nothing to do with another soul-breaking marathon of unrelenting work, because it would require some revolutionary scientific advances to view other planets as close up as Adam 21 was capable of viewing the earth. And then there was the moon observatory project that he had been invited to sign on to as a consultant, a project that tempted him because it was long past due. Why there had not been a manned observatory of the moon, even in the twentieth century, was in his view, one of the biggest scientific mistakes in modernity.

A colleague had given him a collection of New Age music in which sounds of Native American culture were mixed in with faint traces of western cinema soundtracks. The compositions were mesmerizing. He used the collection for background music as he watched hour after hour of Red Cloud's people living along great rivers among vast stretches of plain, skirmishing in battle, practicing for war, hunting buffalo, challenging grizzly bears, and making symbolic gestures to the Great Spirit. When they weren't brutal, these sessions were cathartic, and yet James felt no sense of progress. His keen sense of purpose seemed increasingly diminished, although deep in his gut he had a gnawing sensation that Red Cloud's meeting with nearly all of his lifelong enemies, in August of 1857, along the Belle Fourche River in Wyoming, had something to teach today's world about coming together for a common purpose against a common enemy.

During the development of Adam 21 technology, James had lived through scientific breakthroughs the caliber of Newtonian achievement on a monthly basis. Now, although learning from the past was at some level immensely satisfying, he was left with a deep sense of emptiness, a feeling that maybe his dreams of cataloging the history of Native American culture was a misuse of his talents.

He had to face the truth. For the first time in many years he was bored. And boredom in the light of such great technology some-how seemed like something akin to metaphysical blasphemy. He remembered the words of his great-grandfather, who once advised him to seek boredom as a refuge from those who would otherwise tell him how to live his life. He needed to alter his course in life. He was going to follow his heart and make a trip to visit Angela Black in Denver. He would surprise her, and if what he felt was real, and if she felt as he thought she did about him, then things were going to change. And no sooner he had made up his mind than the telephone rang. It was Angela.

# THE BORDER

THE AIR WAS clear, the sky cloudless, and Win was high enough in altitude to see for miles in every direction. He had the feeling of exhilaration that always accompanied him as he crossed from the Yukon into Alaska. But five hours of waiting for the right moment was taking its toll. He sat at a picnic table near the woods by a roadside campground just a few miles from the border. He could see the oncoming traffic from a long way off, but he was in a position where they would have a hard time seeing him unless he wanted them to.

It was a big gamble, but he didn't know what else to do. There were plenty of places to cross the border on foot, but in doing so he might set off sensors. Border drones would take to the air, launching a search from which there was little hope of escape once they locked onto you. And of course, since today was a cloudless day, he could be located via Adam 21 tomorrow, provided the authorities were that smart. This way was chancy as hell, but if it worked, there would be no manhunt to follow. It was nearing suppertime; RV campers were fewer and farther apart. The tourist season was ending, and he figured most of these northbound vehicles were Alaskans going home.

All at once the opportunity was now. He had only a few seconds to make his move. A pickup pulling a very large trailer drove up and parked. A man and woman got out of the truck and headed for the restrooms. Win was sure that neither had seen him. The moment they disappeared, he ran to the back of their trailer. Sure enough, it was unlocked and no one was inside. He climbed in and squeezed himself into a small closet.

He put his passport in between the folds of his wallet, an old-fashioned billfold given to him by his grandfather that had protective sleeves to keep credit card information from being read. It was the best he could do to prevent his passport from registering at the border.

When the trailer began moving, he held his breath. Too late now, he thought. He had to play this one out. His fate would depend on the luck of the draw, perhaps a whim of a border guard. Sometimes they seemed unconcerned and other times they were thorough as hell. Twenty minutes passed that felt like an hour, and then the truck stopped. Short stops and starts made it clear they were in line at the border. Racing wildly, his heartbeat throbbed in his ears. The door in the back of the trailer sprang open and someone entered.

"Hello, anyone here? Border security enforcement."

# DEVIL DOG

JONAS WAS REFLECTING on his earlier conversation with Samson. The pickup had stopped near the camp, and Samson had asked Jonas to get out so he wouldn't be seen with him and the dog. Jonas opened the door and sat for a moment looking straight ahead. Finally he turned to Samson and said, "Okay, tell me more about this guy you call Red and the business about the dog."

"Well, like I said, man, you won't find anyone in this camp willing to take on Red. If he's in a bad mood, he'd sooner swing an axe handle upside your head as give you the time of day. And up until last weekend, Satan was Red's pride and joy, his favorite pastime. Hell, they have dog fights and human cage matches here most every weekend. And that beast you just took to the vet is one of the fiercest creatures on this planet with teeth. Red tells everybody he bought Satan from a drug dealer in Mexico, where the brute had killed every comer north and south of the border for two years. You can tell by looking at him that he's spent most of his life being munched on. I don't have much stomach for dog fights, but word is that Satan has killed more dogs than any animal in the recent history of dog fighting."

"So what happened to him?" Jonas replied.

"Red had too much to drink a few days back, started to take bets against two dogs at a time. On the third go-round someone threw in a big black mastiff and a full-grown Alaska timber wolf. The two of them teamed up against Satan and chewed him to the bone. If you plan on keeping this dog, you better hide him good. Like I say, you don't want to think about crossing Red."

"I'm not worried."

"You'd better be, man. You damn well better be."

Jonas unloaded the dog and carried him back to his tent. For five days the animal slept most of the time, though he drank water every few hours and ate a few mouthfuls of canned dog food. Jonas slept next to the dog and frequently patted him during the night.

"We're going to rename you," he said to the dog one morning. "From now on, you're going to be Gunny. You look just like the drill instructor that all of us in boot camp thought was the gunnery sergeant from hell. So, going from Satan to Gunny isn't really that big of a deal. I hope you don't feel you've been busted in rank, you big brute," Jonas said, softly rubbing the dog's head.

One of the things most dogs share in common, regardless of breed, is that that they soon learn to respond to their name. But here was a dog called Satan that heretofore had never made a connection between words spoken by men, except for the command to fight and to kill. In the deep recesses of his brain were feelings associated with kindness and frequent petting by a small Mexican boy when he was a pup. Those were all but vanquished until now. He was still very weak, too weak to react to any stimuli, except that the attention he was getting moved him toward a dream-like feeling of affection for the man that fed and frequently petted him. During sleep he trembled in seizure fashion as memories of old battles haunted the dark corridors of his brain. He was, after all, a dog, but he was also a dog killer.

## BUNDY LOGIC

IN WAS LATE evening with lots of daylight still ahead. Vince had returned to the place where the Meyers woman's body was discovered and had parked his Suburban off the road a couple hundred yards. Carrying a small haversack of supplies and a pump shotgun into the woods nearby, he found a comfortable place where he could sit and not be seen from the road.

While watching a recorded interview with mass murderer Ted Bundy, Vince had learned that some serial killers would return to the scene of their crime for a variety of reasons. At the time, Bundy was being asked for his insights into the motives of the Green River killer before he was eventually captured. It was more than a little creepy to hear Bundy claim that the killer was likely returning to the scene where he had dumped the body to have sex with the stiff, but that's what he said, and damned if it didn't turn out to have been the truth.

For a half-hour he sat trying to sum up where he was with this case. Old man Sandburg had obviously thought at first that his granddaughter was killed during a botched abortion, and he'd implemented an elaborate homicidal scheme for taking revenge. Then, once he figured out that he'd been mistaken, he simply forgave himself and hired Vince to find the real killer. What were the odds that Owen had known all along what his father was up to? If he asked now, he'd lose any chance of resolving the case.

As for the actual culprit, if all of these murders were connected, the guy was clearly playing games. This meant the clues being left behind couldn't be taken at face value, and so nothing might be as it seemed. Vince knew that the FBI was very much aware that a select number of serial killers prided themselves on playing mind games with law enforcement. The little things might really amount to big things intended to throw him off or to hide a signature element amid apparent chaos. And if the killer was leaving purposeful clues, then it must mean he was already another step ahead by having an out somehow.

Suddenly hungry again, though he'd eaten supper, Vince reached for the lunch sack that Ginger had fixed. He'd barely bitten into the sandwich when a man on foot with a large backpack appeared in the distance. Vince sat very still, chewing deliberately while never taking his eyes off the stranger. The man was walking slowly, a hitchhiker maybe, but he didn't look at passing cars or appear to want a ride. After ten minutes or so, the man was getting close enough that Vince could see him clearly without the binoculars.

Instead of passing on by when he got to the bridge cutoff, the young man walked down to the river's edge and leaned his pack against a tall birch tree not twenty feet from where Samantha Meyers' nude corpse had lain. He sat down and after a few minutes appeared to be rolling a cigarette. Who in the name of hell would be doing that in this day and age, Vince thought to himself. The lad lit the smoke and sat quietly, seeming to savor the taste. Studying him through his binoculars, Vince could see that strapped to the man's leg was a knife that looked very much like a long hunting knife or maybe a dagger.

He wasn't at the Green River and the corpse was clearly gone, but maybe this guy had simply come back to gloat. Just maybe

Vince's luck had finally changed. He stood up quietly and slowly began a half-circle approach to get close before he could be seen or heard. As soon as he reached soft ground and cover, he picked up the pace. Moments later, he stepped in front of the man sitting on the ground and pointed the shotgun at him.

"Take that knife off your leg very slowly and pitch it out of the way. Make one false move, and I will blow you in half." The young man did as he was told and stood up on what appeared to be wobbly legs for someone in such good physical condition.

"What are you doing here?" Vince asked.

"I'm just resting, mister. Who are you and what do you want with me?"

"I'll ask the questions. What's your name?"

"Win Potter is my name. I'm on my way home to Talkeetna. I've been working the wheat harvest in Montana."

Vince pulled out his PC and called 911. A trooper was only two miles from the location when the call came in, and Vince barely had time get any more information from the suspect before the trooper arrived. Vince handed him the suspect's driver's license. The trooper seemed a little suspicious of the whole thing but took the license back to his car and radioed the information to the dispatcher. Moments later when he came back to Vince, his attitude had changed.

"Well sir, I guess you knew what you were doing. This man is wanted for questioning in Montana. For a homicide, no less." Vince felt a flood of relief and a sense vindication for trusting his instincts. With this kind of luck, maybe he and Ginger should fly to Vegas for the weekend.

## WOLVES

I T WAS AN unusually warm day for the time of year, and the updrafts made for effortless flight. High in the sky, an eagle lay leisurely against the wind as if looking for small prey was too much trouble. A short respite was preferable since being aloft was easy.

On the ground below, the dog was panting. His white fur had already begun to thicken in anticipation of winter, and his tongue languished between open teeth, moving like a starving caterpillar in search of sustenance. There. The sound, again. Faint but unmistakable. His master called his name, but he was undeterred, the urgency of the scent overriding her command. He shuddered as if wet and cold to the bone.

There were five in all, each odor distinct, each filling him with rage. He felt drawn to them with a sense of uncontrollable excitement, something akin to fear and loathing, an ancient vengeance steeped in blinding hatred, one he didn't know from experience, but he understood instinctively that these creatures' very existence made his necessary. They were his primeval blood brothers, yet their savagery and their territorial obsessiveness made them his mortal enemy. They were a threat to his master. This was her territory and because it was, it was his ground. Not theirs.

A deep guttural sound stirred within his large muscular frame, and his lips curled in contempt. He stopped on a ridge, put his nose to the wind, and surveyed the valley below. Another sound, one he'd never heard in daylight, though it was as familiar as his own breath. The primordial wailing howl broke the silence, serving as a warning and an invitation for a very old ritual. He shuddered again, his muscled body quivering involuntarily.

Ellen stopped. Fear ebbed through her spine and seemed to spread over her whole body. This was the first time she'd felt afraid in these woods, except when fresh tracks told her a bear was nearby. Uncle Vince said many times that there was nothing to fear from wolves and she believed him, although he did acknowledge that there were now a few recorded cases of wolves killing humans, even in Alaska. Still, he said it was a rare thing to happen and the people who had been killed must have run from them. "Don't ever do that," he had told her. They had heard wolves howling near the cabin many times, but always at night and never while she was alone. She must be a mile from the cabin, maybe more. There was the sound again, only closer.

A hundred yards ahead she saw him, and her fear dissolved. "Moby, come here, right now!" she yelled. He could see her this time, and so he would obey. When he ran toward her, she grabbed him carefully around the neck and squeezed him hard. "Where have you been? I've been looking everywhere for you." She snapped a leash to his collar and turned toward the cabin. There it was again, then again from another direction and closer, shrill and blood-curdling. Moby growled and trembled, not moving but looking anxiously about and watching his master as if instructions were to be forthcoming.

More fearful than before, Ellen pulled on the leash and walked briskly, tugging to get the massive Great Pyrenees to mind her, which wasn't always an easy task. The more steps she took, the faster she walked. Off in the woods to her left, just for a moment, she thought she saw something. When she looked a second time, nothing was there. She would not look again. The clearing near the cabin was up ahead, and Uncle Vince was waving at her. She was safe. And then she heard it again.

This was a strange exhibition, in keeping with world affairs gone awry—Alaska timber wolves howling in the daytime in the presence of humans. The whole planet seemed to be suffering from a deep-seated brand of social stress, of renewed tribal hatred, grudges made benign by time now being resurrected as though they had happened yesterday.

Could this kind of stress spill over into nature? Could animals feel the tensions of far-reaching human hatred? Ellen didn't consider herself to be particularly superstitious, but surely wolves wailing in the daytime close to humans was a bad omen.

The family had arrived at their cabin late the night before in preparation for the neighbors' annual get-together at Caribou Creek. Every time they visited the cabin, Moby was manic about exploring and re-marking his territory, so Ellen had become accustomed to letting him run loose. He usually stayed pretty close to the cabin because he lived to protect his master.

Until she heard the wolves, she had always felt safe in the wilderness. It occurred to her that whatever threat the wolves might represent, it didn't measure up against the evil she had encountered in cyberspace.

# A SICKNESS UNTO DEATH

SOMETIMES WILFRED FELT himself smirking, and a glance in the rearview mirror confirmed the feeling, capturing the cynicism, the mood, and the unreserved malignant fiendishness hidden beneath his smug face. He was amused that the psychologist friend he'd met up with a few days earlier had jokingly accused him of being a psychopath. Stupid, moralistic bastard, he thought. I was playing him like a fish. If you are born without a conscience, the first thing you have to learn is how to pretend. If you can't learn that, you're doomed because you can't compete with jelly-hearted fools. How else could he have become such a good salesman?

That psychologist had learned everything he knew about psychopaths from books, but Wilfred's knowledge was firsthand. Maybe he would write his own book about psychopaths and psychotics someday. Besides, how could he be at fault if he was born this way? Wasn't it really God's fault that people like himself walked the earth? And if not, how else could it be explained? No evil, no good. Any fool philosopher should be able to see the truth in that set-up.

He had learned from experience, and partly from study, that self-love and self-esteem are just euphemisms for varying degrees of narcissism. If he did not have a conscience, as he clearly didn't, then he would have to take it on faith that his own insatiable, boundless, egomaniacal hunger was an exceptional kind of self-regard that fed on the deaths of others in order to quench an unconscious thirst for his own death. That he had figured this out for himself was, to his mind, hilarious.

He was in good cheer this morning. He'd reread Ian Brady's *The Gates of Janus*, a book about serial killers, written by a goddamned serial killer. It was brilliant, indeed, although he thought it would have been much better if he had written it himself. Brady got most of it right. He had said the great evil in the world is perpetrated not by criminals, but by "bovine conformist cowards." He had also concluded that forensic science can be used effectively against law enforcement agencies by anyone with half a brain. In television crime dramas, law enforcement types are brilliant. In real life they aren't. That fact Wilfred had already proven for himself by mocking up crime scenes to confuse the simpletons, and it had worked to the point of being downright irritating.

Brady was right again in declaring that "the serial killer is in effect your alter-ego," a part of yourself that you must hide from others at all costs. Brady had said that killers would confess to any kind of intention under the sun other than reveal their real motivation, and of course, only a mastermind would know that. One sentence of Brady's had imprinted itself deep within the dark corridors of Wilfred's brain: "Born alone, the serial killer is prepared to die alone." But this was not for intellectual reflection. This was meant for the dark cavity within his body which should have contained a conscience or the metaphorical equivalent of a heart but contained neither. You didn't have to be a goddamned killer to know that every son-of-a-bitch on the planet dies alone.

It was time to up the ante. The feebleminded bastards he was up against still hadn't put it together; he would have to throw them a few bones, maybe even literally, just so they would get the big picture. Brady was also right about it being no fun to kill a person who did not want to live. Well, neither was it fun playing cat and mouse if the mice were idiots.

Because of his superior intellect he would soon give cause to rewrite the record books on the subject of serial homicide. He knew that only a few dozen serial killers were active at present and that the collective body count of all the victims was usually less than a couple hundred per year. Soon he would make adjustments that would warrant rewriting the historical record.

The image was still fresh in his mind from two weeks ago and excited him still. It had looked like a travel postcard or a movie trailer, no, a dream. Just up ahead had stood one of the most beautiful girls he had ever seen, and in Montana of all places, her thumb held high in the air, her auburn hair flirting with the breeze, while sporting a give-me-a-ride pose straight out of a fashion magazine. That he could gather so much beauty at such a distance meant that the day was special. It would be an encore performance of innocence lost. Thank God for cloudy weather.

The memory was exhilarating. Lighting a cigarette, he recalled his words on that fine day, "Hello there, miss. Need a ride?"

# THE DEVIL IN THE DETAILS

WENDELL SMYTH'S PRESS conference, now only a blur in his memory, had been a very awkward and unnerving experience. He wasn't nearly as good an explainer as he thought he was, at least not where the press were concerned. The reporters seemed extraordinarily dense at times and incapable of understanding explanations that he thought were exceptionally clear. The exasperation made him try even harder, putting more and more emphasis on the pronunciation of his words, but that only seemed to make things worse.

He'd never imagined such apathy. He expected his story would be front-page news for days on end and that for weeks it would be the only thing the media would be talking about, but so far it was not the case. His telephone, however, had been ringing constantly from pharmaceutical company executives wanting to make him an offer they characterized as the deal of a lifetime, making him more than a little wary.

It hadn't been that long since his discovery, and yet it seemed a lifetime ago. He'd likely never offered anyone a better explanation of his discovery than what he said to his wife as soon as it all came together in his mind. It was really pretty simple, he explained. He had accidentally found a nonradioactive substance that was nontoxic to the touch, but maintained a Jell-O-like consistency for a brief but predictable period of time before it hardened, with the startling capacity to induce a deranged state of consciousness in brains that were clinically dead. Not only that, but his many years of studying the nature of dreams made it crystal clear that a brain inundated with this substance would stay in a constant dream state of terror, something like the worst dream ever experienced amplified by a factor of a thousand.

The substance induced a sense of dread or even horror in anyone who simply had the misfortune to smell it. The greater the whiff, the more insufferable the feeling, the longer it lasted, and the more it seemed to remove options in one's repertoire of behavior for acts of violence. Moreover, each new sniffing experience increased the amount of dread one had about the potential of having to smell it again. A few whiffs, Wendell concluded, and there would be a better chance for this chemical compound to reform criminal behavior than any kind of therapy that had ever been tried. Furthermore, he thought it had the capacity to be made nearly foolproof in its application.

The material substance maintained almost comic-book strength that made it very nearly indestructible. Any force used against the substance caused it to move away with equal force. If you hit it with a hammer, it didn't absorb the damage but simply moved away with as much energy as was used against it. And after it set up and hardened, it didn't let go of what it was clinging to. Stranger still, it did not require oxygen or any kind of atmosphere to maintain its terror dream state. It was a total environment unto itself, cloaked in something as rigid as the fictional deflector shields of the old *Star Trek* saga.

So, as he had explained to his wife one morning before dawn, imagine giving a criminal several exposures to this material and telling him that if he committed another crime, upon his death the state would inject this substance into his brain and that he would never be able to escape from a horror a hundred thousand times greater than the dread he had already experienced. Nothing could stop it, not even if the earth exploded and his brain was shot into outer space. "And you know the really scary thing about this?"

His wife lay there in the dark, her pupils grasping for light, her mind wondering if this was really her husband or a madman. "No," she had said. "What?"

"Well, just imagine that you would have this horrific dream for no less than 60,000 years."

AMY'S BIRTH WAS one of the most wonderful experiences of my life. Barely six pounds, she looked too fragile to last. After that, everything that happened seems a blur in hindsight. It was as if she sat up one day, crawled the next, walked the day after, then grade school was over in a flash, and then she was in high school planning for college.

The thought that your children will die before you do is an idea so deeply foreign to most parents that it's never given more than passing attention, and yet, as a practical matter, it should occupy our consciousness just enough to establish an ever-present reminder of the possibility of tragedy. Do this and you will benefit in two ways. The first is that it increases your mindfulness in the present, and the second is that it lessens the pain in the event of an actual tragedy. And in that case, you will need all of the emotional advantage and reserve you can muster and salt away for the calamities surely to come, because come they always do in one form or another.

Nothing, but nothing, breeds cynicism in one's outlook about the goodness of humanity than when you are swarmed by media larvae during a personal crisis. These degenerate bastards purport to deliver the news, passing themselves off as public servants, while their imbecilic attempts to display human emotion betray their own lack of character. "Your child has been murdered. How do you feel? What are you thinking now?" Makes you want to say sorry, you stupid son-of-a-bitch, you callous bastard, how would you feel if someone ripped your guts out?

Before Adam 21, the idiots limited their activities to covering public displays of private emotion past the point of banality. Like sharks, these slimy sons of bitches lay with cameras in hand awaiting the arrival of troop ships in port so that they might assail soldiers and sailors and their families in what should be moments of respected privacy. Instead these inarticulate bastards are so far removed from the ability to experience genuine human emotions themselves that their only choice is to prey on people they suspect of having them.

If you can survive a private tragedy made public by these predatory vultures while keeping a high regard for the human race, then you are a better person than I am, Gunga Din. Now in the post–Adam 21 era, the media stooges are likely to say, "What do you think your great-grandfather would have said about your daughter's murder?" Jesus! Best not say it to me, or it may be your last imbecilic question. There are days when I am not a man of reason, but of rage, especially when I don't take my prescriptions.

# THE TASTE OF BLOOD

IT WAS EARLY morning. Ginger had let him go outdoors, but instead of scratching the door to be let back in, Moby was off in pursuit of the trespassers whose scent was in the wind. He had been running at a trot for a long time. The vile scent was getting stronger. A sensation akin to fear engulfed him at times, but the feelings of alarm were overwhelmed by an internal fury over which he seemed powerless to act. The offensive odor was all around him, so they had to be close by. No doubt they could smell him by now, but he had no sense of the tactical details necessary to perform his duty. He was more viscerally aware than consciously aware that this effort he was intent on pursuing was a large part of the very reason for his existence.

His actions were raw and ancient—instinctive movements, requiring no understanding in any conscious animal sense, forbidding thought, and instead summoning the distant past to come alive in the present and do what a creature is on the earth to do, to kill one kind of creature so that other kinds may live.

The alpha male stood on a ridge beneath a large spruce tree. He caught glimpses of the white domesticated animal from time to time and waited patiently. He had known this scent for many days and had noticed splotches of white fur in the brush. This senseless creature had even marked territory as his, which required his death. This would be an easy kill and an easy meal. His subordinates would not even have to pursue the simple animal. This dumb beast was racing toward his own demise and could not possibly be a match for five fully grown Alaska timber wolves.

From his vantage point, the wolf could see that the three youngest members of his pack had fallen in step not far behind the intruder. He and his mate would begin their descent now. They would join the others and put an end to this invasion of their territory. In a few moments there would be nothing of this encounter to be found but scraps of white fur adrift on a light breeze like cottonwood spores in search of deep soil.

Moby climbed a small creek bank and then up and onto a flat but grassy meadow surrounded on all sides by a stand of young birch trees. He jumped through a thicket of brush into the open where he found himself face-to-face with a black and gray wolf, the alpha female. Her mouth was open, her muzzle curled in a grimace, and yet she made no sound. Thirty yards to his left was another wolf, only larger, and to his right yet another and another. Then a black wolf, bigger than all the others, with a splash of white between his penetrating yellow eyes, stepped in front of the alpha female. He was the leader of the pack, and he would once again demonstrate his superiority and dominance by killing this inferior creature in the presence of his subordinates.

Moby's breathing was slowing from his run; a guttural growl reverberated within him, seeming to come from a place deep within his muscular body. He was inexperienced in this kind of battle, and yet he knew what to do without being aware that he knew. From behind him came the sound of snapping teeth as one of the young males struck at his flank. Moby wheeled about to face the attack just as he was hit from the other side. He was knocked off his feet, but scrambled to right himself and then turned and backed up to the brush so that none of his attackers could get behind him. Still he had three wolves in his face and the black monster was near his throat. He could smell blood. A young adult male snapped at his shoulder as the alpha male struck him hard beneath his muzzle in the tender part of his throat.

A shrill note of pain rose in the air and quickly lost its volume and resonance in the woods. Suddenly the wolves were overtaken by a primordial instinct to act without hesitation, and a chilling chorus of howls penetrated the silence. Above the ground now consecrated with fresh blood, a raven commenced a series of truncated caws as if to tell its fellow creatures in the forest what had happened. Or perhaps the raven was just as confused as were the wolves, and that was why the raven's utterances would make no sense to any living being in the vicinity of Caribou Creek.

# CONSULTANTS

WILLIAM DAVID DEE and Angela Black were still emotionally tender from the recent death of the Reverend Sol Worley, their friend and business partner. Worley was the reason their team had made considerable progress in calling attention to so many past injustices in law enforcement, and especially in cases of racial bigotry and racial profiling. Their American Lighthouse organization had even drawn national attention to the dangers of ethnocentrism in South America.

The spirited African-American minister had once been characterized in the media as someone to be laughed at, but over time, his sincerity won the hearts and minds of many of his detractors. Standing up to approach the pulpit one Sunday morning, he'd suffered a massive stroke and had died within minutes. Since Dee was Worley's senior, he felt he was the one who should have died, not the reverend. Dee himself had no family, while Worley's family was the emotional center of his life and of their organization.

If, as it seems, the world is going to war, then our work with Sol may all have been in vain, Dee thought. He had said as much to Angela so many times that he worried she might suspect him of becoming senile. While he didn't think it was obvious yet by outward appearances, he could feel his health ebbing away like a persistent leak in a rust-riddled drum of thinning liquid. That he was beginning to feel exceptionally weak was something of a shock.

Sure, he was incapacitated. That was nothing new. How else would he feel after so many years in a wheelchair? Decades earlier, his police career in Dallas had ended in a shooting that changed irreversibly the course of his life. Without the use of his legs, he'd had to reevaluate everything he thought was important. Immersion in his own education led him to a position in academia teaching sociology, until he was invited to serve as an advisor on Portals and ultimately joined forces with Sol and Angela. The fact that he couldn't walk was an aspect of his life that he'd learned to accommodate. But this recent sense of extreme frailty—coupled with uneven breathing and heart palpitations that he could feel—this was something unusual and unsettling.

Stranger still, was the comfort he experienced from thoughts that he was coming to the end of his life. He had long believed the ancient stoic philosopher's assertion that only people who are unafraid of death are truly free, and at times he could feel the veracity in this idea sweeping over him in waves of blissful sentiment. He'd always thought that human beings have a tipping point, at which time their anxiety level will sharpen and accelerate, finally breaking the barrier, coming to terms with the notion of life approaching a screeching halt, having passed the threshold of too much change, and willing to say, enough already: I'm out of here.

Angela, many years his junior, would soon be taking over their project. He hadn't told her of his decision to retire yet, but he would tell her when the time seemed right. He was simply too old to continue. Sorry he'd taken so long to realize this, he was beginning to wonder if he hadn't already waited too late.

The two of them had been invited to Alaska by former national science advisor James Tall Tree, with whom they were already acquainted and who Dee suspected meant a lot more to Angela than she was letting on. This fact might even be why they were included among those asked to be the guests of billionaire Robert Thornton. The social but strategic get-together, exhilarating vacation, or "relaxing and thoughtful sabbatical," as Thornton had referred to it, would extend for a good three weeks at his secluded sanctuary near America's tallest mountain.

Dee was looking forward to the trip. Time in the wilderness sounded wonderful. He just hoped it would be more of a positive experience and more fruitful than the last time they were all together when the Portals system was first announced. Of course, had that meeting not happened, there never would have been a partnership with Angela and the reverend. If not for that, who knows what he would be doing now? Still streaking up and down university corridors in his lithium-battery-powered chair?

If Tall Tree was involved, the conference must be something monumental, Dee figured, something on the cutting edge of technology and highly important in the scheme of things. The turmoil around the world, the mounting deaths from terrorists and madmen, and the rhetoric now about war coming from countries whose thirst for conflict had long ago appeared almost satiated signaled renewed ethnic hatred coming back with a vengeance.

The only aspect that bothered Dee about his own impending death was that he would not be here to know how things turned out. That would be most unfortunate, he thought, but then in the next moment he would imagine that he really did know what would happen because it would be something he didn't expect. The formula was always the same and it was excellent advice: expect the expected and instead get the unexpected, the really unexpected. Adam 21 had made the point so forcefully, it was now considered common sense that nothing in the past was what we thought it was until technology made verification possible, and even then, actions observed did not always lend themselves to objective explanations.

Shrugging one's shoulders and raising one's hands in the air as if helpless to understand what one was looking at was such a common expression that media pundits were starting to complain about it. One news anchor said, "Please folks, no more expressive hands-in-the-air duhs. Say what you mean, for God's sake, and if you don't know, just admit it. Please."

## ENEMIES FOR LIFE

Life IN THE camp during the day was unusually uneventful, if one could get past the reality of being in the company of so many unsavory characters. At night, things were different. Jonas stayed away from any semblance of action, avoiding eye contact with the others, but he hated keeping a low profile. Steering clear of any possibility of conflict was anathema to his very sense of identity. His creed would never accept turning the other cheek.

He was beginning to resent being among the lowest of lowlifes and was starting to think of moving on when word came from the hill one evening that he would be getting the approval the next day to move up to the higher camp. Good timing indeed, he said to himself, and told the messenger he would be ready to move first thing in the morning. As he packed his duffel bags and busied himself getting ready, he accidentally kicked loose Gunny's chain. But the dog was dozing and didn't move.

After having a bite to eat, he went for a walk. On his way back into camp, he was nearing the pit as the evening crowd was arriving for a night of dog fighting. Just then Gunny ran up to greet him and Red McKinney appeared a few feet away.

"What the fuck," Red blurted. Jonas bent down picked up the weighty dog and walked away. "Where the fuck do you think you're going, asshole?"

Jonas turned to face him and said, "I'll be back in a minute."

"Goddamned right, you will."

Jonas walked to his tent without another word and fastened Gunny to his post. He sat for a moment with his chin in his hand as if meditating and then walked back to what had become a very large crowd consisting of about everyone in the lower camp.

"Get the man cage ready, Max," Red said to one of the men standing close by.

"Don't you want to know how I came to have the dog?" Jonas asked.

"It don't fucking matter, asshole. You don't take my fucking property without asking, ever. Got that, dipshit?"

"Appears to me the only one that deserves the title of asshole or dipshit around here is a big buffoonish looking son-of-a-bitch with shitty looking red hair," Jonas said.

A hush fell over the crowd, color draining from the faces of the men. Butch gulped and mumbled, "Jesus fucking Christ," loud enough that both Jonas and Red heard him. And nearby Samson jumped to his feet as if there were about to be an earthquake big enough to swallow the camp.

Red kicked dirt with his foot, shouting in a rage and screaming, "Get this motherfucker in the cage now!"

Max brought over the leg belts as Jonas entered the cage but Red slapped them out of his hand. "Won't need these," he shouted. "I'm going to kill this motherfucker!"

The crowd settled nervously into the stands in silence, looking at one another with grim expressions in anticipation of a battle to the death, incredulous that anyone on the planet dared speak to Red with so much contempt and disrespect. Max backed out of the cage, leaving Jonas and Red alone, and locked the door. In the stands, Butch bit his lip. Suddenly aware that he had to piss, he said he would be right back. Samson took a seat next to him, mumbling under his breath, "You ain't got time to piss, man. Piss in your pants if you have to, 'cause you'll fuckin' miss it if you don't."

"Rumble time," Max shouted, quickly taking a seat.

"This ain't gonna take long. Don't even look away, bro."

# SENTIMENTS

THORNTON WAS UP earlier than usual. He loved mornings in his wilderness retreat because they were eerily quiet, offering a kind of serenity in which his mind could sort through something difficult, something meaningful, something important. At times like these, he felt a bit closer to understanding the true nature of human beings, because the very promise of the future seemed to depend on reaching an unheard of accord of common ground, a form of cooperation never seen before in human history, something above and beyond the teamwork of the allies in World War II.

The compound he'd built was extraordinarily large, requiring constant maintenance, so he'd hired a full-time staff, consisting of cooks, maintenance workers, mechanics, computer technicians, IT types, housekeepers, and groundskeepers, who also acted as chauffeurs and who did the shopping and ran errands. He even had greenhouse tenders who took care of the livestock, vegetable garden, and bee hives. There were so many bears in the territory that the compound had electric fences around many of the outdoor facilities.

The staff lived in a specially built back portion of the building and were seldom heard or noticed outside their regular duties, except in their large entertainment and recreation room. Most of them worked a two-week-on, two-week-off schedule, like Alaska's oilfield workers. The big difference was that Thornton paid much better than big oil, which made him the talk of the north and the biggest collector of resumes in the state. But when Thornton was alone at the retreat, he often sought out his employees to keep him company, frequently taking his meals with them. Unlike Ruben, who preferred to be alone, Thornton liked to be around people most of the time.

When Ruben stayed at the retreat, he always slept in the original cabin. That way, he could be totally alone. He did make use of the on-duty cook's services, however, as he did not like to prepare his own meals if he didn't have to. On this morning, Ruben was at a table by the large glass window framing the majestic presence of Mount McKinley when Thornton came to breakfast.

"Up kind of early, aren't you, Bob?"

"A little. It's hard to sleep when there's so much to think about. Tomorrow is the reunion, and the day after, I'm going to start trying to develop a plan of action. I've invited some people to help us brainstorm the project. I hope you're up for it."

Nodding his head, Ruben looked out the window without speaking.

"Look, Ruben, I know how things must be for you right now. I know how much you miss Esther and Ben, but you've still got many years left. You might just have a chance to make a big societal contribution in a way that I'm sure you've always dreamed of. I think maybe you should consider checking into the hospital for one of those stem-cell heart regeneration procedures and or maybe get a prescription for depression. Have you ever considered either one?"

"No, I'm not ready to become a zombie just yet, my friend. I'm doing okay. My heart is fine. I just need more time—time to think things through. You know, it's when you're in predicaments like this that you learn whether your established philosophy of life is something of real substance or is just accumulated nonsense. I'll get past this blue mood one way or another."

"God, I hope so," Thornton said, punching Ruben gently on the shoulder.

"Bob, I just can't figure out how you've come to the conclusion that there is really something that you and a group of rich folks can do to have a cooling effect on the levels of escalating testosterone throughout the world. I mean, of course money talks, but Jesus, what a tall order. For God's sake, how long has the Middle East been a powder keg?"

"It's painfully simple, Ruben. One of our conversations from a few years back stuck in my mind, and recalling it the other day gave me the idea. World peace can only be achieved by one thing, one word."

"And that would be?" Ruben asked with a doubtful look on his face.

"Advertising, amigo. What else?"

# BLOOD IN THE SAND

JONAS CIRCLED THE big man, admiring the twenty-inch biceps and thinking what a waste that they were attached to an imbecile who can't help but let his temper get the best of him.

"One last chance to get out of here without embarrassing yourself, you big piece of shit," Jonas said softly but loud enough so those in the first rows of the stands could hear. The men in the bleachers gasped. Max punched Butch in the arm and said, "Goddamn it all, man, you hear that motherfucker? Goddamned son-of-a-bitch has some guts, I'll say that for 'em."

Red let out a war hoop, grabbed a fistful of sand, and threw it in Jonas's face. For a moment, Jonas was blind. A huge fist smashed him on the left side of his face, and he felt he might lose consciousness. But the blow cleared the sand from his good eye, and before the big man could swing again Jonas regained his wits.

When Red lunged with an overhand right, Jonas stepped clear, grabbing the fully extended arm and throwing the hulking giant head over heels into the lower bars of the cage. It was a bad landing. There was a chorus of whooshing noise from the stands as what had just happened registered in the minds of the onlookers.

Red staggered to stand, but before he could rise, Jonas kicked him twice in split-second succession, once to the side of the head and another blow on the chin. Red went down in a screaming rage, but in the next moment was back on his feet, lunging at Jonas like a wild beast lost in darkness, unable to think but for a sense of hatred so forceful there was no room left for thought, nothing to do but act, no instinctive act but to kill.

Jonas kicked him in the chest with his right foot and then to the left side of his head with the left, moving his feet so swiftly that the onlookers had to take a moment to make sense of what they had just seen. Red's knees buckled, but before he could find his way to the ground, Jonas struck him with a left hook to the ribs, a right to the jaw, another left to the gut, and a hard overhand right to the nose just as the big man folded and slammed into the dirt like a bag of wet cement. The men in the stands were awestruck. No one spoke. It was clear Red would not be getting up soon. No one could believe their eyes. The man that each of them had thought was undefeatable, the meanest son-of-a-bitch on the planet, had just been dismantled like an old woodshed taken apart by a master carpenter. Darkness enveloped the pit as the lights went out.

When the lights came on several minutes later, Max opened the cage and Butch entered, whispering, "Man, you gotta get out of here before he wakes up." Jonas was brushing the sand off his face. "Come on, man, I'm serious. He will get his gun and blow you away. I'll get Samson to drive you up to the next camp with your gear. Red won't mess with you there, but if I was you, I'd get out of the whole goddamned state. 'Cause he's going to be gunning for you sooner or later."

It was almost a half-hour before the big man arose from the floor of the pit. No one had been willing to check on his condition or arouse him because they knew that whoever was in striking distance could be in trouble when Red came to his senses. Most of the men who had been in the stands were still sitting there when Red stood up took one step forward and fell flat on his face. A second attempt had the same result before he discovered that his shoe strings had been tied together. Red cut the laces with his knife, stood up, and faced those remaining in the stands. Two of the men jumped to the ground and took off, making strained efforts not to snicker. "Jonas must have tied Red's shoelaces in the dark," one of them said. "What a nervy bastard. Too bad he'll be dead soon."

## SPEAKING FOR GOD

ON THE FOURTH of July, the world was introduced to the National Fundamentalist Radio Network. Negotiations had been underway for years, but it seemed to the public that it had occurred overnight. Without a single day's broadcast history behind them, the network nevertheless claimed an audience three times greater than that of National Public Radio (which, in their wild imagination, they considered their competition, hence NFR). Their announcers claimed that in two months it would be five times greater, and in another two months double yet again.

NFR was an extraordinary alliance of worldwide fundamentalist organizations representing opposing views in many cases but networked and united against the blasphemy of unbelief in whatever form they found it. One zealous announcer characterized it as "The Holy Alliance: My truth, your truth, our truth, God's Truth, an oath in opposition to heresy, a firm stand for God, against evil and unbelief."

It was becoming more and more apparent that the power behind the new broadcast behemoth was a mysterious sage in Missouri known as the Seer. The exact details of the network's closely negotiated arrangements were unknown, but it did appear they had entered into an agreement that allotted broadcast time based upon the membership numbers in their respective groups. In this way, if an organization could produce more members, they would get more air time, and the competition among members would ensure an unrelenting effort to return the listening public to the word and the laws of God.

Their program lineup included names like The Real End Times, Portals of Prophesy, Don't You Be Left Behind, Rapture and the Damned, Escape His Wrath, For the Love of God, Satan and Adam 21, and a whole host of similar titles, "hooks on a trotline for souls," as one Arkansas commentator put it.

According to media watchdogs, the net result was that NFR was now the largest radio broadcast company in the world. They swallowed many traditional Christian broadcasters and a whole slew of network and affiliate stations. Few pundits doubted NFR's ability to produce a gargantuan audience all over the world. Liberal organizations sent a firestorm of complaints to the FCC, but few people felt it would have any effect. It was too late.

The whole thing had occurred without public knowledge, which could only mean one thing: Those whose political power in Washington could be bought had carefully greased this wheel to keep it from squeaking. A subtle but clear objective of NFR appeared to be a full-frontal assault on Adam 21 and every consequential social interpretation that had resulted from the technology. As far as NFR's management was concerned, Adam 21 was the work of Satan, and it was their aim to bring the wrath of God to bear on the blasphemy.

It was not man, but God who was to reveal the truth of the past, they said. That's what the Bible was for. "Stay tuned if you want life everlasting" was one of their standard sign-off messages, often followed by something like, "Heed us not and you will burn forever, in the depths of Hell. You will be doomed to damnation and eternal torment. It is God's promise for all blasphemers. Repent and live forever."

# CARIBOU CREEK

THE SUMMER OF 2028 marked the seventh anniversary of the time a small group of friends with cabins on Caribou Creek first met, as well as the seventh year of Adam 21 technology. So much had happened here, and so much since, that Caribou Creek seemed like a gateway to a different world, a place of pristine natural beauty with the technical capability of gods and a place of enduring friendships.

In 2021, the year Robert Thornton drove to Alaska with Ruben, he'd purchased a pickup from the now-deceased Ben Sanchez in addition to his wilderness cabin. Ruben had accompanied Bob to the site at Caribou Creek to begin setting up. Shortly after they arrived at the property, they met the Terrell family, Adam Whitehead, James Tall Tree, and State Trooper Matthew Sills. An incident involving vengeful drug dealers, who had followed Vince Terrell from Dallas, brought the whole group together, and they had all remained fast friends ever since. They visited one another often when they were at their respective cabins, but once a year, their get-together was a formal event.

This year's reunion barbeque was being held again at Bob Thornton's place. Now a billionaire, Thornton was still celebrated as a hero who had saved the day on more than one occasion with a slingshot, of all things. People continued to talk about it, and news reporters never tired of asking Thornton for a demonstration, just as he never tired of refusing to do so or make any further comments on the subject.

The cabin Thornton had purchased from Ben was beautiful but very small. During his second year on the creek, Thornton had brought in a whole construction company, with helicopters and sling loads of equipment, to create something of a fortress retreat. The original cabin was untouched, but fifty yards behind it now stood a building with 18,000 square feet of floor space carved into the side of a hill. It consisted of three stories: two below ground and one above with a large exterior deck situated for a commanding view of Mount McKinley, or Denali, as some preferred to call it. An argument over the mountain's name had been brewing for decades. Every Alaskan seemed to prefer one name over the other, regardless of the official designation.

In an embankment a few yards down the hill, another excavation contained a generator room, built to supply electricity; it was so well insulated that the generators could not be heard from inside the compound. The basement area housed a movie theater and a state-of-the-art computer and telecommunications room. Wireless video panels hung on the walls throughout the building, exhibiting up-to-the-minute news and selected Adam 21 scenes from the past. And yet, for all the amenities, Thornton's fortress did not detract from the wilderness landscape and was barely visible until one was almost upon it.

With such a facility available, it seemed rather pointless to have the annual get-together anywhere else, so these days no one even broached the subject of having it at one of the other cabins. Doing so would be like going to someone's living room to look at their art collection when instead you could go to the Louvre.

This year was different, though. Thornton had invited some

guests outside of their little group, and Ginger Terrell wasn't sure she appreciated it. Of course, if she had been asked, she would have said sure, but she wasn't asked and that's what bothered her. Maybe she was just being silly. Thornton was consumed by talk of war, so she would just put it out of her mind. Besides, it would be nice to meet some new people, and if they were friends of Thornton's they would have to be interesting people.

At least she didn't have to worry about what she would wear. This was Alaska, after all, not Dallas, and no one paid much attention to your clothes, so long as they were clean. "Ellen, it's time to get ready," she called out the back door, wondering who all was going to be at the party.

"I can't find Moby," Ellen answered. "He's been gone for hours. I'm worried about him, Aunt Ginger."

"He's big enough to take care of himself. I'm sure he'll be along soon."

"But what about the wolves? I know they're still close by because we keep hearing them."

Ginger was concerned, but she didn't want Ellen to know because it would just make matters worse. There was nothing they could do anyway, and she didn't want to spoil the day. "Moby is a very big dog," she said, trying to put the best face on it. "Don't worry, honey. He can take care of himself, and Mr. Whitehead has him properly protected. Get changed into whatever you're going to wear so we can go."

Ellen nodded, but the expression on her face told Ginger she would be worried until the big brute showed himself again. Much as she loved the dog too, Ginger had her own worries.

Vince was beginning to look really frail, and it troubled her no end. Something about the pallor of his skin seemed to foretell illness or a sense of doom. Most of the time, Ginger put it out of her mind, but there were moments like today when she could scarcely think of anything else. She was struck by how much her husband's appearance had changed when compared to the photographs and Adam 21 footage of the incident seven years ago. Vince had always been her tough guy. Now he looked like someone who wouldn't be around for long.

Ginger wondered if Ellen had noticed the change but was afraid to bring it up. Probably I'm just being paranoid, she thought, always expecting another of life's unexpected shoes to drop that won't fit. Worse, if it was like all of the others from the past, it would crush someone, someone close.

She reassured herself with the thought that her best friend, Linda, would be at this afternoon's get-together. Linda was the wife of Adam Whitehead, the scientist for whom Adam 21 was named. Although they rarely ever broached the subject, what both women had in common was the likelihood that they would spend years in the future alone as widows because of the age of their husbands. This brash reality was their unspoken existential connection. Ginger's greatest fear, based on her previous experience, was the virtual certainty that the good in life is fleeting.

# DIRECTIONS NORTH

AT THE HIGHER-LEVEL camp where he lived now, Jonas had already stopped thinking about Red. He was bored, and his restlessness was about to get the best of him. Although he felt like a believer in the midst of services or ceremony, a little distance from it seemed an invitation to doubt. He was simply not cut out for something resembling life in a monastery.

Still feeling obligated to what he'd come to view as a noble cause, he was also a man of habit and he needed a reliable adrenaline rush. Down deep, he knew he was trying to fool himself by acting as if it were in his nature to avoid trouble. As a hand-to-hand combat instructor, he'd become accustomed to living on a continuous supply of adrenaline, and he thrived on it.

This place was the antithesis of action. They wouldn't even let people out of the gate for a walk in the woods. He had come close to leaving when he first arrived, because they objected to his keeping a dog, but they'd relented when it was obvious that if the dog didn't stay, neither would he. Even so, too many more days like these and, one way or another, he would be gone.

The only thing holding him back was that Rev. Baldwin kept seeking him out for a friendly discussion and acting as if he cared deeply about what Jonas was doing and thinking. Baldwin told him that he had originally thought it was over for him when he'd ruffed up Red in the lower camp. He thought the Seer would never let him join the Soldiers for Christ, but his wiping the floor with the big man seemed to have had the opposite effect on the elders. Now Jonas was to be treated with great care and given a mission of great importance.

So, just in the nick of time, Jonas was given a map and expense money and told to set up in an outdoor camp in Alaska. After that, he would receive further orders. This was just the energizing jolt he needed. Alaska. Why hadn't he thought of it before?

# THE ANNIVERSARY

THORNTON HAD BEEN looking forward to the annual Caribou Creek reunion. He thoroughly enjoyed the company of friends with or without a specific agenda, people who would not hit on him in an unexpected moment to fund some kind of a bizarre business scheme. The Terrells, the Whiteheads, Sills, and James Tall Tree were not that kind, and the extra guests he had invited this year were here for a specific task, so this should be an enjoyable afternoon and evening. He thought he had sensed some apprehension when he told Ginger Terrell about inviting a couple of new guests this time, but he felt sure these individuals were cordial enough that they would soon put everyone at ease.

He spent the morning in intense conversations on the telephone in his private office, a *Do Not Disturb* notice hanging on the door. When he came into the main room on the first floor of his grand fortress, he was surprised to find most of his guests had already arrived. He'd sent a limousine to the airport to pick up those coming from other states. They were brought to the cutoff and then given a ride in the Hummer to the fortress.

Thornton entered the room, grabbed a drink from a staff member, and went to the center of the cluster. "Sorry I'm late, folks. The time gets away from me out here. This place is just too quiet and relaxing. I trust everyone has turned their communicators off? Please keep your seats and, if you don't mind, stand or wave as I call your name. Most of us here know each other. This is just for the benefit of our new visitors. I'm sure some of you have introduced yourselves already, but let's make sure there are no strangers among us.

"I'm Robert Thornton, and that distinguished gentleman trying to hide in the corner is our esteemed resident philosopher, Ruben Sanchez. Here to my right are my neighbors Vince, Ginger, and Ellen Terrell, and Adam and Linda Whitehead. To their right are Dr. James Tall Tree and his guests. James, how about introducing the people you brought with you?"

"Sure," said James, rising to his feet and motioning to the older gentleman in the wheelchair. "This is Dr. William Dee, and beside him is Dr. Angela Black. These two took part in our panel discussions prior to the introduction of the Portals system before it became Adam's namesake. Next is Dr. Wendell Smyth, whose recent neurological chemical discovery is mind-blowing to say the least."

"Thank you all, and welcome," Thornton said. "I didn't mean to start off being so formal. We'll know one another better in no time. For those of you who are new to Alaska, you might be interested to know that every year on this date those of us who are locals get together to celebrate the day when we all met a few years ago. Some of you may remember that Vince and Ellen made the national news with the Adam 21 clips of our ancestral connection and of the culmination, when we had an encounter with some drug-dealing assailants from Texas.

"The panel over in that corner explains the whole incident and the aftermath, if you are interested. And, for those of you who are part of our little group, you should know that I've invited these folks here to discuss innovative possibilities for cooling off the warlike tensions in the world. That said, all I want to accomplish today is to make sure everyone has a good time. Oh, and coming through the door as we speak is one of our local VIPs, Sergeant Matthew Sills of the Alaska State Troopers and his wife, Sandra. Matt and Sandra, meet Wendell Smyth, William Dee, and Angela Black."

A hushed roar of small talk ensued. Thornton dimmed the room lighting and turned on the Adam 21 panels centered on each main wall, spaces where, in earlier times, a painting would have drawn attention. The five-by-six-foot panels came alive with screen saver-like snippets of the past taken from time periods and locations all over the world. Since this was to be a happy occasion, the scenes had been selected for beauty and grandeur and for their conversation value.

One screen featured an ancient family of humanoid ancestors, as yet unclassified, who were eating in front of a cave somewhere in France. On the screen on the adjacent wall was a large herd of wooly mammoths. On the next screen was a bustling city in Ancient Greece. An ugly but charismatic and highly animated gentleman was lecturing to a small group of patient listeners. It took only a few moments for most people to feel the high-velocity jolt of recognition that this must be Socrates.

Soft music played in the background with symphony-hall quality. Most everyone stood as they began engaging one another in conversation. Everyone, that is, but Ruben, who was sitting by himself in a corner drinking beer from a bottle. He was staring at the only remaining screen in the room. It was a family of Dire wolves, several adults sleeping while a female nursed her pups in front of an ancient den. These magnificent creatures had been extinct for thousands of years. They were so much larger than the wolves roaming the woods here today that it was hard not to stare at them.

Ruben had already spent many hours doing just that. He paid close attention to everything they did. Somehow their size and strength made them seem extraordinarily savage, and yet he couldn't help feeling a kind of affection for them. Following their daily antics was thrilling. The only thing that eased the effect of their savagery was the fact that many of their prey animals were long-since extinct. Their unfamiliarity added a sense of fantasy to the scene, diminishing the graphic violence of the pack's frequent kills. It was harder to feel sympathy for a creature if, until now, you didn't know it had ever walked the planet.

Some of Ruben's childhood memories of life on a Lakota reservation were still open wounds. Being half Mexican—a half-breed, a breed, a pinkman, a red bean—made him subject to the persistent ostracizing that came with the slurs. Indian-on-Indian racism or intercultural racism—what it was called didn't really matter because the taunting epithets were still present in his dreams. Much as Ruben prided himself on being an objective philosopher capable of understanding what others have no inkling of, he had his own blind spot concerning his heritage.

The racial stigma from childhood insults lingered in the shadows of his mind just below consciousness. He was loath to admit as much, but the feelings that accompanied such an attitude sometimes kept him from applying his usual philosopher's sense of objectivity for understanding discrimination as a soul-killing ethos that stands as a perpetual barrier to civilization.

Nearby James Tall Tree was admiring Thornton's hideaway in the wilderness. He could not imagine how much money it would take to build a place like this so far from civilization and yet with so many amenities. Thornton reminded him that it was a great place to entertain guests. Here he could have their undivided attention, unlike at a hotel in town. With a captive audience, he could get things done.

With her hand extended in greeting, Linda Whitehead approached James. She'd been looking for an opportunity to talk with him. "You know, James," she said, "I like to think that because you can look back in time and observe events as they occur, it makes our existence seem eternal. I mean, as long as this planet and Adam 21 technology exist, our lives will seem to be unending because we will still be observable."

"I agree it's a nice feeling," said James, "but of course, it's an illusion. If you could close the simulated distance at the speed of light, by the time you got to whatever in the past you were looking at, you would arrive in the present. But, on the other hand, time and space are interchangeable, so space is like an infinitely vast recording device keeping a record of everything that has happened as endlessly observable from somewhere else at just the right distance.

"Many years ago, when I was still in school," he continued, "I had already heard of your husband's work and I told my grandmother that space was like a giant DVD player with remote viewing only, that the big bang turned it on and it would take a big crunch to turn it off.

"And, Linda, I don't want to depress you, but the longing for permanence is humanity's Achilles heel. It's the nature of our short lives that causes us to fall for the illusion that we live in a stable universe. Chaos is the signature of existence. Everything is in flux. We are convinced of the stability of our solar system because we take appearances at face value. It comes as a shock to most people to learn that our solar system is engaged in a slow dance of destruction. Our moon is slipping away at the rate of about an inch and a half a year. That doesn't sound like much until you understand that the moon is a quarter million miles away and it used to be about fourteen thousand miles from the earth, towering over the night sky like an ancient, menacing God.

"The moon may go completely AWOL someday, just as the planet Mercury will eventually slam into the sun. Venus may well crash into the earth, but that wouldn't matter much if the moon had already said adios. Mars threatens to escape our solar system altogether and become aimlessly adrift in space. One day the sun will implode, burn to a crisp, and inhale the earth, that is, if the earth is still in orbit."

He looked at Linda and smiled sympathetically to reassure her that, for people living today, there was no cosmic threat. "We should have a few million generations before any of these events occur. My point is simply that if we can become accustomed to accepting the reality of chaos, it can inspire more gratitude, tolerance, and appreciation for the time we are here." Linda smiled and nodded to show she understood.

Noticing Ellen Terrell across the room, Thornton walked to her side. "I haven't seen much of you lately."

"I know, Mr. Thornton. We haven't been spending as much time at the cabin as we usually do. Uncle Vince has been pretty busy and I've been helping him a little."

"I know you still have plenty of time, but I was just wondering if you have any idea what you want to do once you get to college and after."

"Right now I can't decide between being a police officer, a cyber-detective, or a veterinarian."

"Wow. A couple of those choices aren't very closely related, you know."

"I know. Uncle Vince thinks I should stick with animals. Aunt Ginger says both occupations deal with animals."

Smiling broadly, Thornton said, "Tomorrow these people I've invited here are going to try to help me come up with a plan to spend quite a lot of money in order to avoid a world war. I thought it might be especially interesting to get the perspective of someone from your generation. What would you do or say, Ellen, if you had a worldwide audience and you could call their attention to anything you wanted them to think about?" He motioned for Ellen to sit down on the nearby leather couch.

She sat in silence for a couple of minutes while Thornton studied his drink. "Mr. Thornton, have you ever heard of the philosopher Peter Singer?"

"Yes."

"Well, I've read some of his books and I think you can tell a lot about people all over the world from the way they treat animals. If most people are blind to the cruelty and inhumane acts that go on all around them, then they are more likely to be blind about everything other than what they really care about. I think that's really sad. Mr. Singer asks if we were to see a train about to hit either our brand new expensive sports car or a strange child and could only save one, which one we would choose.

"Of course, everyone says the child, but Mr. Singer says that we don't live as if that's true because thousands of people starve to death every day, not for the value of a sports car, but for only a few pennies. I think people who are blind to the inhumane way we treat helpless animals are detached enough from the real world to let people starve to death. If I had the whole world's attention, I would ask them to wake up and see the world as it is and not as the fantasy world they've made up, where the things that are right in front of them are the only things they think are important. I would ask them how they can be oblivious to creatures who are raised for food in conditions so tortuous that they defy any measure of human decency."

"That's a very thoughtful answer, Ellen. Thanks. I'm glad I asked. If you have the time, you are most welcome to join in on any of the discussions going on here during the next few days."

"Thank you. I would like that. Who wouldn't want a chance to make the world a better place?"

As Thornton stood up, he noticed Adam Whitehead standing by himself with a troubled look on his face.

Adam had seriously begun to wonder if he had really done the world a service or had simply condemned it to doom and destruction. Grateful for this chance to discuss his concerns with others, he needed reassurance and needed it soon, because he felt himself slowly slipping away. His forgetfulness stalked him like a predatory creature, waiting at every moment for an opportunity to pounce and blank his mind with a feeling of emptiness, of being lost, wondering what he was thinking and why, as if this moment was not connected to the past, present, or future. If he were lost in his own mind, he would be lost in time, and the thought that such a destiny might be in store for the man who made Adam 21 possible seemed profane and morally blasphemous.

## OWEN SANDBURG'S JOURNAL: JUSTICE

WHEN THE DETECTIVE first came to see me, my first impulse was to put an end to the investigation because I thought I already knew most of the how and why about Amy's death. Continuing the investigation would have been too God-awfully excruciating.

If I thought she was killed by someone in a fit of passion, some-one who had loved her and who would have been tormented by his deed, perhaps I could have let it go. That would have been a tragedy. You might find it strange that I would rather think she was killed by someone who cared for her, but believe me, when it's your only child, any kind of implied affection on the part of the perpetrator that might have lessened her terror and anguish is welcomed. Otherwise, you can't put your imagination to rest. You keep rehearsing the possibilities of the horror she experienced over and over, and you fear you can never stop, not because of what happened, but because you don't really know what happened. It's not the pain that your loved one must have suffered, it's the fear you can imagine she felt that scorches your soul. Great waves of depression roll over you as thick in substance as a Mahler symphony, and it goes on for days, week, months, even years.

So, when Terrell told me that he thought Amy's killer might be a madman who killed for pleasure and not a medical procedure gone awry, as we thought, or an act by someone who really cared about her, I knew that he had to continue on the case and that I should spare no expense in seeing it through. I may be a rich man, but most of my days are spent in a kind of impoverished anguish that only seems to be stilled through the exploration of literature. Oh yes, we have been enamored with Adam 21, just like everyone else, but great imaginings set forth in prose are preferable to the silent horror of visible history, especially at my age.

Her mother used to teach English, and that's all Amy ever talked about doing after completing college. Until her death, we were a family bound together by a love for literature and the arts. The fact that others have thought about the things we care deeply about and have expressed them so effectively adds to our ability to articulate our own thoughts and feelings, and it's through these efforts that I keep nihilism at bay. Amy's death threatens constantly to eat away the remaining vestiges of meaning in my life. Imagine what it's like for a father to realize that his daughter was so afraid of him that she couldn't confide in him if she found herself in trouble. What would this say about his affection for literary pretense and high-mindedness?

If I have any say in the matter at all, good will triumph over evil. The loathsome sick bastard that killed my little girl will find his last days on earth filled with terror. Amy's grandfather, himself a tyrant whose rage touched everyone who knew him personally, would to most people have seemed a greater threat to the perpetrator than myself, but people who frequently exhibit uncontrollable rage are less threatening than those of us who experience a slow and deliberate burning wrath that can easily become an obsession that consumes one's soul. Better to make an enemy of a despot than a real thinker like me, and once I've stopped taking my meds for a long period of time, look out.

# UNSETTLING NEWS

$\mathsf{S}$HORTLY AFTER ARRIVING at the party, Matthew Sills decided he couldn't wait any longer. The latest news broadcast over his police band radio and a world news feed whispering in his ear were too much to keep to himself. As soon as the group appeared to be sitting in places close enough to hear him, he said, "You all might be interested to know that the Israeli police have just discovered a nuclear device in the basement of a building in Jerusalem. So far, it hasn't blown up, but of course there is a massive evacuation underway.

"They have a team in place trying to defuse it because they're afraid to try to move it. All they are saying for sure is that the timer is very sophisticated. The bomb squad and Israeli intelligence agents are working frantically to discover the identity of the group responsible.

"It's also been reported that some 50,000 Indian troops appear to be preparing to cross the border into Pakistan. Pakistani troops are converging to meet the threat. And the unrest in China has escalated to the brink of civil war. The president and leaders all over the world are pleading for calm. In the meantime, Supreme Court Justices Harkens and Monroe and the Speaker of the House are all in the hospital with some mysterious illness."

Thornton could feel the tension rising within the group and decided he should try to refocus their attention. "This is truly disturbing. I know you must be very concerned, and I'm concerned too. But I think we still have a ways to go before our country is involved in a world war. Nevertheless, I will tell all of you here tonight that you are welcome to seek shelter here and stay, if war does become a reality and is felt in Alaska. I doubt it will come to that, so perhaps, for the evening at least, we should change the subject."

The whole group was in close quarters now, close enough so that everyone in the room could hear anyone who spoke, and every person in the room was fighting the urge to turn on their communicators for more news.

Adam Whitehead broke the silence. "Ellen, where is that big slobbering mutt of yours? I think our friends would enjoy seeing him."

Ginger swallowed hard, but Ellen handled it well. "He's worrying us by staying away too long at a time," she said. "And there are wolves close by because we've been hearing them a lot, even during the daytime."

"I wouldn't worry about him. A dog like that is plenty big enough to take care of himself," said James. And then, seizing the moment to change the subject yet again, he said, "I'm anxious to hear about Dr. Smyth's new discovery."

Thornton took the cue. "Yes, Dr. Smyth's work is fascinating. I had a hard time locating him and an even harder time persuading him to join us. Please, doctor, relax. You're among friends."

Smyth shifted in his seat and leaned forward. "What would you like to know?"

"Tell us about Terminal Terror. Explain how you can be sure that a deceased brain can regain a sense of consciousness and also how this substance that the media has started calling the new T&T can be used in a positive way. Do you think that's a real possibility?"

Thornton looked around the room for any recognition that he

had once been referred to with the term T&T because of the way he dressed and because he reminded his office staff of two movie actors named Tom. The nickname had been mentioned numerous times in the media, but he was relieved to see no acknowledgement by any of his guests.

Smyth studied the ceiling for a moment. "T&T is a substance I discovered quite by accident that I think has the potential to scare people straight, so to speak. In other words, get them to refrain from criminal behavior. I can't give you a very satisfactory answer to the question about the consciousness aspect in the deceased, other than to say that in side-by-side comparisons of brain scans during dreaming by living patients and those of the recently expired who received the treatment, it does appear to be the case. Except for the intensity of the dream state, we can't tell the scans apart. Of course, without the ability to communicate with the dead, we may never learn the precise effect. Our research suggests that if we can get to a person within a week of death, we can revive and rejuvenate their neurons and induce what appears to us definitively to be a dream state."

"Excuse me," said William Dee, "but if this Terminal Terror is virtually indestructible and you can revive some form of consciousness in the dead, then aren't you persecuting innocent people simply through your experiments?"

"Possibly, but not very likely. All of the subjects in our tests to date who have been experimented on after death were themselves death-row inmates who were executed. As you know, for a long time we stopped putting people to death, but now it is underway en masse because the latest advances in DNA testing and truth serum technology have reduced to near zero the chances of putting innocent people to death. We obtain the condemned inmates' permission and offer them a last chance to do something positive

for the sake of humanity. We get turned down a lot. And, as for
your second question, it takes a little over a week for the material
to set up into a state where it becomes virtually indestructible, so
we have a window of escape. We haven't let it become permanent
for anyone we've tested who was actually executed. As for an ultimate positive use, it may still be premature to say so, but I think it
might someday eliminate our propensity for evil altogether."

"How the devil could you hope to accomplish that?" Linda
asked.

"Well, deep within our limbic system lie real physical territories
which are necessary for us to engage in acts that we consider evil.
The material I've discovered sets up an obstacle to such behavior
in the same way that a raincoat keeps you from getting wet. We
don't yet understand precisely how or why it has this effect, but
it's very clear that it does. It seems that repeated exposure to the
material simply removes acts of evil as a response option from one's
repertoire of behavior. For example, all of a sudden, the idea to kill
someone in a fit of rage simply does not appear on one's decision
tree as an acceptable option; in fact, the idea seems abhorrent in the
extreme. We know this from brain scans performed while the subjects were given options for acting in highly emotional situations.
So we know that the respondents weren't just telling us what we
wanted to hear."

"You mean this is like giving someone a frontal lobotomy?"
Dee said sternly.

"No, I wouldn't say that at all. We've noted no decrease in a
person's ability to express positive emotion, just negative behavior."

"Sounds great," said Dee, "but too good to be true to me, doctor,
and I would like to be wrong about this one." Smyth nodded in the
affirmative and lifted his glass as if to toast the positive note, and
several others did the same.

Angela Black was seated next to James Tall Tree, and most everyone present was aware that the two were exchanging frequent endearing glances. Dee felt his hunch about his junior partner was on target. She and Tall Tree were involved, and until now it had been a secret. Angela said, "Well, if just being exposed makes a person dread the substance so much that they no longer even consider committing evil acts, then why would you need to threaten anyone with spending thousands of years in a nightmare?"

"Good question," Smyth said. "It just may be the case that psychopaths and psychotics need something more, since some of them revel in their own punishment. Some of my colleagues believe that in order to affect the conscience, a person must actually have one. At this point, though, it seems clear that this substance works especially well on people without a conscience. To have such feelings after never experiencing the benefit of a conscience before seems to really freak out the psychopaths. We've conducted numerous tests in prisons on known psychopaths, and the results are astonishing. I mean, their reactions are often over the top, like suddenly having something that's always been missing is a ten on the psychic seizure magnitude. And then again, there is the revenge factor. Some people would likely derive a great deal of satisfaction out of imagining such a punishment for someone who they thought had it coming."

Angela started to speak but paused for a moment before saying, "Then maybe those people should get a dose of it for themselves. I've looked at your site about genocide, Wendell, and while I think it's well done, it's much too disturbing. You are aware, are you not, that Nietzsche warned of looking too long into the abyss and that the danger in gazing at monsters is that one can become a monster?"

"Yes, Angela, it's ironic you would quote Nietzsche, since it was his writing that spurred my interest in the subject of evil into high gear. I don't recommend looking long into the abyss. Looking too long leads to psychological numbing. But neither do I advocate living a life so sheltered that one lives in constant denial of the diabolical malevolence of the real world we live in. We don't want to become monsters, nor do we want to be eaten by them. So it's important to know their habits, their tactics, their deeds and what they look like in their many disguises."

Ellen sat up straight, tilted her head, and said, "Doctor Smyth, I abhor animal cruelty. I'm always on the lookout for it, regardless of whether it involves factory farming, neglect for pets, or just gratuitous cruelty. I'm always ready to object and speak up. But I don't need to see examples of cruelty to remind myself that it is happening all of the time."

"I believe you, Ellen. That's a good argument," Wendell said with what he hoped was a fatherly smile.

"Okay," Angela continued. "What would have prompted you to create something like this in the first place, and why on earth would it ever have occurred to you to smell it?"

"Well, for decades we have been trying to eliminate or reduce the propensity for criminal behavior with brain chemistry. Years ago oxytocin inhalers were created to help nursing mothers bond with their new born infants. I was trying to improve upon oxytocin with the goal of simply reducing hostility in instances of social conflict when I stumbled onto this new substance. I came up with something similar to oxytocin in some respects but with dramatically different properties and effects. The strangest thing is that it also mimics a radioactive isotope in that it shows no sign of aging, and yet it's still not harmful like radiation."

"Wendell, that's bizarre," said Angela.

"Bizarre it is, but if its power can be harnessed and put to the best use possible, it could change human destiny. I can explain the substance in mathematical terms, but that's probably not the best approach here. Think about it this way: deep within the limbic system in our brains is the amygdala. Somewhere between the kind of fear that gives a person super strength in an emergency and the point at which a person freezes completely, unable to move in a panic, there seems to be a receptor and regulator for fair warnings, things we should avoid, things we shouldn't do so as not to entertain our greatest fears. It would seem that our reptilian brain function realizes at some level that if we don't kill needlessly, then we are unlikely to be killed."

Clearing his throat, Ruben put his elbows on the table, hands under his chin, and said, "Well, folks, Ellen's comment is insightful. Perhaps it's because the general public is so disconnected from the slaughter necessary for the dinner table that when they are confronted with the reality that inhumane brutality is considered routine business, they see the cruelty as never before. This may suggest that we are headed for a big ideological, empathy-based backlash. But then, on the other hand, those who work on the killing floor of factory farms are most likely numbed to the point of being in desperate need of some way to get their empathy back. So a little T&T might be helpful."

Ruben paused for a moment, made eye contact with everyone present, then looked directly at Wendell Smyth and continued. "You know, doctor, in matters of human behavior, your Terminal Terror takes the metaphorical place of God. Mark Twain pointed out that, in spite of all of the evil noted in the Old Testament, it was the meek and the gentle Jesus who turned out 'a thousand billion times crueler' by proclaiming punishment beyond the grave. You, sir, appear to have put hellfire and damnation into a bowl of Tupperware. Anybody drink to that?"

# THE INVINCIBLE

BLOOD WAS FLOWING freely now. He stood facing them: three wolves each bleeding from the mouth and one with a severely torn shoulder, a wound which he himself had inflicted. Their expressions bore a hypnotic manner of confusion, of incidents beyond the comprehension of animal nature, of beasts bred of thousands of years of experience contrary to what had just occurred. They had each struck this domestic brute with killing or disabling attacks, and still he stood his ground, unscathed, defiant, and standing before them with an air of conquest and unearned superiority. He growled savagely, a signal that he could wreak great injury and pain upon his enemies. Lunging forward, he caught the wolf with the injured shoulder off guard, ripping flesh from his hindquarter. Another slash like this and the wild creature would likely not survive.

As Moby moved forward, the wolves slowly backed up, giving him more ground. His confidence was mounting. He had inflicted great damage on his enemies but had not incurred serious injury himself. Most of the splayed blood on his white coat was not his. He lunged forward, missing the alpha male by inches. The pack leader feigned a strike but stopped short of contact. Blood streamed from his mouth. He backed away slowly, turned, and disappeared into a thicket, sprinting off into the dark shade of timber. The others followed him, and in an instant Moby was alone, panting heavily but unharmed. He didn't pursue his enemy and he didn't know why; he just let it be. He turned and headed back to his home at a leisurely gait. Tiptoeing through the underbrush in search of a hare, a frightened red fox, ever on alert for wolves, froze in place. Moby noticed but headed home instead of pursuing the inferior predator.

A downdraft from the mountains brought a hint of colder weather in the wind, and he felt good, strong, and powerful. He had met his foe, head-to-head in greater numbers and had prevailed. Without comprehension of a perspective on his triumph, he had lived up to something he had been born to achieve that required no creature reflection for acknowledgment. It was just the way of the domestic and the wild, it was simply life: animal life.

He could see the cabin, and as soon as he broke into the open, he saw his master, picked up her scent, and heard her call his name. The Terrells had just returned from the anniversary party.

"Moby, where have you been? You bad dog!" Ellen's tone was high pitched and did not match the literalness of her words. She was overjoyed. Her dog was safe after all. But when she grabbed his collar she could see the blood all over his coat. She attached her leash and ran toward the cabin, pulling the big dog in tow behind her like a piece of unwieldy luggage. "Uncle Vince, Aunt Ginger, look," she said. "Mr. Whitehead's suit of armor worked. Moby has been in a fight with the wolves and he's okay."

At the time Adam had first brought Moby to the valley seven years ago as a puppy, he was very much aware of the danger of wolves to domestic dogs. When he gave Ellen the dog, he'd had a suit of armor constructed that could be easily removed for grooming and adjusted for size as the dog grew. It covered all the vulnerable parts of his body. In fact, the more susceptible the area, the larger were the spikes, so any animal striking at his throat or any vulnerable body part would close its teeth on a mouthful of razor sharp metal. Today the titanium suit of linked spikes had worked even better than expected.

"Mr. Whitehead will be very pleased to hear about this," Ellen said. "Moby has been wearing it out here for years, but this is the first time he's ever needed it that I know of." Then she turned to Moby, as if she expected the big white dog to understand every word she spoke. "But that doesn't mean you need to be fighting with wolves." She took his head carefully in her hands. "I'm going to give you a bath when we get back home, but I don't know how we're going to get rid of this blood."

The statement startled Ginger. She put her hand on Vince's shoulder when a lone wolf broke the silence with a mournful howl. Moby stiffened and his fur bristled. All three present thought the same thing: Wolves howling at this hour in the vicinity of people was spooky. It felt strange.

To the big white dog, the call was his reason for being. He didn't know it the way humans know things, but just the same, he knew as he was meant to know, by simply *being alive*.

## OWEN SANDBURG'S JOURNAL:
## A WORLD RUN AMOK

HE DETECTIVE TELLS me once again that there is a good chance Amy was murdered by a serial killer. I've authorized him to hire any additional people and spend all he might need to help catch the bastard. I await his capture with the patience of an eager predator.

There is so much in the news today, it's hard not to get hooked and watch reports around the clock, and many people I know do just that. A revolution is underway in China, thousands of people have taken to the streets, in many cases murdering well-to-do individuals, plundering their property and burning their houses. So many people are taking part in street riots that at times the military personnel sent to control them have broken and run away rather than fire on them. It would seem one too many straws has finally broken the camel's back, one too many peasants starved for want of a bowl of rice, while a few party insiders live like royalty.

A growing fear in this country is that China may soon be taken over by rice farmers, and if that happens, the question becomes, can we trust them with nuclear weapons? Now, just this evening, there is talk of uprising on the streets in India, whose grudge against Pakistan defies easy comprehension. Shots are being fired, and people are dying en masse on both sides of the border, especially in Kashmir.

A social analyst interviewed on television last night declared that there is nothing new in the world and that Adam 21 has made no real difference in our lives. He said we have always been able to look out upon the world and view reality; perhaps it is simply a sign of the times that idiots get free air time. Before Adam 21, the public in every country looked out at the world and saw only what they were taught to see. That's why this new technology is wreaking such havoc. Preferred reality is no longer an option unless one crawls into a hole.

Officialdoms everywhere are losing their ability to justify their existence. For years now, there has been relentless pressure for people to learn to think for themselves, simply because so much we have been taught is clearly and demonstrably false—Adam 21 proves it daily. The trouble is, it's hard to tell if many people are really thinking for themselves, because we have no official way to quantify it. Social media offer clues, but there is no consensus of public opinion or social movement with a clear ideological direction, just the appearance of chaos, revealing no sign of order.

Sadly, the babble of nonsensical ideas about the true nature of the reality we are presently experiencing has long since passed the outer bounds of absurdity, social media having become an exercise of narcissistic madness, of trivia served up as freedom of speech, while amounting to meaningless commercial garbage advocating the consumption of consumption and the assumption of too many assumptions. In other words, people have internalized that which was commercially intended but to further extremes than anticipated. At first, customers became consumers, and then consumers became narcissistic zealots, whose opportunities for originality were smothered by brand names and logos.

To the astute observer, it is clear that human technology amounts to an environmental malignancy for the planet and that our inventiveness leads to an exponential waste of finite resources. This reality becomes ever clearer when one looks back in time via Adam 21 and observes that when the fastest transportation available was horseback, people had to earn their living close to home. These days, people commute long distances, even though working at home has never been more practical or technologically easier. Some even fly to work via commercial jets, often wasting much more in resources than is created in the value of their work. But then, I said astute observers, didn't I? Too bad there aren't many who fit this category. Ironically, a lot of car traffic today is as slow as it was by horse and buggy.

Before Adam 21, sociologists feared that we would amuse ourselves to death with frivolous entertainment. Today they talk of misreading the past and drawing the wrong conclusions about the present, which discounts the future by focusing on enemies real and imagined, mostly the latter. The real confusion comes from watching people engaged in a broad range of activities without knowing what's really on their minds. Every overt action in the past viewed by a million viewers has the potential for a million theories about conspiracy as its cause and for an exponential increase in contempt—contempt steeped in a venomous strain of hatred that self-replicates of its own putrid emotional vapor and self-generating feedback loops.

The interviewer signed off from her conversation with the famous idiot last night by asking how we are to discern good from evil without some kind of authority which we will all be able to recognize as having the credentials and wisdom to tell us the difference. How indeed? Certainly not by listening to imbeciles interviewing idiots.

Here in America, more and more poor people are migrating to southern states simply to keep from freezing to death in winter, in spite of continuous warnings that there is not enough fresh water to accommodate an increase in population and unmindful that home- less people use less water than any other group. Talk of wisdom in such conditions is secular blasphemy. Ironically, mankind finds himself in a pot of water on a hot stove, and we are on the verge of slowly heating to a boil—a boiling over—an evaporation of life as we have come to know it.

My advice is to get ready for chaos. The voices in my head are beginning to whisper, and what they are saying is something that I don't think you are going to want to hear.

## THE SEER SPEAKS

ON THE EARLY-MORNING edition of NFR's feature called the "World of Good News," a broadcaster identifying himself as Benton Barber, or the Seer, as he preferred to be addressed, announced that twice a week he would make proclamations that could not and should not be ignored, that is, if you wanted to go to heaven. He said he was privy to much information that had been classified top-secret in decades past and that he would now reveal truths on a regular basis in order to verify his role as Seer.

"My first proclamation folks, hear me now, is to reveal to you that I know what happened to Congressmen Hale Boggs and Nick Begich, who disappeared in Alaska many years ago in 1972. Why do you think Adam 21 doesn't reveal any evidence of the twin-engine Cessna? The Seer knows the facts. The question is, will you know the truth when the truth is told?"

The introduction of the Seer made the national news in every deliverable format and immediately became the subject of panel punditry. Scores of people who were around at the time of the disappearance of the Congressmen and still remembered one of the largest searches in aviation history were interviewed, speculating about how unlikely it was that anyone could have access to anything that was not already public about the matter. Some said it was a ruse for publicity, nothing more, and then a photo of a downed plane with two men standing beside it was posted on the Seer's web site. The picture was grainy, appearing to have been taken in the rain, but nothing conclusive could be discerned. It couldn't be ruled out or in. It didn't make a lot of sense. What could Adam 21 have to do with it? The photo was obviously taken on a cloudy day. If the aircraft had gone down anywhere near where it was thought to have crashed, there would likely have been more cloudy days than clear.

The larger question was what connection could Barber have had to Alaska decades earlier? He allegedly had explained once to an employee that nothing works its magic in the mind of the public better than the notion of conspiracy. The deep dark secret to keeping a conspiracy alive, he maintained, was to flirt with facts but never provide them in earnest. "You present the lure and set the hook, but you never reel it in all the way. To the contrary, you keep the suspense in play. The whole secret to hyping paranoia is simply to scare people who are easily scared. Scare 'em, tease 'em, then scare 'em and tease 'em some more."

Barber supposedly had said this before acquiring the status of the Seer. The former employee, a technician-turned-disciple who had maintained Barber's radio studio for some years, had further quoted Barber as saying, "Remember, people will go to extremes never imagined possible to once and for all rid themselves of the idea that the world is ruled by chance. Better to have the Devil pulling the strings than face the insane rages of chance and uncertainty. Don't believe it? Look around. Ask questions, teasing questions, but don't stop, ever. And never, but never, tell all there is to tell while a fish is still on the line."

Attempts to fact check and reconfirm that this is indeed what the Seer had said led to a dead end because the claimant had been excommunicated and was reportedly in hiding, insisting his life was in grave danger.

# A HOPEFUL AGENDA

IN THE MORNING, Thornton's guests arrived early for breakfast and eagerly assaulted Ruben's gourmet mix of coffee. They had stayed up late, mostly engaging in small talk to make it seem that things were not as bad as everyone believed. They needed to reassure themselves that they were still the same people they'd always been with the same hopes and aspirations they'd always had.

In the spacious underground conference room, the group seated themselves around a dark mahogany table. The chairs had tall backs with leather cushions, and more than one of the guests judged them comfortable enough to sleep in. Dee was at one end of the table, Thornton at the other, while Sanchez remained in a corner near a scenic window panel by himself. Angela Black, James Tall Tree, and Adam and Linda Whitehead sat together with their backs to the spectacular picture-window view being projected on one wall via camera. Wendell Smyth took a middle seat facing the screen view of Mount McKinley. Thornton opened the meeting.

"I hope everyone had a good time last evening. I certainly did, and I trust everyone got a good night's rest in spite of the news reports." He looked around the room, exchanging affirmative glances with each guest, trying to judge their growing interest in the real purpose of the meeting.

"I wasn't terribly specific when I asked you folks to get together here for what I characterized as a thoughtful and relaxing sabbatical. I very much want you to have a good time and feel at home. Your curiosity must be getting the best of you, so bear with me as the mystery is about to end. Last night's news further underscored the current state of the world and the fact that we may be on the verge of a major conflict or even the possibility of a world war. Well, I've been talking with a group of corporate leaders and philanthropists who propose to come up with a plan to ease some of the tension. We are still in the discussion stages, and quite frankly, things have not been progressing as smoothly as I had hoped. But if we can all agree on a plan, I think we might achieve something worthwhile.

"I had an idea a few weeks ago that I can't stop thinking about, and in the meantime, I've convinced myself, at least, that it has some merit. I would like your input on how we might make it a reality. What I plan to do is to use the only proven power we have to alter opinions around the world. I want to convince the group I'm working with that we can *advertise* our way to a better world. In other words, folks, I want to attack intolerance, bigotry, and global ethnocentrism with the full force of Madison Avenue.

"But before I make my pitch to the group and enlist the help of one or more ad agencies, I want to explore the ethics of the idea and make sure we are on firm moral ground to begin with. I spoke to James about this a while back, and he suggested a group brainstorming session with brains the caliber of yours." Thornton picked up his coffee cup and began to peer into the dark liquid, letting his guests reflect on his message. When it was clear that no one was ready to comment, he began again.

"I feel privileged to discuss this project with the primary architects of Adam 21. I don't think there is anyone here who doesn't know that James still advises the president on occasion and is also still a consultant to the current group of Adam 21 administrators. So,

with the pack of Dire wolves on the Adam 21 panel downstairs. If you didn't see them last night, then you should do so at the first opportunity. Someone sent us their coordinates a few months back, and we've been locked onto them ever since. The wolves have been extinct for thousands of years, but not because of a lack of intelligence.

"Anyway, I call the magnificent creature who leads the pack Machiavelli. He is a beautiful beast, a great provider, and the epitome of strength and vitality, firm but even-tempered with subordinates, and yet he is utterly ruthless with his enemies both real and potential. He has acquired more wisdom about holding on to power than any creature I have ever studied. He knows instinctively who among the younger males he encounters might someday become a threat to his leadership. He allows them into his pack and lulls them into accepting his superiority. And then, when the moment is right and he has them alone and in a posture of total submission, he rips their bloody throats out.

"In the meantime, the pack prospers. Now, I have advocated a democratic approach to global relations all of my life, and I'm not changing my position at this late stage, nor am I contradicting my assertion about neutralizing dictators. It's just that some vicious leaders are preferable to democratic types in some situations, so you have to be very careful in your approach. What I'm saying, based on a lifetime of study and of worldly experience, is that there are different tactics to be applied to those who lead the pack and to those who aspire to lead but aren't smart enough.

"All of the goodwill and persuasion your billions can buy will not have any effect, whatsoever, on those whose thirst for power cannot and will not be satiated with anything short of being at the top of the hierarchy. Don't think for one minute that if any one of those younger wolves had been smart enough to topple the alpha male, he wouldn't have done so. But one has to ponder the benefit or liability of having the best and brightest in command. If his subordinates had known how to go about it, they would have taken the risk, regardless of the cost or who else might be eliminated in the process.

"The trouble is, of course, that people are a thousand times more treacherous than wolves. You want to save the world, okay then. Let's be realistic about what you are going to have to do to achieve your goal. My point in a nutshell is that there simply are no universal rules to follow that will guarantee success. Every situation has to be judged on its own merits. Most dictators are bad news, but some aren't."

"I'm sorry," Linda said, "but you have just made a pathetic case for the justification of evil in the world."

"Pathetic, perhaps, but nonetheless true, my dear Linda. Good and evil reside within us, all of us. We try to keep evil at bay with art, good will, compassion, noble aspirations, and reverence for our fellow man. But don't you see, Linda, don't all of you see, that what people need who are oppressed by power is freedom from that oppression, and they need it more than technical expertise or Peace Corps volunteers?

"When we assist maniacal dictators with foreign aid and technical expertise, we enhance their power to oppress. Moreover, the very people who strive for the credentials to be considered experts crave power, and for some, their thirst is unquenchable. Haven't we learned anything from history? With regard to good and evil in the world, there are and always have been double and triple standards. If you live in a place, even a dictatorship, where the best and brightest is actually in charge, then you are in good stead, but since that's usually not the case, you are subject to tyranny by those desperate to hold on to their power. Period. History is very clear about this.

We Americans are complicit as often as not in further enabling oppression of our fellow man."

Ruben was animated now. "Sometimes I think a case could be made that the ratio of good and evil has pretty much remained consistent throughout history. Had it not been for the Nazis, I would have been the first to argue that education and enlightenment are antidotes to evil. But you don't have to get that serious about the matter to see the point. Just think about what politicians say to get elected and then judge their actions once in office to appreciate the truth of the Machiavellian nature of power. Those who seek it are irrevocably corrupted by it, as surely as the sun comes up somewhere tomorrow morning."

"But what you are saying is that the ends justify the means," Angela observed.

Smyth sat forward. "Perhaps, but think about it this way. If this was 1939 and we had the chance to bushwhack Stalin, Mussolini, and Hitler, are you saying that we shouldn't do it?"

"Well, I don't know about the rest of you, but I would have annihilated Hitler in an instant and never looked back," Ruben said.

"I think most everyone here would do the same, but that's not exactly the point, Mr. Sanchez." Angela's voice was sharp.

"That's precisely the point. You see, if I had killed any of those tyrants before they became tyrants, history would have recorded me as being evil incarnate. Hitler was *Time* magazine's Man of the Year in 1935, and by 1938, economists the world over were talking about the German miracle. So, if one of us were to have been able to go back in time and kill Hitler, we would have to live with knowing a historic reality that no one else was aware of, along with punishment for the deed and the stigma of being one of the most reviled human beings on the planet for destroying the German people's hope for a promising future. And please call me Ruben. I don't know if you are familiar with my work, but I have an extensive web site aimed at promoting self-education."

"I'm well aware of your work, Ruben, but I'm not fond of your methods or examples. If I were promoting self-education, I wouldn't use a couple of misogynists to make my case."

"You mean Jack London and Herman Melville."

"Yes, precisely. London was mesmerized by Nietzsche and his Übermensch superman nonsense. There are myriad examples that you could use without those of clear-cut misogynists."

"Look, Ms. Black, they represent an era in which most everyone viewed the world in the same way. It's only ivory-tower academic types who conclude otherwise. If you want to make sense of the world, you can't apply today's standards to the past. Jack London attacked egomania in *Martin Eden* and Nietzsche's superman in *The Sea Wolf*. What he was mesmerized by was the fact that most of his readers didn't get it and to this day they still don't."

"That is my point. If they don't get it, then it's not working, is it? And, Ruben, please call me Angela." She started to continue, but James kicked her gently under the table, his eyes saying let it go.

Thornton broke in and said, "Well, we don't want to get off track, but Ruben may have a point about people whose thirst for power is never satiated. Does anyone think that Hitler would have listened to any sort of reason as a sound argument to lessen his ascent to power?"

No one spoke for an uncomfortable moment, and finally Linda Whitehead said, "If we're going to be discussing the nature of evil, then why didn't you insist that Vince Terrell attend? I think he might have a lot to offer."

"Excellent idea. He said he had to go to Anchorage this morning on business, and Ellen had something to take care of getting ready for school, but I will ask Vince to spend some time with us if at all possible. In fact, I'll make it irresistible. The pilots have been complaining about not getting enough air time, so I'll tell Vince we'll provide him helicopter transportation. Believe it or not, their dog loves to fly."

"I know he does," Linda agreed. "But if you do that, Bob, you need to invite Ginger. And ask Ellen to come along and bring the dog, if she's amenable to the idea."

"I'll make the call. In the meantime, I'm having the gentleman who brought you here from the airport take you on a Hummer ride on the Denali Highway this afternoon. I think we could all use a break, and we'll pick up this discussion about the world's evildoers again in the morning, if you folks are willing. I have some calls to make."

"Oh, and Adam," Ruben broke in. "You asked earlier about Adam 21 and its effect on people. You can never tell how people are going to react to things. Their reactions have less to do with whether the things in themselves are good or not than with who the people are. Some of us are sensitive to too much of a good thing, and others just succumb."

Continuing, Ruben leaned back in his chair. "Every time I think about this subject, it reminds me of the first time many Alaskans visit Hawaii. Typically they get off the plane and are captivated by the little birds singing, chirping, and whistling. It just blows them away. The melodious singing is magically wonderful, enthralling. But then they get up one morning, say on day three, go to the window, and scream, 'Shut up you little noisy bastards. Let's have some peace and quiet!'

"Some people feel the same way about Adam 21, but perhaps not enough. After a while, too many get hooked on anything hookable, and it's the hookability that does it, not the content. Not only that, but we human beings are portals systems by design.

When we look out at the world, we are actually looking back in time, because most of what we observe is constructed from the residue of memory. We understand now because we understood then, so to speak. Don't ever beat yourself up over your scientific contribution, Adam. You will go down as one of the greatest scientists in history, and this is as it should be." Finishing these words, Ruben noticed a tear streaming down Linda's face.

Linda Farnsworth's parents were killed in a car accident when she was only three. Raised by an unmarried aunt who still clung to the Victorian values of her grandparents, Linda had lived a very sheltered life until she was in her thirties. Tall and slender, with grayish blonde hair and sparkling green eyes, her appearance was striking.

Having married an older man late in life, she wanted to make up for the years she'd spent alone. Now her greatest concern was the health of her aging husband and especially his memory. Her fears were heightened in 2028 because the last waves of the Baby Boom generation were slamming ashore, causing an alarming shortage of gerontology services, particularly in addressing the growing crisis of dementia.

At first, Linda had high hopes for this get-together with close friends, but now she was worried. Adam increasingly experienced bouts of confusion, and he seemed to have become suspicious of himself, as if he were some kind of traitor to his past for questioning his short-term memory. On more than one occasion, Adam had told her he felt his forgetfulness was like accidently hitting the delete key on a computer file. You know the data are still in there, but you don't have the software to retrieve any of the pieces. Such feelings, he had said, cascade into awareness of still being alive but unable to reboot intellectually, a fate much worse than death.

Ruben stood up and walked to the door. Turning back to face

the group, he said, "Folks, we can boil down this discussion to our perception of reality and our relationship to power. It's that simple and that hard because each affects and corrupts the other. But, as long as we heed the connection and remember to keep it in mind and memory, there is hope."

I'M SLIPPING AGAIN. Days without meds. My mind is never quiet. Always noise, talking, incessant talking, never quiet, voices but mostly they don't they speak to me directly, instead they're talking about me. Sometimes I suspect it's because of the Rain Crow.

More than a half-century ago, growing up in southwest Missouri, I lived near a big hardwood forest, where a mighty oak tree suitable for a postcard picture of an English moor separated our property from the woods. One cloudy afternoon, on a still but misty summer day, I heard a haunting bird call coming from somewhere in the branches of that majestic tree. I ran back to the house to ask what could make such a sound. My grandmother said it must be a Rain Crow. I went back to the tree and stood for what seemed like an hour, straining for a view of the creature making that haunting sound. Then, just as the call began again, I stepped to a vantage point to see a beautiful bird sitting all alone on a branch and singing the song of the Rain Crow.

I raised my Daisy Red Ryder BB gun, and in the next instant, that beautiful creature came crashing down through the tired limbs of that vain old tree. The clamor was heart-wrenching, as if the sanctity of a great cathedral had been blasphemed in the plain sight of God. And it was I, Owen Sandburg, who was to blame, barely old enough to know what I was doing but smart enough to know guilt when I felt it. Nearby, the cooing of a mourning dove announced that it had witnessed my depravity.

When I ran home, my grandmother could see I was distressed about something. She asked what was wrong and I said nothing. And then she said that I should always remember that one should never kill a Rain Crow. To do so would mean that dark clouds would follow you around for the rest of your days. She said that every time it rained, it would be a reminder that you had sinned against one of God's most blessed creatures and that whenever you were punished, for whatever reason, it might just be that the spirit of the Rain Crow would have the option of adding a tax to the incident. Every time you heard its call, you'd be reminded of your sin.

A half-century has passed, and the Rain Crow still makes demands of me, excessive demands, when I go without my meds for any length of time, even though I have made restitution a thousand times over. You think that I am mad? Perhaps. The cooing of mourning doves still haunts me just the same. For now, I suspect that no one knows except you, me, and them, along with the dead bird whose decayed body is long gone from the earth.

Oh, and in case I forgot to mention the news, two talk-radio hate mongers, Brandon Murray and Tim Kendrick, have been hospitalized with what is thought to be Fast-Track AIDS. Wonders never cease. I'm thinking maybe there was a tale of a Rain Crow in their past, and I wonder what they will think now when they hear the plaintive song of a mourning dove. I suspect someone will remind them of what it means.

## THE GREATER GOOD

VINCE HAD A full day planned, but when he received the request from Thornton about returning to rejoin the group discussion, he found the idea irresistible, especially when Thornton offered to send the helicopter for the family and the dog. He figured the relief he felt meant he needed a break; it might give him some time to put the Rayburn thing in better perspective. Ellen would come along as there was more crime-scene data she could crunch at Thornton's without anyone even being aware of her presence.

When Thornton opened the meeting he looked at Vince and Ginger and said, "Thanks for coming back on such short notice. Where is Ellen?"

"She's in the IT room," said Ginger. "Thank you for getting us here so quickly."

"She is more than welcome here, and I would very much like for her to attend, if you and Vince don't mind."

"Okay, I'll send her a text." Ginger turned to Vince, who voiced no objection.

"What we are trying to do is come up with a sound approach for cooling tensions in the world through an advertising campaign. If that sounds rather like a squirrelly proposition, let me add that if we go through with this, it will involve billions of dollars." Both Vince and Ginger looked about the room as if to say, "Okay, we're game."

Thornton began, "So far, we've gotten stuck in a quagmire about whether we have to use a different standard when dealing with the general public and with the leaders of their respective countries, regardless of who and where they are. Ruben tells us that people with a thirst for power cannot be dealt with like ordinary folks. Isn't that about the gist of it, Ruben?"

"Yeah, close. I have no doubt you can convince people of just about anything with a good ad campaign. Propaganda is propaganda, but it doesn't work with tyrants. They have to be dealt with separately, in my book, if you and the other benefactors are going to get your money's worth."

"Vince, I'm curious to know. What do you think of Dr. Smyth's T&T solution?" James asked, as Ellen took a seat beside Ginger.

"I hope you don't mind me saying so, but it sounds pretty outlandish to me. I just can't imagine that something as simple a sniffing a substance can put the fear of God into anyone. I think I would have to see for myself before I would believe it. But why do you ask?"

"I'm just thinking that it might be something to use on Thornton's world leaders."

"You're not going to scare people away from grasping for more and more power," Ruben said quickly.

"You're not going to find a consensus for rubbing them out, either," James added.

"You guys think we're nuts or what?" Thornton asked, his eyes on Vince, Ginger, and Ellen. Ginger just shook her head gently to indicate she was still thinking. Vince squirmed in his chair, and Ellen's inquisitive expression said she had nothing to add. After a moment, Thornton said, "Off the top of my head, I would say that Ruben has a good point. We do, after all, have a two-tiered approach in all of society, one for law-abiding citizens and one for lawbreakers. Criminals don't abide by the same rules as law-abiding citizens. So, if you set out to change minds, it might be useful to acknowledge that what works for one category of individuals won't work for another."

"I would need to sleep on it, but instinctively I can appreciate something similar in the criminal mind and those with an insatiable appetite for power," Vince said, leaning back and putting his hand to his chin to think.

Linda Whitehead sat upright in her chair, feeling a sense of vindication for having asked that Vince join the group. Not bad for a cop, she thought to herself, not bad at all. She felt better about today than yesterday because Adam was better and seemed alert.

"So tell us, Vince," said Ruben. "Do you think cops have a privileged view of good and evil? Don't you develop some kind of sixth sense about who's lying and who's telling the truth?"

"That's what most people think, including cops," said Vince, "but it's not really true. The fact is that cops are like everyone else when it comes to reading people. Oh, some do develop an edge, but that's all it is and in most cases not much of one. I have some particular quirks of my own in this regard about the sense of smell, but I suspect all these things do is give somebody a bit of unjustified confidence that may at some point actually become justified simply because it leads to persistence and never giving up. The studies show that the more experience a cop has, the less reliable his instincts are about truth-telling in particular and that's because of a really simple reason."

As Vince paused to get his thoughts together, Ruben broke the silence. "And that reason would be?"

"It's because liars are often psychopaths, and psychopaths are often the most practiced and polished deceivers among us. But, psychopaths aside, anyone who can convince themselves to believe their own lies can be pretty convincing. I'm surprised you aren't aware of that, Ruben."

"Oh, I'm aware of it. I'm just surprised to hear it from someone in your line of work. And it's not often that I'm in the company of people with whom I would feel comfortable declaring that many of our most famous heroes were in fact psychopaths. Psychopaths are manipulative, scheming, deceptive, conniving, charming, and without conscience. Doesn't that sound like a description for a politician or world leader?

"I don't want to burst anyone's idealistic bubble, but we are here to talk about good and evil, so wouldn't it be worthwhile to admit up front that we live in a society that enjoys a significant contribution by psychopaths? If we cut to the chase on the subject of good and evil, I would suggest that evilness is born of the seeds of ignorance, especially when man tries to deny his animal nature, because that's when he begins to do things far worse than any animal would ever do."

"Really?" Angela asked. "Ruben, are you pulling our collective legs or just playing mind games with us again?"

"I'm not playing games at all, but I'm not sure this group readily appreciates the gravity of the situation. Humans are animals from brain to bone. We are gathered here to talk about getting beyond the good and evil in the world in order to ease world tensions, are we not? Well, consider the irony in the notion that in playing devil's advocate, I've already got us to what would appear to be a black-and-white moral dilemma, and yet it is anything but.

"Machiavelli is often dismissed as an immoral dragoon, but he was no slouch when it came to strategies for gaining and maintaining power. This ad campaign that you are counting on, Bob, is but an expression and demonstration of power. Machiavelli was an adman extraordinaire. He also wrote the playbook for political psychopaths. You've only to take a close look at most of the world's leaders to see that these kinds of people are society's sour cream, they rise to the top by the very nature of who they are and how they operate. Now who is being naïve here, Angela? If nothing is done to deal specifically with the tyrants of the world, then nothing gets done. Period."

"So, what do we do, Ruben? Act like psychopaths?" Ellen asked.

"You're catching on fast, young lady," Thornton smiled. Then he turned to James, who had remained unusually quiet all morning. The man could look through you if he wanted to, but now he appeared ready to speak his mind, a detectable anxiousness behind the mysterious eyes and stoic presence.

Sitting up straight, James said, "Sorry if I've seemed inattentive. It's just that I've been here before. It hasn't been that long since Dee and Angela and I, and a few others, were in a meeting very much like this. Actually there were many others because we had lots of groups, so many that I have trouble remembering all of them. They're sort of a blur in my mind, like a fog of concern without real resolution.

"I'm sad to say we didn't accomplish much back then, but what troubles me goes much deeper than that. Before we made our initial announcement about Adam 21 technology, we had scores of meetings hoping to anticipate every possible occurrence so we would be ready for any and all objections. We were so confident, we thought we could handle every problem imaginable. But as fate would have it, we heard what we wanted to hear.

"Bob, you've called us together with the intention of devising an ad campaign to heal the ill-will in the world. Well, it's not that I think your idea is bad. I'm just sorry we didn't do something like that from the very beginning. We knew the technology was going to open old wounds. We said so, time and again, but I guess we just thought that because we knew about it, things would be okay somehow. We went over and over the negative possibilities, and sure enough, they have come to fruition in spades.

"So, don't get me wrong, professor," Tall Tree spoke directly to Adam Whitehead and glanced to Thornton. "It's not Adam 21 technology that is to blame for the current unsettled state of the world. The responsibility for that goes to the managers of the project and to me personally. We knew about the turmoil Adam 21 would produce, but we did little other than acknowledge that we knew. Now it all seems rather like a pathetic excuse to move ahead without bothering further with the problems we clearly anticipated but didn't take seriously enough."

Whitehead said nothing. He sat quietly, gazing at a window panel as if he were a thousand miles away. After a few moments, he asked, "Do you think the world crisis is because of Adam 21?"

The concerned looks on the faces of all present spoke volumes. After a long silence, tears began to well in Linda's eyes. She turned away from the others, gazing at a screen panel to avoid eye contact, thinking perhaps what Adam had always feared was coming to pass—that without memory, life is over. From across the room, Ginger drew Linda's attention with a whisper, after which no words were necessary. The empathetic look on Ginger's face assured her friend that she understood her concern and she was not alone.

sewn into the canvas. The stove took some getting used to, not because it didn't work but because it worked too well. The outside temperature dropped precipitously at night if there were no clouds, and yet, if Jonas didn't load the stove just right, it became too hot to sleep.

The site elevation provided a good view in every direction, save the one in which Mount McKinley blotted out the sky on clear days. Still, he could see a long ways in that direction when he focused on it. The mountain was so overpowering, it took your breath away if you turned toward it suddenly without anticipating its presence.

This was no overnight military operation, so he was determined to take his time making the camp as comfortable as possible. Whatever time he stayed here would likely not be enough. He was well above the creek, but close enough that he didn't have to walk far for water. He erected his tent adjacent to a very large boulder with an L-shaped embankment so that the back of the tent butted up against a rock, and another side rested next to an earth wall much higher than the tent. This being bear country, he felt better knowing a curious bruin could come from only two directions and not four.

In front of the tent he pounded eight-foot stakes into the ground and stretched a long tarpaulin for shelter, enabling him to walk about or sit outside during the rain and remain dry. For drying his clothes, he stretched two lines that would double as guard lines at night with objects hand-tied to hang below the line that would rattle if disturbed. Just inside his shelter, he arranged large stones for a cooking fire, and in a nearby tree, he fashioned a rope-bound bundle to keep the food most tempting to bears high above the ground. A spotting scope set on a tripod provided a wide-angle view of the whole valley.

When he felt mostly settled, Jonas climbed to the top of the boulder to see what more could be seen from the higher vantage point. Just as he turned to survey the valley from the added height, the blind spot in his right eye caused him to misjudge where to put his foot. He grabbed desperately for something to hold on to but fell like a stone, cracking his skull on the boulder on the way down. He lay motionless at the base of the rock.

before knew that when the bright lights came up, the holding chain would be automatically released and the fight was on. There was no barking coming from the pit now, only snapping and deep guttural growling.

The wolf made no noise at all, just crouched low and moved from side to side like a cobra sizing up a nervous rodent. Satan was flushed full of adrenalin. He pulled at the chain with all of his weight, expecting a release at any moment, his chance to rip these beasts apart. It was in moments like these that he became his rage; this was what his life experience up to now had prepared him to do: kill. And he was better at the task than any foe he had ever met in battle. He might be a recent species in terms of evolution, but he was a primordial warrior down to the very marrow in his bones.

Satan found no approval outside the pit; he was only tolerated by humans. Red said petting him would make him soft, and so the dog rarely felt a human hand in any manner, except one given in preparation for fighting or in celebratory attention when he left the dirt floor drenched in his opponent's blood.

The light flashed, and Satan hit the mastiff just below his throat. Fresh blood spurted forth, though the tear was not deep. Before Satan could get a better grip, the wolf lashed him behind the ear and then in the flank and again on his back. As he turned on the wolf, the mastiff bore down on him from above. All three animals spun about the pit with feverish rage, the blood of each mixing with the rich Missouri soil.

The dog killer's specialty was to kneel low to the ground, move in sideways, and at the last minute swing about, grabbing one of its opponent's legs. Then it would throw itself backward as it bit down hard, often snapping the limb and leaving the animal crippled. Not with Satan, though. Satan always moved his head low to the ground, and each time the wolf made for his legs, it paid with a rip to its muzzle.

The skirmish of ripping and tearing went on for more than a half-hour. Satan was slowing down. He couldn't apply his death grip because there were two of them. He had the mastiff in a death clinch numerous times, but the wolf slashed him dearly when he tried to hold on. Warm blood from all three combatants was forming a shallow pool, a symbol of dedication—a sort of implied celebration of their valor as a human would see it. For the beasts, it was simply life fighting to live.

Eventually the fury in the pit began to subside. Red was swearing and drinking in big gulps. He was too drunk to fight, and he knew it, or he would have lit into the phony-sounding Englishman. For the first time ever, Satan was growing weak. He had lost a lot of blood. Most of the crimson-stained dirt represented his courage and commitment.

With increasing frequency, the light in the pit flashed, flickered, and dimmed until finally, just as the mastiff bit into Satan's shoulder and the wolf was on his back, total darkness enveloped him and someone yelled, "It's over. He's done."

# THE MENTOR

INSIDE THE ORIGINAL cabin on Thornton's land was a small area not much bigger than a closet that Ruben used as his music room. There were expensive speakers on three walls and on the floor, and a big leather recliner in the center with massage intensity selections at the ready. Ruben had preselected music set to play automatically when someone entered the room. You might walk in to hear the Platters singing "Twilight Time" or an orchestral rendition of *Clair De Lune*, depending on the time of day.

On occasion, Ruben would hear something playing in his private retreat, only to find Ellen lying back in his chair listening to his music. At those times, he would sneak off quietly so as not to disturb her, thinking if he could pass on an appreciation for such music as the Platters, the Ink Spots, and a dramatic switch to classical, it would be a teaching triumph.

To Ruben, Ellen Terrell had rapidly become a substitute for his absent granddaughter. Ellen was slightly older than Cynthia Sanchez, and yet she was every bit as curious if not more so. He thought them both beautiful and wanted nothing more than to be in the company of his own blood kin, but Ellen was such a pleasurable companion that she helped fill the void. Although he hated to admit it, Ellen seemed to have much more intellectual depth than Cynthia. Her quiet, but seemingly self-assured presence and her well-thought-out questions made him feel that their conversations were indeed something of value. They gave him a new avenue for simplifying his own philosophical views without resorting to longwinded dissertations. He found that if he simply asked Ellen the right questions, listened to her response, and noticed his own reaction, he could clarify his own opinions better than just going on and on about what he thought and why.

Just now the group was taking an afternoon break from the roundtable discussion. Thornton had arranged another car trip for the newcomers to Alaska. So, Ruben asked Ellen if she would like to take a walk and was surprised when she asked if Uncle Vince could come along. He was still puzzling over it as the three of them walked on a trail headed south following the creek. When they were side by side, Vince said, "Ruben, can I ask you a personal question?"

"Sure."

"When we first met and for a long time after, you used to use the word *amigo* all the time, and now it's so rare that I'm sort of startled when I hear you say it."

Ruben laughed and said, "Funny you should mention it. Long ago, Bob bet me I couldn't break the habit in a month. He gave me ten one-hundred-dollar bills and told me every time I used the word I had to give one back, and if I lost all of them, then I owed him money. At the end of the month, I had only one of them left, and I noticed it in my wallet this morning. Both my father and grandfather used the term regularly, and after so many years, it was hard to stop. Why do you ask?"

"Just the detective in me, I guess. I notice small things, and every once in a while they add up to big things, so I always try to get my questions answered, if I can, to keep my intuition tuned up."

They were walking up a steep grade and everyone but Ellen was breathing heavily. "Ruben, what kind of advice would you give someone about writing their first book rather late in life?" she asked.

A startled look crossed Vince's face, and then he broke into a smile, glancing at Ellen in a way that implied the two shared a secret known only to them. It was a moment Ellen would remember for the rest of her life.

"I guess that would depend on what kind of book it's supposed to be," Ruben said.

"Well," said Vince softly, "I've been thinking of writing about my life experience with criminals and/or the nature of criminality. I don't know whether to try a novel or a nonfiction approach, but I think I've got quite a lot to say if I can just get started."

"What's holding you back?" Ruben asked.

"I'm not sure. Maybe I'm just not certain if I can pull it off. Whatever it is, I'm going to have to start soon or it's never going to happen. I've got a huge collection of notes. The only thing I'm telling myself now is that this case I'm working on has to be gotten out of the way first."

"You mean the serial killer thing I read about in the paper?"

"Yeah, that's it, all right."

"Well, why don't you simply start writing about who it is that you think you are dealing with and see where that leads you?"

Ellen could see from Vince's expression that he was mulling it over, which made her feel good about setting up the conversation. "Not a bad idea," Vince said. "The more I think about it, the less I feel that a novel is appropriate to say what I want to say. But it was a novel that really got me to thinking seriously about the idea, so I'm not sure exactly what to do."

"What was the novel?" Ruben asked.

"It was *Wuthering Heights*. It occurred to me as I read it that Emily Bronte was a young woman who died at age thirty, and yet she had insights worthy of a lifetime of reflection about youth and the nature of hatred and evil. It just seemed to me that if she could do that, then with my experience with the shadowy side of criminal behavior, I ought to be able to shine a meaningful light on the subject. I have some ideas I've never seen in print, which is what prompts me to think it might be a worthwhile effort."

They walked on for several minutes without speaking. Finally Ruben said, "Well, you know what occurs to me is that reading is, in and of itself, a lot like detective work. So, I'm betting this venture is even more suitable to your disposition than you can imagine. What you might want to do is mention your intentions to Thornton. A word from him would likely get you a book contract."

"I may do that, Ruben."

They were just about to turn around and head back when Moby, who was up ahead, started barking as if he had treed something. Ellen ran to catch up to him and in an unusually high-pitched voice screamed, "Uncle Vince! Come quick! Hurry!"

## NEW ACQUAINTANCES

LOUD BARKING RANG in his ears, and a thick wet tongue, bathed in loathsome breath and lashing about like an earthworm resisting a fishhook, repeatedly washed his forehead and temple before Jonas could fully realize what was happening to him. Just moments ago he must have fallen. He felt an oozing and matted liquid mass in his hair, and as he began to fully comprehend the meaning of that, a really large white dog started licking his face. He'd always had a way with animals, so he didn't recoil, even though he was startled by the dog's obnoxious breath. A few yards away, his massive pit bull barked and tugged against his logging chain restraint.

"Are you all right?" a man's voice asked.

With three strangers staring at him, Jonas said, "I think so. I must have fallen off this rock and hit my head." He put his hand to his head and tried to get up but became dizzy and nauseous. "Oh, I think I'd better stay down for a minute."

Moby was aware of the other dog but for the moment kept his attention on the man on the ground. Ellen went inside the nearby tent looking for water as Vince and Ruben knelt down beside the man. Ellen returned with a canteen and a towel. She splashed water on the cloth and put it to the man's forehead. She offered him a drink, but he declined.

"I just need to be still for a little while, I think."

"Okay, look, mister," Vince said. "We're going to lift you up and put you in your tent, okay?"

Jonas nodded slightly and braced himself in anticipation of the move. Once inside the tent, he closed his eyes, about to doze off.

"No. On second thought we're going to have to get you on your feet," said Vince. "Once you've had a head injury, you're not supposed to go to sleep."

"Maybe we should put him in a chair," Ruben said. Jonas nodded faintly, as if he couldn't bear to stand on his feet just yet. Ellen moved a canvas camp chair close by, and Vince and Ruben eased him into it.

"Okay, just let me sit here a minute." Jonas leaned his head back and opened his eyes for several minutes, breathing rapidly.

Vince said, "I'm going back and get Hershel to bring the Hummer down to drive this man to the clinic in Talkeetna."

"You think he should go to the hospital? We can get the helicopter going," Ruben said.

"No, the clinic should be good. It's open 'round the clock, and they provide temporary hospital services for people in the bush."

"Okay. Hurry."

Twice Jonas started to speak but thought better of it. He stared at the ceiling of the tent, blinking as if waking from a dream. The older man and the girl were whispering, but not to him. Then she left his side and approached the pit bull. Jonas shouted, "No! Don't go near the dog," and then he seemed to lose consciousness for a few seconds. When he looked up, the girl was petting Gunny, and the Great Pyrenees stood right by her side with his fur standing at attention. "He doesn't usually let anyone near him, miss. And don't let your dog so close. He'll kill him."

Both animals seemed to sense the hazard of the other, and

both growled a low, guttural, menacing threat to warn the other that mortal combat was imminent. "Pull Moby away, Ellen," said Ruben. She attached the leash and pulled Moby far enough away so that the pit bull settled down.

Twenty minutes later, the dark green Hummer pulled up within thirty yards of the tent, and they carried the sleepy man out, placing him in the back seat. Vince and Ellen accompanied Hershel, and Ruben walked back to the cabin.

After a long time on the road experiencing blurred vision, Jonas was faintly aware of Ellen and Vince's presence as a doctor at the clinic examined him for the second time in an hour. The doctor, an aging gentleman with marshmallow-white hair, said, "Well, he needs to spend the night here for sure, but I think he will be able to resume whatever he was doing by day after tomorrow, if it's not too strenuous."

"So you think he'll be ready to go back to his camp tomorrow?" Vince asked.

"I imagine so, unless something changes and we need to transfer him to the hospital in the valley."

"What time?"

"About noon, I would expect."

"Okay. When Mr. Blythe recovers, tell him that Robert Thornton's driver will be here tomorrow about noon to return him to his campsite. We will check first to make sure he's good to go." Jonas had his eyes closed, so Vince and Ellen left the clinic but not before Ellen told him not to worry about his dog.

"Look, miss. You be careful around him. He's no ordinary pet, and don't let your dog get close to him, okay?"

"Okay. Don't worry. I'm pretty good with animals," Ellen said cheerfully.

Jonas grabbed Vince by the wrist. "Careful, please. He's no

ordinary dog, he's a dog killer." Then he lay back as if his head hurt too much to continue talking.

The Hummer trip back to Thornton's place was rough. The nine-mile off-road trail was made for four-wheelers, but Thornton had it maintained with their dozer as often as needed to make it acceptable for the Hummer. It worked, but if the driver didn't hit each slope just right, the jolts could be severe. As they rode a smooth stretch just beyond the roughest spots, Ellen said, "Uncle Vince, why do you think that man is camped along the creek?"

"I expect he's just trying to get away from it all for a while. He has an ID that says he's recently retired from the Marine Corps. The doc says he claims no family in Alaska, so my guess is that he's just looking for someplace to decide what he wants to do next. Why, what do you think?"

"Oh, I don't know. It just seems strange for someone to come so far in off the highway to camp at a place that he's never been to before."

# CARIBOU CREEK PERSPECTIVE

H E INTRODUCED HIMSELF as Hershel Simpson and said he was a driver and special projects coordinator for Robert T. Thornton. It seemed incomprehensible to Simpson that there were actually people in Alaska who had never heard of Robert Thornton. This Blythe fellow seemed like a different person from the one he had taken to the clinic. He was much more self-assured, Simpson thought, and wouldn't have to go far to seem arrogant, but maybe that was being too harsh.

Finally Jonas spoke and offered Simpson a genuinely friendly smile. "Really nice of you folks to take me to the doctor and then come and get me. I don't know quite what to make of that. I've always heard that Alaska is a pretty friendly place, but this is stretching it a bit, don't you think?"

"Not if you know Robert Thornton, it's not. Best boss I've ever had, best job too. All of these people on Caribou Creek are top-notch in my book, though. You won't find a nicer group of people anywhere. What brings you to our neck of the woods?"

"I'm just out of the Marine Corps after twenty-eight years of service. Just looking for some peace and quiet, I guess."

"You should talk to Ruben Sanchez. He's an ex-Marine, Vietnam veteran from what I hear, but I've never asked him about it. He was one of the people who found you after you fell. Ruben lectures a lot, but he's good people. James Tall Tree is a Native American too, a Lakota like Ruben, but some people say he is even more of a talker than Sanchez. Whatever happened to stoic Indians?" Hershel shook his head side to side, keeping his eyes on the road.

"I would never have figured Ruben for an ex-Marine."

"Well, he was one all right. Got a couple of purple hearts in Vietnam, according to my boss."

"Interesting," Jonas said.

"Everything about our place in the woods is interesting, sir. We've got pretty much the best of everything here."

"If you've got the best, why are you still driving a Hummer? They stopped making these vehicles years ago, didn't they?"

"Oh yes, they did, but you can't beat 'em for this terrain. We've got three of them and enough spare parts, some brand new engines even, and 3-D printers to make new parts enough to last a lifetime, I would think. You can't believe how self-sufficient Mr. Thornton's place is until you see it all. We've got huge underground storage tanks for gasoline and diesel fuel. You name it, and we've probably got it."

Both men lapsed into silence, and Jonas dozed off listening to the Hummer's purring sound as they drove north on the Parks Highway. Jonas woke up when the trail to the creek turned rough. With his automatic pilot system switched off, Hershel was concentrating on the road. They followed steep inclines that bottomed out in areas of lush vegetation and climbed out again to high points where they were visually ambushed with scenes that could have been lifted straight out of *National Geographic.*

Jonas was still lost in his thoughts at first and still too unfamiliar with the terrain to realize when he was back at his campsite. Everything was as he left it, except Gunny had fresh food in his dish. From Ellen, he guessed.

Misty clouds, the promise of darkness, and thoughts of winter snow made the prospect of snuggling up in a down sleeping bag irresistible. It must be something special about Alaska, Jonas thought. He couldn't remember getting this much satisfaction out of simply living moment-to-moment with an appreciation of the little things that for most of his earlier life had gone unnoticed.

There was some bear scat thirty yards or so from camp, but nothing was pilfered. When he bent down to rub Gunny's head, he noticed spots of blood on the dog's coat but no marks. Now how in the hell did that happen, he wondered. God, I hope you didn't attack that beautiful young lady's dog.

# SEMPER FI

WHITE PUFFY SMOKE from the campfire rose erratically on the morning breeze, and a cow moose with her young calf nibbled sapling twigs a scant few yards from where Jonas sat drinking coffee. If he spoke aloud, it wouldn't matter. They had already become accustomed to his presence. Nearby a raven and a magpie argued over turf.

His conversion to a religious frame of mind was beginning to puzzle him. He would go for several hours at a time thinking and remembering his actions in the old days, and then, with a sudden shock of recognition, he would recall Rev. Baldwin and the feelings he had experienced at the encampment. Each time it happened, he would spend an hour or two reading the Bible, even though at times his eyesight made reading difficult. Afterwards, he would spend hours reflecting on the new path he was to follow.

On his second evening of being completely alone after his clinic stay, he was sitting under his canvas awning when he saw someone approaching through the woods. It was Ruben Sanchez.

"Well, you look a little different than last time I saw you," Ruben said.

"Yes, and I feel different too. Jonas Blythe here, and if I recall right, you must be Ruben Sanchez. We met before, but my memory is a bit fuzzy. The man who brought me back here in the Hummer mentioned your name and said you're an ex-Marine."

"Indeed, I am. Semper fi, my friend." The two shook hands. "I can appreciate a faulty memory in your case. You took a pretty good fall off that rock. What in the world were you doing up there?"

"Just trying to tell how far I could see from the vantage point. Not far enough to try it again, I'm afraid."

"So what brings you to our part of the country?" Ruben asked.

"Just looking for a place to chill out for a while. I need to figure out where I want to live. Thought some isolation would be good for a change, and I had a map with a notation about this creek that said the water here was drinkable. You a college professor?"

"No. Never been to college. Why do you ask?"

"The driver said you lecture a lot, so just I figured you must have been an officer in the Corps."

"No, just a grunt. I have a little semper fi left in me, for what it's worth. You know the saying, once a Marine always a Marine, although I might be an exception to that rule."

"Why do you say that?"

"Just the philosopher in me, I guess."

"You a Christian, then? Born again?"

"No. I'm born once and am still very happy about it, at least most days I am. I'm not a Christian. How about you?"

Jonas looked surprised, as if he'd been thinking he'd won something at a drawing only to discover that he'd read the winning ticket number wrong. Studying Ruben's face, he stumbled for something to say. "Yes, I've been saved, just before I came to Alaska."

"Well, if I knew you better, I'd ask you to tell me what you've been saved from, but it's too nice a day. So, I'll just leave this with you and be on my way." Ruben handed him a small package.

"What's this?"

"Just something to start your day with. It's my own special blend of gourmet coffee. Folks around here rave about it, and they're constantly perplexed that I won't give them the recipe."

"Well, thanks for the coffee. There's nothing special about the brand I brought with me, so it will come in handy."

"There are a bunch of folks at Thornton's place about a mile up the creek. Stop by when you get a chance."

"I will do that. Thanks again, and tell that young lady and her father hello for me."

"That was Vince Terrell and his niece, Ellen. I'll be sure to tell them."

"Oh, by the way, when I got back here, my dog had some blood on him. I'm almost afraid to ask, but I'm hoping he didn't have a run-in with that big white dog while I was gone did he?"

"Not that I know of. I'll ask Ellen when I get back, though. See you later."

## FRIENDS OF A KIND

GUNNY LAY DOWN, full from eating and with memories only a dog can relive of the visit from wild beasts. He watched Jonas as the images of the night he had been alone in the camp danced about in his brain. With his master gone, he had awakened in the night to a wild stench in the air, an offensive scent that he was deeply familiar with. It signaled to him memories of the beast he had met in the pit, the one that stood tall and accompanied a bull mastiff as they drenched the earth with his blood. It was not yet completely dark when the wolves came for him. Three crouched low, scurrying toward him low to the ground like cats stalking prey. They appeared fearless, as if they had done this before, making an easy meal of a domestic dog tied with no means of escape.

They were just a few feet away and ready to strike when the big white animal approached from behind him. He turned to meet the threat, but the white dog was too fast and went for one of the wolves in a white flash of furry. The wolf slashed at his throat but then made a yelping sound as the dog struck his shoulder, ripping flesh and making guttural noises that seemed to sing of bravado and invincibility.

The smaller wolf made a leap for the white dog but came too close to Gunny, who tore hide off his flank and showered him with droplets of blood. As the wolf wheeled around to strike back, the white dog sank his fangs into his backside, rolling him over. The wound cut deep. In the next instant, all three wolves ran for the woods while the Great Pyrenees and the pit bull faced each other with tongues wagging to cool themselves, waiting for instinct to guide them as to what to do next.

In all of his experience in the pit, in all of his fights to the death, this was the first and only time that another animal had taken Gunny's side in battle. No reasoning behind it, but instead of going for the white dog's throat, he lay down and followed him with his eyes. Moby stood panting for a few minutes and then vanished into the night. He didn't pursue the wolves but went to be near his master. He could go where he pleased, when he pleased, because he was the top dog in this territory. He wasn't consciously aware of the fact, but he knew it just the same.

## PROTECTING PETS AND NEW FRIENDS

CONCERNED ABOUT THE newcomer's health and that of his dog, Ellen put Moby on a leash and headed for Jonas's campsite. As she approached, Jonas yelled, "Hold onto your dog, miss."

"I've got him."

"Don't let him near Gunny."

"He's okay."

"Young lady, Gunny is a dog killer."

"No, they are friends. Look." Instead of growling, both dogs sat down about two feet apart and then lay down as if taking a break from a day's work.

"Amazing. I've never seen him get close to another dog without seeming to go insane with rage."

"I told you they were friends."

"That you did, young lady."

"Call me Ellen."

"Okay, then, I'm Jonas."

"Are you recovered from your accident?"

"I think so. Being out here in the open in all this fresh air is pretty invigorating. Actually I haven't felt this good in a long time."

"Good. Ruben will be glad to hear it."

"Ruben, yes. He came by here earlier."

"He's an ex-Marine, too. Did you know that?"

"Yes, that's what he said. I wouldn't have guessed it. I'm told he's a bit long-winded."

"Even so, he's a great gentleman when you get to know him. I bet you two could be good friends."

"Maybe so. Where did you get that suit of spiked armor for your dog? And what kind of dog is he? I've seen them before but don't remember what you call them."

"He's a Great Pyrenees. His name is Moby, and Mr. Whitehead, who has a cabin nearby, gave him to me when we first moved here. You've probably heard of him. He's the scientist that made Adam 21 possible. That's why they named it Adam 21."

"You're right. I have heard of him. Didn't know he lived around here, though." As he spoke, he looked away so as not to make eye contact. He hated liars.

"He just has a cabin here. He and his wife, Linda, live in Wasilla. He said the Great Pyrenees breed were raised especially to protect livestock from wolves and bears, but they are really no match for Alaska timber wolves. The problem, though, is that they don't know it. They are fearless defenders and will fight to the death to protect their herds and masters. Mr. Whitehead said they look like big, fluffy pushovers until they become protective, and then their fierceness is kind of scary. I've seen Moby get protective just enough to know it's true. You never want to make the mistake of letting another dog eat out of his dish.

"Well, you could have fooled me. He does seem awfully gentle," Jonas said.

"Mr. Whitehead made the spiked body harness to protect Moby from wolves. There are titanium spikes in every place where he is vulnerable to attack. The spikes are beveled in place so they can't turn the wrong way, and his fur is so long that you can't see most of them. We've had to make it bigger a couple of times because Moby

# KILLERS IN CYBERSPACE

ELLEN WAS EXCITED but scared, increasingly experiencing feelings of something akin to paranoia. She was deeply disappointed that Uncle Vince hadn't told her about the arrest of Win Potter at the river. He didn't even mention the incident until the troopers reported that the DNA taken as evidence in Montana wasn't a match and that his story checked out. Had she known, she wouldn't have taken the emails as seriously and she wouldn't be in this situation now. Then again, she probably wouldn't be any closer to catching the killer, either.

At first, the emails came as very subtle warnings. Some were so understated that it wasn't clear if the sender was really a threat, but then they began to escalate in tone. These must be from the killer, she thought, but she could tell from having tried that to track them down to a server to determine his identity and location would be impossible. This guy was way ahead of the game. He definitely knew what he was doing, and it had to be a he, she thought, because surely no woman would act like this.

The emails began to seep arrogance and seething contempt. "You can feel it," she told herself aloud. Ellen knew without any doubt that she was dealing with a true psychopath, but what she did not know was what to do next. If she told Uncle Vince, he would likely forbid her further involvement in the case, and as frightened as she felt, she was even more fearful of being sidelined. She wanted this person caught, but she wanted even more to help her uncle as an expression of the love she felt for him and her gratitude for all that he and Ginger had done for her.

The big problem was in finding this creep's identity and whereabouts. Nothing he had sent so far was of any help. She had the feeling that he was not that far away but couldn't explain why she thought so. Uncle Vince had sent out requests for information on recent homicides between Alaska and Missouri, and there was a message on his voice mail from an investigator in Montana asking Vince to give him a call.

Ellen took a chance and dialed the number. She waited on hold until a friendly voice said, "Lovejoy here."

"Hi, my name is Ellen, and I'm assisting Vince Terrell in looking for a serial killer we believe is active between Missouri and Alaska. We saw a report of a recent homicide involving someone named Amanda Tucker and we have a question."

"Shoot," he said.

"Did the suspect per chance leave behind an Eve cigarette?"

The response was total silence followed by the sound of hard swallowing.

## SCHOOL DAYS

IT WAS THE second week of August, and the Terrells flew home in the helicopter so that Ellen could start school. Although the leaves in town were starting to turn dirty gold in random splotches, the temperature in Palmer was unusually warm. Missing was the customary hint of fall in the air that was already being felt at the cabin up north.

Colony High School had a history of tough football players and a reputation as the home of some of the prettiest girls in Matanuska Valley. Of this group, Ellen Terrell was a top contender, a fact that was distressing to some of the other girls. In the school parking lot, Ellen, Jenny Rice, Hailey Edwards, and Julie Christianson leaned on the body of Jenny's vintage maroon Buick, excited to be back together and catching up on the time they had been apart during the summer.

At first, Jenny had been embarrassed about the old people's car that her father had bought her. But now, since she was the only one in her group to have a car, her mortification was overridden with pride. It had plenty of room for a carload of girls. Her friends supplied the gas money, and Jenny furnished the wheels. Try as the girls might to persuade Ellen to go out for the cheerleading squad, she wouldn't hear of it. She said she was too busy helping her Uncle Vince, and besides she would rather watch football games than have her back to them.

"Where are we going for lunch today?" Hailey asked, directing her question to no one in particular. Ellen and Jenny looked at each other and then focused on Julie, who shrugged her shoulders as if it didn't matter to her in the least.

"Okay then. McDonald's, anyone?" Jenny asked, almost apologizing for the suggestion.

Everyone nodded and agreed to gather at the Buick at lunchtime.

On their way into town, Jenny asked, "Did anybody see that car behind us this morning?" adding quickly, "Don't look now. Wait and make it look normal. I thought he was parked at the other end of the lot this morning, and several times I thought he was watching us."

Ellen stiffened. "Somebody get the license number."

"Maybe it's just a coincidence," Julie said.

"Get it anyway," said Ellen. "Please."

# CHEERS

A SOFT BREEZE SWEET with the humus fragrance of lush forest and ripening wild cranberries seemed to make the sky bluer, the sun brighter, and the air purer. Fall was barely underway, but every now and then a yellow birch leaf would fall silently to the ground just often enough to catch Ruben's attention as he made his way down the path that ran parallel to the creek. He was carrying a large grocery sack and was beginning to tire of his burden when he reached the campsite.

"Hello," Jonas shouted.

"Thought I would bring you some supplies," said Ruben. "Our cook has been doing double duty with guests, and we have lots of food that will go to waste if we don't do something with it. Thought you might be getting tired of your own cooking."

"I'll say. I appreciate your going to the trouble, Mr. Sanchez."

"Call me Ruben, please. No trouble, really, and I need the exercise. But I don't want to get too serious about being overly healthful." Ruben was pulling a cooler in a sling over his shoulder. He opened the lid and offered Jonas an ice-cold beer.

Jonas stared for a moment, as if he were face-to-face with a rattlesnake or cobra, and then in an instant seemed to go weak in the knees. He grabbed a can and popped the top, took a long drink, and shuddered. "God, that's good!" He pulled out a couple of cloth lawn chairs, handed one to Ruben, and said, "Sit down, please. Why do you suppose people like to drink beer so much?"

"I suspect that, in large part, alcohol offers exaggerated feelings of autonomy. Must have blown the folks away who first discovered it, don't you think?"

"Probably did," Jonas replied.

Ruben finished off the can he had been carrying and opened another. "You know, I suspect that in some ways man has changed a lot in the last 50,000 years, and in others not at all. With no books or literacy, people used to read the stars, drawing inference to events in their own lives and always on the lookout for some way to beat the promise of nonexistence. You know, people have been burying objects for thousands of years for use in the afterlife, and even though others have been digging them up—always as they were left and never used—it's done little to discourage the practice. And by what other measure do we have anything in common with our more 'primitive' ancestors? Well, our sophisticated middle class is still distracted by gadgets and shiny things, so in that regard, not much has changed.

"It's conceivable, my friend, and highly likely that there are more planets in the universe than grains of sand in all the beaches on the earth, and for us humans to assume we know the truth of creation because of the hearsay of ignorant people a couple thousand years ago is pure unadulterated insanity. What gets me, though, down to the bone, when I gaze up into the night sky here among all those stars, is how anyone could contemplate the heavens and the sheer size and vastness of space and then conclude that everything in the universe revolves around us human beings and that eternal life depends upon the arrangement and alignment of neurons in our brains. Bat-shit insanity, my friend, that's what it is."

Jonas squashed an empty beer can in one hand, took another one, and said, "So, you lecturing me?"

"No, just making conversation," Ruben smiled.

"Well, I don't know as I'm up for your wisdom, but I do like your beer." Jonas cleared his throat and mumbled to himself, vying for a way to change the subject and said, "How do you keep these beers so cold out here?"

Ruben pointed to his lightweight high-tech container with its own battery-powered refrigeration system.

"Damn, I bet that set you back a few bucks," Jonas said.

"Not that much, really. They aren't nearly as expensive as when they first came out." Ruben paused and then turned serious. "Why are you really here, Jonas?"

The question startled him, and he took another drink, searching deep in the liquid for an answer. "Told you. I'm just looking for a place to relax for a while before I try to find a permanent place to live."

"Why here, though? Couldn't have anything to do with who lives around here, could it?"

"No, I told you," Jonas protested in a voice a little too loud. He was getting angry, not because of the questions, but because lying made him feel like a phony.

Ruben sat quietly studying the man. "Well, if you say so." He pushed the cooler toward Jonas, who opened the lid and took another beer before finishing the one he had. A couple of drinks, and he was nearly helpless to refuse more. Thinking about this very notion as he finished the one and opened the next, he was disappointed to realize this about himself. But he'd always known it was true, so no use pretending that it would ever be otherwise.

"Tell me about Ellen," Jonas said.

"Tell you what?" Ruben's tone had suddenly lost its tenor of cordiality.

"Oh, don't get me wrong. I don't mean anything disrespectful.

I'm not interested as a man-woman thing. It's just that she's so pretty and lady-like that a man can't help but feel protective. I wouldn't dream of deflowering the girl."

"Glad to hear it because you would be on the wrong end of my .44 if you did," Ruben said sternly in a tone that removed all doubt that he might be kidding.

"She's Vince Terrell's niece, his deceased sister's daughter. You couldn't tell it now, but she had a really rough time as a kid, saw some pretty bad stuff."

"I wouldn't have guessed it. Tell you what, though. I would wade into the devil himself to protect that young lady."

"You'd have to get in line," Ruben replied.

"Good to hear. Okay, look. It's obvious you don't believe in God, but in the spirit of semper fi, why don't you?"

Ruben sat still for a moment, scratching his chin. Then, raising both hands in the air as if shushing a crowd, he said, "Jonas, I think most people believe in God with good intentions. They mean well. I think you mean well, but I can't believe in God for conventional reasons and for some not-so-conventional reasons that you are probably not familiar with as most people aren't."

"Which would be what?"

"Look, Jonas. If all life could be sustained without eating other forms of life, it would indicate the hand of a compassionate and caring God, but that's not the way things work, my friend. Adult creatures eating the young of other living beings is not, in my book, the sign of a designer worthy of awe and devotion. Veal is reason enough to be a nonbeliever in Divine goodness.

"Now if the Creator had the power to eliminate the need for creatures to kill to eat, and didn't do it, He couldn't be good, and if He didn't have the power, He couldn't be God. Not to mention how he became a He without a She. And with a little care and thoughtfulness, our species could have been created with the ability to fly and we wouldn't need to drown the world in carbon dioxide, puttering around in combustion-engine vehicles.

"So my question is how could a being so many people think is perfect, design a world that is so arbitrary, cruel, inefficient, and is so outrageously fucked up? If He did it on purpose, He's a sadist, and if He didn't, He's inept and we must return to a lowercase *he*."

For a moment, Jonas looked as if he was going to stand. But then he took a drink, leaned back in his chair, and tried to disguise his grimace as a grin.

"Look, Jonas. All mixed up in the notion of free will is the issue of close-mindedness, which has prompted more and more neuroscientists to conclude that rigid religious fundamentalism is a treatable condition. If the human race survives for centuries into the future, my guess is that fervent religious belief will be considered a malady. Human beings will move toward Jainism and find it horrifying that their ancestors used to routinely kill and eat sentient creatures. They'll have come to the startling mature realization that, because of its tenuous nature, all life is precious.

"Now, I make these claims as a person with Native American blood. My people lived for thousands of years on wildlife. I'm fully cognizant of the fact that the brains of our species didn't really begin to increase in size and complexity until we began to eat meat because of the sophisticated cooperation required to be successful hunters. But factory farming today is a moral blasphemy. It's a hideous enterprise and a crime against nature with no reverence or respect, whatsoever, for the animals. Mankind has created a diabolically gruesome misery among domestic creatures raised for food, more horrific by orders of magnitude than anything our ancient ancestors could have imagined. So, while I don't believe in

God, Jonas, I do believe that if we ever grow up as a species, it will be because we have come to be as compassionate as we hope God would be if God really existed.

"Until we do that, we aren't likely to create a sustainable environment. The forest fires set in motion by global warming are the smoke signals of greed. For millennia, biologically driven evolution has set our trajectory toward the future without regard to the sustainability of our actions. Now, we have to assume the kind of management we would expect of a compassionate deity in order to save ourselves from ourselves."

Jonas started to speak, but Ruben held his hand in the air to avoid interruption. "Wakantanka, the Great Spirit of my people, did not seek to dominate and domesticate nature. Instead the Great Spirit allowed that we are a vital part of nature, making our kinship with all living things sacred and holy, so much so that death was not to be feared because spirits offer an eternal connection among all the earth's species and properties.

"In effect, my friend, the privatization of nonrenewable resources severs the spiritual connection between the people and the land, which should have kept all people both free and conscientious about conservation. We turn our heads to ignore the cruelty of factory farming because we have lost respect for life.

"The white man's actions condemned all the earth's tribes to inevitable poverty. From observing the many tribes of my people, the white fathers should have been able to figure out that all nonrenewable resources should belong to everyone in the country and not just private companies. Now, man's umbilical connection with the land is long gone, auctioned off, sold to the highest bidders. The finite resources we no longer have a stake in will be gone, and we will soon be economically and spiritually bankrupt.

"But it's too late to change course and too early to give up. Like it or not, we are now the genius species on the planet. It's time for us to stop bowing down before an imaginary god and start acting the way we hope a real God or a Great Spirit would act.

"For centuries religion has been a crutch. It's time to discard the prop and substitute the emotional equivalent of a cane if we must. The well-being of all of the other creatures on the earth is in our hands. We have replaced natural selection with human intervention. Like it or not, we are the Creators now. We are the gods now, my friend, not just one, but all of us. We are all responsible. It's time to lighten up on magical thinking."

Ruben stood up, put his hand on Jonas's shoulder, handed him the last cold beer, and headed back to the compound with the cooler. Jonas finished the beer before Ruben was out of sight.

*AMANDA TUCKER'S EXCITEMENT at the prospect of going to Alaska was so forceful that she couldn't calm down enough to make objective decisions about what to do next. She was talking about it nonstop. Win Potter had said he was hitchhiking home so she would do the same thing. She would surprise him by showing up unannounced. The man who was giving her a ride seemed to be losing his smile. His lips were slowly curling into something of a snarl. Now she was getting scared, but it was too late and she knew it.*

Palmer, Alaska, was overcast and experiencing intermittent light rain. With a surge of adrenaline racing through his veins, Wilfred Hopkins speeded up, then slowed down again to make the point that yes, he was following them, but far enough away so they couldn't get a good look at him. Scaring high school girls, he imagined, was the physical and emotional equivalent of a wolf playing with rabbits. He had been cautious at first, but now they knew he was there. This is the exhilaration that makes it thrilling, he thought. They were all watching, all but the driver, who had speeded up and was now exceeding the speed limit. A hundred yards ahead of the Buick, Hopkins saw a state trooper parked in a lot near the road. He took the next right, and just before losing sight of the girls, he saw red lights begin flashing on the squad car.

Trooper Sid Reynolds stopped behind the vehicle. Instead of

adopting his usual cautious manner, standing a bit behind so as to make the driver have to turn to see him, he walked beyond his usual stance so he could see all of the girls. It was immediately obvious that they were all very pretty and all extremely excited about something.

"Hey, ladies, what's the hurry?" he said.

Four shrill and excited voices made it clear that the girls were frightened. Reynolds had already told himself that nothing these girls said was going to talk him out of issuing a ticket for speeding, but now he wasn't so sure. They were shook up, no doubt about it.

"So, who was following you and why does it matter, miss?"

"We don't know who he is. He was watching us at school earlier this morning. We've never seen him before," Jenny said.

"So where is he now?"

"He must have turned off. Really, officer, we're not making this up," said Ellen.

"Did you get a license number?"

"It was a silver car, pretty new, I think a Honda or a Toyota, and all we could make out was that it began with WW."

"Alaska license?"

"We're not sure, but we don't think so," Ellen said.

"Then why didn't you call it in? You have phones don't you?"

"We did, officer," Hailey said from the back seat. "I did."

"Okay, just sit tight for a minute." Reynolds stepped to the rear of the vehicle and spoke into his radio, "1-17-B to dispatch. Have you received a report of a car following some high school girls in Palmer?"

"Affirmative, 1-17-B. We were just about to put it out on the air, but they couldn't tell us exactly where they are and we lost the call before we could get a GPS fix."

"Okay. Thank you. Any units on the air, it is reported to be a late-model, Japanese-make silver auto with WW in the license plate number, and it may now be on the Glenn Highway. These young ladies don't know who it is or why this person is following them. Over."

"1-28-B to 1-17-B."

"Go ahead, 1-28-B."

"Sid, a vehicle matching that description just passed by me seconds ago on the Glenn, headed toward Anchorage. I'm going to turn around and stop him. Will advise when I get him."

"Thanks, Bill, I'll be right with you." Reynolds returned to the Buick. "Okay ladies, slow down. Write your names and telephone numbers down on this paper in case we need to contact you, and I'll be on my way. Please hurry. A trooper close by thinks he's spotted the car."

Five minutes passed before Reynolds pulled away. "1-17-B to 1-28-B . . . 1-17-B to 1-28-B . . . 1-17-B to dispatch. Has 1-28-B checked out on traffic?"

"Negative, 1-17-B. Dispatch to 1-28-B . . . Dispatch to 1-28-B . . ."

There was no answer. "Okay, dispatch, this is 1-17-B. I'm turning onto the Glenn. Keep trying to raise him."

Reynolds picked up speed and turned on his red lights. Passing a gravel turnoff, he thought he caught a glimpse of flashing lights. He made a U-turn and then took a hard right. Fifty yards ahead was a squad car stopped in the right lane with red lights flashing. The door on the driver's side was open. Pulling even with the car, he felt sick, tasting bile rising in his throat. He knew what this meant, even before he saw Trooper Bill Welsh lying in the road, in front of his car. His gun lay close by his empty hand. The position and demeanor of his body left little doubt: Bill was dead.

Reynolds scanned the scene over and over in every direction but found nothing. Kneeling beside Welsh's body he didn't see it at first because it pierced so deeply: Dead center in the man's heart was a slightly protruding shaft, the arrow bolt from a crossbow. He hadn't been wearing his body armor.

# OWEN SANDBURG'S JOURNAL:
## CLOSER TO EVIL

CLOSER TO EVIL, closer to evil, every report from the detective suggests he may be getting closer to identifying the killer, and yet the only feelings I have are vile, so vile that it seems to be me who is really getting closer to evil. The Rain Crow has finally caught up with me, and the price of knowing this must be paid in vengeance, not in the creature against me, but in my vengeance against the person or persons who killed my daughter. You may not understand the logic in such a twist of fate, but then, if you aren't inclined to be irrational at times, how would you? How could you?

You must realize that the will to live, the drive to stay alive, is the same source, the same stream in which evil is born, which is why we can experience pleasure from another's pain. Nothing is mysterious about the nature of evil except where it comes from. It's an innate part of our humanity, as good and evil are bound together in a dance of absurdity, locked together in perpetuity, while effort—strenuous effort—to purge evil very often actually yields more of it, a deeper, darker strain of evil.

The greatest misunderstanding about good and evil stems from being unappreciative of just how futile, limited, and short-lived, most expectations about human happiness are, and how not knowing this sets us up for unrealistic goals. And then, when the goals prove impossible, we find someone to blame, someone to take the brunt of our dissatisfaction in life and to stand in as the distraction needed so that we can avoid facing the inevitability of death and the destruction of every memory, every thought, every act of kindness and good we have ever known. But if we accept that life is good, then death must be evil, so then we are back where we started from, are we not?

Are you confused? I am. But then, we have no choice in the matter. That's who we are and why we are. Good and evil—never mistake them as being unconnected or as opposites, as if one does not reside deeply in the other, because only fools believe such artless fallacies. I'm no fool. Are you?

# HOMICIDE INVESTIGATION

VINCE WAS BESIDE himself with worry. He gunned the Suburban, throwing loose gravel as he entered the school grounds. Six trooper units were in the parking lot and three Palmer police cars. The trooper dispatcher had offered few details, except to say there had been a homicide, that Ellen was fine, and that he was to meet a supervisor in the principal's office at Colony High.

Inside the building, students crowded the hallway, and through the window of one room Vince could see Ellen with three of her friends talking to troopers and police officers. He didn't see anyone he knew, but he burst through the door. Everyone turned toward him as he entered.

"What is going on here?" he said, searching the room for someone who might answer his question.

"Mr. Terrell, I'm Sergeant Spurgeon," an older trooper said. "One of our men was killed earlier today just off the Glenn Highway by someone we have reason to suspect might have been following your niece and her friends. From what she tells us, it appears she might indeed be the one he was after."

Momentarily speechless, Vince positioned himself on the edge of a desk in an effort to regain his balance and asked Ellen to explain what had happened. He was furious when she told him, not with her, but with himself for letting her become mixed up in an investigation that likely involved a cold-blooded killer. When he asked to speak to Spurgeon alone, the two men left the room and stepped into an empty classroom down the hall.

"Is Matthew Sills around?" Vince asked.

"He's been in Anchorage in court, but he's headed out here now. He's going to take this hard. Welsh was a close friend."

"God, how could I have let this happen?" Vince said.

"What do you mean?" Spurgeon asked.

"You heard what my niece said about the call she made to Montana and the emails. I should never have brought her into such a thing. Why, why didn't she tell me about the messages?"

Spurgeon said nothing, and Terrell didn't appear to be looking to him for answers. He was just questioning himself.

"Did you get any kind of description on this guy?" Vince asked.

"Only that from a distance he was thought to be white and wearing and sand-colored jacket," Spurgeon said.

"Anything on the camera in the squad car?"

"It's really strange we got nothing. It doesn't even show Welsh going down after he was hit. He must have been hit and then pitched in front of the car to get him out of the road. The person who did this had to be strong. The whole thing happened so damned fast. Trooper Reynolds was just minutes behind him, and he saw nothing. We've got drone units in the air with instructions to report anything resembling the vehicle description, but I think it's likely our suspect has ditched the car out of sight and stolen another. The only thing we have from yesterday's Adam 21 feed is that the car the suspect was driving was stolen, but we didn't get a visual on the driver. This guy knows what he's doing, but he's also lucky. The unit Welsh was driving was brand new, and it didn't have the full set of cameras installed yet."

"I'm going to take Ellen home now, if you're through with questioning her."

"Okay. Let us know if she thinks of something she didn't mention or if you see or hear anything suspicious."

They rode home in silence, save Ellen's soft weeping, something Vince was thinking he didn't ever want to hear again. It was heartbreaking and all his fault. He had to fix this.

# A CHANGE OF PLANS

RUBEN WAS UP early, enjoying a rare third cup of coffee. He was seated at the long kitchen table by a window that should have been filled with a view of Mount McKinley but wasn't because of cloud cover that appeared only at the mountain. William Dee wheeled himself to the table near Ruben and was quickly joined by Angela and Wendell. "You guys are up a bit early, aren't you?" Ruben asked.

"Too much going on to sleep, especially when you're in a place this beautiful," Angela said.

"That it is," said Dee.

Wendell nodded affirmatively as he took a sip from his mug. "This coffee is really good."

"Special blend," Ruben said, waving his hand. "There's been a change in plans, folks. Thornton and Tall Tree left out of here in the middle of the night. James told me to ask all of you to wait for him to get back if you can."

Angela looked stunned. "Why didn't he wake me—or us, I mean?" she asked.

"They left like bats out of hell. Bob called me in the night and said a helicopter was about to land on the helipad to take them to the airport in Anchorage. I'm surprised you guys didn't hear it. Thornton said the president was waiting for them to get to

Washington. That's all I know, but I'm sure they'll call as soon as they can."

Ruben picked up a remote control and turned the wall monitor television on to the Adam news network. Something was wrong with the sound, but the picture showed a mushroom cloud in the distance. There were no news people on the set, but the copy streaming at the bottom of the screen said a small nuclear device of some kind had gone off in Pakistan near the border with India. The four concentrated on their coffee and avoided eye contact. No one spoke because there wasn't much to say that wouldn't sound trivial.

An hour later, Angela got a text message from James. It said, *Sorry to leave in such a hurry. Miss you already. Will be back soon. Please stay if you can and ask everyone to sit tight if they can manage it. And try to make peace with Ruben if you can. Thornton asked me to ask you. Love James.*

## NIGHT LIGHTS

AFTER THE INCIDENT with the state trooper, Vince and Ginger decided to return to the cabin and have Ellen attend school through online correspondence until the murder suspect was caught. Ruben and Vince tried in vain to cheer Ellen up, but it wasn't working, so with Ginger's permission, they offered to take Ellen to the high school football game in Palmer on Friday night. Ruben asked Jonas if he would like to go, and he jumped at the chance.

The trip from Caribou Creek to the game took a little more than three hours in the Hummer. They stopped at the Terrells' home so that Vince could drive Ginger's car to Palmer to meet Matthew Sills at the trooper headquarters. He would come to the game when he was finished, and they would follow him back home to leave the car behind.

It was the first game of the season for the Colony Knights and the Palmer Moose. The air was warm, the sky overcast, as dusk approached. The stadium lights were already on. Ellen was sitting between Ruben and Jonas in the stands. Ginger had insisted that the only way Ellen could attend the game would be with able chaperons. It had only been a week since the trooper was killed. Vince couldn't tell for sure whether that incident was connected to the case he was working, but he and Ginger were taking no chances. Ellen was instructed to stay with Ruben and Jonas at all times.

Not far from where they were sitting in the bleachers, some of Ellen's classmates kept looking her way. Since she'd been attending school from home, she texted with her friends and engaged in small talk, but she made it clear that she would not discuss the murder investigation. She was too embarrassed. "Anybody want anything from the concession stand?" she asked. "I think I'll get a Coke." What she really wanted was to get her fellow students to focus on something else besides her.

"No, I'm good," said Ruben, "but one of us has to go with you."

"You can see it from here," Ellen said.

"Not good enough," said Jonas, standing up. "Let's go."

As usual for the early season, the game was getting off to a late start. Officials were on the field arguing about something, and then all of a sudden someone blew a whistle and said "Game!" on the loudspeaker.

Darkness had begun slowly closing in, and the concession line was not moving very fast. Waiting there with Ellen, Jonas turned briefly to look for Ruben in the stands, and in that moment Ellen screamed. Someone had grabbed her arm, pulling her out of the line. He had a stocking mask over his face, and when he saw Jonas break from the line and come toward him he put a long knife to Ellen's neck. He didn't speak, but he didn't have to. He meant to kill her, and Jonas had no doubt that he would do so. Otherwise, why would he be so bold as to do this in a public place? There was an air of desperation in the act.

Something about this shrouded stranger convinced Jonas that if he successfully got away with Ellen, no one would ever see her alive again. Jonas made eye contact with Ellen and jerked his head slightly, hoping she would take it as a sign to try to escape. Instantly she dropped to the ground before the knife wielder could stop her, and Jonas made his move.

In a split second, he was all over the man, dislodging the knife from the assailant's hand with simultaneous chopping blows to both sides of his arm. The knife fell to the ground, and in one seamless movement, Jonas knocked the man to the ground and kicked him in the groin. As he stepped forward to pin him, the downed man struck Jonas on his blind side, burying another knife nearly to the hilt in Jonas's leg. The blade struck an artery, and blood shot forth like a broken water line. When Jonas knelt to apply pressure to the wound, the masked assailant escaped through the crowd of confused and spellbound onlookers. Frozen in place, no one tried to stop him.

"Is there a doctor here?" Ellen shouted. A man raised his hands above his head in the stands nearby, saying, "I'm a paramedic," and rushed to where Jonas lay on the ground. He quickly applied a makeshift tourniquet, and moments later, an ambulance arrived. Ellen rode along with Jonas and the paramedic while Ruben followed in the Hummer. In spite of the tourniquet, blood gushed irregularly from the wound every time the ambulance hit a bump. Ellen held Jonas's hand, speaking softly to him as he seemed at time to struggle to maintain consciousness.

"I'm so sorry, Jonas," she said. "This is all my fault."

# A WALK IN THE WOODS

AFTER SPENDING SEVERAL hours at state trooper head-quarters in Palmer and picking up Jonas at the hospital, they drove back to Caribou Creek. The next day, Ellen still appeared to Ruben to be an emotional wreck. Vince and Ginger had gone home to Wasilla, grateful to Ruben for looking out for Ellen while they handled some things in town. He kept trying to make conversation, but after each encounter, she would begin to tear up. Finally he persuaded her to ask Angela and Wendell to go on an afternoon walk with the group of stay-over guests. Ruben assured everyone that Thornton and Tall Tree would be back at least by the day after tomorrow. In the meantime, a walk would be good for Ellen and would help to set Angela's mind at ease. Besides, Thornton had asked Ruben to make peace with Dr. Black.

"Hello, Angela," Ruben said, nodding his appreciation to Ellen for successfully getting Angela to come along. "You ladies up for a walk?"

"Sure, why not? Dee is resting," Angela said.

Adam Whitehead joined the group, and they all headed down the trail that ran parallel to the creek. "Heard from Thornton or Tall Tree?" Ruben asked.

"James called me last night and asked me again to urge every-one to sit tight and wait until they get back, Monday morning at the latest," said Angela.

Ruben already knew as much but didn't say so.

"I hope you don't mind me saying this, but it seems like you and James might be getting serious," he ventured.

"Maybe," said Angela, offering no further comment.

Forcing herself to be sociable, Ellen asked, "You haven't met Jonas Blythe yet, have you, Angela?"

"No, I don't believe I have. Who is he?"

"He's an ex-Marine camped on the creek. Night before last, he saved my life."

"Oh yes, of course. We heard about that. How is he doing?"

"He sounds fine on the phone, but we're going to see for ourselves and you guys will get to meet him."

"Seems like a nice fellow to me and, my God, what a dog he's got. I bet that animal would tear into a bear without hesitating," Adam said.

"Ruben seemed a bit suspicious about him until we went to the football game," said Ellen softly. "I spent some time with him last week, and he's very nice. So is his dog, Gunny. My guess is that Ruben wants to get everybody's opinion of him."

"No doubt about it, Ellen. You are going to make a fine detective," Ruben said, laughing. "You may as well give up on being a veterinarian." As soon as the words were out of his mouth, he bit his lip—stupid thing to say after that trooper was murdered in Palmer. Both he and Vince had spent hours trying to convince Ellen that, even though it was a mistake not to tell Vince about corresponding with the possible killer, she was still not responsible for murder; no one was but the murderer himself. Seeing Ellen look away to hide more tears, he cleared his throat to change the subject quickly. Pointing ahead, he said, "Jonas," and then called out, "Hey Marine! How you doing? How's the leg?"

"Okay. It's just a little stiff. I think they sutured the wound with some kind of superglue," Jonas said. "Hello, Ellen. How are you?"

"I'm fine, thanks to you. Angela, this is Jonas Blythe. Jonas, this is Angela Black and Wendell Smyth. You already know Mr. Whitehead." Saying this, Ellen realized she had beat Ruben to what must have been a rehearsed introduction.

"What brings you folks today? Looks like rain any minute. Been misting all morning."

"Yeah, typical cloudy and rainy day in Alaska," said Ruben. "One that rains all day but you can stay out in it for hours and still not get wet." Then he rubbed the back of his neck with his hand and added, "Our group of guests up at Thornton's place have been discussing good and evil. We thought, since you've recently been to war, you might have something to say on the subject."

Jonas looked as if someone had punched him in the gut. With a very stern look on his face, he sat down, motioning for the others to take seats on the big logs he often used for chairs. The logs formed a square around a fire pit in the center. He said nothing for a few moments and then began to smile in a way that his visitors could see was mostly forced. "I'm probably not one to ask much about such a subject. I've spent most of my life soldiering and not that much time wondering about why. Sitting here alone, though, for the past few days, listening to the radio and knowing what's going on in the world, I can't help but wonder, if it wasn't for people like me, maybe the world wouldn't be such a mess."

"What do you mean exactly?" Angela asked.

"Well, maybe if there weren't people who would go to war simply because folks told them to and without asking lots of questions, maybe there wouldn't be so many wars."

Angela smiled, looked at Ruben, and then back to Jonas, saying, "I think you may be more of a philosopher than you give yourself credit for, sir."

"Wendell, here, has a new substance he invented that he believes will cause people to avoid conflict," Ruben offered. "Isn't that about the gist of it?"

"Pretty much sums it up, I think. But it may be a very long time before we figure out how to best use it, if ever."

"Why so long, and how would such a thing work, anyway?" Jonas asked.

"Oh, it's a very complicated subject." Wendell shook his head. Then Ruben broke in, saying, "Jonas, why don't you join our group for breakfast in the morning and we can talk some more? Okay?"

"Sure, I could really use a good breakfast."

"How is your dog's suit of armor working out?" Adam asked.

"Fine, Mr. Whitehead. I really appreciate it. I've just started to let him roam free since he's been wearing it. Just the same, I hope he doesn't need it. There's been a lot of wolf howling around here lately, though. Ellen told me she's heard them howling during the daytime, and right after she left the other day, so did I."

"The world's angst is in the air, I'm afraid, Angela," Ruben said, smiling at her.

# ENDS AND MEANS

THE SMELL OF waffles, bacon, eggs, ham, and biscuits with gravy filled the crisp morning air. Greetings at breakfast were short, the ravenous group seeming to want food more than conversation. Jonas was eating like someone who had been picked up after weeks abandoned at sea. Breaking the silence, he said. "God, this is good food."

"Thank you, sir," said a rather tall Asian gentleman wearing a cook's hat and carrying an enormous plate of biscuits fresh from the oven.

"Should we continue our talk about good and evil so that we might have something to share with Bob and James when they get back?" Ruben asked.

"Why would Mr. Thornton be interested in our opinions when he is likely to have access to many of the most renowned experts in the country?" Wendell asked.

"Oh, he will have a passel of papers from so-called experts, but he likes to compare those assessments with people he considers just friends, and he will also have the same conversation with all of the people who work here. When he asks for opinions, he wants to know what everyone thinks, and I mean everyone," Ruben added.

"Isn't all that Machiavellian wolf business you've been going on about just another way of saying the ends justify the means?"

Angela said, looking straight at Ruben. Realizing her tone was a little harsh, she recalled that she was supposed to make friends with the man. Not that she considered him an enemy. It was just that the two of them seemed always on the verge of setting the other one off.

"In a way, you're right, Angela. You have a point and a good one. Is everyone here familiar with what was known in psychology circles some years ago as the trolley dilemma?" Ruben asked. Several blank looks answered the question for him, and he continued.

"Okay, let's assume you are facing a runaway trolley headed in a direction that is going to kill five people unless you flip a switch and send it onto another track where it will kill only one person. Do you flip the switch?" Ruben looked into the face of each person seated around the massive table.

Angela was loudest in a chorus of affirmative responses. "Of course you do," Ruben said. "Okay, now the same scenario, except this time you are standing above the track on a bridge and instead of flipping a switch you have to push a big man off so he will fall onto the track below and save the same five people. Do you push him?" Again Ruben sat way back in his chair to study faces.

Jonas was first to speak. "No, I wouldn't do it."

"But you were a professional soldier, a Marine," Ruben said.

"Yes, but it feels wrong."

"Agreed, it feels wrong and it should feel wrong, but the result is the same. One person dies and five live on," Ruben said.

"I know where you are going with this," said Wendell, looking at Ruben.

"Tell me then."

"I've been studying this subject for many years, and what you are aiming at is that our instincts are imperfect, that it feels wrong to push someone in order to save others, and not simply because it is an evil thing to do, but because our intuition is subtly suggesting that if we push this person to his death, he may have friends or family who will retaliate against us. One death instead of five is still the best moral option, but it just doesn't feel that way." Wendell glanced around the table.

"Thank you," said Ruben smiling, delighted to have someone knowledgeable and articulate who seemed eager to support his views.

"So, killing the one person is what you are implying when you suggest that the ends justify the means?" Angela looked at Ruben in a way that appeared to be more earnest than arrogant.

"In a nutshell, yes, it can be, though I'm not saying it's often the case. The notion that the ends justify the means is always provisional and dependent upon circumstance. Joshua Greene wrote a masterpiece of moral reasoning years ago titled *Moral Tribes: Emotion, Reason, and the Gap between Us and Them*. A big part of his thesis was that the best way to settle differences between groups of people when they are deadlocked about settling the dilemma is to aim toward a utilitarian goal, and in my view it makes as much sense as any argument I've ever considered on the subject of morality. Greene, a neuroscientist, considered himself a deep pragmatist, and for the life of me, I can't think of something better to aspire to."

"So what exactly is deep pragmatism?" Jonas asked.

"It's sort of like going to whatever trouble is necessary to find the best possible answer that will do the most good for the most people in any given situation," Ruben replied. "In every instance where a resolution that requires that some win and some lose, making whichever decision serves the needs of the most people is as good a criterion as I can conjure. You can make a case against Greene, but you can't dismiss him out of hand. Got something better, do you, Angela?"

"I'm just wondering what the long-term consequences might be if suddenly it became fashionable not to heed one's inner sense of right and wrong," Angela said. "Isn't that the expressway on-ramp to evil? And isn't it easy for fascists to use doing the most good for the most people as an excuse to justify all sorts of evil deeds? I mean why fuss about people having a conscience if they are expected to circumvent it? Wasn't it Thoreau who argued what's the use of having a conscience if we don't put it to use?"

Wendell suddenly became animated. "Sure, but as soon as we become aware that our intuition is faulty, we have to compensate for it, don't we? All this talk about evil, and we've been getting hung up on the subject of nature. Nature is not evil. Wolves are not evil. Nothing wolves do is evil. Nature is amoral. Nature just is, that's all.

"You want to really probe the subject of evil, I'll give you some examples: Joseph Goebbels, Reinhard Heydrich, Heinrich Himmler, and Adolf Eichmann. Goebbels said if your lie is big enough and you keep repeating it, people will come to believe it. Heydrich chose to believe the lies of the Third Reich, and the vicious predator's ambition knew no bounds. Himmler said that cruelty commands respect, and Eichmann said he would laugh falling into his grave with five million lives on his conscience. He said he regretted nothing.

"You want evil. That's evil. And my point is that the only thing that has changed since these men lived is the fact that now there are many more just like them and worse. Too many like them are in positions of power, only now they have communication capabilities like that of ancient gods, and their weapons, compared to those of the Nazis, are terrifying. So when we chalk something up as simply being evil, the reaction of most people is just to drop the subject, and that's what helps perpetuate evil. Can't all of you see that?"

A long silence followed. Ruben cleared his throat and said, "Wendell, I've looked at your impressive web presentation. Why don't you feature any examples of the genocide that occurred right here in this country under the guise of Manifest Destiny?"

Wendell sat for a moment in deep thought, "I'm afraid I don't have a good answer, Ruben. I guess I just overlooked it."

"Yes, Wendell. One can hardly expect the people of a nation to understand the ethos of good and evil, when its very foundation is based on a mythological past that disregards and conceals some of the most egregious acts in human history. Adam 21 is revealing these atrocities daily, but most people misinterpret what they are seeing. Until people understand this about human perception, those who call themselves Americans won't know the first thing about good and evil, especially if not knowing suits their life's objectives. What do you folks think? Is there some group of people we need to get rid of now to make room for our egos?"

# A CALL IN THE NIGHT

IN THE WEE morning hours on Saturday, Vince had dozed off only minutes before the telephone startled him awake. He picked up the phone on the night stand just as Ginger raised her head off the pillow to ask who was calling.

"Mr. Terrell, this is Heather Rice, Jenny's mother."

"Yes, what is it?" Vince said, suddenly struck with a tightening in his chest.

"Jenny didn't come home after the game tonight. She doesn't answer her phone, and nobody knows where she is. Could you ask Ellen if she might know?"

Vince put the call on hold and called Ellen at Thornton's compound. He listened to Ellen explain what he knew she would say, that she had no idea where Jenny might be. She hadn't gone to the game because it wasn't safe, and the last time she'd heard from Jenny was a phone call earlier in the morning.

Vince stayed on the line after Ellen hung up and gave Mrs. Rice his cell number. He told her he was going to the school grounds and would be in touch, then stepped into the shower for a five-minute wake-up, knowing this was likely the end of this night for him.

Viewing himself in the mirror, he got the usual feeling of dread, wondering where the muscle that had once covered his body had gone. He was constantly looking at his own arms and questioning who they could possibly belong to, surely not Vince Terrell. Then he would simply tell himself he was an old man and no different from anyone else in this respect. Sometimes it helped, and sometimes it didn't. Like now.

Walking onto the football field in the crisp air would normally have been a refreshing and invigorating experience, but he had really bad feelings about Jenny's disappearance. He had known Jenny for a long time, and he felt in his gut that this must be connected to the attempt to kidnap Ellen the week before.

What was so deeply disappointing was his failure to see it coming. The curse of knowledge and experience is that it makes us more responsible, he told himself, although it was more of a feeling than an articulated thought. But he knew just the same. He knew this as he knew about the depth of madness available to those who explored the notion of evil in the middle of night and just as he knew that Ellen's sweet young friend was dead or worse. He also knew that such news would completely devastate his niece, who would never forgive herself for how she had handled the communication with an alleged killer. Right now, he would call the FBI. Ellen and her other friends, Hailey and Julie, had to be protected.

No sooner had he hung up with the night-shift agent at the FBI office and turned on the squawking police radio in his car, than chatter began to give hints of what he already knew to be the case. The Buick that Jenny had called an "old people's car" had been found on a back road, and Vince could tell from the beating around the bush in code talk that they had found Jenny's body.

He was going to be sick. All of Ellen's friends should have been protected as an act of common sense after the murder of the state trooper and the attempt to kidnap Ellen. Twenty years ago, would he have been this thoughtless? Simply posing the question scared him. "Why did we let this happen?" he said aloud. Ellen is going to be shattered, and once again it's all my fault. She had even commented on the killer seeming to be the one in control of things. What better way to jerk his chain than to kill someone close to his niece? For the first time in his career, Vince felt incompetent.

## ANIMAL NATURE

ROBERT THORNTON AND James Tall Tree had returned during the night, but as they were finishing their breakfast, they got a call prompting them to fly to Anchorage in the helicopter for a meeting. They didn't say what the meeting was about or who it would be with. The rest of the group left the breakfast table and went topside to the grand rooftop patio with a view of Mount McKinley. The air was cool but not uncomfortable, and everyone but Ruben was dressed for the outdoors. He always claimed that his Indian blood ran hot.

"So, it feels good out here, don't you think?" Ruben's comment was directed to everyone and no one in particular.

Angela thought he was showing off and frowned before she could catch herself. "Yes, it feels good, very good, Ruben. Why don't you tell us some more about your theories of human versus animal behavior?"

"You know, Angela, most of the time when this subject comes up, especially in the company of academics, I'm always reminded of the propensity to judge our distant predecessors by today's moral standards. It's not only unfair, it just doesn't make a lot of sense."

"And that's because?" She cocked her head.

"Well, ever since European settlers first arrived in this country, in my country, there has been a big dustup about goodness versus evil, a big part of which has involved just trying to avoid the reality that human beings are both good and evil. Good and evil are part of our biology. Some people's genes don't allow them to produce oxytocin, so, in effect, they are born psychopaths. There is nothing mysterious about the nature of evil except for the fact that so many people don't seem to understand its ubiquity and its universal potential for sudden appearance.

"To the pilgrims arriving in this country centuries ago, wilderness represented the very possibility and potential for evil, of savagery, moral depravation, idolatry, and the hidden but subconscious fear that cannibalism existed as the basest level of such savagery, a simple means of survival effected at the expense of all that is good.

"And yet, the great irony is that what they feared they really brought with them. It was a biological part of them embedded in their genes, a part of their own forgotten history. Seeing evidence of it in the new world threatened to remind them of their base animal nature and make their true nature public. So they hated Native Americans because they posed a threat—the threat of bringing to mind their own inherent propensity for evil, forcing an unwelcome reflection on the prospect that, at a base level, we are all savages, given the right circumstances. And there's something that goes even deeper in that troubling, idealized notion of the noble savage, namely, the idea that man, unencumbered by the arbitrary trappings of civilization, is really and truly free. I say it's best not to entertain this view because it can cause intellectual constipation." He shook his head before going on.

"Metaphorically, looking at the people whom they assumed to be barbarians was similar to our present experience with Adam 21. They were looking back in time. Of course, they weren't consciously aware that this was the source of their fears, but it was, just the same."

Ruben glanced at Angela, inviting her to reply, but she just nodded her assent for him to continue. Feeling a sense of relief, he said, "Literate America has viewed my people as vicious beasts, devil worshipers, murderous wretches, blasphemers, cowards, noble savages, and brave warriors. Then finally, after centuries of criticism, they stole the plains Indians' stoic persona and mythologized it as the boldness of the Western gunfighter.

"Now I know you don't have much use for Herman Melville," he said, looking directly at her, "but he put the whole thing together when was only thirty-one years old. In Moby-Dick, which I still maintain is the greatest novel ever written by an American, Melville swept up a couple of centuries of mythology and wove it into a narrative from which it's still possible, with a little representational imagination and tweaking, to foretell a likely future. We're all metaphorical passengers on board the *Pequod*.

"Take Ahab's hatred for the white whale, and substitute the loathing that those of us feel who are concerned about America's lust for wealth. The next chapter—in fact, I think the last chapter—for humanity can be surmised because the underbelly of wealth is greed. And greed is but a cousin to hatred because the pursuit of great wealth gushes contempt and resentment as surely as whales create water spouts. Greed is a malignancy. Greed leads to scarcity, scarcity to starvation, and we are back in the bowels of evil when things become so severe that once again people are eating one another. Selfishness belies self-hatred, as Erich Fromm argued, not self-love, because of our inability to experience self-satisfaction.

"Now, eating to survive is not evil, in and of itself, but we make up for this fact because the otherwise tortuous things we do to one another based on ignorant assumptions provides the justification for viewing others outside our group as things to be used for our pleasure at their expense. Our means, their end. What do you think, Angela?" Her expression suggested she was still willing to listen, and she nodded slightly for Ruben to continue, trying to suppress a faint smile.

"When I was a young man just getting interested in philosophy, I thought the pessimism of Arthur Schopenhauer was over the top and completely absurd. I felt the same way, but with even more objection and outrage, about Gottfried Leibniz's notion that this is the best of all possible worlds because it makes what is good possible by posing the very opportunity for evil to exist. Now I'm an old man and am no Dr. Pangloss, but with one foot in the grave, I find myself caught somewhere between Schopenhauer and Leibniz, and I'm not sure I have time enough left to work my way out of the dilemma.

"In my view, if we were not genetically bound biologically to evil, life would be worse than empty. If, for example, it were possible to live on eternally after our physical death in a state of perpetual bliss, such an experience in my view would amount to the embodiment of hell."

"If you think that is the case," Angela ventured, "then why are you so critical of formal education at a college or university level? A college education can help immensely in encouraging people to figure these things out for themselves."

"I think you misunderstand my objective from the get-go, Angela. You're right that colleges can do this, but as often as not, they don't. Nothing but nothing is more important educationally than learning to deal with your own existential angst without the need to blame others for your own fears. Human angst, human anxiety, is the bedding ground for evil."

"Then what are you trying to do, if not encouraging one over the other? It's not as if academics haven't given centuries of thought to what people should learn in order to live better and get along with one another. Decades upon decades of liberal arts professors work tirelessly trying to identify those things in life that will help their students live better, and yet you seem to think people can just stumble onto these things by themselves."

"I don't disagree. The goal of self-education, in my view, Angela, is simply to disabuse ourselves of the notion that we are very special people and everyone else isn't. The objective of education should be to spark the pilot light of curiosity and ensure that it stays lit, to inspire people to read, read, read, and to think, think, think. Voracious reading enables one to live deeply, and to absorb a level of articulateness that will enable one to dissipate some of the anxiety that comes with the human condition, simply by being able to explain away the angst instead of being consumed by it.

"Look, Angela. If we cut to the bone, culture is just an oppressive lie that's agreed upon by a consensus of those afraid of the truth, those whose lives will be spent looking out for troublemakers bent on opening the window and throwing back the curtains on festering hypocrisy and the existential fear of the doubters who suspect they are being swindled out of what could otherwise be a decent life. Nothing is more stressful than being versed in only one way to live.

"Humans who are ignorant of other cultures and the range and scope of human behavior are virtual repositories of stress, and they can never rise above the kind of vulnerability that makes them reliably easy to manipulate. We need to challenge the stupid convictions we internalized before we learned to think. We need to tamp down the narcissism born of the arrogance of Western culture that assumes we hung the moon. We need the ability as human beings, not as human doings, to see beyond the prepackaged platitudes and fermented clichés that come with too many of what colleges and universities claim is a liberal education. A lot of it is just feel-good nonsense.

"I say, the pursuit of happiness is a lame exercise. If America's founding documents had focused instead on the pursuit of wisdom, more of us might have something to be happy about. Educators talk incessantly about the need for a core curriculum but not that much about the need to understand the core issues of humanity and the fear that comes with knowing one is a mortal creature. Humans don't come with a user's manual, but we've learned enough to help people deal with their inevitable human torment without needing to find fault in others—knowledge that's subject, of course, to endless revision."

Ruben stood up suddenly as if preparing to leave, but then sat back down and continued before anyone could speak. "Look, we are wired for conflict over petty differences because that was a sustaining evolutionary factor in prehistory. The ends, as terrible as they were in many cases, justified the means by keeping the populations of tribes in check with available resources. Speculate and moralize about this all you want, but the facts are indisputable. Early humans kept their numbers in check and their imprint on the earth small by methods we view today as barbaric. I'm not suggesting they weren't barbaric or that we should follow suit, but I *am* saying we need to understand their predicament and ours. Thanks to Adam 21, there is no way to hide the fact that, over the long term, the effects of human beings on other species and the environment have been profound. We are pedaling close to the edge of a very big drop that may end our kind.

"Religion enabled tribes to become ever larger because of a shared sense of the sacred. But when it was discovered that unwitting believers could be psychologically manipulated as a means of gaining power, human relations became corrupted. And when believers began to burn nonbelievers at the stake, the whole notion of civilization went south. Disingenuous intent is an expression of scorn for the very notion of morality. Scheming to justify greed gives rise to an insatiable cauldron of evil deeds with an ethos of 'whatever it takes,' because our kind is worth any price and all others simply aren't.

"Formal education has a place in the world, but today there is a desperate need to show the world that, in order to make the best of their brief time on the earth, the education human beings need most is free for the taking. The only tuition required is the desire to become knowledgeable enough to put one's life perspective into the context of a meaningful existence—meaningful in the sense of doing something worthwhile instead of focusing obsessively on happiness bullshit and on economic growth and riches.

"The philosophical question, Angela, is about how one is to live, and it can't be addressed fully without taking into consideration how we relate to and get along with others. In prehistory, the ends justified the means without anyone being aware that their abhorrence of otherness was helping them to keep a check on population. Today, people who live on fear are pathetically easy to manipulate. What the whole world needs desperately is for people en masse to learn how to deal with the ambiguity, uncertainty, and angst that come part and parcel with being human without the felt need to take out their torment on scapegoats." Angela raised her eyebrows and smiled, urging Ruben to continue.

Ruben took several swallows of water and put the glass down. "Greed, despair, contempt, hatred, genocide—all of these maladies exist as a psychological on-ramp to evil, as you said earlier. Our ancient ancestors didn't know any better. We do. Hatred is a great unifying force. Hatred and contempt thrive in that part of the human psyche that fears death and the unknown.

"The lunatic fringe in this country, the ones who are stockpiling food and weapons to survive as they cheerfully and gleefully embrace what they presume is the prophesied Armageddon that will give those outside their group their comeuppance, is bearing down on us, and the reality that these people are glad should give us pause."

Pausing himself, as if to accentuate the point of it all, Ruben was silent for two minutes and then asked, "What do you think, Angela? Anyone?" Ruben looked from face to face, inviting a response. When no one spoke, he turned his gaze toward the great mountain.

Angela pursued her lips and finally said, "But aren't we sitting here in this beautiful place with enough stockpiled supplies to ride out a global catastrophe?"

## MONTANA

ALTHOUGH VINCE HAD Adam 21 video from the Amanda Tucker crime scene in Montana, he still wanted to see it in person. If he could establish a personal relationship with the investigators there, he might be able to get some additional help from them. Plus, if he took Ellen along, he could keep her out of harm's way and stop worrying about her long enough to think clearly. It's not that he thought she would be in danger at the cabin or at Thornton's place, but having her with him would put his mind to rest about her safety, period.

Even if he didn't find anything of value, just ruling out the possibility that something was overlooked would help ease his mind, and of course, the bastard might have left purposeful false clues, which might prove insightful. After discussing the matter with Ginger, Vince asked Ellen to go along. Besides, being in a different place might help Ellen with her grief, which for her was excruciating at times and worse for him.

They took an overnight flight from Anchorage, arrived in Helena, and rented a car. After lunch they drove to the northern-most office of the Montana Department of Justice. Before leaving, Vince had called Detective Lovejoy to explain what had happened in Palmer and that he was not aware that Ellen had called him when she did. He thought it best to get these questions out of the way for Ellen's sake so they would not come up in casual conversation.

While Lovejoy drove them to the crime scene where Amanda Tucker's body was found, the nearly indecipherable chatter of the police radio interrupted frequently enough that no one felt awkward for not talking. Twenty minutes later, they arrived at a large bridge over a creek that appeared to be posing as a river. There was no sign to indicate the name of the small stream.

Vince and Ellen followed Lovejoy for a hundred feet or so, and then he stopped in front of a diagram of a body drawn in the shoreline. Fraying yellow tape still clung to brush and small trees marking the perimeters of the homicide.

"She was naked," said Lovejoy, "lying here with one foot in the water, when she was spotted by a local resident."

"The woman in Palmer lay in exactly the same manner, with one foot in the water," Vince said. "What could that possibly mean?" He seemed to be asking himself the question as he walked in a tight circle, glancing at Lovejoy.

Focused on the scene, Ellen cleared her throat and said, "Maybe it's some kind of metaphor, Uncle Vince. Maybe the water is supposed to carry away the sin and absolve the killer of the crime. You know how a river can represent many things? It could mean something about life as a journey, or maybe about all rivers coming together before emptying into the sea, into something bigger than any of us. Or maybe this psychopath is just toying with us, like he's trying to get us to make connections when there really aren't any."

She knelt on one knee and paused for a moment, her eyes on the crime scene tape. The two men looked surprised but made no reply before she continued. "He obviously craves notoriety. I read somewhere that time is a serial killer. Maybe this guy is just jealous because time is a more infamous serial killer than he is."

Getting to her feet after another long minute, Ellen observed what Vince had already noted. "Some of his scenes seem planned but others don't. You think he's purposely trying to confuse us? I mean, we still don't know enough about this guy. He might have no clue why he wants to place his victims near rivers or streams, but one thing is for sure—if he can make us think what he wants us to think, then he is the one in control." Her eyes were still locked on the place where the body had lain. Though her voice was calm and unemotional, tears streamed down her cheeks.

Vince and Lovejoy looked at each other as if struck by a newly charged Taser, stunned that a person so young, right or wrong, could surmise so much with so little to go on. Ellen's comments reminded Vince of his fascination with the little things and how important it is to keep digging for details.

Snapping pictures to busy himself, he now felt certain that Amanda Tucker and Samantha Meyers were murdered by the same killer. Both women had one foot in the water, and yet neither crime scene photo showed as much because, in each case, the first peace officer to arrive had pulled the victim closer to shore for fear the body might be carried away by the current. It was unlikely that two such staged scenes were accidental or coincidental. He might never learn the full significance of it, but undoubtedly it meant something to the killer.

Lovejoy hadn't mentioned the fact that the victim had one leg in the water because he didn't know it himself until shortly before he met Vince and Ellen. Just this morning the highway patrolman who had first arrived on the scene happened to mention the fact as an afterthought. For his part, Vince had learned these details about the Meyers woman by persistently questioning everyone involved.

On the flight back to Alaska, Vince kept telling himself that his niece was no longer a child and wondered if Ellen knew him better than he knew himself. Her growth these last few years was one of the most amazing things he had ever witnessed. Everything about her had changed. She had never been unattractive, but she did seem ordinary when she was younger. Now she was not only beautiful, she was genius-level smart. Her auburn hair enhanced an intellect that made Vince shudder at times.

Seated next to him on the plane, Ellen stayed unusually quiet, keeping her eyes closed most of the time and listening to music. Every once in a while, Vince noticed tears spilling from her eyes. He knew that, no matter what anyone said now or in the future, she would always blame herself for the deaths of Jenny Rice and the trooper.

He hoped her experience on this case would not weigh too heavily on her future, whatever she decided to do. If she chose to go into law enforcement, she would very likely be better at it than he was. But if he didn't catch this bastard, she might never have the chance.

## AROUND THE TABLE

ALL HAD ENTERED the conference room when Ginger came in to announce that Vince couldn't make it because he and Ellen had just returned from their trip. She told the assembled group about the murder of Jenny Rice and explained that Ellen might be the target of a killer. She asked everyone to please be thoughtful because Jenny had been a close friend.

Thornton said how sorry they all were and assured Ginger that Ellen should stay in the complex for as long as she thought it necessary. She could continue her schooling from there. "I've instructed our IT guys to raise the security level around here and to activate all of our sensors and security cameras. Anything you need, Ginger, anything at all, you let us know." Ginger nodded, barely able to hold back tears.

Changing the subject, Thornton said, "James and I are going back to D.C. again in a few days. When we were there earlier, I spoke to some of the others involved in the peace project, and we have retained three New York ad agencies to begin work on a campaign. They will be doing all of the really hard work. They have two weeks to pitch us their approach. So all I want to do here is to make sure we've thought this thing through well enough to know the right campaign when we see it. Ad agencies will sell what they think they can sell, period. But I want to convince myself beyond persuasion so that I am fully committed about what needs to be done and won't be inclined to change my mind because of some simple aspect that I haven't considered. I don't want something to pop up that we haven't thought of already."

Ruben sat staring at wall panel as if he were not aware of the others.

Looking in his direction, Angela said, "Care to join us?"

"I've said my piece," Ruben replied.

"You still think the answer is with the leaders and not with the people right?"

"Pretty much," Ruben said, continuing to study the view.

"I think if the campaign is convincing enough, the leaders will be bound to pay attention to the will of their people," Angela said.

"Maybe," said Adam, and Linda added, "It would depend upon how much money you put into the effort, I think."

Ruben's head was bent, his face in his hands, as if he had seen something no one else could.

"Something you want to say, Ruben?" Ginger asked.

Without looking up, Ruben shook his head to say no.

"Well, something has to be done quickly," Adam said. "That the whole world is a powder keg was yesterday's truth. Today it's more like 'let's light the powder and blow everything up.' More than 80,000 people were killed in the Pakistani bomb, and they still aren't sure who is responsible. Or if they know, they aren't saying. Luckily the fallout is not moving fast and it's not currently headed toward the U.S., but the long-range weather report suggests it will in time, maybe sooner than thought. It's a miracle that there isn't an all-out nuclear war between India and Pakistan already. The influx of UN troops and the pall over the fallout area might be the only thing stopping escalation. We might have already reached the point when no one is able to turn the tide. Two weeks is a long time, if you ask me. I thought it would be sooner.

"I've heard there's not much fallout danger for us," Angela said, watching Ruben shake his head. "Go ahead, say what's on your mind, Ruben. You are driving me crazy."

Ruben looked at the floor and then toward the ceiling. "Maybe just another way to think about the situation, I suppose. Good and evil seem to be at the core of the dilemma, at least that's what I think some of you are implying. But we don't have a lock on morality in this country, even though we are accustomed to acting as if we do."

"What do you mean by that?" Angela asked.

"Okay, picture this. You are an Ethiopian parent, mother or father, take your pick, and you are being interviewed by the press. You're standing in front of your starving children, whom you are trying to shelter from the cameras because of their emaciated condition. The reporter shows you a video clip on a hand-held PC of Americans drinking coffee in an espresso joint in Seattle."

"What's that got to do with it?" Angela sounded impatient.

"Let me finish. The reporter asks you if you think it's fair that these people are paying four, five, or ten bucks a cup for their coffee while you try to scratch out a living growing coffee, barely making enough money to keep your children from starving to death.

"Imagine that the reporter then asks you if you think Americans are a good people, a moral people, a caring people, a responsible people. How do you answer? Do you say, 'Yes, of course they are; they're just not very thoughtful'? Do you say, 'They're like most everyone else in the world, mostly concerned about themselves. They care only about what happens to them, and now that what happens elsewhere is going to affect them, suddenly they care about everybody'? Is that your answer? Not likely.

"Are we assuming the rich and starving poor will suddenly be friends? Should the poor care about us the way we care about them? Think before you answer. You see, just because we are facing war, nothing has really changed for the very poor as we sip gourmet coffee. Has it? What am I missing that is going to cause these poor wretches to suddenly jump on the bandwagon and to engage in gestures promoting world peace? What about the wholesale price of coffee? They are simply worried about their next meal.

"The great moral question, folks, is how do those of us in the developed world stand by and watch millions of people starve to death for want of pennies? Unless something big changes in the lives of those still on the precipice of starvation, why should they care about what we want?" Ruben raised both hands in the air. "What am I missing? Tell me, please."

# KILLING THOUGHTS

H E WOULD LEAVE no cigarettes behind this time and carry none with him. Just the thought left him pissed because he could really use a smoke. For months he had been leaving clues behind to toy with stupid law enforcement types. Now, though, someone was a little too smart by half, and she could be getting closer than he expected, although her warning was more than likely a bluff. A pretty redhead no less, much smarter than the one he picked up in Montana and the one in Palmer that he had followed home, who'd had the prettiest legs he had ever seen. No, this young lady was in a class by herself because she was apparently more intelligent than the police, the FBI, the state troopers, and her aging uncle, so it might be better not to take a chance that she's pretending.

He needed to fix this situation before going back to playing cat and mouse with the usual dimwitted clowns. It needn't be that hard. Anyway, he could use a good hike for the exercise, and he needed a fresh kill to quench his insatiable thirst. No one knew what he looked like, so he could walk right up to his victim and take her out. He wouldn't have his usual fun with her, but this was business, strictly business, and he should act soon. He wouldn't even take a weapon, only a can of bear spray, to make sure he couldn't be considered a serious suspect. He would kill her with his bare hands, and in the remote possibility that he was arrested for any reason before doing so, it would simply work to his advantage because the evidence from past crimes would clear him.

Using an Adam 21 connection and map, he studied the trail from the Parks Highway to Robert Thornton's famous retreat. He would eliminate the young lady, hide her body in the woods, and simply walk back out and be gone. All he had to do would be to wait for the first cloudy day, and in Alaska that would always be sooner than later. Time to check the forecast.

## SCENT OF EVIL

THE GROUP HAD earlier split off in private discussions while Robert Thornton and James Tall Tree were away. Now the two were back, prompting everyone to take their seats around the table. Ruben sat by himself, away from the others as usual. He told Bob and James about Jonas and introduced him as the man who had saved Ellen's life. Both men thanked Jonas profusely and welcomed him to the group.

Thornton said, "I really appreciate it that you all have stayed on board here. On the way back from Washington, James and I read scores of synopses prepared by a slew of experts in their fields, and I'm loath to report that while there are lots of interesting ideas about how we might proceed to promote world peace, we don't have anything close to what we would call a consensus."

Ruben cleared his throat and squirmed about in his chair as if he were sitting on tacks.

"Something you want to say, Ruben?" Thornton asked.

"Yes, I think I may have confused things a bit when we were all talking in your absence, and I just wanted to make some things clear to the group, Bob, as you and I have had this conversation before.

"I have a habit of beating around the bush and never getting to my point because I often get sidetracked, but the point I was

trying to make is this: Human identity and the ignorance surrounding it are both the source and eminent domain of good
and evil. In prehistory, people didn't know there was a better way
to live than killing one another to keep the total population in
check and ensure there were adequate resources available. When
humanity did figure this out and then didn't do anything morally
to compensate, that was the beginning of sin, in my view. These
days we experience a similar dilemma with regard to people living
longer lives, pitting generations against one another for limited
resources.

"Evil centers on the notion of identity and ignorance of the
other. That which polarizes evil-izes. Change and otherness represent the enemy because group identity requires a stable self-image
and a shelter from reality. Undermine a group's self-image and
you pose a mortal threat. Look, folks, what I'm trying to say is, it's
as if a river of ignorance and arrogance runs between groups of
people at the geographic, ideological, or even generational borders
that divide one group from another. And in this river is a seething and festering stream of contempt and vitriolic hatred that, in
a heartbeat, can turn a tribe into a fascist herd under the guise of
patriotism, which really amounts to a raging expression of ignorance intended to shelter one's group from the ideology of another.
Freud characterized this borderland divisiveness as the *narcissism
of minor differences.*

"To drink from this river without reflection is to be poisoned by
hatred and to succumb to collective delusion. This river between us
and them flows over the bedrock of evilness, its waters representing
the potential and possibility of harm to us by them, and then the
body of the *they* that's represented by *them* poses as a mortal threat.
If we are successful in eliminating them, then we will have to find
another *them* to distract us and thus protect ourselves from the

reality that we are mortal creatures and from the fact that we die. We need someone to blame because the existential angst is just too much to bear without distraction.

"And one more thing: I'm not a carte blanche advocate for the end justifying the means. Instead, I'm an advocate for the notion that there are no general principles one can follow that will always prove to be the right choice. Sometimes the ends can justify the means, and sometimes, maybe even most of the time, they don't and can't. But my point, in a nutshell, is that it's just not practical to think that a person can say I'm always going to react to certain situations this way or I'm never going to act like that, because it's just not a realistic way to live. Not to fully understand this is to have been intellectually dogmatized." Finishing with those words, Ruben folded his hands and slumped in his chair. "That's all."

"Yes, indeed, Ruben," Thornton said, slightly shrugging his shoulders. "We have talked about this before, and if I recall correctly, what you are forgetting to add is that if there is no such thing as free will, at least in the abstract, then the subject of good and evil is moot. Do I have it right?" Ruben raised his hand toward Thornton, thumb up.

"Okay, then, back to business at hand. Nothing has changed our resolve to go ahead with our advertising project, and as we speak, the agencies we have selected are putting together something for us to look at. While James and I were in DC, we met with the president's chief of staff on several occasions and tried to describe Wendell Smyth's T&T innovation. We were met with great skepticism, so I've asked Wendell if he would be willing to fly to Washington and give them some kind of demonstration. He's agreed, but only after he does something here to convince us, because we need to assure the president that it won't be a waste of his time. So, Wendell, are you ready?"

Wendell stood up and said, "I am, but I hope you folks won't be offended if I ask you to sign an agreement before we proceed."

"What kind of agreement?" Ruben asked.

"Just a note to hold me harmless if your reaction is so negative that it causes you problems in the future. I really don't like the idea of doing it, but my attorney insists."

"How could it be that bad?" Angela asked.

"So far, my experience suggests that individuals vary greatly in how they are affected by the substance. But, as I said before, this material brings to one's consciousness those things that remind us of our involvement in wrong doing. We know that we human beings have an inborn sense of morality, and this concoction I've come up with makes one aware of it as never before. You all know what oxytocin is, Ruben mentioned it earlier. It's the caring substance secreted by the pituitary gland that helps us bond and care for one another. We often call it the moral molecule. Well, T&T is the anti-moral molecule, in a way, and in another it reinforces the effects of oxytocin by making the very idea of harming others in any manner something to dread in the worst possible way. Perhaps T&T is the real moral molecule on steroids. It may go even deeper so as to discourage cheating and thus guard against the social taboo of free riders.

"Vasopressin is also produced by the hypothalamus, and it helps make us protective of the things we love. Now, there is an awful lot that we don't understand about oxytocin and vasopressin, but we do know that increasing them doesn't necessarily get you more of their effect. For example, increase the level of oxytocin, and you might get a reduction in caring instead of more. Oxytocin is a bonding agent for in-groups, but it also seems to be capable of upping the hostility toward out-groups. With both these chemicals, and I suspect the same is true with T&T, an optimum amount is what does the trick. Just keep in mind, folks, that the animal instinct in our DNA is still very much alive and is constantly tweaking our emotions, which means we are not yet suited for an advanced civilization."

Wendell sat down and looked around the table at each person to see whether what he had said registered and to judge their reactions. For a few minutes, no one spoke, but most of the faces present expressed some level of both doubt and concern. Finally, Ruben said, "So, what you are telling us, Wendell, is simply sniffing this substance may mess a person up psychologically. Is that about it?"

"Possibly. At least, I suspect it has that potential, although I don't think it's happened so far, not to my knowledge. And look, you folks are under no obligation to do this. I would really hate it if any of you had a bad experience. I've tried it myself and am about to my limit, I think. The effects seem to accumulate over time, and the negative feelings escalate if you smell the substance without much of a break in between times. My experience suggests that one whiff is not going to really mess a person up as Ruben suggested, although I guarantee it will get your attention. But if you don't think you should try it, then by all means don't."

"How bad could it be? Give me a form," Vince said, picking up the paper and signing it quickly without reading it. "Give me a whiff." Ginger had pleaded with Vince to take a needed break and attend the discussion sessions, since he had been visibly shaken by recent events, but taking something that could be stressful and potentially harmful wasn't what she had in mind.

Wendell reached into his briefcase, pulled out a metal cylinder, and removed the lid. He walked around the table and stood directly facing Vince as he turned his chair away from the table. Ginger touched Vince's shoulder and said, "Are you sure about this?" Vince nodded, and Wendell held the container up toward Vince so that he would have to bend down of his own volition to sniff the substance. Vince leaned down and inhaled deeply through his nose.

At first nothing. He sat still and slowly looked around the table at the expectant faces. He was about to speak when a deep sense of dread reminiscent of a fog in a moor adjacent to a cemetery for the damned engulfed his senses. All of the bad thoughts that had ever appeared in his mind seemed to threaten him as if on the verge of flooding his consciousness all at once, competing with one another to override his ability to think of anything else. All of his twilight sleep and purposeful dreaming in his attempts to enter the minds of the criminally insane seemed present and on the verge of assaulting his senses.

He took a deep breath, putting his head in his hands and resting his elbows on his knees. Ginger grabbed his arm and held on when he made a moaning sound, the faces of Vietnamese prisoners of war forming a surreal collage in his brain. In his mind's eye, the ghostly face of Jason Spangler appeared to gaze into his eyes with an accusing smirk. Vince had been responsible for Spangler's death while serving as a police officer in Dallas. It was the only true black mark on his career and a specter that still haunted his dreams more often than he was willing to admit. He opened his eyes, stood up, and said, "The goddamned stuff works. Take my word for it. Don't try it. Don't even think about it." Before anyone could respond, Vince left the room and Ginger followed after him.

Jonas stood up and said, "Give me a form."

# THE PROTECTOR

ON A MOUNTAIN slope far ahead on the horizon but clearly
in view, a small black bear grazed on blueberries, unaware
that an old boar grizzly was fast approaching. Ellen turned her eyes
to the ground as she knew from experience that the old boar would
likely dispatch the intruder without hesitation. She didn't want to
watch. To see any animal killed was too much too soon; it was all
she could do to go a whole hour without tearing up. Just then, Moby
began acting antsy and getting hard to manage. Kneeling down,
she unsnapped his leash and let him run free.

It was as if a primal instinct had spoken to him in a language
neither he nor anyone else would ever be able to fully comprehend, except for the innate need to perform, to act as if there was
no other thing to do but what a creature was meant to do. The
message was clear, and he felt it in every cell of his being. His
white fur bristled, standing on end, and an involuntary growl
began a curdling slow rumble from deep within his gut. Ellen
shuddered at the sound.

The group was taking a day off from their conversation, and
she had offered to deliver some leftovers from Thornton's kitchen to
Jonas at his campsite. Although he still walked with a slight limp,
the knife wound on his leg had mostly healed, and Ellen knew how
much he liked the cooking at Thornton's place. Jonas was now a

hero in the eyes of everyone on Caribou Creek. He had kept Ellen from a fate that all who knew something about the situation thought would have been fatal. She'd asked Robert Thornton if there might be any possibility of Jonas finding work with his enterprise, and he had said most certainly. Now she could find out if Jonas would be interested.

The sky was overcast, and occasional raindrops teased of the potential need to take cover. Ellen was about a hundred yards from the turnoff trail to Jonas's camp when she saw someone walking toward her on the trail. He was still too far away to see clearly, but she could tell that he saw her because he waved. She raised her hand slightly and then abruptly withdrew it.

Moby knew that the stranger approaching his master meant to do her harm. It mattered not a whit how he knew, but there existed no doubt in his canine brain. As the stranger got closer, Ellen could see that he was smiling, but she felt anxious and wasn't sure why. She hit speed dial on her PC, and Jonas answered.

Looking at the caller ID he said, "Yes, Ellen, how are you today?"

"Jonas, I'm walking to your camp and there is a strange man coming up the trail. Are you expecting a visitor?"

"No, Ellen. I'll be right there. Stay clear of him. Don't let him get close to you."

Scared now, Ellen stepped off the trail into the woods, and now the man was running toward her. Turning to see how close he was getting, she tripped and fell face first, dropping her bag of food. When she managed to get back on her feet the man was only a few yards away. Ellen screamed just as the raging white dog flashed by her, bolting onto the scene as if from out of a cloud. Her big gentle dog was at this moment a ferocious avenger with one reason for being, which was to protect his master. Moby hit the young man mid-chest knocking him to the ground, sinking his teeth into the man's shoulder. The man on the ground grabbed the dog and screamed when spikes pierced his hands.

Jonas appeared, speeding toward them on his four-wheeler, and when he was close, Ellen shouted for Moby to stop. Ellen grabbed Moby around the neck, feeling carefully to avoid the barbs, and Jonas jumped between the dog and the man on the ground. Moby stopped his assault, but his low guttural growling continued. Ellen snapped on his leash and held him tight. Jonas reached down with a grip of iron and pulled the man to his feet and said, "Who are you and what are you doing here?"

"I'm just hiking to see some country."

"Where is your backpack?"

"Wasn't going far. Didn't think I needed one."

"You don't think eight miles from the road is far?"

"Didn't know I'd gone that far."

"Oh, I think you do. I think you know exactly what you are doing here and why. I think you know who I am, too, and the girl. I think I owe you for a knife wound."

"I don't know what you're talking about, mister."

"You aren't fooling anyone. Turn around and put your hands behind your back."

"Hey."

"Do it, or I'll turn the dog loose on you. Ellen, call your uncle and let's have the troopers come after this clown." Jonas took a piece of rope from his four-wheeler and tied the man's hands behind him, then put a rope around his chest and tied him to a tree.

"Jonas, how do you think Moby knew this man meant me harm?"

"I'm just guessing, but I figure he thinks it's his job, and damned if he's not pretty good at it. And here I thought he was a big fluffy pushover." When he and Ellen were far enough away from the intruder, Jonas said, "Ellen, this is the same guy from the football game in Palmer."

"How can you tell?"

"I don't know how I know, but it's him. I'm sure of it."

## EXISTENTIAL EXCLAMATION POINTS

THE CONFEREES TOOK a break to admire the real-time view projected on the screen from outside. Overwhelmed by the grandeur of it all, Dee turned his head to one side a second too late. Angela and Adam had seen tears on his face. Adam started to speak, but Angela touched his hand. Dee wheeled himself out of the room, and a long silence followed before Adam whispered, "What's that about?"

"He does that a lot lately," said Angela. "It's sad. I asked him about it a few months back, and he said that when you are very thoughtful and you reach a certain age, then frequent tears occur as exclamation points for memories that are too good to let die once you are gone."

"What did you say?" Adam asked.

"What could I say? I mean, how do you top that with something that's supposed to make someone feel better about the fact that they are nearing the end of their life?"

"Aren't we all?" Adam replied.

"Yes, but for most of us, the end of our life is an open-ended question because we don't know for sure when we will die. The when seems as if it could really be never, or at least it can feel that way."

"No, Angela, that's something only young people think. When you get to be Dee's and my age, and unless you are very obtuse, you think about death all of the time. Don't you see, Angela, the very existence of death sets up the economy in which human values are born and are able to flourish? It's the temporal nature of life that makes love possible. Since nothing lasts forever, we naturally love that which is fleeting *because* it is fleeting. Thinking about death doesn't have to be a bad experience at all. To the contrary, it gives us the opportunity to appreciate those exclamation points as we mine our life experience for something worthy of leaving behind."

"Nicely put, Adam, but like what, for example?"

"Like the kinds of things you would want to pass on, the lessons you've learned the hard way, those things you've learned the easy way but seem hard for others to learn, the memories that you find hard to let go. Not to mention all of the things that you have truly enjoyed in life but in all likelihood will never experience again— simple things, natural things, sounds, smells, weather, memories of people long dead, thoughts of family members to be born after you're also long gone. Worthy stuff, Angela, worthy stuff, but things so simple and so seemingly insignificant when they happened before that you would have never thought them important enough to get upset about when faced with the possibility of never doing them again."

"Such as?"

"How about never picking ripe wild persimmons again after the first frost in late fall, their taste like nothing else under the sun? How about never again standing outside on a hot summer day and feeling the sudden cool downdraft from an approaching thunder storm, or standing outside in the rain to get soaking wet on purpose, or the sound of crickets on a hot summer night, or a largemouth bass breaking the surface of the water trying to break your line? How about watching the sunset over the ocean off the shores of Hawaii, driving with your windows down in the countryside with the scent of freshly cut hay in the air, or just lying in bed at night listening to the rumble of distant thunder?

"These sorts of things aren't such a big deal until you realize the likelihood that you will ever do them again is pretty much nil. At this juncture is where I say they become life's exclamation points. And worse, much worse, is living with a condition which makes it doubtful that tomorrow I will remember that I told you this."

"Your memory seems as good as mine or better, Adam."

"Well, it does at the moment, but I can no longer count on my memory, especially short term. I guess it works until it doesn't, as the saying goes. We view the things I mentioned as having value, Angela, because we are predisposed to see ourselves as being at the epicenter of meaningful experience. I mean, when you think about it, how could we manage to live our lives in any other way than by soaking up significance and gleaning it from every little thing we do and feel? The trouble is that, when you reach a certain age, you begin to realize just what little impact our individual lives have on the world and that, once we are gone, life will go on without missing a beat. In a short span of time, it will be as if we never existed at all.

"But cheer up, Angela. It's not so bad, really. Think of all the aches and pains we won't need to experience." Grinning from ear to ear, Adam put his hand on Angela's shoulder and said, "I wish you and James the very best life has to offer, and I think Dee is right when he says the secret of life is having the opportunity to do things worth remembering. Yeah, he said that to me the other day. At least I think it was him." Adam was still grinning as he exited the room.

# KILLER IN CUSTODY

THE TROOPERS DIDN'T have a vehicle handy that could travel the nine-mile drive to the creek, so Vince and Jonas took Hopkins in one of the Hummers to the Parks Highway to meet the state troopers, who were waiting when they arrived. Vince told them that he would call the FBI and provide information as to why this suspect was very likely the serial killer that had been active between Missouri and Alaska for several years.

Later in the morning he placed a call. "Agent Sowell? Vince Terrell here. Remember me?"

"Yes, what can I do for you?"

"Remember I told you about the serial killer theory I have been working on? Well, we've got him this time. We just turned him over to the troopers, and they are taking him to jail in Palmer, although they may move him to Anchorage without notice."

"What makes you sure he's the one? You thought the Potter kid was the killer for sure because he was a seasonal worker traveling the Alaska Highway. But he was cleared by DNA."

"I know he was. But, as I know you are already aware, my niece has been helping me with the investigation. Although she is a teenager, she is an expert with computer technology and software, and we are convinced this guy has been making contact with her via email, although at this point we can't prove it. He was hiking into our place on the creek when a fellow camping out here kept him from attacking Ellen. Her dog, who is very protective of her, attacked the suspect, whose name is Hopkins. The guy lives in Springfield, Missouri, and every year he travels to Alaska selling medical supplies and lab equipment. It has to be him. Everything fits. And Jonas, the one who was stabbed in the leg when he kept Ellen from being killed before, says he knows it's him by the way the guy carries himself."

"That's still a bit weak, Terrell. You thought everything fit with the young man you found at the river, too, you know."

"I know. We make mistakes. Who doesn't? But I'm telling you, this is the guy. You can smell it on him."

# DOOMSDAY

WHEN THE PRESIDENT made the announcement, James and Angela were on a short trip to Montana to introduce her to his family. At Caribou Creek, the strategy discussions had ended early to allow everyone time to take care of some personal business. In a spontaneous gesture, Thornton had invited his neighbors to dinner, so the Terrells, the Whiteheads, Dee, Thornton, and Sanchez were all together when they heard the report.

The telecast aired a 5:00 p.m. Alaska time. The news it contained revealed the nightmare of nightmares, a horror unimaginable but nonetheless declared as a certainty. It was one of the few discoveries that made Adam 21 technology seem unimportant, frivolous even, and of little consequence. The president's announcement and simultaneous declarations by heads of state around the globe left the world stunned and in shock, deep shock.

Listening to the report, James had a determined and hopeful look on his face. The president said that a recently discovered, very dim and hard-to-detect binary star was thirty-three years away from obliterating our solar system with gamma rays. What he described was like a death star, or "doomsday star," as media pundits would thereafter refer to it. There was no doubt about the data. Scientists from nearly every country in the developed world had been over and over the information to confirm it before the broadcast, with no holdouts making statements to the contrary, none of the usual naysayers.

The fact that the event would not occur until thirty-three years in the future, precisely on Saturday, August 27, 2061, did not diminish the public anguish. Even the major news organizations and their pundits, anchors, and talking heads seemed cowed and subdued, as if they had been slapped silly and simultaneously overcome by astonishment and bewilderment. Some made efforts to downplay the actual doomsday event by stating that it wouldn't be a catastrophic explosion all at once. They suggested instead that a brief flash of light would be followed by deadly radiation, destruction of the ozone layer, and ultimately the support systems that make life possible. These ideas only made matters worse.

News panel members talked less to the camera and more to one another, speaking in quiet tones and holding one another's gaze for distracting periods of time, often with their voices trailing off before the end of a sentence, as if they were losing interest in their own thoughts while they spoke. Reporting on an Adam 21 piece about an ancient battle, one network anchor broke down and in tears said, "What good can come from understanding the past, if there is no future?"

Back at Caribou Creek, Bob Thornton stood watching from the side of the room with his arms crossed. His guests sat in stunned silence for what seemed like a very long time. Then, apologizing to everyone, Thornton excused himself to make some urgent phone calls. Ruben began pacing impatiently along the back wall, muttering to himself. Holding hands with Adam, Linda Whitehead whispered private words to her husband. Dee shifted restlessly in his wheelchair, deeply concerned about Angela, wondering what she was thinking, and wishing she were by his side.

Ellen was the first to address the group. Nestled on a couch between Vince and Ginger, she'd been counting on her fingers. With eyes fixed straight ahead she said, "I'll be fifty when the world ends."

# WHAT'S WORTH DOING

THE GROUP REASSEMBLED the next day as soon as James and Angela returned from Montana. Most everyone had spent the morning making calls to family and friends. Too restless to take seats, several of the guests stood staring at a wall panel with a view of the great mountain. The doomsday address was less than forty-eight hours old, and the nation and the world were in a precarious psychological state.

The president and every leader around the world, save a few despots, had made the announcement at the exact same time in an effort to avoid a panic of misunderstanding. In some time zones, the address occurred in the middle of the night, so the speeches were being replayed over and over to reach as many people as possible in the shortest time possible and to keep conspiracy theories from going viral. Nevertheless, a chorus of social media denial chatter encircled the globe. Some groups were being asked to have faith that God would save the earth, that this kind of Armageddon was not what had been foretold in prophesy, so if one was simply true to one's faith, there was really nothing to worry about.

Thornton had asked his guests to gather right after lunch to discuss the truncated future. Around the big conference table, the somber mood seemed contagious. There were no smiles, no private conversations in progress, only faces with subdued expressions, as if too much reflection would come at a cost, a price too high to discuss in polite conversation. But they didn't appear fearful. Rather, they were experiencing something closer to remorse or a strain of melancholia that inhibited their ability for self-expression, a kind of existential bewilderment or accelerated angst.

Thornton looked around the room and started to speak several times but didn't. Finally, he said, "It's really hard to know what to say, considering the circumstances."

"Well, James was apparently wrong about us having a few million generations left before the end of things," Linda said. "I wonder what else we are wrong about." The group avoided eye contact, and no one attempted to respond to the comment.

Ruben got out of his chair and took a seat at the table. "Well, I guess the apocalyptic lunatics won't get to have their sweet revenge now," he said. "They may experience an opportunity to become human beings before they die. Even so, I would wager there is not a chance in hell they will take it."

Dee pushed his wheelchair back from the table and said, "The only people in this room who will likely be alive when the time comes are Ellen, Jonas, and Angela. I would like to hear their opinions, since those are the only ones that really count in this instance, don't you think?" All eyes turned to the three who were sitting at the far end of the table.

"Do you have any thoughts to share, Ellen?" Ruben asked softly.

Ellen sat up straight, moving closer to the table. "I guess it's because I'm only seventeen that thirty-three years into the future seems like such a long time. Except Jenny. . ." She broke into tears before she could finish the sentence. After pausing for a few breaths, she continued. "Even so, it's hard to see how anyone who expects to be alive when the world ends can ever make a major decision about anything that won't be influenced by thoughts of the event to come. I can't help but wonder if, long before the time comes, everything will just fall apart. I mean, what's the point of people working, paying bills, and acting like they have a future, if they really don't have one?"

"Good point, Ellen," Thornton said. "What do you think, Jonas?"

"I never thought I would live to be an old man anyway. I guess I would think about it differently if I had a family, but I don't. So I don't quite know what to think at this point. Something like this needs to weigh on a person for a spell before you can really make sense of it. I mean, doesn't every person alive need to give some thought to how they would feel about the end of the world? Isn't this a good way to put your life and all life into some kind of perspective?"

"Jonas, I think I was right about you being more of a philosopher than you give yourself credit for," said Angela. "Speaking for myself, I have nothing to add right now."

"Indeed, Angela, I think you were right about Jonas," Ruben jumped in, seizing the moment. "I'm not being disingenuous or flippant when I say that, for the first time in history, we now have a democratic future on the horizon. Most of us in this room will be gone in a lot less than thirty-three years. But, for everyone else, it's just reality, or life without illusions. Death awaits us all and always has, but we've always been able to distract ourselves from facing the impending reality of death. Now it's front and center, where it should have been all along, to help us appreciate our lives and stop squabbling over stupid issues."

"Some democracy, Ruben. We have to lose everything to gain something, is that what you're suggesting?" Linda asked.

"Well, for the first time, we've got something before us that the rich can't buy their way out of, and it very well may be the case that, in a comparatively short period of time, there will be a lot of things people prize more than money. Think about it. All of a sudden, the curtain on reality has been pulled back and the most important thing in the world is *time*. Time isn't money anymore; it's something much more precious.

"When we use Adam 21, we see value in snippets of time, a view of the earth from space that can give us perspective about what is valuable and what isn't. For most people, the idea that their time should be spent doing what they themselves perceive as being valuable, as opposed to what society says they should be doing, comes too late in life, if at all. Too many people live the whole of their lives set on automatic pilot with their free-will gear disengaged.

"The sad truth is that this realization could have always been the case, had we not had our better judgment overridden by a society driven by mindless commerce, a commercial obsession that likely would have destroyed us, anyway, in the not too distant future. So, the question is, folks, what do we do now? How do we spend our remaining days and years? What's worth doing and what isn't? What should we care about and what should we push aside? What should we raise up and what should we bury?"

Resting his chin in hand, Thornton studied the group and exchanged glances with James, who was still feeling a bit of jet lag. They had both agreed they would sample Wendell's new potential miracle moral cure, but they would do so privately. If they were going to advise the president about the significance of the chemical, they would simply have to test it themselves first.

Jonas had taken one of Wendell's hold-harmless forms to sign at the earlier meeting, but they had decided to break off and do it another time. Now Wendell was whispering to Jonas, who nodded and looked at Robert.

"Go ahead, Wendell," said Thornton.

Wendell walked around the table and stood in front of Jonas's chair, holding the container such that Jonas would have to bend down to sniff it, and waited.

Jonas took a deep breath and inhaled through both his nose and mouth. Then he sat back in his chair, alert to whatever was next. For a full minute, nothing happened. His face began shaping a grin to express his doubts about the effects, when he suddenly felt as if he had been mentally slapped silly with a confused but tortuous sense of dread. Images of dead bodies in wartime flooded his mind and then began to swirl in a macabre dance.

The very notion of evil, evilness beyond any words to describe it, and seeds of hatred and disgust began to well up in his head with the sense that he would drown of dread and apprehension without even knowing what it was that was so deeply horrific. This is hell, he thought. Plain and simple hell. Like some kind of mental hemophilia, each of his thoughts splattered blood on the walls of his mind.

And then something far beyond the pale of comprehension seemed to devour the walls and partitions in his mind and his very sense of consciousness, a frightened awareness of evil so over-whelming that the only release was to weep, his tears forming a sea of anxiety intent on drowning mankind and every living creature that drew breath on this earth. He felt he was choking, out of breath, starved for oxygen, but also allergic to that upon which he depended to live. His sobs grew so loud that Thornton was about to call a medic. And then he was quiet long enough to make everyone in the room uncomfortable. Finally Jonas said, "Oh God, no. Don't anyone else try this. Don't, please. Take my word for it, just don't do it." Tears were streaming from eyes, and a look of terror took hold of his ghost-white face with a grip that seemed too powerful to turn loose.

For a prolonged moment of silence no one spoke. And then Ruben announced, "I'd say it works."

# REGRETS

THE CLOUDS APPEARED restless and indecisive about whether to clear out or stay put. The wind seemed to be playing silly games, pushing the cloud cover this way and that, but never far enough in any direction to fully change the coloration of the sky. Dee was sitting topside in his wheelchair, hoping the great mountain would show itself, at least one more time. He had a blanket wrapped around himself and appeared to be on the verge of dozing off. Angela pulled a chair close to him and said, "How are you doing?"

"Not so good, Angie. I'm pretty weak. Not much time left, I think."

"Dee, we can get you to the hospital."

"Oh, no. For sanity's sake, no. I don't want anything to do with medical treatment. I was just sitting here hoping the mountain would say hello so I could say goodbye."

"Don't talk like that, Dee. You have lots of time left."

"We both know better than that, Angie. I've been going over something like a life review in my mind, thinking mostly about the things I regret, things I'd like to remember differently if only they could have happened differently."

"Care to talk about it?"

"Oh, I don't know, maybe a little. You know what I regret most?"

"What?"

"I regret that, when I die, all of the living memories of my grandparents' generation will be gone. That's one of the casualties of living to a very old age. We put my grandmother, bless her heart, in a nursing home one day out of the blue, moved her there without warning and never let her return home, because that's what the idiots who ran the nursing home said was best and we were stupid enough to believe them."

"I'm so sorry to hear that, Dee. You never mentioned it before."

"I know. When she was dying, she lay in that bed for months by herself. Her mind was mostly gone, but there were times when she seemed to know her family. All of us, including me, couldn't wait to get out of the place. Now, though, near the end of my own life, all I can think about is how much I would like to go back and while away the time sitting beside that bed holding my grandmother's hand."

Angela moved her lips but said nothing for fear she would start crying.

"You know something, though?"

Angie shook her head slowly so as not to send tears flying about.

"The whole secret to life, in my book, is living so that what you do in life is worth remembering. Life without good memories is worse than meaningless, Angie. It's an egregious waste of opportunity and a sacrilegious act, regardless of whether or not a person is religious. Beats me why, exactly, but knowing that the world is going to end pretty soon helps a little against the loss of memories about my grandparents' generation. I guess it's because, this time, the end will close the chapter on humanity and there will be no more memories, period. But then, like Ruben said, nothing has really changed except our perception, because as individuals we have always been going to die and the same has always held for our species. Makes a big difference, though, when you know when it's going to happen, even if you know you won't be here to see it.

"I think Ruben may be right in concluding that this situation amounts to a new kind of freedom, a kind of freedom where authority loses lots of the implied cultural power that prompts people to do things they know they shouldn't do but play along with anyway because it's expected, even if they think doing so is absurd. They're too afraid of the penalties of not conforming. Maybe you should advise James and Bob to have the ad agencies play the new freedom angle." Dee turned away from Angela and set his gaze on the horizon where the great mountain should be.

Angela patted him on the shoulder and went inside, thinking that perhaps the portending doom had changed the whole meaning of existence. The final question might be the most important one: What do we do now? What is still important and what isn't? How do we tell the difference? To whom should we listen? Who decides what's important, if not each of us as individuals? Now that we are face-to-face with total oblivion, what's next? The inevitability of total annihilation has always been a blatant and profound truth. How could every human being on the planet not have always been aware of this fact?

# PLAN B

*S*HE WAS SO *relieved because getting a ride without having to call home was one step closer to attending to her problem without her father finding out about the trouble she was in. The man driving seemed nice, sort of cute even, until they were a long ways out of town and his smile turned into a grimace. The more scared Amy became, the more sinister the look, until Amy thought she knew what lay ahead.*

Hopkins had hired the best criminal defense attorney in the state of Alaska. Even before his arrest, he already had the man's telephone number in his communicator set on speed dial. Now, the next step was to get a restraining order against Jonas Blythe and Vince Terrell. That should be easy, given the circumstances. Once that was behind him, he would finish what he'd started.

Jonas Blythe and the white dog had taken him by surprise, and he would have been upset with himself had he not been prepared for being arrested for any number of reasons in pursuit of his new quarry. Even though Vince Terrell had claimed Hopkins was the number one suspect in a string of homicides, he would soon be cleared of those by DNA. This would mean that he would be able to travel freely without worrying about being stopped and searched. He would just have to be very careful driving stolen vehicles. If stopped, he would simply wave the restraining order in their faces.

He could also show them a copy of the lawsuit he was going to file to collect damages from having been attacked by Terrell's dog.

Blythe had insisted that Hopkins was the man who had stabbed him at the football game in Palmer, although there was not a shred of evidence to support the claim. The inevitable clearance of the DNA report would cast a lot of doubt on his involvement in anything thought sinister. He was through wasting time. As soon as he was released, he would wrap this situation up and start his drive south before the snow and cold would hamper his trip. He was through playing cat and mouse. It was time to pounce, but the weather was not cooperating and his quarry was no longer attending high school in person.

The lawyer had assured him he would be released today, and when he'd asked about the weather, the attorney read him a PC forecast indicating that a ridge of high pressure would likely cover Southcentral Alaska for a week, meaning clear skies. He didn't have the time to wait it out. Only one option was left: Go back to Caribou Creek at night and stay completely out of sight during the daytime. Kill the girl by any means possible in darkness and then get the hell out without being seen. He would have to steal another car or hitch-hike to avoid leaving a vehicle where it could be spotted via Adam 21. The car he'd driven to Alaska was parked in the airport parking lot, and he would not drive it again until it was time to leave. All he had to do was to pack and get his thoughts in order.

They had moved him from jail to the court earlier in the day, and in the few minutes he spent outside, the hint of winter in the crisp Alaska air brought a flood of memories, six or seven years back it must have been, two young ones, high school age, both sweet, both dead—seeing the first little redhead having car trouble outside the grocery store in Wasilla, giving her a ride to a friend's place to get help, not noticing she was pregnant until she got in his car, and then the tall princess with orange hair waving at them in the parking lot, representing unfinished business.

Funny thing is, the police never reported the condition of the pregnant chick's body, likely because it turned out she had wealthy parents. He'd never thought of delivering a baby post mortem until then. Hadn't done it since, but maybe he should do it again sometime. After all, it had been interesting, if messy, and life without novelty was unbearable. If a conscience is as wonderful as they say and you don't have the sense of empathy that stimulates it, then what else but the thrill of vengeful excitement could possibly compensate for the loss?

## OWEN SANDBURG'S JOURNAL:
## THE NEW OUTLOOK

WHEN THE VOICES became too loud, my wife convinced me to begin taking my medication again, although there are times when the temptation to stop is so severe that I give in. Our president announced that in about three decades from now, thirty-three years to be precise, we will finally get our apocalypse, our final comeuppance. No doubt some will think that, instead of the situation being an act of cosmic chaos, the event will be punishment for our intellectual immaturity and for giving reign to our evil nature, the inevitable result of deep-seated tribally based ignorance. I am sympathetic with the sentiment, although I don't really believe it, because if it were true, it would mean someone or some kind of entity is in charge that gives a tinker's damn about human beings, and I don't for a second believe such a thing.

I find some relief in the notion that, not very long after I am gone, the whole world will end in a solar blast of radiant damnation. Still, there are moments when I find the annihilation of all that there is to be a very troubling thought. But how could we ever have lived in the first place without the dominant role irony plays in our absurdly short lives?

The viral strain of nationalism that savaged the twentieth and much of the twenty-first century to date is beginning to depressurize like an automobile tire with a bad puncture. Nationalism is a primordial pathogen of the psyche, a cultural bonding mechanism driven by a fever of zealotry that enables a people to behave as if it were a reigning organism. But without a future in which to wage war, without the ability to feel the enthrallment of being alive in the face of orchestrated conflict, the worldview has turned somber, melancholy, and reflective, with public brooding and pensive citizens visible anywhere and everywhere. In other words, more and more people are facing the reality of having more drama ahead than the human condition calls for. Ethnocentric hatred appears to be dissipating like a cool mist on a warm spring day. All of a sudden, introspection would be the new rage but for the fact that the very notion of rage itself seems to be ebbing.

Interestingly enough, psychiatrists and psychologists report that, since the doomsday announcement, many of their patients with a whole host of phobias have been canceling appointments, claiming they no longer feel the need for assistance in coping. It seems something really big and concrete to worry about has pushed the small stuff aside. If you listen closely, I suspect you can almost hear a collective sigh of relief accompanied by a stifling sense of utter befuddlement.

World peace, increasingly referred to as an existential truce, now seems possible, if still somewhat remote. I find the whole thing deeply ironic, since the very reason we humans have big brains to begin with is to spur cooperation, and yet the smarter we get, the more obstinate we become.

Lamenting the end of life on earth in harmony with former enemies now seems decidedly preferable to dying before it's time. And the preliminary news about the ad campaign being directed by Bob Thornton that Wendell Smyth told me about personally sounds as if it will be zeroing in on the sentiments of empathy, sympathy, and an existential twist of nostalgia that targets the very core of our primate sense of identity, the longing for belonging, the striving for social approval, and the sense of attachment to something strong, something stable, something that now doesn't even seem to exist except as a desperate human aspiration to transcend existence and leave a stain of our having existed somewhere in the universe that some future creatures might discover and say, "Wow look at that! There was a being that really lived."

Instead of asking people to forgive their enemies of their past hostile acts, the campaign appears to be singling out the very things they might value or miss about their adversaries, like their music, for example, or art, literature, philosophy, or poetry. More and more it seems that letters to the editors of publications are not followed up with antagonist comments from the usual hate mongers. There seems to be instead a flood of concern, empathy, and admission of regret for past accusations.

On the local news this morning, it was reported that Wendell Smyth is still at the Thornton compound north of here. I am most intrigued by his innovation, which the press is calling the new T&T. I told him so when Terrell set us up with a video conversation. Said I've been interested in laboratory science for a long time. If his discovery is at all as advertised, I may want to make a purchase and perhaps invest in his product development, even though the horrific news hanging over the world makes the very notion of investing seem like an archaic idea.

Terrell and his niece seem to have made some progress in the investigation. I'm most anxious to see where their efforts lead but am sickened by what happened to the young lady named Jenny Rice and the state trooper. It was very disappointing to learn that the suspect that they thought might be the serial killer wanted for the south-to-north killing rampage has been cleared by DNA evidence. He seemed to fit the description by the FBI profilers. I'm anxious to find out what they discover next.

Time is short. But I'm heartened by the fact that the conflict between India and Pakistan seems to be focused mostly on helping those who have suffered injury. It would be a hopeful sign but for the reality that time is running out on mankind—hell, on every kind.

It makes me sad to realize that with no future for our kind, scores of great minds, the likes of Newton, Galileo, Copernicus, Leonardo, Darwin, and Einstein will not be born. Some of the most magnificent works of literature and art that ever could have been will instead never be.

# ECCLESIASTES

IT WAS SUNDAY morning, and Robert Thornton's guests seemed to be sleepwalking through a wide-awake dream, switching back and forth from denial to deep melancholy, from a sheltered past to a dead-end future. Immediately after the doomsday announcement the group members' first impulse was to go home, but then their objective seemed more important than ever.

Ruben, to everyone's chagrin, seemed to be in a chipper mood. He asked for the group to convene after breakfast but had to do some verbal arm-twisting to get everyone to agree. Ellen, with her hair in a tangle, was the last person to enter as Ruben got up from his chair and said, "I can see from your expressions that you folks have not yet come to appreciate the opportunity before us. Before the whole world.

"I spent last evening reading Schopenhauer, and it may seem completely counterintuitive, but I swear there is a great deal of solace to come from the experience."

"Joy comes from reading the words of a dyed-in-the- wool pessimist. Is that what you are telling us, Ruben?" Angela asked.

"In a nutshell, yes."

"And you expect us to believe you?" Linda added. Ginger shook her head as Vince bit his lip and Jonas rolled his eyes.

"No, not without giving it a try. What do you have to lose but some time spent in obvious psychological torment? Look, nothing at all has changed for most of us here. Ellen, Jonas, and maybe Angela are the only people here facing an eclipsed future, and Ellen has already said she feels as if the event is a long, long way off. For the rest of us, absolutely nothing has changed. Our future is just as limited as it has always been. The only big difference is that it's now front and center on our minds where it should have been all along because not thinking about our long-term responsibility screws things up." Ruben sat down, drank from his coffee cup, and leaned back in his chair.

"Is that all you wanted to say and the reason you asked for this meeting?" Linda asked.

"Well, it's a big part of the reason. But I thought you knew me better than that, Linda. Schopenhauer got me to thinking, and I just wanted to share it because I hate to see you guys so down and out when there is so much opportunity ahead.

"Schopenhauer said something to the effect that once people reach their seventies, they can begin to appreciate some of the first few verses of Ecclesiastes. Now all of you know me well enough to know it's rare for me to be referring to the Bible for any reason whatsoever, but there is a bit of wisdom to be found there about putting our present reality in perspective. What I wonder is how such a book got into the Bible in the first place, because, when you read Ecclesiastes in depth, it's an exposition on uncertainty that's capable of inspiring an awakening to there being something virtuous in doubt. The greater the skepticism, the greater the awakening."

Jonas sat up straight in his chair with his eyes locked on Ruben as he continued.

"Remember the assertion that 'All is vanity,' that generations come and go, but the earth is forever, albeit an assertion that we may now have cause to question. That there 'is no new thing under the sun,' that there is no remembrance of things past or in the future, and that with wisdom comes grief and 'behold, all is vanity.'"

"Kind of a truncated version, Ruben," Wendell said.

"Granted, but I know you guys get the idea. Look, without some sense of permanence, America's obsession with the philosophical idea of freedom has to be deeply discounted. Permanence has always been an illusion, and so is the satiation of human desire. No one knew this better than Schopenhauer. He argued that our species is a bad idea to begin with. That the tax of our existence by far outweighs the benefits of living; the more things we get, the more we want, and the more we think we need. Life wants, life gets, life eats and wants more.

"It's a dismal affair in a very real sense, especially for some people, because every goal achieved brings on a degree of despair in an endless chain of wants, gets, and gots. Then it repeats, over and over, never stopping, the insatiable feelings never letting go, often giving way to deep despair, like a famous movie actress past her prime, despondent because she is no longer recognized nor does she know anyone who cares who she is or was.

"And so, my friends, freedom for our species has always represented an elusive grasping for something unattainable by design, and as soon as we meet a goal, the satisfaction gives way to angst, which makes us slaves to circumstance. One goal just leads to another and another with angst and disappointment as the ultimate reward because we live in a trajectory that, once it starts going downhill, there is no stopping it."

"I don't see what you are getting at, Ruben," Angela said.

"Nor do I," Linda echoed.

"Look, folks. Now, for the first time in another sense, we are free. We are free of our greatest existential illusion, or at least we can be, if we seize the occasion. Don't you see, not facing death is no longer an option? Now we can spend our time trying to rid the world of evil, like sweeping the floor and tidying up before company comes for one last visit. We can counter the argument that all is vanity, and if indeed our species is finished on this earth, at least we can bid adieu with a moral exclamation point and defy the notion that our existence wasn't worth the effort.

"Schopenhauer, as I'm sure most of you know, argued that what he called the Will is an underlying life urge at the crux of all life that is independent of consciousness and that lives on without us. I've never fully bought into the notion, but now I find it sort of comforting. Think about it. We are made of star stuff, and perhaps it's back to stars we go. I think, in a very ironic sense, that it might be possible to imagine religion as something more powerful as a philosophical consideration without the existence of God. A religiosity of and for life, just as Emerson advocated.

"Wouldn't it be a great thing if, before the end of human existence, we could send a message into deep space to the effect that we as a species grew up and fully matured before we died? Nietzsche said, 'Become who you are,' so let's do it. What do you think?"

Ruben looked around for a friendly face and finally got a few weak smiles. Angela shook her head and walked to the door. Ellen lay back against her chair and shut her eyes. Rubbing his neck, Jonas limped out of the room, and the rest followed.

# FATE

IT WAS LATE afternoon and Thornton's guests were scattered about, some walking in the woods, some watching newscasts, and some were just lost in doomsday reflection. Wendell was topside looking toward Mount McKinley and wishing the clouds would rise so he could see the great mountain. Vince walked over and said, "Can I join you, Wendell?"

"Sure, pull up a chair. Just sitting here realizing that I've only had one short peek of the mountain since I've been here. Is it always like that?"

"Unfortunately, yes. The mountain is so big it makes its own weather. Sometimes you can see it a hundred miles away but not if you're only ten miles away. Maybe that's why it looks so magnificent when you do get a glimpse."

"Well, I've already been here longer than I expected to be. I need to get home and I have to go by the White House first, so I can't stay but another couple of days."

"I hope you can come back every once in a while."

"Yes, I would sure like that. My wife would love this place."

"Wendell, after you spoke to him via video feed the other day, Owen Sandburg said that he is interested in investing in the future potential of T&T and would like for you to come to his home and discuss the matter. He said he would make you an offer that would be hard to turn down. I'll give you a ride if you like."

"Well, there's no shortage of people interested in putting up some money. Only problem is, in spite of all kinds of possibilities, I don't have a sense yet of how we might put the substance to practical use. You can imagine how long it's going to take to get the FDA to approve it or if even they will."

"You know, with the Sword of Damocles hanging over us, so to speak, I think there could be a big change in the way people make such decisions. Sandburg said he would offer you an investment with no strings attached."

"Interesting. You may be right. I'll see him again, if you wish, since he is a client of yours. When would he like to meet again? It'll have to be soon."

"I'll give him a call. He's pretty excited about the potential, but he wouldn't say why exactly."

# EVIDENCE

VINCE, ELLEN, AND Ginger were stunned when they learned from Agent Sowell that Hopkins had been released from custody. The word was that he, too, had been cleared because of the DNA evidence. The FBI had given the case top priority, although a delay occurred when a lab technician mixed up the names of Winston and Wilfred, insisting the tests had already been done. The results were expedited, checked, and rechecked: Five different individuals had been involved in the last ten homicides, and none of their DNA matched the sample taken from Hopkins.

At the family cabin the morning after receiving the news, Vince was shaving at the bathroom mirror when Ellen knocked on the door and called his name. "What are you doing up so early?" he asked, opening the door.

"Uncle Vince, I know how he did it. I know what he's been doing to hide his involvement."

"What? What do you mean?"

"He works for Sabastian Laboratories, right? So that means he could have access to their sperm bank. He just takes samples with him and leaves them so they can be easily found. He didn't seem at all upset when he was arrested, and I bet it's because he's been wanting to get caught so he can clear himself of suspicion. I think it's all a part of his plan. I found a note in one of the case files by a

Canadian detective who said it looked like the sperm sample was left so she would be sure to find it. It all fits. If I had only figured this out earlier, Jenny and the trooper might still be alive."

"Ellen, you mustn't think like that. It's not your fault that a psychopath chooses to kill people. The reasons and responsibility are all on him—it's all on him—and if you're right about the lab connection, we will get him. Please don't beat yourself up over this. I know how it feels to assume responsibility for things you have no control over, like crimes other people are committing, but you can't be a cop and take that on. It will eat you alive."

Vince cupped both hands with water and washed the shaving cream from his face. He was shaken a bit by her sense of guilt. The fact that Ellen spoke causally about sperm banks reminded him again that she was an adult, but mostly he was upset because, under the circumstances, he should have considered a lab connection possibility himself, not to mention the FBI. In fact, it was such a no-brainer that he guessed the FBI would get defensive about the subject if he wasn't careful in bringing it up.

"Jesus, Ellen, the more I think about it, the more I think you could be right. We should have considered his lab connection and the fact that so many crime scenes had different DNA, even though evidence of the others made us think we were dealing with one suspect. I'm going to call Sowell."

Vince was in no mood to beat around the bush. He decided to accept the blame for not considering Ellen's theory himself and apologized to Sowell. It seemed to work. Sowell said it might be easy to check. They would send someone to the lab and see what they could find out.

Early the next morning, Agent Sowell called to report that the lab was missing sperm samples and eight of them were from donors that still had other deposits in storage. He would get a court order for a test comparison and assured Vince he would hurry. Vince felt flush, feverish, breathless.

# RAINBOWS AND THE DEAD

WATER DROPLETS GLISTENED like gems in bright sunlight as the huge rainbow trout danced on the river's surface, trying to spit the lure back at the angler whose excitement was surging for fear of losing what appeared to be the biggest trout he had ever hooked. The drag began screeching when the beautiful fish ended its dance, hit the water, and plunged to the depths. Hoping not to step into a hole over his waders, the man inched carefully forward so as not to snap the line. For ten minutes that seemed like an hour, he played the line, letting it out and reeling in the slack until the fish began to tire. At last, his quarry seemed finished.

One final tug, and the rainbow was on the bank. The man stepped forward so fast that he brought up a big mound of mud and dirt from the riverbed and flung it onto the shore. Feeling a burst of exhilaration at the size and weight of his catch, he lifted the trout in the air in triumph, the colors of the rainbow sparkling like polished jewels. Then something at his feet caught his eye.

There, gleaming Colgate white in the morning sunshine, was the lower jaw of a human being, the upper and lower teeth still intact and appearing as if they had just been polished by the dentist. He stared at the fish, then the thing at his feet, from one to the other, back and forth. Finally, he walked up the bank, sat down on a fallen tree, and called 911.

## EVIL AND FREE WILL

RUBEN WAS TOPSIDE, hoping the majestic mountain would show itself, when Jonas pulled up a chair and said, "Can I asked you some questions?"

"Sure, fire away."

Before he could speak, Angela approached them, and Jonas said, "Please sit down. I'd like to hear what you think about the questions I'm going to ask Ruben."

Angela took a chair across from Ruben and said, "Well, if I wasn't concerned about the end of the world, I would be intrigued, but seeing as we have some time, I don't have anything better to do."

"Well, you folks may think I was born in a cave or something, but I can't help but wonder about something. You've been talking about the Will as if it's something independent of us but also living in us. So what might it have, if anything, to do with the idea of free will?" Jonas looked back and forth between Angela and Ruben for an answer.

Finally, Angela said, "Ruben, do you still believe in free will? Bob said you used to be a strong advocate of free will."

Ruben took a sip of coffee and put a hand to his chin. "Angela, most of the time I consider myself to be a compatibilist, but I am often ridden with doubts. I believe in both free will and determinism, in a sense. But this is a complex and highly arguable subject, so sometimes I vacillate and seek the shelter of rethinking my position. That said, I'm not so sure I would want to live in a world where most people didn't believe in free will, even if it were provable that we don't really have it, because I think in such a world evil could quickly get the upper hand. Sometimes I suspect it already has, even though most people believe they have free will."

"You mean you don't think we're free to choose what we're going to do from one minute to the next?" Jonas asked.

"Choose? Sure. But choice? Not so much. Bear with me for a minute. First off, as I was saying earlier, Schopenhauer likely would have called consciousness a cosmic malignancy, and yet, one can tell from his prose that he got a great deal of pleasure out of thinking and writing. Now, my take on the Will is not nearly as sophisticated as his. I view the Will as being nothing much more than a bias for survival that's written into DNA, all DNA. When we witness a beautiful sunset and find it awe-inspiring, I think what we are doing is simply affirming our bias to live, and in the same moment, we are lamenting the temporary nature of existence, which most of us remain consciously unaware of, even though our unconscious may very well be obsessed with the fact that you, we, and it are all running out of time.

"This bias, I believe, is an acknowledged or unacknowledged tip of the hat to the grim reaper, which explains why things that are beautiful seem to move us so much emotionally. We think these moments are special because deep down, way down, our subconscious is savvy enough to know that, while the beauty we are witnessing is timeless, we most assuredly are not. Our subconscious knows it, even if we don't.

"Now I suspect Schopenhauer's Will can also help explain the process by which the activities going on in our brain at any given time decide what we are going to do next and then inform our consciousness in such a subtle manner that we automatically think we are the ones deciding. We're unaware that the circumstances and the values present in our minds are in collusion with our biology and that our unconscious mind has already set a course of action. How ironic that our hardware is shrewd enough to let us think we are supplying the software as our own ideas.

"Let's say you are a student in medical school. Everything you decide to do from one day to the next is born of a message that your unconscious decision-making process sets in motion and then clues you in on. But your conscious decision to become a doctor, to stay in medical school, to defy your subconscious inclinations— that, my friends, I would argue takes a measure of free will. Maybe free will is as simple as *life goes on*, because we are never likely to understand the elusive nature of our will, period. Perhaps what we think about the notion of free will is never going to matter.

"Now, the essence of free will, in my view, is simply the same force that causes grass to grow or flowers to bloom and that gives every living creature a strong urge to keep breathing so forcefully in some species that cannibalism is preferable to death. Of course, this predisposition can be short-circuited by an act of suicide, but the Will is still involved, and if the Will can't be destroyed anyway, then no big deal, right? I mean, in the great scheme of things, nothing has changed." Ruben sat back in his chair, took another sip of coffee, and smiled at Angela and Jonas, awaiting a response.

Finally Angela said, "So, Ruben, what you are saying is that whether or not one believes in free will doesn't matter. We have to act as if we do because we have no choice. Am I right?"

I

T WAS EARLY morning and Vince was on his way to the Anchorage crime lab. Matthew Sills had called him about human teeth being found at Willow Creek. They had found a match by checking with a local dentist's records, and he preferred to show Vince the evidence instead of telling him about it over the phone.

Nearing Seward Meridian on the Parks Highway, Vince noticed a vehicle in the left lane pulling alongside. A passenger in the vehicle held a badge to the window and waved furiously. The glass was dark, but Vince could read FBI well enough. The person motioned for Vince to turn right at the exit, which he did, the other car falling in behind and following him around the corner to the big paved lot at the corner. Yet another car with three men inside was already parked there, and occupants from both vehicles were signaling Vince to pull alongside and stop. When he parked, the men got out of both vehicles and climbed into his Suburban.

Getting into the passenger seat, one of them said, "Lots more room in your vehicle, detective Terrell. Better that we talk here. We've spoken on the phone before. I'm Special Agent Ed Sowell." He extended his hand and motioned to the others. These are agents Wexler, Simpson, Gates, Stubble, and Picket. We can get better acquainted later, but right now, we need to be brought up to date about your affiliation with Robert Thornton, James Tall Tree, and Adam Whitehead.

"Have you been in Alaska very long, Agent Sowell?" Vince asked.

"Only six months. I transferred up from Denver. Why?"

"Most folks around here know the story about my friendship with those gentlemen. It was all over the news years back. Were any of you here about seven years ago?" Vince asked, glancing at the suits in the front and back. Two of the men nodded affirmatively.

"I don't mean how you met. We are all aware of that. I'm asking about your relationship now."

"But why is that important? What am I missing, gentlemen? I would think you'd be asking about my progress with the Alcan killer, and whether or not it has a connection to the attempt on my niece's life, the murder of Jenny Rice, and the trooper who was killed in Palmer, not my friends. Have you had any DNA hits from the lab where Hopkins works?"

"No, we should have them soon, but this is a different case altogether," Sowell said.

"Aren't you working on the Palmer murders?"

"Yes, we are, detective, but that's not why we're here."

"I'm retired, you know that, right?" Vince continued, annoyed. "As I said before, I think Hopkins is our guy. I've given an extensive progress report to the Alaska State Troopers and to your office as well. Do you guys not read any better than you share information?" Vince looked from face to face for some kind of reassurance, while the agents looked at each other bewildered.

"No, detective, we are working on the serial killer case, and I agree with you that Hopkins may very well be your man, but like I said, this is something completely different. Have you got something new that can't wait?"

"No, my niece is working on some Adam 21 searches, and I'm on the way now to meet Trooper Sills in Anchorage. You guys know about the human teeth found at Willow Creek, right?"

"Yes, we know quite a lot about you, and we know about the evidence found at Willow Creek, but right now we just need to know what your current connection is to the people I mentioned. You may be retired, but you are still a detective in thought and practice, are you not?"

Vince nodded but didn't answer the question. After a moment of silence, he said, "Okay. Look, there is nothing to hide here, but I would like to know why you are inquiring. Is that too much to ask as a professional courtesy?"

Sowell studied Vince for a long minute and said, "Okay, Terrell. I'll say this much. We have reason to believe that James Tall Tree and Adam Whitehead have been targeted for assassination by a group of fundamentalist radicals, and we suspect that Robert Thornton has been added to the list. You could wind up on it yourself if you spend much time with them. In fact, we aren't sure that you aren't already in on it. I'm sure you also know that Tall Tree is well connected politically, and if something were to happen to him and Whitehead it would be considered a national disgrace. Those of us in this nice Suburban sure as hell don't want it to happen on our watch, now, do we? Is that enough to quench your professional curiosity, detective?"

Vince's stern look of concern hardened. "Have you told them about the threat?"

"No, but we are going to let them in on it now. And here is what we want you to do. We are going to insist that Tall Tree and Whitehead tell no one that they know, and I do mean no one, not even you, detective. Now, if this information gets out, I want to know immediately."

"But."

"Look, Terrell, money means nothing to this Missouri group. If this information gets out, it means people are talking and it could mean there are spies or bugs in Thornton's place. If that's the case, we need to know. Okay?"

"Okay. Got it." Vince nodded.

"You don't want your friends killed, do you?"

"No, I don't," Vince said.

"So, who are you actually working for, now that Buck Sandburg is dead?"

"I'm working for Owen Sandburg, his son."

Sowell studied Vince's face another moment longer and said, "You know he's bat-shit crazy, don't you?"

"Seems perfectly normal to me. Where did you hear that?"

"I thought most everyone in these parts knew it. Hell, I do, and I'm new here. Ask around, and I expect most people here will tell you that Owen Sandburg, as they used to say in the old days, is certifiable. Word is, it runs in the family. They say Owen had a grandmother that was stark raving mad." He put a card in Vince's hand and said, "I expect a call if you hear anything out of the ordinary, and I mean anything."

In seconds, the men were out of Vince's Suburban and assembled around Sowell's sedan. Opening the door, the agent said to his men, "Jesus. You don't suppose the Palmer homicide was the start of this thing, do you?" Then he started the engine and left the scene without waiting for an answer.

Vince was shaken by the discussion. He pulled out his cell phone and called Ruben. "Ruben, Vince here. What do you know about Jonas? I mean, what do we really know about him?"

"You know him nearly as well as I do, and if it weren't for him, Ellen wouldn't even be here. Doesn't that speak for him?"

"It does, Ruben, it surely does. But there may be more to it, and if so, it's really important that we get to the bottom of it quickly. Ruben, find out all you can about him and get me enough information to get him checked out as soon as you can, please. I'll fill you in this evening, but please check him out."

"Vince, he almost got himself killed protecting Ellen."

"I know how it sounds, Ruben, but please. It may be important. Okay?"

"On my way to his camp."

## BELIEVERS UNTO DOUBTERS

FOR DAYS AFTER the doomsday announcement, the Seer's Christian network was unusually subdued, but the wheels were turning. The word was that soon there would be a declaration much more credible than the one put forth by the president and his cabal of stooges from around the world. "Stay tuned" was the message, but it seemed to be suffering from persistent postponement. Then, the second Sunday morning after the doomsday announcement, the Seer appeared on camera. He wore a white robe and a purple headdress adorned with pearls in the shape of a cross, immediately above his hairline.

He stood silently at a podium for five full minutes without speaking. He wanted those watching to become anxious and emotionally ready to hear what he had to say. Finally he stepped aside from the podium to show he wanted to be closer to his audience. "Hear me brethren, brothers and sisters. The end is not nigh. God will choose the end times. In fact, God has already done so, as the Word tells us in the Book of Revelations.

"The doomsday announcement that you heard recently by our president and the sycophant leaders of other nations around the world is nothing more than a conspiracy for one world government. Behold the warning of false prophets and the call for one religion. Satan is present. He is among us, as is the Antichrist.

All that will happen is foretold in the Bible. Read Revelations and repent. Before the great harvest of souls will be the battle of Armageddon. The beast will come out of the earth. He has already come out of the earth, and he walks among us now, today. There will be a great White Throne of Judgment and the blasphemers among you will be condemned to eternal damnation for your evil deeds.

"Believe what I tell you. All of what is to happen was written long ago by the hand of God. Pay no attention to those who say the earth will be destroyed in thirty-three years, it is but a trick to manipulate the minds of men. God will handle the end times as He has promised. Believers, believe what I tell you. There is nothing to fear from the starry heavens but the wrath of God when He smites the unbelievers and sends them into the flames of Hell for all eternity. Keep the faith and stay tuned for the voice of the Almighty. Heed not, and you will burn forever in the cauldrons of Hell's fire."

# RUBEN'S EMAIL

WHEN RUBEN SENT a brief email to the subscribers of his blog, it went viral and was picked up by other blogs and major outlets around the country and across Europe and Asia. Some radio hosts read it on the air. The header was simply: *Still Time for Carpe Diem.*

"Here on planet earth we live still," it said. "There is time to seize the day. If you are reading this, you are already one of the most fortunate creatures in our solar system because you are experiencing consciousness—an act of improbability off the charts, with the chances against it having happened or occurring again, perhaps one in many trillions.

"Remember what the twentieth-century philosopher Alan Watts said: If we can't live fully in the present, then the future remains a hoax. It was true then, and it's still true today. Far too many of us have lived most of our lives in the future—a future that never arrives. Someday, when this or that happens, we are going to do this or that, but we don't. Ever. We never catch up to tomorrow.

"The recent doomsday announcement is a clarion call to live now, this day, now, this instant, to live in the moment. Let's do it. Watts made the point frequently that 'belief clings, but faith lets go.' He noted that mankind has spent centuries enthralled with ideas that offer permanence, and yet it is clear that chaos, chance, and change rule the cosmos. They always have and always will.

"In seeking permanence we destroy the present, and, as Watts said, 'the desire for security and the feeling of insecurity are the same thing.' Furthermore, 'if the universe is meaningless, so is the statement that it is so.' And yet, the fact that some of us really do experience meaning in our lives trumps the inevitability of despair.

"Death is the real secret of life, and once we understand this, we live, really live. For centuries, our philosophers have been trying to awaken us to the fact that looking death in the eye enables us to see as if for the first time and to live accordingly. Rousseau held that simply being conscious of time is to be continuously made aware of the inevitability death.

"The quality of what remains of our future is in our hands, yours and mine. There is no time for wallowing in pity, no time for sorrow with so much left to do, so many days left to learn and reflect, so many opportunities to ensure that the legacy of mankind as a species is that of having achieved adulthood before our demise ripples through the cosmos until the end of time, even as we realize that it matters not if others learn of it, because while we were here, we did. If it is ever the case that a future species of archeologists discovers artifacts of our having existed, we would want them to recognize that our lives, while brief, were worth the effort and that meaning is simply art brought to life in celebration of life. We will want them to know this by the degree of our efforts.

Yours in Perpetuity,

Ruben Sanchez"

# NIGHT WORK

THE PROSPECT OF hitchhiking didn't look so good. After all, there would be a witness as to his whereabouts and proximity to Caribou Creek, and there was also the timing issue. He couldn't afford to be seen during the day near his victim, so he stole a pickup from a space where Wasilla commuters parked to get a ride to Anchorage to work.

At the end of his three-hour trip, he found a pull-off less than a mile from the trail to Caribou Creek. He drove the truck into deep brush and then cut some limbs to cover the cab and bed. It wasn't an easy task in the dark, but he had a headlamp and infrared night goggles for the trail.

Walking with a heavy pack was harder than he'd thought it would be, and even though he could see pretty well with the glasses, he kept stumbling. If things went according to plan he would find a good place to spend the day under cover, do his deadly deed tomorrow night, and be gone. Just gotta keep walking. When the GPS on his PC indicated he was getting within two miles of the Terrells' cabin, his PC downloaded a security text asking him to identify himself. So he backtracked a hundred yards, sat down, and dozed until the first sign of daybreak.

In the morning, his biggest worry was confirmed—it was going to be a clear and sunny day. When he found a pile of dead trees clumped together in a dry creek bed, he crawled underneath, thinking he would sleep there until nightfall if no clouds appeared.

He turned his PC off, hoping that if the security system didn't confirm its message, then the motion detected could simply be considered a moose or a bear. Tonight he would have to find another place to hide and remain hidden until he had an overcast day, or else he would have to take care of the girl during the night, which might be too risky. Just after dark, he began walking again, stiff and sore from being holed up in a tight space.

He headed toward the Terrell cabin without his GPS turned on and was beginning to worry about finding cover again when he saw a cave in the creek embankment. This meant the cabin was close by. The water didn't appear very deep, so he waded across and entered the darkness. Switching on a flashlight, he could see the entrance of the cave was three feet above the water level, and the dirt on the floor was dry. Lots of animal tracks were evident, bear, wolf, maybe dog, and some he couldn't guess. It was troubling, but at present he was clearly the only occupant. This would be a perfect place to hide. He would rest again here today and explore tonight to see if he could get close enough to kill, and if not, the cave would be just fine until he had a cloudy day. Sitting down and leaning against the cave wall, he pulled a can of Red Bull from his pack. He needed to think.

Security sensors were not in his plans, and he was visibly upset because surprises represented opportunities for making mistakes. He should have known after watching the Adam 21 clips of the Thornton compound that anything this sophisticated would have a state-of-the-art security system. If he didn't acknowledge and identify himself, wouldn't they just think he was a large animal walking about the territory? Surely this sort of thing happened all the time. But what was the complexity of the security system? Was it simply a motion detector or did it detect the presence of a PC? This was not a part of his strategy.

At midnight he left the cave. A few yards outside in the dark, he tripped another security alert, and a red light flashed on a tree nearby. He ignored it, but after another few steps, he tripped another sensor, and then a second red light began blinking on a post near the trail. There was only one thing to do now: Get the hell out of here and make another plan. This was infuriating and scary because it revealed a flaw in his judgment, making him vulnerable to being caught. Next time would be different.

He must not act in haste and do something stupid. He often reminded himself that Dennis Rader, the infamous BTK killer, had always stayed way ahead of the law, until he made the mistake of including a floppy disk in one of his letters intended to taunt the authorities and it was traced to his church. Imagine that, a bloody floppy disk, a relic from the early days of computers. But the lesson was clear: You had to be very careful in teasing the simpletons. Overconfidence could bite, especially when using technology you'd not yet mastered.

# FORENSICS

EARLY ON IN the development of Adam 21, the Federal Bureau of Investigation had been instrumental in the creation of a global weather database in order to check as quickly as possible to find if cloud cover might hinder a crime scene investigation. The database was created to save time, but because large amounts of data can be toxic, it also led to mistakes when investigators put too much trust in its accuracy. Critics in forensic science warned repeatedly that relying too heavily on the data was risky and that nothing save a real-time Adam 21 check would tell whether or not there was something worth looking at.

Vince purchased a Q-Vision stage about the size of an average coffee table to play Adam 21 events. It was the first model commercially available, and he charged it to the Sandburg case. He thought that, because it was three-dimensional, it had the potential to be faster than a standard Adam 21 search algorithm, which proved to be correct.

Ellen programmed some instructions to produce Adam 21 queries for as many of Uncle Vince's victim timelines as she could think of. She searched up and down the highways in Montana for any possible signs of the killer of Amanda Tucker. She did the same for the Meyers woman murdered recently in Palmer, but she found nothing worthy of a follow-up.

It was when she looked for Celia, the young woman Uncle Vince told her about, whose teeth had been found at Willow Creek, the one with orange hair, that what she saw made her heart race. The investigators looking for clues in the disappearance of Amy Sandburg did not know about the connection with Celia. The weather database showed the whole period with intensive cloud cover, so they must have taken the report as a given without double-checking.

Indeed, there was a heavy cloud cover, except for a brief interval of less than a minute when the clouds parted. Ellen found the last known Adam 21 clips of Celia before all traces of her vanished beneath the clouds. She wrote a program to search a fifty-square-mile area for any person with orange hair and asked for a report on any hits within a thirty-day period, beginning a week before Celia was first reported missing and ending a month afterwards. Now she had the smoking gun.

The clouds opened up for only a brief moment, but there was no mistaking what was visible. There on Main Street in Wasilla, Alaska, stopped at a red light, was a vehicle with its turn indicator suggesting a turn to the north on the Parks Highway. In the passenger seat with the window down sat Celia, her orange hair stunning in pigment. Sitting behind the steering wheel was none other than Wilfred Hopkins. This time she had him cold.

# ORDERS AT LAST

RUBEN'S QUESTIONS TO Jonas about his being in Alaska were borderline accusatory. The answers he got seemed to satisfy him, but the experience left Jonas a little nauseous. Sitting under his extended canvas awning for shelter from the evening drizzle, he was thinking about his response to Ruben's questions when the communicator in his breast pocket vibrated. The encrypted device through which Rev. Baldwin was to send his orders had received nothing so far, so its sudden activation startled Jonas.

Opening the unit, he was mortified by the simple message: *Eliminate everyone in the main compound and those who live in the cabins. Eliminate the employees only if they get in the way or if you otherwise feel it is necessary to complete your mission. God speed, Jonas. Do us proud! Amen.*

He sat on a log staring at the text, reading it over and over to make sure he hadn't misunderstood what he was supposed to do. Unbelievable. What in the name of anything good could justify killing these fine people? It made no sense, but then again, in coming here he had assumed the role of soldier. So, what should he have expected? He didn't realize it before because he had never really thought it through, but neither had he suspected he would ever have to kill anyone, even with all of the combat language they'd used to describe his duties. You just don't do that sort of thing unless you're really at war.

But, he decided, it didn't make any difference what they thought he was going to do or expected him to do. He was not about to harm these people. They were his friends, and he loved Ellen in something of a fatherly way, seeing himself as her protector. For an hour he sat with his head resting on his folded hands and tried to decide what he should do. Finally, he texted a response, sat for another five minutes and then hit send. It said, *Out of the question. These are decent people. I will not do it.*

An hour passed with no response, then another. Just as Jonas was lying down to sleep, the device vibrated again. *You must. It is your sworn duty. This is God's plan.* His reply was quick this time: *Doesn't matter whose plan it is, the answer is no, and it is final.*

He put the device back in his pocket, brought Gunny into the tent, and crawled into his sleeping bag. Only then did he realize how ridiculous it was to expect that he could fall asleep. He didn't think he would be getting any more messages tonight and he was right. Now what? He didn't know, but he was worried, so he got up again and went outside.

The sky had cleared, and bright moonlight flooded his campsite, as commanding as a lighthouse beacon trying to warn a wayward vessel to halt: rocky shoal dead ahead. He wasn't superstitious, but just the same it felt like an omen, perhaps his shipwreck death-trap was a mile north. Maybe he should pack up, forget about the Missouri folks, and just strike out for parts unknown, take things a day at a time and go where he willed. He could change his bank account online, throw away the phone he was given, and simply pretend this whole venture up until now was but a dream forgotten. Yesterday, that would have been an option, but not now. He had to warn his friends. If he didn't and something happened to them, it would all be on him.

He sat down beside Gunny, who had one lazy fluttering eye open and the other shut tight. "Sampson was wrong about you, you big brute. You are a fine pet and good company," he said, patting the dog's scarred nose. "But I wish you wouldn't growl when you dream because it wakes me up."

Early the next morning, Jonas called Sally's Dry Cleaning store in Missouri and asked to have Butch call him. He said it was very important. Hours passed and he heard nothing. What next? He feared he must do something soon, but just what, he still wasn't sure. The thought of having to tell the folks on Caribou Creek why he really came to Alaska filled him with dread. Why indeed? The whole thing seemed suddenly absurd, deeply embarrassing.

The first thing he felt he must do was warn everyone he thought might be in danger. He also needed to destroy the GPS. Better yet, he thought, use it as a lure to draw anyone else the Missouri bunch might send to finish the job to a place of his choosing. That's what he should do, but where? And how should he go about warning his new friends? What would they do when they found out about his connection with the Seer's group in Missouri? He should have said something earlier. Now it was going to look bad, really bad, and he didn't have much time. None of his options were good. Some could be fatal.

# TURBULENCE

FOR RED, THE flight to Alaska was a nightmare. He craved control, could barely function without it, and nothing emphasized his lack of authority like turbulence. Instability in midair was proof positive he had no control over the aircraft, which scared the big man because his size and ferocious nature were rendered irrelevant by something as transparent as the air we breathe.

When he first got word that something was wrong and that the Seer and his bunch were extremely upset, Red had wondered if it had something to do with the ex-Marine who had embarrassed him in front of the men in the camp. His hunch was right, and he jumped at the chance to go to Alaska and regain his reputation. He would bring something back, an ear, or the scalp of Jonas Blythe, and hang it above the man cage for everyone to see.

Red didn't like to fly, ever, but driving to Alaska was out of the question. Not only would it take too long, but he and the three henchmen with him would never be allowed to get through Canada with their weapons and gear, to say nothing of the criminal records of some of them. Checking their weapons as airline luggage for hunting was not a problem.

Even though Rev. Baldwin had provided Red with a fake ID tied to a credit card so that they could rent a vehicle, it wasn't proving to be that easy. The auto rental dealer at the airport had turned him down flat, even when Red offered to leave a large cash deposit.

They took a taxi to another rental agency, where the clerk asked so many questions that Red finally reached over the counter and put a hundred-dollar bill in the young man's face and mumbled something that sounded like a borderline threat. A half-hour later, the four men left in a Jeep Cherokee.

They had a perfect cover story. It was hunting season, and the Seer had a hunting guide in Alaska who was a devotee. The guide would fly the men to a short airstrip that was inaccessible by road, roughly ten miles from Thornton's place, and would pick them up whenever they called. He didn't want to know anything about what they were up to. He was breaking the law already by simply dropping off out-of-state hunters in an area that was not his territory, but he would do as asked because, as the Seer said, this would be God's work. Even so, he wouldn't fly them to the location or pick them up unless it was a cloudy day, and making the trip in the dark was out of the question. If the men were caught for any reason, he would deny having ever seen them or having had anything to do with them. He made that very clear.

Red and his cohorts had to spend the night in a motel in Wasilla, and Red came close to getting arrested at a local tavern for punching out a man who had the temerity to smart off about the four strangers in the place. With one short overhand right, Red broke the man's jaw, and the four men escaped arrest simply because they left before the local police arrived.

Now he had a hangover, and he also had to endure another small plane ride. He wasn't happy, but he wanted his pound of flesh from Jonas Blythe, and it would soon be his. It wasn't enough that Jonas had beat him in hand-to-hand combat; he'd also had the gall to make him look foolish in public, a capital offense in Red's mind. No one embarrassed Red and got away with it. No one.

One of the twins in the seat in front of him yelled and jerked forward, clenching his left hand as if holding on to a saddle horn and raising his right hand in the air like a bull rider in a rodeo. A tremor of fear engulfed Red as the small airplane shot upward a hundred feet, then down again just as far, before turning so far sideways that Red was looking out the window straight down, his face pressing the glass. Then, in a split second, they were bouncing on air like butterflies in a wind tunnel. The turbulence seemed to go on and on, each jolt stronger than the one before, each boosting the levels of panic and frenzy, something that Red could only combat later with rage to balance the scales of retribution real or imagined. Now came a stiff jolt, a straightening up at the last second, and a hard hit and bounce on soft tundra.

Having just experienced the worst flight of his life, Red was drained and weak. They had taken off from a small airstrip in Wasilla, and the flight had been smooth until a few minutes before touching down, when the pilot yelled to hold tight that it might get a bit rough on landing. "A bit rough," the man had said. Red had been tempted to bust the pilot's jaw when he got out of the aircraft but restrained himself because this guy was their getaway ride, their only exit plan.

Outside the plane, they gathered their gear, strapped on their backpacks, and shouldered their rifles. Red grabbed the pilot by the arm and said, "Don't pick us up if the turbulence is bad. Wait for smooth flying. Hear? I'll walk out of this goddamned place before I do that again, and I'll leave your dying ass in the dirt to boot."

## A CALL FROM MISSOURI

JONAS WAS FAST asleep when his PC rang. He didn't look to see who was calling; he just answered.

"Yo JB, I mean Jonas, that you? Butch here."

"Yes, how ya doin', Butch?"

"Way better 'en you, man. Way better 'en you. What did you do to upset everybody down here so much? I've never seen such a ruckus and people running around here asking questions about you. Red and three of his monkeys are coming after you, man. They might already be there. Don't know how long it takes to get up there, but they left late last night. Made out like they were going big-game hunting in Alaska, took guns and equipment with them. They'd skin me alive if they know'd I was telling you 'bout it."

"They can't find out, can they, Butch?"

"No, I'm using my aunt's phone. But, man, you gotta get out of there fast, man."

"Who is coming with Red?"

"Mean sons-of-bitches. Don't think you know 'em 'cause I don't. Didn't recognize 'em when they met Red here in camp. Bad-looking dudes, looks to me, though, and I know bad 'ens when I see 'em. One black, two white twins, I think. All big and all got that look."

"What look?"

"That look like they'd just as soon kill you as go eat breakfast.

That's what. I don't know what you done to get people so jacked up, man, but it must be somethin' big. I never knowed 'em to send anybody anywhere straight from the lowdown camp. Shows they must be desperate, would be my guess, or else they want 'em to do something they don't want their true believers to get caught trying. 'Cept you went from the true believer camp, so I'm not sure what's up with it."

"Thanks, Butch. I really appreciate the heads up. If you learn anything, give me another call, okay?"

"Okay, man, but you gotta get out of there and get rid of your communicator 'cause it's got a GPS and they can find you anywhere you go with it. Oh, and before I forget, Red killed the Brit a week ago Saturday."

"Killed who?"

"The one we called the Brit because he talked like an Englishman. He was the guy with the beasts that almost killed Satan. Reminds me, how are you and that fierce set of jaws gettin' on?"

"We're getting on fine. Tell Samson I said the dog is a damned fine pet."

"I'll do that when one of us gets the hell out of here. Can't let anybody know I've been talkin' to you. But yeah, man. Red just walked up behind the Brit and crushed his skull with one blow from a hickory axe handle. Don't know what they did with the body, but I 'spect it'll never be found. Gotta run, Jonas."

"Okay, Butch, thanks. Watch your back."

"It's your back that worries me, JB."

## HIGH GROUND

LIVING ON HATRED and pumped up by seething contempt, Red had been in such a hurry to get to Alaska that he hadn't thought much about an actual plan to take out the people on Caribou Creek. He figured it was his pure determination that convinced the highfalutin bunch in Missouri to let him take this assignment. Plus, in the event he failed and the men were caught, Missouri could deny any affiliation with the likes of him and his companions. Red knew everyone on the list by sight from hours of watching Adam 21 clips the Seer had authorized before he left camp. He figured as long as the targets didn't know what was underway, it would be easy because they wouldn't be expecting trouble.

Things would be much better, though, if not for the fact that he detested the men who were sent along with him. Twice he and the black fellow named Les had almost come to blows. The guy seemed to have a chip on his shoulder, and every time Red asked him a question, he just grunted. The twins from Alberta weren't much better in Red's eyes. They were French Canadian and kept to themselves, constantly looking at each other, apparently sending mental messages. Red couldn't pronounce their names and would make no effort to learn how.

Once they left the aircraft, Les said, "Okay, what now?"

Red got out a tablet and pulled up a map of the area. "First, we get to some high ground here," he said, pointing to a place on the screen. "From there, we can see some of the ground in Blythe's camp, and it's only a mile north to the main place where we will find the rest of the lot. If the sky clears off, we may have to sit tight for a few days. When we're ready to roll, we turn on the jammers."

"We know who is on the list, but what about the people that just work there?" Les said.

"They don't see us, no sweat. If they do, we leave no witnesses. Got it?"

Les nodded but didn't answer. The twins just looked at each other and smiled as if they had just won a prize.

It took almost four hours through the rugged country because the soft, spongy tundra made for difficult walking. It also took some climbing through dense vegetation to reach the high ground spot. As soon as they arrived and set up camp, the sky cleared and the temperature began to drop. Red looked at the sky and said, "Might as well camouflage our site and get some rest and sleep. Goddamn it, we can't do anything till it clouds up. And then, goddamn it, we will cloud up and storm."

# SNIPER

L ES COLEMAN HAD been a Marine Corps sniper for sixteen years. At one time he had been considered one of the best of the best. He didn't talk about the number of kills he had accomplished, but everyone knew they were substantial. After killing a civilian in a bar fight at Big Bear Lake in California, he had been kicked out of the service for manslaughter, even though the civilian had been the one to start the fight. As a result, Les lost his retirement and his wife. Luckily, they had no children. Now he had nothing, and he was increasingly bitter. A friend had told him he might find some kind of mercenary work at the Missouri religious compound, and it worked out. The pay promised upon completion of this job would be a big help.

He had nothing personal against the people he had been sent to assassinate, but they sounded like a bunch of elite, sanctimonious bastards anyway, so what the hell. Still, he wondered how and when his killing had reached a point when it no longer mattered who the people were that he was to kill, it was just a matter of how. What would his mother say, if she were alive? He didn't really have to ask. He knew the answer.

So far, he had dismissed the morality of it all and just pushed it out of his mind. He had never in his life thought of himself as a criminal. The idea took some getting used to. The only relatives he had were distant, people he had never even met. He wasn't very introspective, but he understood himself well enough to know that if he had close family members who were still living, he would never have taken an assignment like this. Assignment. Even the word seemed phony under the circumstances. The military gave assignments. He wasn't sure what this venture should be called, but the whole thing was beginning to gnaw at whatever he might have left that could be called a conscience.

The most distasteful thing about the trip was the big redheaded buffoon who had been given command of the job. But for the promise of the big payoff, Les would be tempted to gut him and leave his entrails for scavengers. When it was over, he might just do it anyway. The twins were weird, but they weren't so hard to be around. They pretty much kept to themselves.

He was beginning to obsess about strategy. If this were a military operation, they would have a very specific plan and fallback plans if things didn't go well. The big oaf in charge, however, acted as if everyone would just know what to do without needing to discuss it. Stupid. Les might have to take charge himself, regardless of the consequences, or there might not be a payday. He would find out soon enough.

Having to hide during the day was really getting on his nerves. They had pitched camouflaged tents with a small awning in front so a man could stand and take a piss without being seen from the sky, but this lack of being able to move around was getting really old. Come on, cloudy days, so we can be done with it and get the hell out of here.

A drop in temperature honed his senses. Pangs of hunger began to sharpen his hunter's sense of awareness, adding a sense of urgency that contrasted sharply with the unrelenting boredom. Les felt like someone at the starting block in a foot race, with one leg fastened to the ground after the starting gun had already fired.

He decided to turn on his PC and learn more about his quarry, since their faces were the only thing he was really familiar with. Of course, everything he watched would likely be scrutinized by his employer, but if he stuck to the subjects of his business they should be able to see the value in it. He pulled up an Adam 21 piece about the Terrell family, their encounter with James Tall Tree, and the history of both families. There were clips of a Civil War ancestor and a wagon train headed west with a team of horses driven by a young woman who looked very much like one of his targets. Indeed, it turned out that she was Sara Spencer Peek, the great-grandmother of Ellen Terrell.

Tastefully edited clips showed Plains Indians, said to be James Tall Tree's ancestors, chasing buffalo and engaged in battles with other tribes and the U.S. Cavalry. The most impressive scenes were of a coming together of scores of tribes—all former enemies—in the summer of 1851, somewhere in Wyoming. The wide-angle Adam 21 view from high above, with several thousand Indians on horses converging toward one location, was mesmerizing to watch. It almost looked choreographed, but of course it couldn't have been.

There were sub-links to explain the strained relationships among the tribes—who hated whom the most and why. The narrators didn't come right out and say it, but it was clear that this must have been where the strategy was hatched among all of the tribes that having the white man as a common enemy was enough to put their quarrels with one another aside. In other words, this was likely where the thinking took place, years earlier, that did Custer in. Nothing like having a common enemy, Les thought to himself. If the Seer's common enemy was simply nonbelievers, what the hell was he thinking? He too was a nonbeliever.

Another clip explained how Ruben Sanchez had met Robert Thornton and how the two of them had joined forces to do some good in the world with scores of education programs and efforts to fight hunger, poverty, racism, and genocide. Through shrewd trading, the narrator said, Robert Thornton had become a billionaire and had also become one of the world's most ambitious philanthropists. And then there was an elaborate tribute to Adam Whitehead that told the story of how he had come to do the work that led to the development of Adam 21.

Les realized that two hours had passed and that he had barely taken his eyes off the screen. Now he was stricken with questions for which it was too late to find answers, the first being, what in the hell had these people done, precisely, to deserve to die?

And then there was the haunting effect of the doomsday announcement to contend with. He kept trying to put it out of his mind, but it kept roaring back. Every time the subject popped up in his mind, he quickly tried to concentrate on something else, anything. At night, though, he was aware that the doomsday scenario was a big part of his dreams, making him thankful that he couldn't remember all of the details of his dreams. People had always said that Les was moody, and he had mostly brushed it off. But now his moodiness seemed to have taken over, with anxiety rendering him so confused, so overcome with uncertainty, that he felt he might be on the verge of a nervous breakdown. This was clearly not the time for going mental, though. He needed to think. Because of the cosmic catastrophe to come, he would never be an old man, and thinking about the fact made the idea of spending his remaining time in prison seem horrifying.

There was something about being in wilderness that made him hyper-aware of death, the fragile nature of independence, and the fact that he had never in his life felt free to speak his mind or spend his time as he wished. This reality seemed to make a mockery out of the very idea of freedom. Hell, up to now, his whole life had been dictated by the whims of people he didn't even like, meaning that he had never really and truly been free. The sudden realization felt unbearable.

# LIFE WITHOUT ILLUSIONS

OWEN SANDBURG HERE again. I stopped keeping a formal journal a while back. I guess it no longer makes much sense, since before long no one will be left to read it. It may seem a little daft that I'm so disappointed about the scheduled construction of a manned observatory on the moon being canceled. I mean, why that even seems to matter in light of what the future portends may sound silly, and yet it does matter to me, if only because it confirms the worst is nigh. I stopped taking my meds again. I mean, what's the use? What's the point of anything anymore?

The long shadow of no future is starting to show itself in the behavior of the rich and poor. Time itself is rapidly overtaking wealth in more and more people's minds as to what really matters and what doesn't. Business associates tell me that people who are already wealthy are leaving the financial industry in droves. And at the low end, people striving to climb their way out of poverty, people who have already learned how to manage on very little income, are living pretty well, and the stress they have usually felt so strongly because they can never get ahead is evaporating, the question being, get ahead of what? The end? Really?

Still, millions of people, it seems, are just plain paralyzed about what to do next. Most of the shooting wars around the world have achieved some kind of truce. Apparently the willingness to die, when there isn't a possibility to live very long to begin with, makes the time that's left seem all that much more important. The commercials across all sorts of media are less and less about commerce and more and more given to a humanitarian calling for reverence and introspection, forgiveness, courage, empathy, and a concern that we look out for one another until the end. Whether it's a clever way to sell or a real concern, who knows and who cares? I keep thinking things will turn sour and that people will start fighting over resources, but sharing is the in thing right now. I hope it lasts.

Politically it seems that a good many tyrants are losing a great deal of their authority. The old saying that nothing concentrates the mind like the notion of being hung from the gallows at daybreak rings true, even if that moment is three decades ahead. Just the certainty of a formal ending is enough to cause people to sit up and take notice. It makes you wonder why we haven't had the wisdom to do so all along.

Human life spans are pathetically short, but our kind have always thrived on the denial of such a reality, even though now it's becoming crystal clear that our species cares a great deal more that life will continue to go on without us than was thought to be the case in the past. I guess it's because the issue never really surfaced until now. But people do care. Do they ever. Some are shocked by the realization of how much it matters to them that there will be no generations to follow, no more future, no more past, and no more history, no more anything.

Some folks keep saying nothing has changed: It was always true that we are all going to die, and soon, so what's really new? Nothing, of course, but the pressing reality we are facing at this time reveals the great flaw in our makeup. The human predisposition to view the future as something open and unlimited, regardless of one's age, has always been both a social asset and a crucial defect. Early on it no doubt helped us survive because it made us daring enough to take the chances necessary for our respective groups' survival without weighing the risks, but in hindsight, we human beings clearly overdid it. Hindsight, these days, the very word seems a waste of breath and a sacrilegious and very decadent remark, because in a vacuum of nothingness, what the hell could possibly matter?

Perhaps the most positive thing, or maybe it's just the irony attached to one of my pet peeves, is that media pundits now seemed to have stopped asking people the state of their emotions in emergency situations. It appears they may have discovered that they have emotions of their own. After all, they are going to die, too, and soon. Are we starting to figure things out? Does life make sense now, or have we discovered instead that it never has and now it never will? You tell me. For the first time in history, it's now clear that each and every one of us needs to figure out the answers to such questions for ourselves because, if we don't, the voices in our heads will begin to whisper about us instead of to us.

If time is on the verge of ending for human beings, perhaps Wendell Smyth's T&T potion can be put to use in stretching time's parameters for some who deserve special consideration. I'm going to make him an irresistible offer.

## ANY PLAN BETTER THAN NONE

A CLOUD BANK FAR on the horizon to the southwest appeared to be moving in ever so slowly, as if it were lost, searching for an easy place to rest. When Les checked his PC for the latest weather, it said a cloud cover could be expected later in the day. Well, that much he could see. At this point, though, it was hard to tell because the clouds would move forward a little and then back. It was time to get this waiting off his mind.

The twins appeared to be asleep. Under the awning, Red was smoking an E-cigarette, probably loaded with marijuana, since weed was legal once again in Alaska after having been voted in and out two or three times. The same kind of referendum had occurred with the right to carry a concealed weapon. Les and the twins had waited on Red for a half-hour outside a cannabis dispensary shop, and now the idea that he was involved with someone who didn't have sense enough to stay clear-headed was also starting to bother him. "So, what's the plan, Red?" he asked.

It was Les's first clear utterance that hinted at awareness of and a willingness to acknowledge Red's authority, and it startled the big man. "We take them out and then get out, that's what."

"I know that, but we have clear orders to make sure we get Blythe first. We can't leave him to talk, assuming he hasn't given us up already. The rest of them are just bonuses, but once we start, we have to mop this thing up fast or we will never get out of here alive, man."

"I know that."

"Okay, then. Any plan is better than none. Let's figure things out and get it done. Clouds are moving in and we need to be ready. Another couple of hours and we should be ready to turn on the communication jammers, get it done, and get the fuck out of here."

# THE WARNING

B OB THORNTON WAS sitting in a recliner, studying papers on the world peace marketing strategy when his PC vibrated. "Mr. Thornton, this is Special Agent Sowell with the FBI. We are on our way to your location via helicopter and want to alert you that you and your neighbors on Caribou Creek have apparently been targeted for assassination by a religious movement in Missouri that is run by the person they call the Seer."

"Are you sure about this?"

"Our information has been checked, double-checked, and verified. We have an informant in Missouri. We just now learned that, earlier this summer, they sent someone ahead, a Jonas Blythe who is supposed to carry out the plan, or at least put it into action, only it seems he may have changed his mind. Now it appears at least four other mercenary types have been sent to your location to ensure the plan gets carried out. We talked to Vince Terrell, and he informed us that Jonas has twice saved his niece from dangerous situations, which doesn't make a lot of sense. Do you know where Jonas is at the moment?"

"Jonas has been here with us on several occasions lately. I can't believe he would intend to do harm to anyone here. I'll call you back when I find out something more. Thanks for the warning," Thornton said, realizing he might have hung up prematurely.

"Ruben, do you know where Jonas is?"

Ruben hollered from the next room, "Yes, Ellen went to take him some food and then walk the dogs. Why?"

"I just had a call from an FBI agent who says Jonas is connected to that Seer outfit in Missouri. He says they have us targeted for assassination."

"Bullshit. Jonas has been doing nothing but looking out for us. I already gave Vince all of the information I could get from Jonas about his past so he could check him out. Neither of us found anything to make us think he's a threat to any of us."

"I don't disagree, Ruben, but we need to find him and get to the bottom of this now. Get Vince on the line and tell him to head that way. I'll hook up with him."

"You're going?"

"Yes, I'm going. You have a heart condition, remember? Have the IT guys put some spies in the sky. Our chopper is down. I'm taking a four-wheeler. Keep in touch with Ellen."

"Okay, keep me posted."

Already outside, Thornton consulted his GPS. "Okay." According to the coordinates, Ellen and Jonas weren't that far away, but some of the terrain was rough, so rough that a four-wheeler going too fast could easily flip over. He had barely gone a half-mile when he heard Vince coming fast behind him, threatening to overtake and pass him. "Vince, slow down. If we crash here, we can't help her."

Vince nodded as if he heard, but the look on his face was nothing short of absolute panic. Vince the lawman, who always stayed cool when things got really hot, was now on the verge of losing it. Life without his niece would be unbearable.

Thornton kept looking at the screen on his machine's console, expecting Ruben to link him up with Ellen and the FBI, but so far, nothing. And then came a security alarm that said someone was approaching on a mechanized vehicle from the trail off the Parks Highway. The trespasser had ignored the warning to identify himself. What the hell else could go wrong?

# THE TRAP

ELLEN WAS WALKING Moby to Jonas's camp when her communicator whistled a loud warning. Before she could take it out of her knapsack, Jonas appeared, coming toward her with Gunny on a leash. "What are you doing out here, Ellen?"

"I was looking for you," she said, reading the message on her comm screen. It said: *Stay away from Jonas until we talk. Bob Thornton.*

From the look on her face, Jonas could sense that the truth about his mission for the Seer had been discovered. "Ellen, I'm not going to hurt you. I hope you know I would never hurt you. I got mixed up with some very unsavory people, and I came here to await some kind of assignment. I had no idea it would mean harming the folks who live here on the creek."

Stepping cautiously away from his reach, Ellen swallowed hard and looked at Jonas with a grim smile. In a weak voice she said, "I want to believe you, Jonas."

A rifle shot rang out from a ridge several hundred yards north as a round hit the ground less than two feet from where Jonas stood. "Quick! We need to get into the woods," he shouted. They ran straight ahead into a thick stand of timber as another shot rang out. Both dogs were excited simply because their masters were animated, but there seemed to be no immediate threat once they were in dense cover. They ran for five minutes and stopped behind a huge stand of ancient cottonwood trees.

"Ellen, my PC has a GPS, so these people shooting at us know exactly where we are. Take Gunny's leash. I'm going to run back to camp to get my four-wheeler and come back here and get you. Okay?"

"Why can't I come with you?"

"It may not be safe. One of them might be waiting at my camp. Sit down and stay behind these trees until I get back. I will be exposed for a few moments before I turn in here, but I will go very fast. Don't move away from here unless you see someone you don't know approaching, and if you do, turn the dogs loose, okay?"

Ellen nodded but didn't speak, and Jonas ran as fast as he could toward his camp. He stayed far enough into the edge of the timber and away from the open spaces and trail that he wasn't worried about being shot. What he feared most was that they might move in on Ellen before he could get back. The distance took him nearly ten minutes, and he was gasping for breath as he broke into the open at his camp.

He grabbed his AR-15, the Smith and Wesson .44 on his gun belt, and a knapsack of magazines and ammunition, then turned the key, and sped out of camp as if the Devil himself was gaining on him. He zigzagged on and off the trail, enough to make himself a hard target. Just before he turned in to where Ellen was waiting, a shot rang out and he heard the screaming sound of the bullet pass by. It was close, very close, but, from the sound of the rifle, the shooter must still be in the same place as before.

When he pulled in, Ellen stood up. "Turn the dogs loose and get on quick," he said. Ellen unsnapped the leashes and climbed on the four-wheeler behind Jonas. "This may be rough, so hang on tight.

I'm going to try to stay in the edge of the woods so they can't get a clear shot. We're going to have go back to the camp and I will leave the PC there this time. As they rode through the camp, he threw the Missouri PC as far as he could into the brush behind his tent and then sped away on a game trail into deep wilderness with the dogs in hot pursuit. Coming to a small clearing but still surrounded by old-growth forest, Jonas stopped and turned off the machine.

"Jonas, I thought I heard a wolf a minute ago."

"I didn't hear anything."

"I'm sure that's what it was because I've heard them before, lots of times recently, and Moby and Gunny are not behind us."

"They are fine, well protected."

"No, I forgot. I didn't intend to turn Moby loose, so I hadn't put his spikes on yet. I have them in my knapsack."

# WOLVES IN THE WIND

H E RAN DOWN a steep ravine, the invasive scent overwhelming him, flooding has senses, building in him a sweltering rage, an animal-bound sensation of all-out loathing. They were close by—he could both smell and feel their presence. He sat down, panting to cool off from the run. Moments later, a flurry of gray appeared in the brush ahead. Then another, and another, and as they started toward him, the black alpha male broke into the clearing a hundred feet from the others. Moby held his ground but slowly backed up to a stand of new-growth aspen trees so close together that there would not be enough room for one of them to get behind him. The slow-burning growl began from deep within his gut as he moved his head slowly side to side to watch his enemy close in.

There were five wolves now. Four to his right and the leader of the pack to his far left. The smallest of the four lunged forward with lightning speed. Her aim for his shoulder was accurate, and she drew blood. It was his blood this time, and as he positioned himself for another attack, the largest of the four targeted his flank with another sudden strike, drawing blood. This wound was deep. The success of the first two led the others to strike now, the alpha male sitting idly by as if watching a show put on to demonstrate the pack's loyalty.

Two wolves struck simultaneously, both drawing more blood.

So far, Moby had exacted no price from his attackers. All four were now poised to attack. As the first to do so lunged forward, a brown mass of muscle and scar tissue jumped between the white dog and the wolf. A loud guttural sound and then a snap as the pit bull broke the wolf's left front leg—a tactic he had learned from a wolf trying to snap his leg.

The largest of the four jumped onto Gunny, muzzle first, and made a shrieking noise as warm blood rushed from his mouth. Another wolf attacked Gunny from the other side with the same result. A sense of quiet and calm ensued in which all of the animals present froze in place and seemed to try to make sense out of what had just happened. Gunny moved forward and the wolves backed up. The huge spikes on the pit bull's armor glistened in a small ray of sunlight breaking through the clouds. Whitehead had told Jonas that because Gunny did not have thick fur, he had made the spikes longer and sharper to compensate.

Suddenly the alpha wolf disappeared into the woods. The others followed, and the wolf with a broken leg hobbled into the brush to rest. What it should do next would require some time to work out. The domestics went to find their masters.

## SHOTS FIRED

THE LOW-PRESSURE SYSTEM finally seemed to make up its mind, covering Caribou Creek with billowy white clouds. The men could move about now without worry of being caught on video from the sky. Red had spotted Jonas about a half-mile from his camp and was waving wildly and pointing. He held up his arms as if aiming a rifle to indicate he had located their target.

Now Les would have the opportunity to eliminate Jonas and get this show on the road. He got into position with his portable bench rest and looked through the rifle scope, faintly realizing that his whole life could be judged by crosshairs, by targets, by acts in which a split second meant death and a ripple in future events. Instantly his mind was filled with last night's dream, a vivid vision that he was remembering only now.

In his dream there were news screens of every size and shape everywhere he looked, and they all carried headlines announcing that some of the world's most life-worthy citizens had been killed, murdered in fact. And then there was a picture of him on a wanted poster declaring the incident to be a crime of the century.

The memory affected his breathing rhythm, and when he squeezed the trigger and heard the thunderous but muffled sound through his earplugs, he was shocked by what he saw. Then he was even more surprised by his reaction. For the first time in his memory of combat operations, he had missed his target. He fired again at a tree for Red's benefit. The real kicker, though, was that this time he was glad. He figured the old Les, the one he used to be, must be speaking through his subconscious. It was as if the weight of the world had lifted from his shoulders.

Somehow he felt it was deeply connected to the fact that the world was going to end, perhaps in his lifetime, if he should live so long. Suddenly time itself seemed more valuable than money ever did, and now that he was actually willing to give it some thought, he realized that there could be nothing worse than facing a future in prison while waiting for the end of the world. It would be hell on earth and clearly not worth the risk. He saw the direction his quarry took on the four-wheeler, and he would follow, but this time his objective would be different, very different. He fired again and again with no intention of hitting his target.

Red and the twins were staring at him. Red with his hands on his hips as if waiting for news that his team had scored. The twins were having one of their indecipherable private conversations. As quickly as he could without appearing in too big a hurry, Les collected his gear, put his pack on his back, slung his rifle over his shoulder, and took off in the direction of his shot. Red was shouting something, but Les was still wearing his ear protection and pretended he couldn't hear him. Red and the twins scrambled to gather their guns and backpacks. Fifty yards down the steep incline and once into deep forest, Les changed directions.

He wasn't exactly sure what had come over him, but he made a good guess. He had been brooding about the doomsday message, and then, once he had watched the profiles of the people he had come to eliminate, the two things had merged in his mind. What felt like a fire had been burning in his brain, and when the smoke cleared everything looked different. So he didn't have his military retirement. So what? He was still alive, still free, and now suddenly time itself, moment to moment, seemed to matter more than anything else. There were still plenty of things he wanted to do in life, and they didn't all cost money.

It was as if he'd had a stroke or a heart attack or had been unconscious and at death's door only to awaken in a different world where the things he cared about didn't matter. For the first time in recent memory, Les was actually anxious to find out what would matter in the remainder of his life.

Right now, though, he was in big trouble. He would have to figure a way to extricate himself and be quick about it or it would be too late, if it wasn't already. He was gaining distance now, as Red and the twins weren't prepared to leave in a hurry, which reinforced his contempt for Red's apparent incompetence. He would likely have to deal with Red himself, and the thought was the most pleasurable idea he'd had for days.

SITTING ON THE four-wheeler with Jonas, Ellen was frantically trying to communicate with Ruben. Finally she connected. "Ruben, I'm with Jonas in the woods. We're 2.8 miles north northwest of you. Someone shot at us near Jonas's campsite."

"Are you okay? And Jonas?"

"Yes. We're both fine but we think we were probably followed. Moby is gone, too. I didn't have time to put his armor on and I'm afraid the wolves will get him." As she looked away toward the hill that they had traversed, a muscle-bound pit bull ran out of the woods followed by Moby, his white coat crimson with his own blood. Ellen screamed into her PC, handed it to Jonas, and ran to meet the dogs.

"Oh my God! Look at you Moby-dog." She put her arms around him and held him gently to examine his wounds. Then she carefully fit the suit of armor around him and leashed both dogs.

"Ruben, it's me, Jonas. The dogs are back. Looks like Ellen's dog is a bit chewed up. Think you can get someone here to look after her?"

"They're on the way already, Jonas. Be careful, and for God's sake don't let anything happen to her."

"Okay. Who's coming?"

"Vince and Bob."

"You mean, Mr. Thornton is coming?"

"Yes, he is. The helicopter is down for maintenance. They are coming on four-wheelers."

"Okay. Let me know if anything changes."

"Jonas, Jonas," his name was being shouted somewhere nearby, the voice unfamiliar.

"Who are you?"

"I'm coming out of the woods. Don't shoot." Les walked out in the clear, holding his rifle with the butt toward Jonas and the barrel toward himself.

"I said, who are you?"

"I'm the one who shot at you."

## ON THE RUN

THIS WAS ALL too confusing. For some reason, Ellen could raise no one on her PC. Her system was still online and her GPS still tracked her precise whereabouts, but no one answered her calls and the message system was still down. None of it made sense. Of all the IT problems she'd experienced at Caribou Creek, this was the first time she'd seen a communication blackout. One of the last things Uncle Vince had told her was that the FBI was on the way. Maybe they had something to do with it.

Now this stranger, who gave his name as Les, was telling Jonas that three people were coming to kill them and that Ellen should get away immediately.

"Run, Ellen. Run!" Jonas shouted in response. "Take the dogs and go. Now!"

Ellen grabbed both leashes and ran down a steep incline toward a dry creek bed, hoping this wasn't some kind of trick. Recalling the remnants of an old cabin another mile ahead on a small lake, she decided to continue in that direction. She would go there and no further until she could contact someone and find out what was going on.

The dogs were manic with excitement. When Moby barked twice, Ellen stopped and took hold of his muzzle, softly shushing him to stop. When they got to the creek bed, the going was easy, and the dogs grew more manageable. As soon as her PC showed that she'd covered more than half a mile, she slowed to a walk. Twice she thought she heard a helicopter, but nothing now. Occasionally she heard shots, and she cringed with every discharge.

When she reached the old cabin site, she walked to the edge of the lake and let the dogs drink. A slight breeze hinted of autumn, causing her to shiver. Everything everywhere seemed chaotic. The character and personality of the whole world were changing in plain sight, and no one knew what to expect. The things people valued were taking new directions as frequently and dramatically as cracks of a whip. Worldly ambition appeared to be dissipating like fog on a hot summer day, and here she was running for her life for reasons that seemed insane.

Suddenly, in the far distance, rapid gunfire erupted. It sounded like war.

# PANIC

VINCE'S HEART WAS beating so hard, he could almost hear it, the incessant racing and pounding in his ears giving no signs of letting up. He kept gunning the engine of the four-wheeler every time he hit a straightaway, but Bob Thornton was ahead of him and kept slowing down and waving his hand to warn Vince to be careful. Of course, he knew he should be cautious, but he also knew that if something happened to his niece, his life would effectively be over.

Always before in emergency situations, Vince had been the calm in the storm. When people all about him were losing their heads, he was revered by his law enforcement peers for keeping his. This time was different. This time he had too much to lose, which he knew deep down was precisely why he had to get a grip on his emotions. Swallowing hard, he tried to concentrate on the rough road ahead.

Something was wrong with their communication system. The screen on his four-wheeler was blank, but it still registered the GPS location where Ellen was when she first contacted Ruben. They shouldn't have far to go. His mind kept sliding back to the Ellen he took custody of in Texas and the young lady she was today in Alaska. Most of the time, the Texas Ellen avoided eye contact, so shy she was. The way she carried herself and her facial expressions seemed to be a means of apologizing for her mere presence, as if she believed herself to be something to be tolerated, endured, and suffered. All of that was gone now, forgotten, erased from memory, and Vince would have guessed it was even gone from her dreams. Never before had he witnessed such a transformation.

If something happened to Ellen, it would be his fault, and no one would ever be able to convince him it wasn't. This much he knew about himself. So he began to repeat a silent mantra in his mind: Stay calm, stay calm, stay calm.

There was a small clearing up ahead and a stand of big trees where Ellen should be hiding, according to the GPS. Just ahead of him, Thornton slowed down. Vince spotted Jonas and then another man that he had never seen before holding a scoped rifle. Before he could stop and dismount, a long burst of fire from an automatic weapon several hundred yards away shattered the silence. Jonas and the stranger took refuge behind enormous cottonwood trees as Vince and Thornton raced toward cover.

Two more weapon bursts filled the air, and then Thornton's four-wheeler turned end over end, throwing him headfirst to the ground. When he hit the ground, he didn't move. Vince grabbed his arm and Les jumped forward while Jonas fired a pump shotgun at where he thought the assailants were hiding. When they were all safe behind the big cottonwood trees, it was clear that Thornton was unconscious. Seconds later, another four-wheeler burst into the clearing. Jonas could see that it was Ruben.

"Shoot!" Vince shouted. "Give him cover." Jonas emptied the shotgun, and Ruben drove into the woods.

"Ruben, I thought you were our communications link with the FBI," Vince said.

"Communications are down everywhere. Thought maybe I could help out."

"Where is Ellen?" Vince asked.

"We told her to take the dogs and run," Jonas said, pointing to a slope behind them. "She headed down that gulley."

"I know where she's going," said Ruben. "I got a partial message from her when the system came up for a minute. She's going to be at the old burnt cabin site near that little lake where we fish sometimes. You know where I'm talking about, right, Vince?"

"Okay. See if you can get Bob awake. I'm going to find her," Vince said, heading down the hill on foot.

"Okay go. Be careful. Communications are sporadic but mostly down. I don't get it. We've never had this kind of a problem before. Keep checking your PC," Ruben called as Vince disappeared in the timber.

"I know what it is," Les said. "I could have been one of them."

"One of who?" Ruben said.

"One of those bastards shooting at us."

"It's a long story," Jonas said, "no time for it now. We've got to figure out how to get out of here alive. I have a box of shotgun shells on my ride, but we don't have enough to fight a war. I lost some weapons and ammo on the way here because they weren't tied down."

"I've got a box," Ruben said as he rubbed Thornton's forehead with a cloth damp from his canteen. "Bob, you okay? Talk to me."

"We don't have enough ammo," Jonas said.

"I have enough," said Les, holding up his sniper rifle. "Can one of you spot for me?"

"Sure," said Jonas. Taking the binoculars Les handed him, he began to glass the hill where the shots had been coming from. "Give me a couple of minutes."

"Be careful," Les said. "They have those new AR-19s and shotguns and handguns. No scopes. That was my job."

"Okay, okay. See that cluster of yellow leaves to the right of that big cottonwood?"

"Got it."

"Now, down at the bottom of the tree, and to the right about a foot." As he spoke, Jonas suddenly felt nauseous. A deafening shot rang out, and far away on the hill, a scream followed. For a moment, there was a hushed silence and then another blood curdling scream of anguish.

With teeth clenched, Les exhaled and lowered the rifle. One of the twins was dead, which meant the other one would be insane with grief and a desire for revenge.

# CHOPPER DOWN

AGENT SOWELL GRABBED a canvas strap and held on tight. A burst of gunfire hit something vital, something in the engine or rotor. It was clear they were going down. The helicopter had an emergency safety rotation mechanism to ease the rapid plummet of an impending crash, and it seemed to be working, but still, it felt like they were dropping like a rock. And then they hit the ground hard. It was teeth-jarring and loud. Sowell swallowed so much air he thought he might hyperventilate. But he was alive and clearly uninjured, and so, apparently, were the rest of his men. The pilot, however, was dead. A tree branch had penetrated the fuselage, impaling Sowell's best friend.

There was nothing they could do for him, so Sowell yelled at everyone to get out quick. As the last agent and state trooper ran clear of the downed craft, the fuel tank exploded and the blast nearly knocked the men to the ground. Sowell began to run, shouting, "Straight ahead, we're about a mile from Blythe's camp. Keep a lookout. The shots that brought us down came not far from there. Take these sons of bitches alive if we can, but don't take any chances doing it."

Sowell was breathing too hard to keep yelling as the five men ran abreast of one another, dodging trees, young stands of willows, and devil's club. When they came into the small clearing where

Blythe's tent stood, there was no sign of anyone. The only thing obvious was that the pit fireplace where Jonas cooked his meals was still smoldering, giving off an occasional puff of smoke.

Distant shots to the northwest, automatic bursts followed by single shots, fired at uneven intervals. There was no need for discussion. With firearms at the ready, the men took off toward the gunshots. The going was tough, the ground soft and spongy. At times it was almost like running in place without gaining much distance. As time passed, Sowell began to think they should be there by now even in rough terrain. No shots had been fired for what seemed like a long time. He raised his hand high in the air as a signal to stop. The men stood still for a few moments catching their breath, and then, just when Sowell started to speak, more gunfire rang out, this time sounding as if it had come from their crash site. Again without discussion, they changed direction and resumed the pace. Sowell's confidence was shaken.

# SAFETY

VINCE WAS RUNNING at a jogger's clip, breathing heavily and feeling sick when he came to the clearing at the lake. Moby met him, blood-stained but with tail wagging, and Vince could see Ellen sitting on a cabin log. A flood of relief washed over him when he saw that she was okay. The pit bull sat at Ellen's feet as if he was bored or tired. "God, what happened to you, Moby?" he said.

"He was loose without his armor," Ellen said, "and he must have gotten into it with the wolves again. He has some pretty deep cuts and needs some stiches, but I don't think it's too serious. I'm so sorry. Is Jonas okay? I keep hearing gunshots."

"They were all okay when I left them. Thornton is hurt, though. He flipped over and bumped his head, and he hadn't come to yet when I left. But he'll be okay. I'm sure of it. God, Ellen I'm so glad you're safe. Nothing to be sorry for. This big mutt doesn't mind, do you, you big brute?" Vince stroked the dog, being careful not to cut himself on a spike.

A moment later, far off in the distance, they could hear the intermittent sound of a helicopter that was obviously in some kind of trouble because of the erratic rotor noise. Then came a loud crashing sound, and moments later an explosion.

"FBI," Vince said. "Must be. Gotta be. Let's head that way and see if we can lend a hand. Sounds like the crash happened a good distance from where Jonas is pinned down. Keep checking, Ellen, and let me know if communications are back on. Let's stay off the open trail and walk in the woods."

"Should we keep the dogs leashed?" Ellen asked.

"No, it will slow us down too much. They'll be okay."

As quickly as they could, they headed for the smoke of the downed helicopter. Running into willows thick with the stench of a carrion-eating bear made them stop and seek another route. Moby and Gunny, however, were intrigued by the bear scent and stayed behind to investigate.

## AN UNEXPECTED VISIT

HE PUT ON his best clothes, dark green Filson trousers, and an expensive khaki shirt. Having watched Robert Thornton on Adam 21, he knew that these were the kinds of clothes he wore. So, if he looked the part, maybe it would help him fit in. He unloaded his newly purchased four-wheeler out of the back of his new second-hand Ford pickup and headed up the trail to Robert Thornton's property. The place had been described as a fortress, a compound, and a mansion, but from the Adam 21 views, it was hard to tell which one was the better description.

Today felt like a truce between fall and summer. Clouds were moving with sunlight fading. The great mountain sent an occasional faint whisper of icy breeze throughout the region. His new machine had a great suspension system, computerized to ease the bumps from the rough terrain, and he was feeling glad that he'd spent the extra money to buy the best.

A console beneath the handlebars housed an Adam 21 screen, a GPS, a communicator, and a sophisticated radio that could be set to monitor emergency channels. About five miles into the trail, an incoming message from Thornton's resident security system asked him to identify himself at least a mile before reaching the property. He wasn't at all sure that it would be a good idea, considering the circumstances. Maybe he should turn around and forget about it. If he said who he was, they might try to keep him from reaching the place, and yet they might also try to stop him if he didn't identify himself. Well, if at all possible, this was something that needed to be done in person. Even if he tried face-to-face communication via PC, it wouldn't be the same. Maybe, when he only had a mile to go, he would speed up and get there before anyone could stop him.

Then, in the far distance, came the sound of gunshots—not single shots but rapid fire, staccato bursts, one after the other, as if an all-out war had suddenly erupted in the vicinity of Caribou Creek. What should he do now? He had a bear gun on his gun rack, but what he was hearing sounded like automatic weapons. Maybe it was just target practice. Surely that was it. When he reached the mile marker, he saw a small sign with a security notice to self-identify before proceeding. Okay, he might as well tell them who he is and why he is coming for a visit. But when he awoke his PC, there was nothing save a system notice announcing that communications were down.

Okay then, one problem solved. But the shooting continued, becoming more and more sporadic. Then came the sound of a helicopter getting louder by the second and in some kind of distress because the rotary signature was clearly missing the harmony of a precision-engineered machine. Next came a crashing sound, and a couple of minutes later, a massive explosion with billowing black smoke rising fast as if pushed aloft by an enormous fan.

God, now what? Now he had to proceed because these people must need help. Keeping his eyes on the horizon, he opened the throttle as much as the trail would allow. What felt like fifteen or twenty minutes later, he came to the top of a hill, where he could see for some distance and spotted a man running in a windbreaker with FBI on the back. He stopped his machine and sat still wondering what to do.

In the distant sky, the black smoke began to flatten out, rising no further but expanding as if being compressed top to bottom. That's where he should go, and up ahead was a trail to the west that might get him close to the crash site. What he was seeing didn't make sense because there might be passengers who needed help. He decided not to make contact with the FBI agents and instead took off again in the direction of the smoke.

When he hit a smooth straightaway, he opened the throttle, then started down a steep grade and up another hill. On reaching the top, he could see the downed helicopter fully engulfed in flames. No one to help if they were still in there, for sure. It was obviously too late. Still, he headed toward the wreckage as fast as the terrain would allow, just in time to see a man and woman coming out of the woods. Even from the distance he could tell that this was the man he had come to see. It was Vince Terrell, and that must be his niece, the one he'd seen on the local news.

The moment he raised his hand in the air to wave, a shot rang out and Vince Terrell fell to the ground.

Win jumped off his machine and ran toward them as fast as he could. Another shot rang out that hit close by. Ellen was on her knees beside Vince when he reached them. She was pressing her hand on his right side to stop the bleeding.

"Let's get him into the woods quick," Win said. Reaching down, he grabbed Vince by the shoulders to pull him into the trees, and Ellen held his legs.

As soon as they were out of the line of fire Vince said, "What are you doing here?"

Speaking at a breathless pace, he said, "Sir, I'm Win Potter, remember? You thought I was wanted for murder, but the DNA cleared me. I wanted to see you in person. I heard you are still look-ing for the person who killed Amanda Tucker, and I came to see if there is any way I can help. It's my fault she's dead. If she hadn't been coming to see me, nothing would have happened to her." He took a deep breath as if suddenly starved for air.

The impact of the bullet left Vince with a foul taste in his mouth. He didn't have to look at the wound to know that he was in serious trouble. As he began to regain his breath, he could feel the warm wetness of bleeding and the first signals of pain threatening more to come. "We don't need any help, son."

"No disrespect, sir, but I think you do." With that he ran erratically to his four-wheeler, grabbed his shotgun and ran back. There was no gunfire. Vince had been holding a shotgun but had dropped it when he was hit. As soon as Win reached Vince and Ellen, he handed his gun to Vince and ran to pick up Vince's gun. Even as he ran back, still no shots were fired.

When he knelt down beside them, his eyes met Ellen's, and he was smitten. "I'm Win Potter, miss. You must be Ellen." The way she looked at him made him think that, emergency aside, she might be interested. He put his hand on Vince's shoulder and said, "Who shot you, sir? How many of them are there? It sounded like a war going on a little while ago, and I saw an FBI agent running in the woods a ways back. What's going on?"

"Which way was the agent headed?"

"Couldn't tell for sure because of the terrain. Maybe back this way, sir, but it's a long way on foot and hard to make good time."

Bursting instantly out of thick brush, a huge redheaded man came toward them so fast there was no time to react. His eyes ablaze, his face the shape of hatred, he swung a rifle with one hand, the butt knocking Win to the ground, and grabbed Ellen by the waist with the other hand, scooping her up and disappearing into the woods as effortlessly as if he had casually snatched a beach towel to dry himself after an ocean swim.

Vince was doubled over in pain and had barely seen what happened. Terrified that he would never see Ellen alive again, he tried to get up time and again, but could do nothing more than lie on his side holding a hand over his wound to stop the bleeding. Win Potter lay writhing on the ground in a semiconscious state, trying desperately to clear his head.

## FACE-OFF

JONAS AND LES reached the crash site just in time to hear Red shout at the top of his lungs, "Get me Jonas or I will cut this girl's heart out and feed it to animals. You hear me?"

Vince finally gained the strength to struggle to his feet, while Win Potter twisted, turned, and thrashed about on the ground as if trying to awaken himself from a bad dream. Taking aim with his shotgun, Vince said as loud as he could, "Let her go. Take me." Through the trees Vince could see the man who had taken Ellen, but he couldn't see her. He had a clear shot but couldn't bring himself to squeeze the trigger. The dilemma made him sick and on the verge of retching.

Before Red could reply, Jonas yelled, "I'm here. Come out, you big coward. You have to hold a girl hostage to show us what a big man you are?"

"You need to catch up first. Come alone or I will cut her up here on the spot." And with that, the big man tossed Ellen over his shoulder like weightless duffel bag and headed down a deep draw covered with willows and devil's club. Vince was nearly insane with remorse that he had not taken the shot, wondering what on earth had come over him.

Jonas ran down the steep incline and found no sign telling which way they went. As he desperately scanned the terrain, Moby and Gunny appeared out of the brush, greeting him as though he'd been away on vacation and had just returned to a kennel to pick them up. "Moby, go find Ellen. Go find her."

The dog seemed to get excited hearing Ellen's name, but he was otherwise confused. Since Ellen was being carried, her scent was not to be found on the ground. Jonas began to walk in larger and larger circles, thinking that Red would have to put Ellen on the ground at some point and that, when he did, the Great Pyrenees would recognize it.

Twenty minutes of searching revealed nothing. The dogs followed Jonas as if they were on a carefree romp in the woods. He was dripping with perspiration, worried about what the vengeful bastard might do to Ellen to get even. Then, just as they were on the high point of a sparsely timbered hill, Moby let out a high-pitched part-bark and part-yelp and took off, heading back toward where they had started. Jonas thought Red must be lost, not realizing he was going back to where he first found Ellen. Moby was way ahead of Jonas and then, in the dense underbrush, he let out a noise as if he had been hurt. Silence followed.

Running straight ahead into a clearing not twenty yards from where they had started, Jonas saw Red standing with one huge hand around Ellen's neck and a rifle in the other. Moby lay off to the side unconscious, and Gunny sat by, panting and apparently confused by what was going on and by an old familiar scent.

Red let go of Ellen to use both hands for his weapon, and the instant she fell to the ground, Jonas covered the short distance and kicked the big man in his chest, causing him to drop his gun. He hit Red so hard, he lost his own footing and both men fell, one atop the other, an entanglement of writhing malice.

With both arms choking Jonas around the neck, Red was about to twist when Jonas struck a backwards blow to his groin. Red let go, falling back and doubling up, but sensing he could take no time to favor his pain, he picked up a dead tree branch, jumped to his feet, his face seething in rage, and with a sweeping blow hit Jonas on his blind side. Red took a deep breath as if doing so would relieve the pain in his groin. Still lying on the ground, Jonas opened his eyes, stared at Red, and pulled a small revolver out of his back pocket. But when he pointed it at Red, he felt reluctant to fire.

Red's face bore a wide grin as he realized that Jonas couldn't bring himself to shoot. Standing over Jonas, he lifted the limb over his head, readying himself to bring it down for a final blow, when a red dot appeared on his forehead. A gun blast echoed through the forest, and he collapsed in a heap of instantly relaxed muscle, dead before he hit the soft tundra.

Jonas, still too dizzy to stand up, crawled over closer to Vince and Ellen. He found he couldn't look them in the eye for having failed to shoot Red himself. Blood flowing freely from his wound, Vince lay on the ground a few yards away, aghast that he had almost lost a battle to save Ellen because he too seemed to have lost his nerve for the first time in his life.

Ellen ran to Vince, knelt down, and applied more pressure to his wound. A loud crashing noise sounded through the brush, and suddenly it appeared to be raining FBI agents and state troopers. Agent Sowell bent down to Vince and Ellen and said, "Medevac helicopter on the way. Should be able to hear it any minute. How many others are there, do you know?"

"I think that's it," Vince said.

"No," said Les, approaching Sowell, "there is one more. He might be trying to get a ride out with a hunting guide, but I don't know for sure if he even knows how to contact the pilot." He gave the FBI the name of the guide service, and then Sowell took Jonas and Les into custody as suspects in the assassination plot.

Lying beside Ellen, Moby regained consciousness but was in bad need of a veterinarian. It was all he could do to just stay awake. Win sat close by with his eyes shut, gently petting Moby while nursing his own splitting headache. It seemed too much effort to speak, but he refused medical treatment and would not get on board the helicopter.

Sowell seemed satisfied that Potter wasn't a threat of any kind and showed no interest in detaining him. So Win leaned back against a big cottonwood and watched the medevac helicopter fly south. He was in no hurry. He would just rest here for a while and soak up the scenery. For the first time since returning to Alaska, he felt good about the future. He wasn't sure what he was going to do, but he made a silent vow that his career in the wheat fields was over.

# DEAR ANGELA

THINKING THAT HE might be asleep, Angela stepped softly into Dee's quarters, but it was readily apparent that the room was empty. There, on the nightstand by the lamp, lay an envelope. She reached for it and flinched when she saw her name. Taking a seat in the leather recliner next to the bed, she paused for a while before opening the letter:

*Dear Angela,*

*If you are reading this, it no doubt means I am gone. I can say this with confidence because I can feel the end. It's almost as if I can reach out and touch death. I've thought often of telling you these things, but so much of the time I feel my attempt is just senseless rambling, and it's always been easier to remain silent and procrastinate. Most people, I suspect, have never looked directly into the abyss without blinking. Now, maybe, at least young people will have to. Oh, I know most people think about dying, but I've always wondered how many stare down the abyss refusing to look away, wondering as they might about the mystery of nothingness and the absurdity of squandering so many opportunities in life and spending so much time worrying about matters that in the final analysis don't make a fly swat's difference to any living soul.*

*All of my years in a wheelchair thinking about walking, all of the papers I wrote but never published, all of the psychological and sociological inferences I made but never made note of, all of the petty grievances I held against others, and theirs against me, are now evaporated into a vacuous plane of ethereal absurdity.*

*I trust we have done some good in the world, and I don't mean in any way to take away from it, but of late I've come to the conclusion that all that is important in the world is obscured by the frenzy of busyness most people pursue to keep from facing the certainty of oblivion. I've known for some time now that my death is close by, so close that I can feel my life force shutting down. I didn't think I would make it to Thornton's retreat. And then, getting here, I knew I would not leave alive.*

*You may share this letter with the group if they have not disbanded yet. The good vs. evil discussion is off track. Face the abyss, and the conclusion you reach will make a lot more sense. Don't do that, and your time will be wasted. Death is reality. And all of the things we do to put off thinking about it keep us from figuring out what is important and what is not. Real meaning surfaces in thoughts and implications when we're facing nonexistence and the absence of time. The real reason for politics is to enable us to forget that we are going to die. Everything that doesn't come to mind when one is facing death is bullshit to begin with.*

*I wish you the best in life as you have been the best in mine. Scattering my ashes near this place would be nice.*

*With Love,*

*Dee*

Angela went topside, and there, sitting in his wheelchair, nestled in a blanket and facing America's highest peak in full radiant view, sat the corpse of William David Dee. Clouds covered much of the sky, but it looked as if the mountain had appeared just in time to say goodbye. Far away to the south, Angela thought she heard gunshots.

## SORROWFUL NEWS

COMMUNICATIONS WERE BACK on line. Troopers found two battery-powered jamming devices in the woods and put them out of commission. They also found the body of Jacques Archambault where Les Coleman had shot him, and later, ten miles away, they found his brother, Toussaint, dead of an apparent suicide.

The medevac helicopter sat down first at the compound, and Ruben jumped aboard to help Thornton, whose concussion still left him wobbly. No sooner had they achieved altitude than they descended, landing again to pick up Vince. Straining, Ruben picked up the mountainous white dog and put him aboard the helicopter too. When Ellen jumped in after him, Vince said, "Stay here, Ellen. I'll be all right. Go find Ginger and make sure she's okay. And take care of Jonas's dog."

"Don't worry about Moby, Ellen," Ruben said. "I will see that he gets to the vet's office in Wasilla."

"Okay," she said, reluctantly stepping out of the aircraft. "Call me and let me know how you're doing. Don't forget." She felt great relief that her uncle, Mr. Thornton, and Moby were on their way to medical treatment, but she couldn't shake a sense of dread that it was a mistake not to go on the helicopter. Still, she did need to find Aunt Ginger, hard as it was to think clearly. The troopers had taken Jonas, and she didn't know where he was. What was going to happen to him? Had Uncle Vince lost too much blood? Where on earth was Gunny? She had seen her abductor hit Moby with a gun butt, but once the redheaded monster was shot, Gunny had disappeared.

Two FBI agents and two troopers walked Ellen back to Thornton's compound. When they arrived, Ginger and Gunny met them out front. "Oh my God. I was so worried about you," Ginger said, embracing Ellen.

"Uncle Vince is on the way to the hospital with Mr. Thornton," said Ellen.

"I know. They just phoned me." They walked arm in arm inside the main building. A half-hour later, Ginger's PC rang with an urgent ring tone.

"Ginger, this is Ruben. Vince is in cardiac arrest. We are still a few minutes from the hospital, but there are two medics here with him. Thornton says his helicopter will be ready to fly shortly and the pilot will bring you and Ellen to the hospital. Okay?"

Silence and a burst of tears from Ginger's face told Ellen her fears had been justified.

# A TROUBLED LEGACY

I T WAS HARD getting a grip on his new sense of disappointment. The whole thrust of his ambition had been to have his reputation as a cunning serial killer survive him in the history books. Now, all of a sudden with the doomsday announcement, there was to be no history. His own life would stop short of old age, his name would not be remembered and discussed in police academies, in college history classes, and in forensic labs. Like everyone and everything else, he would simply be nonexistent.

This new reality left him empty. Something was missing, a gnawing hunger, an insatiable force, but then, wasn't that what prompted him to kill in the first place? Why let himself be troubled by his very nature, his core, his very reason for being? Why was he having so much trouble pushing these anxious thoughts aside? Time to get back on track.

Marking time, waiting for a cloud cover, was irritating. He told his employer at the lab that he wasn't feeling well and that he would make some cold sales calls, but he would be late getting back to Missouri. They wanted to know when, and he said he would let them know in a few days. He could tell they weren't pleased, but then, what were they going to do? Fire him? Not likely.

During the night, a low pressure system moved in and clouds covered the valley. No Adam 21 recordings would be made, no big screen depiction of the Palmer postman with an arrow bolt through his heart, no film on the nightly news for days, because the body would not likely be found until he was gone—long gone—but not forgotten, at least not for three decades. Now he had the perfect escape vehicle. Who would suspect a mail truck driving away from the scene of a crime, a crime where a beautiful and smart young lady would die at the conclusion of her dear uncle's funeral service?

To a homicidal psychopath, Vince Terrell's memorial service seemed over the top. Why so many people for so little accomplishment? Why so many dignitaries? Why use a public facility and not a church? Too much for a man of such little achievement, a law man at that, not even smart enough to solve a simple puzzle, a puzzle laden with purposeful clues, and demanding respect for the puzzle master, a puzzle that could only be solved by a girl. And what a girl. She reminded him of the pregnant chick years before, the one whose deformed fetus he fed to the fish in Willow Creek, the one who before she died told him where he could find her friend with orange hair, the one who wanted to live so badly that simply remembering her filled him with pleasure as if it had just happened. The memory would have to do, because he couldn't take his time with Ellen Terrell. This was simply a quick hit, and he'd be gone.

His adrenaline and sense of invincibility surging, Hopkins congratulated himself on his sheer genius. Ellen Terrell would be hard to get close to in private, but in a crowd of people, many of whom were themselves in law enforcement, the confusion when his victim went down without a sound would amount to total chaos, and he would simply drive away to deliver the day's mail, rain or shine. Was that not the motto?

Sitting in wait, deep in a lush hedgerow of thick shrubbery forty yards from the covered door of the building where the services were being held, he recalled his cleverness years ago when, after he had disposed of the pregnant girl's body, he'd gone back to the grocery store parking lot, jump-started her car, running the engine long enough to charge the battery, and then parked down the road a ways so no one would know how he had made contact with her. He had been lucky that it was a cloudy day because that was before it was common knowledge that Adam 21 was a law enforcement tool for solving crimes. After he was through with his first quarry, he'd picked up the girl with orange hair under the pretense of taking her to meet her friend, and his luck held: it was still cloudy then as it was here now. Lucky for him, not for her. Her body was never found and never would be.

The service was over. The big doors opened, and the mourners began to emerge in a slow stream. Twenty, forty, maybe fifty people now, maybe double. And there she stood. Clear shot. Low in the shrouding shrubbery, he steadied himself against the corner of the building, then *fire*: he pulled the trigger, releasing the arrow.

## SERVICES

GINGER AND ELLEN were staying at the Caribou Creek cabin to avoid well-wishers, and to grieve in solitude. On the second day after Vince died, Hershel had picked up Moby from the vet in Wasilla and brought him to the cabin. Moby had a pretty bad concussion and was still heavily medicated and listless. For reasons that would remain a mystery, once Gunny had been found in the woods, he seemed bonded to Ginger, so much so that he didn't like to be away from her. When she sat in a chair or on a couch, he was nearly always to be found at her feet. Ginger got word to Jonas, who was still in jail in Anchorage, that Gunny was with her, and Jonas told her she was welcome to keep the dog.

The drive to Wasilla was sad, too sad for words. No one spoke. Soft whispers and flowing tears set a cadence of remorse, in tune with the whir of tire tread on a newly washed Hummer bound for the funeral service. Ginger and Ellen sat in the front, Ruben and Thornton in the back, looking out opposite windows so as not to find something that would require spoken words.

Hard feelings had been put aside because of the service to come. Jonas and Les were both in police custody pending charges, and every time the group discussed what should happen to them, arguments erupted. Ellen wanted them both freed; everyone else seemed to be less sure of what to do about their situation.

As they parked at the sports center on the Palmer-Wasilla Highway, the only place deemed big enough to accommodate such a service, Owen Sandburg waved and then turned and entered the building. Ginger and Ellen clasped hands as light rain turned to heavy rain. Ellen thought tears from above were called for, as the dearest man on the planet was now lost to her forever. Such a short time and so much grief: first the trooper died, then Jenny, then Dr. Dee, the kind man in the wheelchair, and now her Uncle Vince. All this at the same time as the doomsday announcement lamenting the end of the world while she was still young. What next? Who next? She knew at the time that she was making a mistake by not riding with Vince in the helicopter; it felt wrong. She should have insisted.

The service lasted an hour and a half; the crowd was huge. So many people Ginger and Ellen had never seen, so many well-wishers surrounded them, and yet there was nothing, but nothing, to feel good about. Grief foreclosed their ability and willingness to pay attention to anything save that Vince was gone. Even the dignitaries were a blur. Both Ruben and Thornton avoided eye contact with close friends.

In the background, "Liebestod" from Wagner's *Tristan and Isolde*, Vince's favorite piece of music, played softly and then began to gain rigorous volume, bringing the service to a close with Wagnerian crescendos so loud that speaking was out of the question. For that, both Ginger and Ellen were grateful. Ever since Ginger had seen the movie *Melancholia* years ago, this music had never seemed the same. Now the piece always brought the end of the world to mind. How fitting, she thought, how appropriate of Vince to set the stage of his own departure with that of the whole planet.

Vince had asked long before that he be cremated and his ashes strewn along Caribou Creek on a summer's day. Remembering his wishes, Ginger dreaded the coming year. People were walking up to her and Ellen on the way out, letting their sad expressions speak for them, some nearly blinded by tears, some too moved to exchange glances, and some so stricken by the overpowering hold the music had on their emotions that they feared looking directly at family members might reduce them to uncontrollable sobbing. A few people hugged or touched them, speaking in whispers so as not to have to compete with the music.

Leaving the building, Thornton told Ginger and Ellen to wait out front and Hershel would bring the Hummer around. The rain had let up to random sprinkles, but dark clouds still blanketed the horizon. Owen Sandburg walked up and gently put his hand on Ellen's shoulder, causing her to recoil and move ever so slightly backwards.

"I'm sorry," he said, but before his words could be heard, the bolt from a crossbow pierced Ellen's shoulder and Owen jumped away. Instantly he came forward again to shelter her from harm. Screams went up as the milling crowd realized what had happened. With blood from Ellen's shoulder soaking his shirt, Owen held on to her, desperately searching for another shot to come.

Just exiting the building, Matthew Sills ran toward Ellen, shouting to the crowd. "Did anyone see who did this?"

A man twenty feet away shouted back and pointed, "Over there."

## THE NATURE OF BEASTS

MOBY WAS RESTED and fully alert now, still tender from the concussion and stiches, but allowed to venture outside from time to time. When Hershel opened the cabin door to drive Ellen and Ginger to the funeral service, the two dogs had slipped out. Later in the day, when there were no humans in the area, they both became aware of the beckoning allure to follow a female wolf prancing about at the edge of the woods near the cabin. This was something beyond the instinctual demand to kill an enemy—a female wolf in heat was inviting two male domestic canines to follow her into the deep forest. She was summoning them into the silent, unfathomable underbrush of terrain that two-legged creatures could barely traverse.

Gunny followed close behind Moby for a mile until they reached a low point in what had once been the deepest part of an ancient creek bed, where limestone banks surrounded the opening and steep sides made escape impossible. It was a perfect place to kill. The domestics stood their ground, still swaying side to side from the run, panting to cool themselves, their tongues flipping rhythmically like fishermen's fly lines in search of famished trout.

The she-wolf blended magically with the underbrush, disappearing ghost-like into the woods, the stench of the wolves now overwhelming their distant cousins. Moby and Gunny backed up against the limestone as a mass of black and gray fur closed the escape route. Twelve full-grown Alaska timber wolves, for the first time the whole pack, faced the two dogs in an age-old test of might. This, however, was not a contest, or at least, it should not have been but for technology.

The scent of dried blood on the white dog's fur added a primordial sense of excitement from wounds already laid open. The wolves moved in, as if they were but one body, like a school of piranha bearing down on plucked chickens, any sense of memory of their first encounters with these domestic creatures forgotten by the success of their last confrontation with the white dog. This kill would be effortless, representing a collective instinct without regard to the action of individual members of the pack, this was the way of the wolf, the way of the wild.

As the first pack members made contact with the tame creatures, the tenor of whining yelps, wincing sounds echoing pain, gained an audible crescendo, getting louder by the second, injury to the intended victims of the well-orchestrated strategy being marginal at best. The flow of blood increased with each strike, the wolves not noticing the sharp cuts incurred on their own muzzles until moments after their attacks, prompting them to strike again and again, even as their injuries mounted and they became less and less of a threat and more of a defeated force, like a vastly superior but weaponless army.

Moby and Gunny fought defensively solely by instinct. Neither animal had ever been under siege by so many attackers at one time. There were simply too many attackers to take on one enemy with the intent to impose a serious blow or to kill. After a few moments, the whimpering began to subside, and the wolves, one by one, began breaking off the attack, backing up a few feet, lying down with muzzle on the ground, blood oozing, and yellow, penetrating eyes riveted on the two invincible creatures before them, straining to gain an animal's comprehension of something beyond their natural ability to understand, a means of resolving why they were impotent against inferior creatures.

After a half-hour standoff of nothing but gazing at their quarry, the alpha male disappeared into thick brush, followed moments later by the individual pack members, until the two invincible domestics were alone, muddled by circumstance, miraculously still alive without serious injury, and triumphant as a couple of Piper Cubs after holding off a squadron of Japanese Zeros, the attack pilots having flown away dispirited, failed Kamikazes.

## COMBATANTS

A ROAR WENT UP from the crowd outside the sports center, women screamed, men shouted, some people began to run without first deciding where to go. And then a tall man with a loud voice shouted a second time, "Over there in the bushes," and pointed to the corner of the adjacent building. The dense, expansive hedges had mostly concealed Wilfred Hopkins, but now a flurry of twisting and shaking brought him into view for those close by.

He was attempting to reload his crossbow when a young man, seeming to appear from nowhere, jumped into the hedgerow as if he were practicing the high-jump at a track meet. He landed on top of Hopkins, the crossbow lost in the foliage, and the two men became locked in furious combat, with those nearby unable to discern what was underway, only that the struggle was fierce and unrelenting. A gunshot rang out, the movement slowed, and moments later, stillness prevailed—no sound, no movement, no indication of what had occurred, and nothing visible except a big, beautiful row of emerald evergreen shrubs and what appeared to be a morass of flesh underneath.

People were screaming and running in circles, looking about for someone to explain what was going on or to tell them what to do next and where to go. Two state troopers and two local police officers arrived at the hedges, and without hesitation, the three men and one woman pulled the downed combatants out of the shrub-bery. A search through wallets revealed that the man who still had a pulse and a bullet wound in the stomach was one Winston Potter. The deceased subject with a knife in his heart was one Wilfred Hopkins.

The wounded man and Ellen were rushed to the hospital, accompanied by two state troopers in the ambulance. The coroner's vehicle took the dead man's body to the morgue. The wounded man would come to be a celebrated hero, the deceased, a diabolical but failed killer not worthy of the archives of famous criminals except as a footnote and as a warning to law enforcement and juries that sperm samples could indeed be planted at crime scenes.

On the second day after its arrival, Hopkins' body was stolen from the morgue. The incident made headlines everywhere, but there were no leads, ever, fueling a mystery that would haunt the Internet and social media for years to come.

## RECONCILING RELIGION,
## RED CLOUD, AND RACISM

THE SUMMER GUESTS were gone from Caribou Creek. Only James Tall Tree stayed behind to help Bob Thornton prepare for another conference on the growing world unrest. Ruben had spent several days in Anchorage and was just returning with Hershel in the Hummer when he saw James walking along the trail a hundred yards from the compound. "Where you headed, James?"

"I'm going to Jonas's camp. Bob thought we should have a look and see if anything needs to be put into storage, and I need some excercise. Want to come along?"

"Sure." Ruben got out, waved Hershel on, and the two men began walking.

After five minutes of silence, James said, "You know, Ruben, we've known each other for a long time, and I don't recall your ever asking me about the folks back home. I mean, we grew up not that far apart."

"My apologies, James. I guess it's a holdover from the old days. Not all of the people back home took to those of us with mixed blood. I know it's silly, but I guess I've always been a little stand-offish when it comes to discussing our people with full-bloods like yourself."

"Well, first off, I wouldn't be that sure about anybody being a full-blooded anything, but I'm really surprised to hear that you would give a second thought to such nonsense, Ruben."

"I know."

"You understand, then, that I'm not like that in any way, right?"

"I do, James. No worries. It's me, not you. It's just old feelings that are hard to shake and that have more influence than I would like to admit. I realized just recently that when I'm talking to non-Native Americans, I frequentlty speak of my heritage as a Lakota tribe member, but when I'm talking to full-bloods, I don't."

"I never would have guessed as much."

They walked for another five minutes without speaking, and then James had a question. "Bob said you were going to visit Jonas in jail. Did you?"

"Yes, and I can't stop thinking about it."

"What do you mean?"

"What he said was stunning."

"Stunning?"

"Yes, he said he'd watched an old archived lecture by the religious scholar Karen Armstrong that helped him get clear on some things. She spoke of a competition held among tenth-century Indian priests to describe the essence of God or the reality of God, and the winner of the debate was the one whose comments left the others dumbstruck and speechless. 'That's it,' Jonas said. 'That's what religion should be. Not something about beliefs. It should be about behaving honorably and relating to others with compassion, like the woman said, and whenever religion comes up against an unknown, it should bloody well stop and contemplate the mystery in silence as the ancients are said to have done.'

"He said that silent reflection and contemplation are open to everyone, and the people who keep making things up when they should be silent do so strictly for the purpose of gaining power over others. He's wishing he'd been smart enough to figure that out before he got himself in trouble. I have to say, I was sort of dumbstruck myself by his assessment, and that doesn't happen very often. I mean, to me, it was like a left hook to the jaw."

"Well, it seems like awfully good counsel," said James.

"It fits Buddhism's notion of enlightenment, and Kant might have likened it to doing the right thing for the right reason and not because it was thought of as one's duty. It certainly lines up with Wittgenstein's assertion, 'Whereof one cannot speak, therefor one must remain silent.' If religion were to devote itself to relating to others with compassion and to contemplation when dumbstruck, religion would stand for mature inquiry. Such conviction could become an effective viral antidote to conflict and war, and we wouldn't likely be in the God-awful mess the world is in today.

"Just imagine, James. What if we could substitute wonder for belief? I mean, Jesus, pursuing a subject to the point of being dumbstruck is the reason I get up in the morning. If the point of religion was to focus on learning to the limits of our knowledge, behaving with compassion, and connecting with those outside of our respective tribes, the world would be a very different place and I might be amenable to being considered a religious person.

"Instead, what we have are millions of members of the clergy, all over the world making shit up, professing to know the unknowable, professing to know the mind of God and to speak for God. The end result too often is contempt for nonbelievers at best and fanaticism at worst."

"What you're saying puts me in mind of the powwows back home when we were kids and how hearing a persistent drumbeat used to feel like a means of making a spiritual connection with visitors from different tribes."

"I witnessed war dances and powwows but wasn't allowed to participate."

"Sorry to hear that, Ruben. You know, don't you, that, speaking philosophically, I'm a Lakota Indian and a scientist, and yet I've never been able to reconcile the two worldviews. Angela told me what you said about tribal hostilities over the centuries and how they kept the population from outstripping the resources. She was dying to argue the point with you, but I asked her not to until after Bob got what he was looking for from the group.

"I have friends in the field of anthropology, who make a compelling case that over the long term, the very long term, it's actually war and oppression that have given us the wherewithal to realize a scientifically technological existence. War, they claim, has been followed incrementally by societies with larger and larger governments who over time are better and better at enforcing peace. Prosperity follows as the whole thing plays out, repeating itself over and over."

"You know," said Ruben, "there is a universal but seldom-acknowledged moral lesson here. We now have the most unbelievable technological tools in history, and the more nations can move their people out of poverty and into leisure, the more innovation surges. The past shows unmistakably that a hand-to-mouth existence stifles modernization."

"I agree. Good point. Imagine what it would be like if the Europeans had never landed on these shores. Would I still be riding a pony and chasing buffalo?"

"You might be chasing buffalo, James, but it would be on foot. The Spanish brought horses to this continent, remember?"

"Touché. Well, it would still be a good life. But warriors in Red Cloud's tradition couldn't stop an asteroid from hitting the earth, and I can."

"True, James. But for an asteroid, we wouldn't be here anyway, right?"

"Yes, my point precisely, because that goes for everything that's happened up to now, the good and the bad. But hey, I can watch Red Cloud as he lived, even though he's been dead for more than a hundred years."

"So where does oppression figure in?" Ruben asked.

"Well, look at how many centuries passed by, eons really, with very marginal technological advances because a hand-to-mouth, hunter-gatherer existence didn't lend itself to enough leisure time and enough diverse experience or interaction with those with different customs to inspire a truly creative and inventive culture."

"The Aztecs were an advanced culture," Ruben observed, and just then a slight breeze sent a burst of yellow birch leaves fluttering. Close by, a raven began to caw as if preparing for debate. Both men paused for a moment before proceeding.

"Yes, and they were hellishly oppressive," said James, "and they did indeed create a ruling leisure class. Looking back in time, it's clear that slavery and oppression gave the oppressors the time and where-withal to tinker, while the oppressed toiled and did the heavy lifting. Today, when we watch Socrates via Adam 21 babbling to his listeners, we can clearly see the work in the background being accomplished by slaves. America's rise as an agrarian power did so on the backs of African slaves, and Adam 21 makes that very clear, too.

"Look, Ruben, I'm not saying that the injustices of the past were absolutely necessary to get us where we are today technologically, but there are clearly grains of truth in the big-picture version of how we got here, precisely because of what actually *did* happen. We are all indebted to the oppressed souls of history because, without their contribution, our lives as they are now would simply not have been possible.

"Today, the increases in productivity that our technological advances have generated should stand in for the utility of historical oppression and offer enough leisure to all of our citizens to spur an exponential increase in the creativity we need to meet the challenges of the future. But then, that would require wresting power away from entrenched plutocrats.

"We have the technological sophistication to create such a society, but what we lack is the will, the political smarts, and the appetite for revolution, although the current state of world affairs may present a once-in-a-lifetime opportunity.

"You know, Ruben, sometimes I think the scientific mindset might be explainable in terms of human intelligence as an aspirational metabolic force, a fervent imagination forever in search of a way to emerge and grow larger. I mean, human intelligence is like a viral outburst of energy that strives constantly to up the ante of its being in the world."

"You aren't headed toward the incomprehensible notion of what is being called the Singularity, are you, James?"

"No, not at all. I mean an effort in pursuit of Einstein's space-time as a fifth-dimensional reality, with the realization that, if we were to prove a unification theory, it might qualify as something comparable to the mind of God.

"Is God hiding behind hyper-dimensionality? Dammed if I know, but neither do those who speak falsely from lecterns in churches. It's ironic that the ancient religious leaders most often quoted today were ignorant by our standards, but the fact that they weren't literalists shows they had more common sense than lots of people demonstrate in the present."

"By my reckoning, James, ancient Christianity was more like Buddhism is today than the preposterous pulp fiction of today's crazed evangelists."

"You might be right about that. I think human intelligence, if given free rein and enough room for expression, can best be described as a positive life form that has the potential to turn negative and metastasize in a heartbeat.

"So, that being the case, the negative is a malicious source of energy every bit as powerful as the dynamism of intelligence and curiosity. It's a dark force of inborn ignorance, the same substance that has made a scourge of religion. It's a seething malfeasance born of the fear of death and driven by contempt for the unfamiliar, a strain of smoldering hatred that feeds on its own paranoiac assumptions. Remember our discussion about the human need for some semblance of permanence? The need for certainty and permanence is a crippling trait.

"Tribal cultures, as you well know, Ruben, serve as shelters from threats and objectionable behaviors. Strange customs are often perceived as putting one's tribe at risk, so here we have the justification for all manifestations of prejudice simply as a means of protecting one's cultural sense of reality.

"The predisposition for racial prejudice in prehistory provided the emotional impetus to form war parties as an offensive or defensive tribal strategy. The trouble is, we should have learned enough by now to compensate and overwrite the malignant aspects of our tribal instincts. Instead, we have made very little progress, and now it has all come to a head.

"I mean, think about it. How long have we known that human brains are virtual bias machines that snapshot reality beneath consciousness and then subconsciously nudge us toward rationalizations to match our internalized biases, all of which we just identify as common sense or intuition? In this day and age, we—and especially you, of all people—shouldn't be plagued by our primitive predispositions.

"That's your good and evil dilemma in a nutshell, Ruben. So, a few of us have to resort to lies and trickery to keep people's base instincts from destroying the planet. In other words, we have to stop evilness from short-circuiting the whole enterprise of civilization.

"The savage dialectic toward stronger cultures with less and less violence and greater prosperity is in danger of ending abruptly. We are near the end of the existential human equation, if we don't act against evil in the defense of the good. The very well-being of the planet itself and the existence of human life are at stake. Don't you agree?"

"Yes," Ruben nodded. "But I'm still a little skeptical. By doing so, we too are making shit up and acting like God all at the same time, are we not? And I'm not at all sure that we wouldn't be better off chasing buffalo, asteroids be damned."

# REFLECTIONS ON MEMORY

DARK CLOUDS, CLINGING fog, and a forgiving rain gave Caribou Creek a socked-in feeling. Ruben had called earlier to ask Ginger and Ellen if it was okay to stop by. He put on a windbreaker and rode his four-wheeler to the Terrell cabin. Cleansing raindrops on his face reassured him of better times ahead.

A state trooper murdered, a failed attempt on Ellen's life, Jenny Rice slain, followed by William David Dee dying unexpectedly at the compound, and then the big shootout leading to Vince's death, and an end to the reign of a serial killer. How much more could they take? Surely his news would help lighten their emotional stress. Cheering them up about their loss wasn't likely, but chances were good he could lift some of their depression.

As the drizzle added mass, the temperature dropped, turning the rain to wet snow, sticking instantly with the promise of a blanket of whiteness to come, recreating a picturesque landscape, long overdue for this time of year. It seemed another hopeful sign. Maybe a fresh white backdrop would make the world feel clean again.

He stopped his machine a few yards from the Terrell cabin and walked the rest of the way, then stood on the porch for several moments before knocking. The security sensors had probably picked up his presence by now, and if not, the dogs barking inside the cabin surely had.

Opening the door Ginger said, "Come in, Ruben. Ellen's taking a nap. Her shoulder still bothers her since the surgery."

"No, I'm fine," said Ellen, entering the room. "It just throbs a little."

The pit bull sat near Ginger, studying Ruben with anxious eyes, awaiting any chance of a threat to his new master. Moby lay by the couch watching Ruben with one eye open and the other eager for sleep. Ruben smiled at Gunny and laughed aloud as if he and Moby were longtime friends. "I was wondering if I could get you two to put on your coats and take a little walk with me."

"Where to?" Ginger asked.

"Not far, just down to the cave. You might need your rubber boots."

"Why the cave, and what are you carrying under your arm?" Ellen wanted to know.

"I've got three canvas sitting stools, and I want to keep them dry. I have some things to share with you two, and I thought it would be nice if we could sit at the edge of the cave, watch the snow, and talk. What do you say?"

Ginger and Ellen exchanged mystified glances and, instead of speaking, proceeded to dress for the occasion. Then Ginger locked Gunny in the bedroom.

The cave was only a couple hundred feet from the cabin, and with a little wading through still unfrozen, ankle-deep water, they reached the interior. Ruben unfolded the chairs for all of them to sit down. After a few moments of silence watching the gently falling snow, Ginger said, "So, Ruben, what's on your mind?"

"Wait, Ruben. Bob said you went to see Jonas in Anchorage. How is he doing?" Ellen asked.

"He's doing fine, Ellen. He said the FBI arranged a phone call from a preacher in Missouri named Baldwin, who said Jonas had no idea he was going to be asked to kill people on behalf of the Seer. Baldwin is going to testify against the Seer's organization. I'm guessing Jonas isn't going to be charged with anything serious if Bob and I can help it. I'm not so sure about the other guy, though. He may be in big trouble, but Jonas really wants him to be let go. He says we would all be dead but for Les Coleman.

"Jonas appears to have learned his lesson about falling in with nut cases. And that reminds me. I forgot to bring it today, but he sent you and Ginger a package."

"What is it?"

"That I know, Ellen, because he had it delivered to my address in Anchorage. He sent you a couple of dog collars that have a GPS, a camera, and voice communication capability that you can activate remotely with your PC. So you can talk to Moby and Gunny and tell them to come home. All you have to do is click and you can turn on their camera and see what they're looking at. I'm guessing it will really freak them out that you seem to be everywhere they are, but they can't see you or smell you."

"That's very thoughtful," Ginger said smiling. "Something like that will no doubt come in handy, although watching what the dogs are seeing might make us decide to keep them indoors."

After a pause, Ruben lowered his voice to a near whisper and said, "Ellen, I want you to know it was Vince's hope that you might write the book he intended to write someday—your version anyway. He said when you and he went to Montana, he realized you're already smarter than he ever was or could be.

"And then there is the reason we're sitting in this cave on a bright snowy day. You will find this mentioned in Vince's will. If we were to go toward the back here and shovel some dirt and shine a light, we would find this cave is hiding an incredibly rich gold deposit."

"What? You're kidding. We would never want a gold mine here."

"I know that, Ginger, and that's why Thornton wanted me to tell you that if you and Ellen ever need the money the mine would have produced, he will form a partnership with you and give you your half of the wealth without ever putting a shovel in the ground except as a way to estimate how much gold is recoverable. In other words, it will be a way to have your cake and eat it to. He said for you to think of it as a bank account to draw on anytime you need to, but that there will be no need for mining here, ever, while we are alive, any of us." Ellen and Ginger looked at each other, both near tears.

"Another thing that's important for me to say. Vince knew he had a bad heart, and he felt guilty for not telling you two." Looking at Ginger, Ruben added, "He was worried sick that you and Ellen would blame yourselves in some way for what has happened. He made me and Bob promise to do everything in our power to convince you otherwise. And I can tell you without a doubt that he would be deeply disappointed if we fail. Vince wanted you two to remember the good times you had together and forget the rest.

"Which reminds me of something else. Angela shared a conversation she had with Dee shortly before he died. The more I think about what he said, the more I think it may be one of the most valuable pieces of self-help advice since *Poor Richard's Almanac*. It's sort of like a fundamental open secret to a good life. It's an admonition long overdue." Ruben stopped talking when he noticed an empty can of Red Bull on the floor of the cave.

"Are you going to tell us what he said?" Ginger asked.

Returning his gaze to her, Ruben continued. "Dee said simply that one of life's greatest pleasures is to lay down good memories because of the reward that comes from recollection. Now, think about the wisdom of starting each day with a goal as unpretentious as setting out to do things worth remembering. I'm going to start a social media effort called the *nostalgia project.* Just think about the difference such a strategy could accomplish by making nostalgia the coming attractions in one's life—something to expect as a reward of having lived well. Stack up enough good memories, and before you know it, you have a legacy, something worthy of reflection and something worth being remembered for."

Ruben appeared to drift away in thought for a moment before resuming. "Well, anyway, as I was saying. Up topside a few days before he died, Dee seemed mesmerized by the mountain. He motioned me over and out of the blue asked me if I knew why old people sometimes cry when they hear stirring music. I said I would have to think about it, and he offered to save me the trouble. He said whether we will admit it or not, most of us reach an age when we know the curtain is about to fall.

"He'd realized that all of the memorable events in our lives—the good, the bad, the happy, the sad, the feelings we had when things were so hopeless we thought we wanted to die, and the reasons we still want to live forever—stay lodged in our gray matter. Our vault of reminiscences is so crowded with these emotions that when we hear beautiful music at an advanced age, we experience a flood of memories competing to reach the surface. But there isn't room, so the tears are simply spillover from the congested struggle to express our gratitude for having lived and our regret that it will soon be over.

"'Memories,' Dee said. 'Just try to think what life would be like without them and how unfortunate it is that so many people never stop editing them. We are rigged for self-deception, you know.' Then he stopped cold, as if I wasn't there, and he and the mountain went back to studying one another.

"So, later that day, I asked him to elaborate more about self-deception. He said what's been missing from the discussion about good and evil is that making sense of the subject is all the more difficult because we human beings are a seriously flawed species, predisposed as we are to constantly strive toward a preferential reality that includes magical thinking and memory revision. I asked him what he meant by that, and he said when we call up a memory, we don't put it back as we found it. Instead we create new file, a brand new version, and in that way, we can act irresponsibly and dishonestly. We can deceive ourselves a little each time we recall a memory, and over the long term we can distance ourselves from unpleasant events through revision.

"But then Adam 21 comes along and a preferred reality is no longer an option. The past is not changeable to suit us because even our magic won't change the reality of Adam 21. 'We are tribalistic as hell,' he said, noting the group's discussion, and went on to point out that the World Wide Web promotes retribalization based on echo-chamber ignorance and social misperception.

"I don't recall exactly how Dee put it, but essentially his point was that it's little wonder there is so much social angst in the world, because we are no longer as adept at manufacturing the past to exaggerate our worth and degrade the value of others. Memory, he said, is the meaningful fabric of human existence. Nostalgia represents what we have internalized as having been sacred experience. Post-traumatic stress disorder, on the other hand, consists of horrific memories so indelibly etched in one's mind that they resist revision.

"With memory comes responsibility, he said, and we have to know this to be able to compensate for our faulty wiring. Unless and until most people understand their propensity to gravitate toward ignorance-based bonding, achieving civilization isn't possible. Of course, in light of doomsday, he recognized that the point was moot."

"What did you say, Ruben?" Ginger asked.

"I said amen. The memory overlay he was talking about is called reconsolidation. It's not quite that simple, but it's close. Couldn't have made a better case myself. James and I both knew that Dee used to be a firebrand, a free thinker with a passion for combative debate, and yet in all of our discussions he didn't have much to say. Maybe the change in him was simply the wisdom of age. Anyway, I feel sad that he's gone."

With that, Ruben froze, slowly putting his finger to his lips. "Out there," he whispered, pointing with his head so as not make a sudden move. There, in a clearing barely fifty yards on the other side of the creek, stood a black wolf looking straight at them. Contrasted against the fresh snow, the creature appeared majestic.

The instant Ginger and Ellen saw him, Gunny and Moby let loose in the cabin with a crescendo of aggressive barking. Undeterred by the threat from the dogs, the wolf stood his ground motionless for a full minute, staring at the people in the cave. Then, as if he suddenly lost interest, he turned his nose to the wind and vanished.

The three exchanged glances, and Ruben shook his head, trying to conjure the words to describe what had just happened. "And to imagine that something like this would occur when we are talking about things that are unforgettable. I've been coming out here for years, and this is only the second time I've see a wolf up close. It's ironic how eerie it feels to see such a creature in the wild and to realize my Indian ancestors were thought to be no less savage than those regal animals. Did you guys know that none other than George Washington, our first president, likened Indians to being wolf-like beasts of prey?"

Ruben looked away, not expecting an answer to his question. He picked up the empty Red Bull can, studied it at length, and crushed it with both hands. Then, exhaling with a heavy sigh, he said, "Okay. Now for the real reason we're here. I didn't think it was going to be so hard to tell you the secret of the ages."

# THE CIA

THE CENTRAL INTELLIGENCE Agency, with the assistance of NATO and foreign ambassadors, arranged for a summit of dictators to be held in Qatar. The subject of the meeting was declared top secret. Invitations were issued by a select group of NATO members to the leaders of thirty-two countries. Twenty-seven autocrats accepted and all were present, but the meetings took place in three separate rooms because some of the relationships among those invited were hostile at best.

Jane Preston, the director of the CIA, presided over the gatherings. Through interperters she told those present that, because of the recent doomsday announcement, they were being offered unconditional assistance in the event of citizen uprisings. There were multiple levels of assistance, including conditional financal aid, but what she wanted to help them with specifically today was to enable them to deal in the immediate future with countrymen who might engage in criminal or treasonous acts. Peaceful behavior and calm in the face of an uncertain future were what was being offered. She introduced the idea of pathological altruism, explaining that it was specficially intended to deal with their enemies, the kind of people who might martyr themselves in order to assassinate them and thus become heroes of the people by removing them from power.

What she proposed was exposure to a substance that would make dangerous zealots such as those less likely to break their country's repective laws. If the leaders would agree to sample the substance themselves, and if they were satisfied that the substance would be helpful to them, then at their request, she would see to it that samples would be provided for use under strict supervision. The substance, code named Patriot, would remain in the custody of the CIA, but all a leader had to do was ask, and arrangements for exposure for chosen subjects would be forthcoming in a matter of days.

The immediate reaction among the dictators, across the board, was that to the last man they were suspicious and more than a little wary of sniffing and inhaling something offered up by the CIA. But, given a few hours of cajoling, and with CIA personnel present who were willing to try the substance themselves, some success was achieved. Of the twenty-seven present, nineteen agreed to participate, and early the next morning, three more called and said they were also willing.

Only three of the dictators seemed to understand that if the substance was supposed to work on their enemies, it would likely have an effect on them as well. So, they agreed to subject some of their citizens to future use, but declined a sample for themselves. Some of the others, however, seemed to think that sniffing the Patriot substance was an act of bravado and submitted to several samplings as a means of outdoing the others, even when doing so brought them to tears at the very thought of doing it again.

The results were classified, but it was reported that when the CIA director met with the president to be debriefed, she was grinning from ear to ear. A shriek of enthusiam was heard as the door to the Oval Office closed.

# STATE OF UNDERSTANDING

THE EFFECT OF the doomsday announcement was strange and also ironic in some ways. People afraid of the dark see things very differently once the light has been turned on. In similar fashion, when death was suddenly real and there was no longer an option to deny or ignore one's ultimate demise, no one to stand in as a scapegoat distraction, it was like having the light on all of the time and still feeling the essence of darkness.

Everything looked different, although not much changed, except that more and more people began to actually face reality. Knowing that the whole of mankind was destined to die at the same time felt like an emotional earthquake that never let up. The constant shaking of the passionate ground that people had always stood on made it difficult to feel that anything much mattered anymore. The very notion of value became suspect because the very notion of a concept without minds to ponder it became patently absurd.

Contemporary philosophers had a field day pointing out that man is primarily a territorial animal, that the only difference between humans and lower animals is the sophistication of what we claim are our territories and how we mark them—everything from families, careers, land, clubs, and associations, to cities, states, countries, nations, and even sports teams. But now that the lease was about up and wouldn't be renewed for any of these entities, the resulting disenchantment sucked the meaning out of our here-tofore shortsighted reasons for being. Our very identity was born of these associations, and without them, the rug was pulled out from under all of us. The result: we no longer know who we are, and it's becoming even clearer that we never have known. So many wars, so many crusades, so many jihads in search of an identity worthy of celebration, and all for naught. It's almost as if God said, *Humankind, never mind. Big mistake.*

In the West, people en masse began to awaken to the reality that too much of their lives had been spent in the thrall of fashion. Now under a sentence of doom, fashion was at last revealed to be the shallow herd mentality that it truly represented, a pursuit suddenly thought so vacuous as to cause millions of people to feel that they'd been lulled asleep and cheated by a frivolous mirage, nothing more than narcissistic trivia like that of primitive tribes and the history of shiny objects.

Nostalgia soared in popularity, and it's little wonder why. Indulging in memories past and longing for the serenity of times that were safe, secure, and enjoyable are ways of reaching out to those no longer with us without actually admitting that this, indeed, is what we are doing.

With the end of human life in plain sight, products for con-traception in developed countries skyrocketed, portending a population dive. In less-developed nations, the trend was less severe, but still noticeable, and the birthrate was thought likely to soon drop like a rock. After all, bringing another life into the world with the expectation of having it end abruptly and prematurely was viewed by some as an expression of cruelty. Media headlines mim-icked examples of when to tell your child, when do you deliver the news, when do you tell them the only reason you brought them into the world is not to enjoy a short life but to die young?

Experts said that all it ever would have taken to get the population of the earth in sync for sustainability and back down to less than two billion, as it had been in 1900, would have been for every nation to adopt China's twentieth-century policy of one child per couple, although now it appeared to be a moot point.

The promised apocalyptic end of humanity had myriad unexpected effects, with groups of individuals coming together around different ways of coping. A new Thoreau society emerged, in which great numbers of people gave up all of their PCs and any kind of gadgets for communication or social media, savoring instead group discussion, face-to-face conversations, an aggressive pursuit of solitude, and a vociferous argument that a quiet mindfulness, by measures of magnitude, is the best way to spend one's remaining years.

Other groups came together with a reverse approach. Instead of avoiding social media, they embraced it wholeheartedly, believing that the experience of sharing one's moments with others is the most meaningful way of facing the abyss.

Millions of people who otherwise would have spent many more years working, opted for retirement. The demographic drop in unemployment sent shock waves through the business sector, pushing wages up and—for the first time in the memory of any living person—putting employees in the driver's seat. Suddenly corporations had to compete aggressively to hold on to their workforce. Also for the first time in the memory of anyone alive, significant numbers of both liberals and conservatives agreed that capitalism was finally working as it should, although there was a publicly shared sentiment that it was too bad that the specter of nonexistence was necessary to bring it about.

People began dropping out of school in alarming numbers. Others dropped in, with philosophy and liberal arts experiencing an upsurge of interest as a means of coping, an exercise in acquiring and maintaining mindfulness. Rich people everywhere began to lose interest in getting richer. Suddenly time was deemed more important than money, more important by orders of magnitude, because time was sold out, off the market, unavailable for purchase, superseded by the promise of universal equality in the simultaneous distribution of death and a desperate desire for the wisdom necessary to squeeze the last remnant of meaning out of existence.

Historically the threat or even a reminder of one's impending demise had led many people to render themselves overly susceptible to the influence of charismatic charlatans, and the impending human extinction was no exception for many. But, surprisingly at first, millions of people the world over appeared to be having a contrary reaction, a reaction that assumed universal annihilation to be a profoundly democratic opportunity, an opportunity calling for nothing less than accepting one's final fling at life as something not to be wasted by submission to anyone's authority except one's own volition to live for all one's worth, as if one's remaining years of life mattered, really mattered.

The threat of doom seemed to diminish people's insatiable drive for status. With the realization that one day soon the dust and ashes of the rich and the poor would be indistinguishable, they began placing more value on simply being alive and in good health. All they would have to do to make their lives as interesting as anyone else's would be to dramatically increase their level of curiosity.

## OWEN'S FAREWELL

CAMUS WROTE, "THE future is the only transcendental value for men without God." God or not, I doubt that it ever would have occurred to Camus that man would have only a short time to contemplate the end of everything as the ultimate expression of existentialism. I wonder how he would have reacted to the ironic and cynical advertising slogans like: *Be Ready for the Big Weekend in '61.*

Long before the end of the world, my wife and I will be gone and most of the people I really care about will be gone as well. I don't envy those who will live to see all life come to an end. In some ways I find it hard to believe, and in other ways it feels as if our ship of fools has finally lost its mooring, that the tattered line holding us at the dock has been severed and we're about to sail off into the abyss, that the earth was flat after all and we are poised to slip over the edge into oblivion.

For all living creatures, the past is their place of birth and the future is their psychic and literal cemetery. Uncertainty for some has always represented a reminder of their mortality, their greatest fear, but when certitude takes the place of uncertainty in the matter, confusion reigns and time screams. Environmental scientists have for years now claimed we are experiencing the sixth major extinction of life on the earth, but they expected it would play out over a few centuries, not three decades and change.

Next year in April, the asteroid Apophis will come somewhere between eighteen and nineteen thousand miles close to the earth. Because of its erratic wobble, scientists are still arguing about its potential for actually hitting the earth when it comes around again in April of 2036. I wonder how these events will be viewed against the 2061 gamma rays. Maybe now they won't be thought of as that big of a deal. Just a left jab before the lethal overhand right to come. It reminds me of some of the things I've read on the subject of mortality that I've never been able to forget.

Blaise Pascal said something to the effect that we should imagine men in chains sentenced to die, with some being butchered in plain sight while those awaiting the same fate look on, sharing their grief and despair with one another. This, he said, is an explicit image of the human condition. The doomsday scenario, like war, is an in-your-face reminder of Pascal's observation.

Marcus Aurelius suggested that death is a mystery of nature, that composition and decomposition are the same, and that we should be ashamed of neither. "Always reflect that soon you will be no one, and nowhere," he said. And he asked us to remember the wisdom of Heraclitus, who pointed out that "soon the earth will cover us all," that the earth will change too and continue to change forever, and that the death of one thing means the life of another: water becomes air, and "the death of air is to become fire." Simply put, we once were star stuff and may be so again.

Freud reminded us that "no one believes in his own death," and that if we aren't vigilant, our fears of passing can lead to a life of cowering risk avoidance amounting to existential impoverishment. But that was when the future seemed endless.

He asked us to recall frequently that "if we desire peace, we must prepare for war." But I'm wondering now if he may have been wrong about that because he also worried that our predilection for aggression might lead to our ultimate self-destruction, and that's where we find ourselves today. Whether or not the world is prepared for war doesn't seem to have mattered. Ready or not, here we come, but for 2061.

In wartime, people experience intense adrenaline rushes that offer a sense of ecstasy from simply being alive in the face of death, in contrast to the petty and often boring nature of their peacetime lives. For many people, war is a chance to live, really live. The rush of meaningfulness from combat for some is both intoxicating and addictive, and when war is over, the absence of a reliable source of horrific experience can make the prospect of creating new enemies enticing.

The current doomsday scenario hypes the significance of being alive in a similar way, minus the addictive nature of experience. It subordinates fear to a present-tense exhilaration for just being. So, perhaps for the first time in human history, the news hanging over us renders the whole world stone-cold sober and simultaneously obsessed with the notion of finding some sense of meaning in life. All of a sudden, living a passionless life seems unappreciative to the point of being sacrilegious.

Because of 2061, we've become hyperaware that we have been wasting our lives by engaging in mindless conflict to distract ourselves from the inevitable. Now, though, we realize that our existential angst has never been anything more than a contagious form of innate insanity called tribalism. So, Tolstoy was right in saying that, to end war, we have to abolish patriotism.

I find this sad, very sad, because from the day of our birth, we await our turn to die, just like Pascal said. We don't need wars, natural disasters, or celestial threats from the heavens to find meaningful reasons to live. The mortal fate that awaits us all is reason enough, if only we think it through, while the hatred, angst, and mindless destruction we've always engaged in for the purpose of distraction is a blight on the ideal of human character and a blasphemy on the soul of our species.

It's such a juvenile convention that the quest for safety and order in a cosmos driven by chaos will morph into a need to believe in immortality. Purposeful self-deception is preferable to facing the vacuum of nonexistence. Thus, whenever nonbelievers raise doubts about the possibility of eternal life, they incur a barrage of contempt, hatred, and in some cases bloodshed.

Achieving symbolic immortality trumps belief in an afterlife. It always has, and it always will, at least until 2061. Symbols, art, icons, family, kin, ideas, work, and our existential acts as individuals, these are the things that make our lives seem worth the effort. But make a big enough splash in your generation's pond, and you will be remembered by the ripple of your deeds.

We strive for a measure of immortality, for the most part unaware that what we are really trying to do is time stamp the present with a meaningful performance, something that will outlast us. Unfortunately those without hope of a legacy sometimes choose a violent end, believing that flaming out is better than dying a nobody. That's why in cultures where despair is more prevalent than hope, suicide bombers become martyrs. Nothing is more horrific than acknowledging that one has lived a life that mattered not a whit. And so we kill one another to feel truly alive, to pass the time, and to mask our insignificance.

During the past century, roughly more than a hundred people per hour, 365 days per year, have been killed in wars, in which the vast majority of the casualties didn't even know the real reasons why they were fighting. Now, though, 2061 puts the need for diversion in a new light. We no longer need enemies to distract us from our mortality. The big question the whole world seems to be asking today is why, up to this point in time, we have settled for lives so shallow in substance and so filled with scorn and derision. Now, letting past resentments go while appreciating the present seems the best option.

For me, thinking about the end of everything is a kind of solace, an exclamation point on the trials and tribulations of humanity, and a moral comeuppance that we have squandered so much life for reasons which today seem beyond insanity. Perhaps Freud was right about our species having a death drive. The idea that nothing really matters is, in a way, kind of exhilarating. If the death of all is an evil event, then it must still have a positive side in that it eliminates the perpetuation of evil. Is this, then, the genocide of evil? Can the end of evil not in some manner of thinking be considered a good? After all, time enslaves us in preparation for the slaughter, does it not?

Or could it simply be true that the machinations of human beings will fall flat in a universe that couldn't possibly have cared less and that if no one hears the end of humanity, then in effect there will have been no sound of it? The realization that our respective cultures represent a sacred shelter from uncertainty and that they have always offered us little more than symbolic immortality seems to have come too late to the party. This oversight about how we are influenced has kept us from realizing that if our species ever gave up on the quest for immortality, it would be because we have lost the will to live, and the immediate future may bear this out. Before the doomsday announcement, falling leaves reminded me of decay and renewal. Now it's worse. Now they just remind me of death.

There are so many different ways people are coping with the prospect of the big ending to come. Pundits keep saying we have to face it, yet many people still find purposeful distraction, as has always been the case. I have one friend who spends his time watching Adam 21 episodes of Field Marshal Erwin Rommel's exploits in North Africa during World War II, another who watches the ancient Aztecs, and another, America's Revolutionary War, not to mention the dinosaur enthusiasts, who long ago started clubs and social media organizations to discuss the beasts of prehistory and four centuries of gladiator blood and gore in the Roman coliseum. The asteroid that killed the dinosaurs 66 million years ago has also been the focus of a lot of attention, but the earth's being shrouded for years in cloud cover has led to endless arguments about what was actually taking place.

Since the advent of Adam 21, scientists and thousands of laymen have focused on revealing man's early ancestors. Homo sapiens, homo erectus, homo soloensis, homo neanderthalensis—these ancient kin were well known, but portals into the past have revealed scores of other candidates. Arguments about their relationship to modern man are rife with personal attacks among those making claims. That humankind's impact on countless animal species has resulted in mass extinctions is now a settled issue. All doubt is removed. But with the end for man in sight, those whose arguments are the most ad hominem are beginning to soften their tone—a good thing I think.

And then there are the conspiracy buffs, who routinely trade one debunked conspiracy for another that hasn't yet been deconstructed. They cling to conspiracy rather than face the horrifying reality that chance rules our lives. They would rather be ruled by sinister plots than subject to the perils of uncertainty, and they seem to be suffering dearly at the thought that a gamma-ray burst is not part of somebody's plan. What a plot, though, were it true—a cosmic conspiracy.

But by far the most popular and powerful doomsday diversion has been the introduction of Q-Vision. By the time this new technology hit the store shelves, the cyber gaming industry already had apps enabling us to copy a 3-D Adam 21 episode and then select our own avatar and enter into past actions as a participant in what amounts to a metaphorical application of time travel into the past. Perhaps it will enable us to amuse ourselves to death before the actual death rays arrive.

A New York ad agency is supervising a campaign for world peace, and they have been clever enough to sponsor contests for amateurs to create meaningful ads, some of which are quite amusing. One I saw this morning featured rats side by side, running as fast as their little creepy legs could carry them. Finally, as they are about to reach the finish line, one of the furry creatures jumps ahead and crosses the finish line first, raising his paws to celebrate victory, while a large furred caricature of a rodent steps in front of a microphone and in a very deep voice says, "So you've won a rat race, big deal. You are still a rat. Think, people! Deconstruct the Skinner Box that conditioned you to pedal for contemptible rewards. The rest of your life depends on it." And then the furry creature resumes running with the rats. A friend recently described the absurdity of so many lives stuck on automatic pilot like this: stockpile, stockpile, stockpile, oops death.

The upside of life, the side that manages to have some semblance of power, is the part that provides a platform for attaining satisfaction—the satisfaction of vengeance for whatever one has been cheated of by social design. That the weak and powerless masses are beginning to comprehend that universal death is democracy at last, the ultimate schadenfreude, the comeuppance of all comeuppances for all of those against whom they have held grudges for myriad reasons, makes one wonder what the world would have been like if the same thing had been realized much earlier. But for the indoctrination to run with the herd, the possibility for this kind of justice was always present. The realization, it seems, is just too late in coming. Assholes are often considered winners, but they are still assholes.

Perhaps Shakespeare summed up the futility of our kind when he said in *Macbeth* that life "is a tale told by an idiot, full of sound and fury, signifying nothing." The more times I repeat it to myself, the truer it seems. The goddamned signifying just gets louder and louder.

That this world has had a share of evil equal to or beyond the good seems unquestionable, and it feels foolish now to even spend much time thinking about it. There is but one savory bit of compensation, which I will take to my gamma-burst-ridden grave, and that is the pleasure and satisfaction I feel in thinking about the nuclear nightmare the fiend who murdered my little girl will experience for thousands of years to come.

Thank God for revenge. Thank God for His gift of the Rain Crow. I've always heard it said that revenge is a dish best served cold, but it's better yet, much better, if the dining lasts for millennia. It's almost as good as Nietzsche's Eternal Return. I do love it so. Like father, like son. Yours, Owen Sandburg.

# CARIBOU CREEK SECRETS

WARMED BY THEIR closeness inside the cave, the three sat in silence as the forlorn look on Ruben's face gave Ellen and Ginger pause about pressing him to continue. Finally, he straightened up, leaned forward, and said, "Okay, I know that if I ask for you two to keep a secret, I can trust you. You don't even have to promise to do so because I know when you hear what I have to say, you will realize it should never leave this cave." Ruben sat for a moment without speaking, patiently watching the snow fall. Then he said, "I'm more than a little happy to tell you that the world is not really going to end in thirty-three years. Thornton, Tall Tree, and the president's advisory committee, along with some of our allies and many of the world's top scientists, have been using it as what they are calling a common-enemy strategy."

"Oh, my God. Do you mean the Seer's religious group is right?" Ellen gasped.

"The Seer is right in one way, but wrong in another. He totally misreads the motivation, but he is indeed right that there is a conspiracy. Well, I guess it's time he's right about something. Fearful people fueled with hatred and egged on by despots confuse revenge with justice, and they are likely to follow up with vestiges of belief that amount to the reification of stupidity. Of course, the shame of it all is that the Seer is promising vengeance against nonbelievers

in the next life for everyone who's willing to postpone the punishment of heretics in the here and now. All they have to do is to stop
thinking, be submissive, and worship him."

"Ruben, how long is our government going to let people believe
that the world is doomed?"

"First, Ginger, let me ask you how the prospect of the end of
humanity affected you personally."

"Affected me? It pulled the emotional rug out from under me.
Except for Vince, I've had a hard time thinking about anything
else. In my dreams, I keep seeing Ellen at the end of the world as
we know it. It's the most psychologically threatening thing I've ever
heard of. That's how it has affected me."

"I hope I can explain the whole thing without sounding overly
paternalistic, but your reaction is the point, Ginger. What the
world has needed, indeed what it has been desperate for, is an aha
moment of epic proportions, or else this epoch that our lives are a
part of may come to an end. This whole thing is just a *psychological
time-out*, so to speak. Thornton's group along with the president's
staff and a dozen or so world leaders entrusted all of the information and recommendations they had gathered to David Webster of
Webster and Horton, the big ad agency.

Webster is the genius who came up with a plan that the whole
group has bought into. The first thing he pointed out was that to
get a stubborn mule to do something it doesn't want to do, you
have to get its attention. That's what the doomsday announcement
was intended to do, and by all measures, it seems to be working.
Webster knows that advertising is a Machiavellian enterprise and
that myth and symbols will always trump moral arguments, which
is precisely what it is going to take to do the trick of giving the
world a chance to chill out and pull together."

"Trick? Ruben, people are going to be furious when they find out this whole thing was nothing but a hoax."

"No doubt, Ginger, no doubt. But we have an old scientist who wants to accept the blame for having made a mistake in his data, with the truth of the matter to be revealed fifty years after his death. By that time, maybe the world will have grown up. Better yet, perhaps we should appreciate the doomsday scenario as a useful fantasy or fairy tale but apply to the fiction the kind of logic that will work in the real world.

"Once we have a general acceptance of the notion that humanity is soon to end, and once we have examined and studied the reactions, the ad campaign will proceed full speed ahead. You see, what I said a while back about this being an opportunity for humanity to grow up to full adulthood still rings true.

"What we expect the doomsday scenario to prove is that we human beings have a huge psychic investment in the idea that, even though we will die as individuals, life will go on. And if life doesn't go on, the psychological shock value is the equivalent of an existential black hole that effectively sucks the meaning out of existence. It amounts to a two-by-four upside mulish heads. It gets our attention."

"When will they tell us that predicting the end of the world was a simply a mistake?" Ellen asked.

"Months, likely. I doubt it will go on for a year or more, but I'm guessing. Here's the thing: Webster argues that he can use the shock value of the doomsday expectation in the minds of people the world over to clearly demonstrate that all humans, regardless of race, creed, or color, have a compelling interest in life's continuation long after each of us has died as individuals. He's certain he can show that this is true in a way that's clear to everyone.

"The next stage is to show that if we do not come together as a planet and if we continue to bicker and fight with one another as if we're schoolyard adolescents, then we are indeed going to put an early end to mankind, which could be avoided with a little bit of wisdom and maturity.

"Look, I know this whole idea takes some getting used to, but this is good news. I know that, on one level, it is a very paternalistic thing to do, but the thinking is, and I agree, that this is one of those times when the end justifies the means."

"You mean, if it works," Ginger said.

"Indeed, yes, only if it works. But it seems to be having a positive effect already. All of the hot spots in the world appear to be cooling down. Actual shooting has stopped in most places, and the vitriolic rhetoric is way, way down."

"Well, I can't say I'm sorry the world is not going to end when I'm fifty," said Ellen, "but I can't help but feel angry about having been lied to, especially with all of the worrying this thing has caused."

"I understand completely, and this strategy would never have been used if not for the fact that we were on the brink of a world war and the kind of conflict that could finish off civilization for sure. People are still dying daily from the nuclear blast in Pakistan. I think it's something of a miracle that so far there has been only one detonation and that the fighting hasn't escalated.

"Look, we could be saving the lives of a couple of billion people, or maybe even most of the people on the planet. This is just an existential time-out, a stopgap measure, and a chance to wake up and look at the world anew, a chance to see the incessant need for growth of GDP for what it is: a malignancy on a frail planet about to enter stage four of a fatal disease of irresponsible resource consumption."

"Why did they come up with gamma rays?" Ellen asked.

"Well, science has not yet reached the kind of expertise that can predict an impeding gamma-ray blast, but it is clearly sophisticated enough to make people believe we can. So, deception seemed to be an easy way forward. James says we view ourselves as masters of technology, but when it comes to cosmology, we are still just feebly trying to interpret the shadows on the wall of Plato's cave.

"When Bob and James were soliciting input for this planned intervention, they put the quest to Hennessey, you know, our know-it-all search engine, and it kept coming up with scenarios in which some kind of a common enemy seemed the best option to gain the most worldwide support. It's a simple but really powerful premise.

"Try to picture a set of concentric circles, where family is at the center core of our feelings of loyalty. This center is surrounded by the wider rings of tribe, city, state, region, nation, race, religion, and ethnicity, with mankind itself as the outer circle. To expand people's sense of loyalty to one of the outer rings, an enemy or threat must endanger that ring. When a ring is threatened, everyone in that circle rushes to defend it. So mankind itself has to be in danger to rally the earth."

"Won't people just figure out that the whole thing has been a lie from the beginning, Ruben?" Ginger asked. "Isn't there likely to be an enormous backlash?"

"Well sure, there could be. Some people haven't believed it from the beginning, and some will continue to express disbelief. But many of them will nevertheless experience haunting doubts. The science involved is so complicated that there are only a handful of people in the world capable of understanding it, and most of them are on board. That's what Bob and James were doing in Washington, convincing folks of the urgency of the effort. And then they met with the president and Webster and Horton. The rest, as they say, is history.

"So, no doubt, there will be lots of speculation, and of course, not everyone can keep a secret, even for a few months. I am telling you two, after all, and there are sure to be others who spill the beans, but we've known and expected that from the beginning. James explained the program to Angela, and Bob is telling everyone here on Caribou Creek today. I mean, lots of people are going to be in on the secret, and it may start to unravel at some point, but if it does the trick, so be it. If we can prove the notion that a common enemy can bring the world together in a ruse, we may be able to use the fact that we did so in a way that keeps the idea going.

"James wanted to call our group together at the time of the doomsday announcement and explain what we were up to, but Thornton convinced him that as many people as possible should be exposed to the shock in order to comprehend the full effect of the strategy. James was so distraught at not being able to tell the folks here on the creek the truth that he took Angela on that one-day trip to Montana so as to be gone when it happened.

"Now, both of you know me well enough to know that I'm not bashful about telling you what I really think. Doomsday notwithstanding, another century may well be all that mankind has left on this planet anyway, if we don't grow up as a species. We may indeed be living in the end times, but not for the reasons cited by religion. If the world stays the course of seeking perpetual growth via the greed path modeled by the West, then we will have already entered the final stage of the metastasis that will finish us off. We've already lost most of the winter ice in the Arctic seas, and flooding in wetlands near the coasts on every continent is a constant occurrence.

"We've learned through spectrometry that organic life exists on other planets. We just don't know what kind of life it is. But our species won't be going anywhere in space to a new world because we don't have the speed or life span necessary to find another resource-rich rock like this one. Ginger, we are close to a mass extinction event with more possible fronts that I can recall at the moment: viruses, natural disasters, acts of terrorism, not to mention asteroids and comets.

"Look, when you consider the dynamics of in-group, out-group politics, the collective delusions that make each group think theirs is the only one that counts, and their relentless striving for the power to prove their group is naturally superior, then is there really any doubt that a scientific conspiracy may be the only remedy?"

"What about Wendell Smyth's substance for reducing the tendency for violence?" Ellen asked.

"Yes indeed, Ellen, what about that stuff? If we try to further domesticate our species, I worry that we will destroy ourselves by stamping out our creative nature. I suspect that in a few years, the pharmaceutical industry will have quashed the notion of free will, forever, while at the same time having developed a psychoactive substitute for the very idea of God, which of course will be expensive and will be available by prescription only. To save ourselves, we must learn to see our species as one tribe without the necessity of having everyone believe the same things. We have to move the peoples of the world to the outer ring and feel the connection both emotionally and intellectually.

"So, until that time, should those of us who care enough to want to save the world stand by and watch the end unfold without doing everything we can, even if we have to lie? But here is the thing. This Webster adman is all over the problem. He is preparing a campaign to educate people everywhere in the world in a manner that resembles an existential education because it teaches the humanities at an emotional level. He knows that, if an anti-intellectual population continues to outbreed truly educated people, a democracy based on such a worldview will be doomed because they will always default toward ignorance." Ruben leaned forward, put his head in his hands, and fingered his hair. For a couple of minutes no one spoke.

"Ruben, I wish Vince had known the truth before he died," said Ellen.

"He did know, Ellen. Bob and I told him. It's painful for me to tell you this, but it was clear to me and Bob that Vince knew he was dying. Vince asked the medics on board the helicopter with us for some privacy, and once he told us what was on his mind, Bob told him the truth about the doomsday announcement." Ruben picked up the crushed Red Bull can again, turning it over and over as he caught his breath to continue.

"Vince was so relieved. That's the other part of why I wanted to come out here in this cave to share Vince's last wishes. As I said, he wanted you to write the book he had planned to write, Ellen. He told us he had a PC in the bottom drawer of his desk that has all of his notes for the book he was going to write about the nature of good and evil and man's nature and predisposition for both. He said the file is huge and it contains comments on Michel Foucault's observations on the genealogy of power and punishment. God, I didn't know Vince even knew who Foucault was. I'm so sorry I didn't know him better.

"And speaking of knowing people, it turns out Vince and Dee knew each other in Dallas, from around the time when Dee was shot on duty and Vince was a police rookie in training. But I never saw them speak to one another during or after our discussions. Not knowing that Dee had died, Vince asked us to tell Dee he was sorry they didn't talk. Now, I guess we will never know why they didn't. The last thing Vince said to me was semper fi. Hell, I had no idea he was an ex-Marine too."

"I'm so thankful Uncle Vince knew the truth."

"Yes, for sure. I do feel better," Ginger said, wiping a tear.

"The doomsday announcement has brought all of humanity's

problems to an existential point, and it's nudging us toward the outer ring. We are all going to die. So what? It's nothing that we didn't already know. We just have a different perspective today. But if there was ever a time to assume responsibility for the creation and careful maintenance of our memories, it is now.

"I mean, look. The whole world is going through a seismic shift of consciousness in which people all over the planet are becoming less materialistic and more focused on personal relationships and just getting along well with others. Billions of people are now sympathetic with the core reality that good memories are what have made humanity worthwhile. Dee nailed it. This is a fleeting opportunity for a perceptually opened window on attaining wisdom and for living one's life accordingly without need of a rules manual.

"If we're careful, the doomsday scenario can be the most nourishing intellectual event in history. Just do something that's worth remembering, damn it, and substitute wonder for beliefs based on faith. Then humanity will achieve adulthood. Now is the time to drive the point home.

"For decades, Thomas Paine's notion that 'we have it in our power to begin the world over again,' has been used mostly by political cynics as a way to make fun of idealists. But now, for the first time in our written history, there really is a chance to start the world over for anyone and everyone willing to make the effort. I say, living a life worth remembering is a good start, don't you think?"

# EPILOGUE

FOURTEEN MONTHS TO the day after the doomsday declaration, world leaders made another simultaneous announcement to the effect that the doomsday forecast had been a mistake, a miscalculation, that there would be no gamma-ray blast, and that humanity would survive if we willed it so and behaved accordingly. Celebrations the world over went on for a week, but once the elation began to die down, queries were initiated about the whole doomsday scenario, with the promise of legislative hearings to come. The media coined it Doomsgate.

The plan had been to let the doomsday threat go on for at least three years, but after eleven months, the suicide rate spiked upward, as it was learned that the absence of a future for mankind created what was increasingly referred to as an existential black hole voraciously devouring the joy of existence. Mental health professionals on the president's advisory panel were warning of an emotional backlash, saying that the initial appearance of having a choice about how to spend one's last three decades was giving way to a morbid and potentially scary form of anxiety for a large portion of the population, with dreadful consequences likely to follow. But the real kicker, the nail in the coffin, so to speak, was that people were rapidly losing interest in sports. If that were to happen across the nation, the economy was expected to collapse in total.

The point was driven home by a prominent television sports announcer who was asked the score of a football game occurring on another channel. During a live broadcast, he seemed to awaken from a trance to reply, even as he silently read the score on his PC to himself. He summed up the growing public sentiment when he said, "Who really gives a shit?"

Research papers in psychology and neuroscience suggested that belief in the reliability of a future for generations to come turned out to be even more important to people than faith in an afterlife. It seemed clear to those in positions of authority over the common-enemy strategy that, at the core of what our species truly values, humanity itself trumps religion, and that, for millions of people, once the realization fully sets in that nothing will survive them, despair is inevitable.

One month later, Webster and Horton kicked off the second phase of what would be the beginning of the largest public relations campaign in the history of the planet. The developed nations of the world, along with private donors, pledged an additional $300 billion toward the Campaign for World Peace. The movement stressed the fact that the total destruction of humanity was still a distinct possibility through mindless animosity and common misunderstandings attributed to misreading the motivations of others. A lack of sincere effort by the peoples of the world to understand the human condition and the short-circuiting effects of tribalism remained the most intractable problem we faced.

As soon as people realized the world was not going to end, the cyber-gaming industry exploded, with Q-Vision technology becoming the largest software company on the planet, not counting Adam 21. Gaming apps became so sophisticated that players could have their avatars enter into a copy of, say, the Civil War battle at Gettysburg and change the outcome. Competition among players garnered the kind of enthusiasm that had formerly existed for World Cup soccer or American football playoffs. Critics argued that, just when the world had become truly thoughtful, giving traditional sports the back seat, now the public would be swallowed by another meaningless distraction.

James Tall Tree and Wendell Smyth joined together to give a global media presentation in many different languages to make the point as tastefully as possible that all peoples of the earth have been guilty of evil actions toward others. No group is without blame or without the potential for despicable behavior, they said, but with our lives being as short as they actually are in reality, the only sensible way to respond to the frequent horrors exposed on Adam 21 was to forgive, forget, and make our remaining years on this planet worthy of our existence.

With Angela's assistance, James and Wendell made a four-hour Adam 21 feature film with a narrative encapsulating the founding of America. It included the genocide of indigenous people and the enslavement of Africans, making a compelling argument that it is simply not possible to truly appreciate what it means to be an American if this historical understanding is omitted.

Two months after the doomsday correction announcement, James and Angela were married and moved to Montana. Wendell was still without official partners for T&T, but he appeared to have enough funding so as not to be in a hurry to find investors. Owen Sandburg checked himself in to a mental hospital facility in Anchorage to avoid the media and hopefully escape continued public scrutiny.

Jonas Blythe and Les Coleman spent six months in custody, most of it in the Anchorage jail, while three law enforcement agencies argued over their fate. The authorities were very concerned with Les Coleman's involvement with the assassination plot, but

Jonas pleaded for leniency, and Sanchez and Thornton said they would accept responsibility for Coleman. So finally, both men were released and employed by Thornton Enterprises as all-around roustabouts at the Thornton compound. They would fill in where needed, in whatever capacity required, until such time as they assumed another role.

The two men worked as alternates on a two-week-on, two-week-off schedule. They rented a condo in Anchorage, where they lived on their time off. Thornton liked both men personally, but he made it clear to them that they were on probation and that, were it not for Ellen, they would both still be in jail.

The Seer went into hiding. He was thought to be somewhere in Jerusalem or maybe even South America. His media network still broadcast 24/7, but seldom was he quoted now, except when it was possible to claim it was something he had said before the incident at Caribou Creek. Butch Cassum had testified as to the involvement of the Seer's group in the attempted assassination plot and had gone into the witness protection program.

Bob Thornton met a Russian anthropologist named Iskra Ivanov at a New Year's Eve party in Washington D.C., and they were married the following June. Iskra was even more outgoing than Thornton, and her perpetual cheerfulness quickly made her the most popular person at the compound.

Adam Whitehead had to be admitted to a nursing home in Palmer. He experienced some good days, but not many, and those were occurring less frequently. New medications mitigated Alzheimer's symptoms in some people, but Adam was not so lucky. Linda spent her time between the nursing home and Ginger's. On the weekends the two women would take Gunny to Caribou Creek and spend their time walking in the woods, visiting with the Thorntons, and reminiscing.

Moby-dog would meet the black wolf two more times, and each time, the wolf paid him little attention, simply moving along as if Moby were a shadow. A year to the day after Ruben had his talk with Ginger and Ellen, Moby-dog died in his sleep. Trying to be thoughtful and kind, Ruben told Ellen he was probably dreaming of fights with wolves to the very end. Two months later, Ruben died of a stroke, a week before he was to get a stem-cell heart-repair treatment.

In the spring of the following year, Win Potter and his wife, Ellen Terrell Potter, moved to Barrow, Alaska, where Win would begin his first assignment as an Alaska state trooper. There, Ellen would spend the long winter days and nights writing *A Genealogy of Evil*, while working on an online advanced degree in criminology. After an eighteen-month assignment in Barrow, Win was posted in Anchorage for six months before finally getting stationed in Palmer, which was where they most wanted to live. And it was there in the valley that Vincent Terrell Potter was later born.

In her book, Ellen would explain in detail her interpretation of how her Uncle Vince viewed the subject of good and evil from a police officer's perspective. She would also reveal that two Supreme Court justices, the Speaker of the House of Representatives, and two nationally known conservative radio talk-show hosts were murdered because Alaska business tycoon Buck Sandburg thought that his granddaughter had been butchered during a botched abortion attempt. He had thought that those individuals were to blame and deserved to die because of their unnecessary meddling in the lives of young women.

Ellen's work brought another amazing discovery to light, one that would be headline news for months to come. Once she had the evidence in place, it didn't take her long to extract from Uncle Vince's notes that the young man named Paul Rayburn, who had been instrumental in the deaths of the Supreme Court justices, had a personal physician named Dr. Evert Mendelsohn. Digging deeper, Ellen discovered that Mendelsohn had other patients who had died of Fast-Track AIDS, and that he had a sponsor—a sponsor who most assuredly had backed the creation of the disease.

The conspiracy theorists were right this time: the disease had been manufactured in a laboratory, and the financier behind the manmade disease, motivated by his father's outrage, was none other than the man who had saved Ellen's life by touching her at her uncle's funeral service, the man who declared that his being there to save Ellen was the providence of fate—namely, Owen Sandburg.

Sandburg's attorney furnished strong evidence that Dr. Mendelsohn was at the center of three right-wing hate groups. He had been introduced to Owen Sandburg at a Chamber of Commerce meeting and had subsequently become his personal physician. Even though he was not a psychiatrist, he had taken over prescribing Sandburg's medication.

Ironically, Mendelsohn already had connections to people close to Buck Sandburg, and his ultimate goal was said to have been to ensure unlimited funding from the Sandburg fortune by threatening to expose their crimes, even after he himself had made those crimes possible. While the evidence for Mendelsohn's complicity was compelling, it wasn't absolute proof, and sorting out the details would take time and a series of congressional committee hearings.

Ellen would write in detail about how deeply ironic it was that Owen Sandburg had continued to employ her Uncle Vince to find the killer of his daughter, an investigation that had led to his own exposure as the financer of a criminal enterprise based on mis-information and the emotion of revenge, in spite of his professed love of literature and his frequent eloquent narrations of hope for the future of humanity. But then, Uncle Vince also uncovered the blatant fact that, without strict adherence to his medication, Owen Sandburg was mentally unstable. In truth, without his medication, the man was certifiably insane.

After turning over her discoveries to the authorities, Ellen also offered a brief history of the known deeds of Wilfred Hopkins. Shortly after his death, Hopkins' car had been found at the airport, and the FBI had put together a solid story about his history and even his ambition to live in infamy. His notes on the subject were found in his home in Missouri, along with eighty-one individually numbered locks of human hair, the seventy-sixth being orange. But they found no list of names to match the numbered list.

The consensus among law enforcement agencies was that Hopkins was simply trying to make himself out to be the most effective serial killer in history. He had failed. And although there was a relentless search underway for more victims, he never received the kind of notoriety he apparently craved. Instead, after a reporter got access to the information, it became widely known that Hopkins detested being called Willie, and so "Willie the Wily Killer" went viral in social media, where he was mocked as a failed wannabe. Conspiracy buffs insisted there had to be some kind of a Missouri connection between Hopkins and the Seer's organization, but none of their claims withstood scrutiny.

Ellen's piece on Hopkins was countered by a prominent psychologist, who argued that people like Wilfred Hopkins are born psychopaths, that they are freaks of nature and should be understood as such. How do you hold people criminally accountable, she asked, without some measure of compassionate medical treatment, if they are born morally blind with specific malformations in their brain structure? If morality is a product of hardwiring, do we execute people simply because their wiring is faulty? Is being physically atypical a crime?

"Psychopaths have abnormal brains," the psychologist said. "Lock them up, of course, by all means, but they didn't choose to be born and we need to be careful about our penchant for wanting retribution. This is a physical condition, and as such it needs to be treated as a medical problem." The same expert then went on to suggest that Owen Sandburg's mental illness was likely a ruse to escape prosecution.

In a follow-up article, Ellen quoted Hopkins' parents opinion that their son was indeed born evil, without a conscience, without sympathy, and without empathy. She ended the piece with rumored speculation about what had happened to Hopkins' body. Ellen thought she knew, but she wasn't going to say at this time. Let someone else figure it out, if ever.

In the meantime, someone kept anonymously flooding the web with statements like *Please Do Not Disturb: Willie Hopkins Is Dreaming.*

# ACKNOWLEDGMENTS

THIS SEQUEL TO *Portals in a Northern Sky* has been a work in progress for twelve years. I began writing it as soon as *Portals* was published in 2003. I got about 50,000 words into it but then put it aside for five years, although I still thought about it frequently. My hope is that this novel will offer readers profound insight into the philosophy of good and evil, lead them to greater appreciation for the ways in which we relate to the subject of mortality, and inspire continued reflection and introspection long after they finish reading the book.

Over the years, I have heard from many readers who have told me that because of the depth of thoughtful material in *Portals* they have read the novel numerous times. That being the case, I would expect the same will apply to *A Mile North of Good and Evil*, because there is even more philosophical material here to contemplate.

I'm grateful and deeply indebted to LuAnne Dowling, my editor for nearly three decades, without whose help I would be lost. I'm also thankful for those who read and commented on the manuscript: Steve Heimel, Scott Morrison, Paul Peterson, Randy Presley, my wife Nancy, my son Charles M. Hayes, my nephew Aaron Hayes, and my granddaughter L. Emily Hayes. Their ideas and suggestions have been invaluable.

# ABOUT THE AUTHOR

CHARLES D. HAYES is a self-taught philosopher and one of America's strongest advocates for lifelong learning. He spent his youth in Texas and served as a U.S. Marine and as a police officer before embarking on a career in the oil industry. Alaska has been his home for more than forty years.

Promoting the idea that education should be thought of not as something you get but as something you take, Hayes encourages readers to pursue learning throughout their lives, to stay receptive to new ideas, and to consider their legacy to future generations in the actions they take and the wisdom they convey. In 2006, he established www.septemberuniversity.org, a site devoted to ongoing dialogue among September University participants in search of the better argument.

Hayes' work has been featured in *The L.A. Progressive*, *USA Today*, and the *UTNE Reader*, on National Public Radio's *Talk of the Nation* and on Alaska Public Radio's *Talk of Alaska*. His web site, www.autodidactic.com, provides resources for self-directed learners—from advice about credentials to philosophy about the value that lifelong learning brings to everyday living.

All books and shorter works by Charles D. Hayes are available at:
**http://amazon.com/author/charlesdhayes**

I hope you enjoyed reading this book as much as I enjoyed writing it.

I would be very much interested in your comments.

You're welcome to contact me at charles@autodidactic.com

Proof

Made in the USA
Charleston, SC
19 June 2015